Praise for Michelle Collins Anderson

"Anderson weaves a rich and poignant tale of a
small Ozarks town's factual tragedy, its generational
secrets and the juxtapose of searching and belonging.
Vivid and evocative, this is a debut to savor."
—Kim Michele Richardson, *New York Times* bestselling
author of *The Book Woman of Troublesome Creek*

"Michelle Collins Anderson delivers what every booklover
craves in her absorbing and exhilarating debut. Combined
with an intriguing historical event and charismatic characters
with deeply held secrets, the end result is a mesmerizing
story about reconciling guilt and letting go of the past so
new beginnings are possible. Anderson's talent is undeniable
and held me spellbound until the very last page."
—Donna Everhart, author of *The Saints of Swallow Hill*

"A vivid blend of sensorial writing, historical detail,
and memorable characters await on the pages of *The
Flower Sisters*. Poignant, compelling, and surprising,
here is an insightful story of the weight of long-held
secrets and the resulting hunger for truth."
—Susan Meissner, *USA Today* bestselling
author of *Only the Beautiful*

"Michelle Collins Anderson has taken a tragic footnote
of small-town history and turned it into an absolutely
absorbing novel, brimming with atmosphere, heart,
and winning characters. A wonderful debut!"
—Dominic Smith, *New York Times* bestselling
author of *Return to Valetto*

THE
FLOWER
SISTERS

MICHELLE
COLLINS ANDERSON

JOHN SCOGNAMIGLIO BOOKS
Kensington Publishing Corp.
www.kensingtonbooks.com

JOHN SCOGNAMIGLIO BOOKS are published by

Kensington Publishing Corp.
900 Third Avenue
New York, NY 10022

All Kensington titles, imprints, and distributed lines are available at special quantity discounts for bulk purchases for sales promotion, premiums, fund-raising, and educational or institutional use.

Special book excerpts or customized printings can also be created to fit specific needs. For details, write or phone the office of the Kensington Sales Manager: Kensington Publishing Corp., 900 Third Avenue, New York, NY 10022. Attn. Sales Department. Phone: 1-800-221-2647.

ISBN: 978-1-4967-4828-7

ISBN: 978-1-4967-4829-4 (ebook)

First Kensington Trade Paperback Edition: May 2024

10 9 8 7 6 5 4 3 2 1

Printed in the United States of America

To Mom, for everything, forever & always.
And Clay, for your love & unwavering belief.

THE
FLOWER
SISTERS

PROLOGUE

August 13, 1928

She leaned against the front balcony of the dance hall and shook her shiny dark hair in its neat, new bob, reveling in the delicious sensation of goose bumps on the back of her bare neck. Through the open door came the wail of Mo Wheeler's saxophone, bluesy and beckoning, while the plaintive piano answered with a seduction of its own. She smiled, realizing that one of her patent leather pumps was tapping the time with Dale Diggs' trap drum. She loved this new "jazz," the way it snaked through your veins and made you want to writhe and sway, to merge with that resonant, relentless beat and sing your blessings out loud. *Amen.*

And she was lucky tonight, wasn't she? Despite her mother's admonition to skip the dance: "It's Friday the thirteenth, you know." But her twin sister had practically pushed her out the door at the first honk of Charlie Walters' Plymouth—his father's car, actually. The gang packed in both seats tighter than ammunition, Dash unfolding himself out of the back, gallantly throwing open one silver door for her. She had ignored her mother's dark, meaningful look—a nice young man comes to the door!—and shrugged off the subsequent twinge of guilt almost as easily as the gauzy beige hip-length jacket she would shed at the dance.

Now she leaned over the rail and breathed in a deep lungful of the August night, a mixture of sunbaked earth and the slightly cool damp of leaf decay. Lamb's Dance Hall was the top floor of a two-story red brick building that housed an auto dealership and garage on the bottom floor, the smell of which left the slightest metallic tinge of grease on her tongue. From her perch, she could see a few young men talking through the open windows of their cars on the downtown square in front of the solemn courthouse, while others stood near the streetlamp, smoking cigarettes.

Which reminded her: cigarettes. The reason she had excused herself from the dance and her date in the first place. Her sister had shoved a half-open pack of Lucky Strikes into the beaded blue purse that now hung from her shoulder: "Here. You'll need one for a smoke break with the girls."

Her twin had cocked an eyebrow at her. It was always alarming to see her own exact features—large brown eyes in a pale face, pointed nose, small pink bud of a mouth—configured in an expression she would never use herself. Perspiration had trickled down her underarms as her sister scrutinized her head to toe, from the narrow-brimmed blue cloche hat to matching shoes, a peacock in borrowed finery. Then: a sudden frown.

"Just a minute."

Her twin had disappeared to their small shared bedroom and returned with a gold heart-shaped locket with a single diamond chip embedded in its center. "Let me put this on you."

"I shouldn't."

"I insist." Her sister sounded the tiniest bit bitter as she closed the minuscule clasp. "There."

The sisters looked at each other apprehensively for a moment and shrugged at exactly the same time. And then they laughed together, an identical charming giggle.

"Have fun tonight. Just be yourself." Her twin smiled, but her face was gray. "Or on second thought: don't."

"Thank you," she had replied, pulling her jacket closer around the thin lavender drop-waist with a beaded fringe hem. She reached up self-consciously to pat the back of her hair, surprised once more to find the length gone, what was left curving at her nape with a slightly longer frame around her face. This could take some getting used to. "Feel better, okay?"

"Wake me up when you get home. I want to hear all about the dance. Every. Single. Thing." Her sister winked. The car horn sounded two sharp blasts. "Bye now."

Then she was off into the car and the hot Ozarks night.

And so far, so good. She had hardly stepped off the dance floor. And managed to keep up with Dash in every department but drinking.

"Violet! Thought you'd skipped out on us." Fern and Ginger edged in beside her, one on each side.

"Can I bum a cigarette?" Fern Watson was always well turned out, with stylish dresses and shoes to match. But a closer look revealed ragged cuticles and nibbled nail polish, and her dark brown mass of natural curls may or may not have been combed all the way through underneath. Fern was a little haphazard, the type who would forget her head if it weren't attached, which was why she never carried a purse. But she had an easy charm about her—much like her father, the Mayor—and felt no compunction about asking for smokes, rides or even the answers to her math homework.

Ginger sighed and tapped out a cigarette for Fern before placing her own between her bright red lips and lighting it. Her family owned the pharmacy, so she always had the latest lipsticks and powders to help compensate for her plain features. Not to mention cigarettes. And a pocketbook full of cash.

"Dash is on the prowl for you. It's almost intermission." Ginger released a lazy cloud of blue smoke through her nostrils with a sidelong look. "I don't know how you keep up with that boy."

"Yes, *do* tell, Violet." Fern's giggle was punctuated by a couple of hacking coughs as she choked on her last inexpert inhale.

"Oh, we all have our little secrets." She fingered the locket at her throat, reminding herself that she belonged here.

"Until he gets bored with your little secret and wants to uncover someone else's." Here, Ginger gave a lazy, feline grin.

"Well, it definitely won't be *yours*." She watched Fern's jaw drop and Ginger's kohl-rimmed eyes widen slightly. That felt good. "Tootles, gals. See you on the dance floor."

Dash Emmonds was stinking drunk. Not that it was anything unusual, especially on a Friday night. He noticed it after the Lindy, when he attempted a low bow to his dance partner of the moment, Hazel, and had a hard time pulling his upper body vertical again. She reached for his arm to help right him, letting her hand rest there for a couple of beats too long. His eyes bounced around a bit before settling on her face. A nice face with a lovely mouth. Forgetting himself, he continued down her neck—long and pale—to her breasts, which seemed bound tightly beneath the shapeless, sparkly dress. Why did these girls want to look like boys these days? He liked curves, he couldn't help himself. Anything but the straight and narrow for Dash Emmonds.

Hazel was blushing when he finally looked up, but her eyes didn't waver from his. Definitely something he wanted to keep in mind when this thing with Violet went south, as he knew it inevitably would. He wasn't the going-steady type. Scratch that. He wasn't the going-steady-for-long type.

"Bye, toots." He caught Hazel's hand up in his and put it to his lips and then headed crookedly for the door. He nodded at Mo and Dale, who had started up a slow, lazy tune and caught the eye of Beebe Monroe, who peered at him over the top of her upright piano and winked. Where was Violet, anyway? How long can it take to smoke a damn cigarette?

The dance floor was filling up again as he pushed past the crowd at the bar and the coat-check counter and through the open door at last. He reached up and straightened his tie and then smoothed his hair back with his hands except one dark blond curl, which he allowed to fall onto his forehead. More than one girl had let him know she liked that curl, starting with his own mother, who used to train the lock of hair with a lick of spit and her forefinger. His father had shaken his head against their vanity, Dash's and his mother's, but then, his father was against most everything: pride, envy, vanity, gluttony, drunkenness, dancing, sex (not that he ever said that word out loud). Everything fun, anyway. God, he hated being a PK: preacher's kid. He was twenty-five now—practically an old man—with no real prospects. Most of his buddies had gone to college and were either back in town learning the family business or off to the big cities—St. Louis, Kansas City, Chicago—to seek their fortunes. He'd tried college, too, which he had loved right up until the moment he flunked out. And to his father's unvarnished disappointment, he wanted nothing to do with God or the church. As far as Dash was concerned, religion was for the stupid, the unimaginative and the chicken-hearted. People who were too afraid to admit there wasn't anything after this life and spent their time banking their prayers and good deeds in hopes of eternal reward. He was having none of it. He'd take his rewards now, thank you very much.

"Hey, Violet." Dash lurched right into his steady, who was coming in the other way. He slid his arm around her bare shoulders and gave her a small squeeze. Her skin felt cool to his touch and he had the urge to rush her off to the Plymouth in the back parking lot and explore some more of it. She'd let him that once, hadn't she? They had both been drinking that night. Gin. He had started gently at the nape of her neck, brushing back her bob with his hand and discovering a dime-sized birthmark at the hairline, an ink stain on pale onion skin. He had kissed it reverently. And then, not quite so slowly, he had worked his way around her throat and down. And further down, his hand finding his way beneath the slippery dress and her stockings while his mouth stayed on her breasts. She may have protested a little bit, he couldn't remember. But she let him push all the way into her with just the slightest moan, her arms wrapped tightly around the back of his head. Now *that* was heaven. Every girl just a different window into it.

"Want to go out back with me?" He hoped his tone sounded light.

"Dash, are you drunk?" His date hesitated a brief second before reaching up to hold his face in her hands, searching his eyes. He couldn't quite focus on hers, although they were as large and shiny as a wild animal's.

"I might be." He smiled crookedly. "Pretty please?"

"Mmm. I'd love another dance? It's almost intermission."

He felt her steering him back the way he came. They had just made it through the door when a large young man with brilliantined black hair and his striped tie askew pushed them both roughly to one side as he parted the sea of merrymakers in his path, his face dark and thunderous.

Dash had heard that Jimmy Jeffers' girl had given him the heave-ho. He scanned the room for her. Nell. Dancing with someone Dash didn't know, probably from somewhere outside of Possum Flats. People came from fifty or more miles away for the Lamb's Hall dances each month. He reached for Violet's hand and wondered, ever so briefly, what it would be like to be thrown over for someone else. Not his experience. He typically broke up with a girl before it crossed her mind to drop him. Not that any girl would ever drop him, of course. But his attention span was short. And so was life. Too short to be tied to one girl, no matter how gorgeous or witty or charming. Even Violet here, her sweet breath against his chest as they moved onto the dance floor. At her throat she wore the gold heart he had given her, but he knew—even if she didn't—that it was a useless talisman against his restlessness.

He felt himself strangely moved by this thought. Or maybe it was just the gin. He drew her closer, wanting to protect her somehow, from the inevitable. Not tonight, of course. But soon. He would miss Violet, he really would.

* * *

She let her cheek rest against Dash's chest. She tingled, like her nerves were on the outside of her skin. The band was winding up the first set with "At Sundown," and practically everyone was out on the floor, each couple jostling for their square foot of space. At the piano, Beebe had sweat on her brow as she teased out each melancholy note; Mo's eyes were closed as he blew sweet agony on the sax, his fingers moving up and down the keys like a lover's spine. She wanted to be held like that. Like this. Before Dash, she had never done more than hold the clammy hand of that splotchy, nervous boy from the funeral home. She had refused the silver flask that Dash had offered earlier, but still, she felt like she must be drunk anyway. It was intoxicating, breathing in his smell and seeing how all the eyes in the room watched him—either with thinly concealed desire or naked jealousy, depending on the gender. These were not parents, of course—those looks might have contained disappointment, disbelief or even a bit of contempt for this beautiful man who lived with absolutely no thought of the future. These were his contemporaries. She felt Dash's hand slide down to the small of her back and pull her in close. She shut her eyes and let the beat of the drum take over for thinking, the rhythm of it a question that made her body want to answer: *yes, yes* and *yes*.

Then: a flash so bright she could see it through her eyelids. Her eyes flew open and she turned her face up to find Dash's, surprise written in the "O" of his mouth and the crease of his brow. Almost instantly, a deafening explosion followed and she felt the floorboards rising beneath their feet, as she and Dash continued *up, up, up,* as though they were flying, launched into the sky and literally dancing on air as the floor and walls fell away around them. She felt the night air on her cheek. The ceiling had opened up into a brilliant night sky, stars in their stasis coolly winking at the dancers, frozen in the air at their apex for those few unbelievable seconds, still embracing their partners. She saw Nell, Charlie, Beebe and her piano, Mo with his mouth still on his horn, all suspended against the inky sky.

"How impossibly beautiful," she thought in the strange sliver of silence before the screaming started and the dancers began their terrible fall. As she was ripped from Dash's arms, she heard the cries of women and men, crying out for their husbands, wives, partners. Their mothers. God.

She clawed desperately at the air as she watched the ground rushing up to meet her, a horrible black smoking hole where the dance hall had been.

Then: a sharp rip of pain in her shoulder as she was halted in her fall while Dash continued to plummet.

"Violet!"

No. She hung suspended from a still-standing timber, stuck through the shoulder and left armpit and what remained of her dress by a large, pointed piece of wood. She knew she should feel pain, but she felt nothing but wonder. She saw the bodies and bricks and beams begin to fill the hole beneath her, felt the rain of rubble and rock on her exposed flesh, marveled at the bloody wound around her left armpit and ragged flap of her naked left breast. Her purse still hung from her right shoulder. Her feet were bare.

People were littered everywhere, covered with debris and screaming and crying for help. Some didn't move at all. But she was alive. *She was alive.*

A light caught the corner of her eye and she watched with morbid fascination as the dark pile of rubble was overrun with bright orange and blue flames, and frantically writhing victims worked to free themselves, screeching in agony as they were engulfed. The flames reached higher, and she felt her dangling feet warm and then grow hot as the fire licked at her, gently at first and then with a pitiless greed. Her nostrils filled with the smell of burning flesh. She was going to die. God, she didn't want to die. *Please.* It was her first dance. She had just found out what it felt like to be alive.

It hurt. It hurt to be alive and be on fire and God, *please, please, please* make it stop. She screamed, just once, and everything went black.

* * *

She seemed so far away from him as he lay there in the pit that used to be the dance hall and garage. He watched her, dangling above him by an arm—or was it her dress? He saw that she was practically naked, a beautiful pale angel against the night sky.

"Violet!"

He tried to free himself from a large timber that had wedged his ankle under the pile of debris, pushing against the wooden beam and trying to lift it with both hands. But it was no use. He heard the flames before he saw them, racing toward him with a roar in a menacing blue line. He heard Violet's scream, like the terrible shriek of a wounded rabbit, before her body lit up completely in a brilliant flame and that quickly extinguished itself, leaving her hanging there, charred and lifeless as a piece of meat.

No. I will not die like this. Dash struggled to pull his ankle free, pushing up on his elbows and bracing his arms behind him.

"God, help me," he whispered. *If I make it out of here, I will be a different person. I swear.*

The fire was at the timber now, slowed only briefly by the bricks and rocks. He felt the heat of the wall of flame on his face and turned his head. He tried to brace himself. He wasn't going to make it. His mind flashed on his father. *You were right*, he thought. *I have gone to hell.*

He felt movement at his ankle as the timber shifted, then the excruciating relief of freedom and the simultaneous searing pain of the crushed bones as he tried unsuccessfully to stand. Then two strong arms were lacing themselves through his and dragging him backwards, away from the fire.

"Hang on, Dash. I got you."

It was Jimmy. Dash watched as his own legs jounced along the ground in front of him as though they belonged to someone else. They passed the piano, upside down and splintered, Beebe crushed and lifeless beneath it. She lay on her back with her arms outstretched, staring at the sky as though she had been trying to catch her dear piano, to break its fall.

After about twenty yards, Jimmy dropped Dash to safety on the sidewalk, and ran back to the rubble. Dash lay with his cheek scraping against the rough concrete, which still held heat from the summer day, curled onto his side and watching the fire rage and burn, unable to do anything but weep.

DAISY

May 1978

I know what she's doing down there.

I heard the hearse pull up to the basement garage around five this morning, when it was still dark outside. And now I can hear her, knocking around like a clumsy ghost, doing her dark magic on God-knows-who. Some old guy, maybe. She won't bring him back from the dead, but she can at least make him look alive.

My grandma, the funeral director.

It's bad enough I have to live with her; I barely know her. But on top of a funeral home? It's so creepy, with disturbing sights, sickening smells and people showing up at all hours, bawling like babies about losing Uncle So-and-So or Grandma What's-Her-Face. Maybe some are sincere. But from what I've seen, most of them can't wait to get out of here. Get the corpse in the ground and get back to living—watching TV or eating Cheetos or complaining about Jimmy Carter and the price of gasoline.

Grandma says she actually enjoys it. That being a funeral home owner is her "calling." She doesn't mind dead bodies. In fact, she likes to say she puts the "fun" in "funeral," and then laugh herself silly. I've been here a month and I've heard it a billion times, which really gets on my nerves.

"I ought to put that on a T-shirt," she'll say, wiping away a tear. "I'd be rich."

I guess it could be considered a fun, party atmosphere around here—if you ignore the dead part. Like some weird spa weekend, with Grandma giving all her guests shampoos and shaves and manicures. She puts the old ladies in curlers and "Brylcreems" the geezers. Finishes them all up with a little makeup. *Poof.*

But it's the other stuff that is super gross. That's what she's getting ready to do right now. Draining the blood. Pumping in the preservatives. Kind of like making a pickle out of a cucumber: It looks the same on the outside, but inside? All smelly, bitter vinegar.

I hate pickles.

Then there's the clothing. People don't usually die in their Sunday best but that's what they're buried in. I can't imagine trying to wrestle some cold, naked grandpa into his boxers and bowtie or wriggle a stiff old lady into a pair of pantyhose. Even Grandma has to have extra help with that part, which is where Roger comes in. He is her "right hand man," she says, a big, barrel-shaped guy who does all the heavy lifting: body pickup and delivery, funeral setup and cleanup, maintenance, janitorial and even chauffeur services. Roger's a regular jack-of-all-trades in the funereal arts.

He and Grandma go way back. She says Roger will take over the funeral home someday, but as she puts it, he's no spring chicken, either. Roger started working here when Grandma's husband died back in the '50s and left her in charge of the family business: Steinkamp & Son Funeral Home. I saw the old rusted sign in the basement, painted sheet-metal with black, Old English lettering. Grandma married "Son." She changed everything to her maiden name, so it's Flowers Funeral Home now. My mom was long gone by then.

The tarnished brass clock with the glow-in-the-dark hands says it's nearly eight. I haven't even gotten up yet and I'm already bored.

I'm in the old mahogany canopy bed that used to be Mom's.

Right now, I'm rereading *To Kill a Mockingbird*. I've already read everything on her bookshelf, which is a mix of Nancy Drew, The Bobbsey Twins, The Five Little Peppers and the *Anne of Green Gables* books. All a little Goody-Two-shoes. But tolerable if your life's as much of a yawn as mine. All I've done since I got here a month ago is read books and go to the library. And write letters to Mom, begging her to rescue me and take me to California, too.

She is being unreasonable. I mean, she has never said *anything* good about this town. Or much about Grandma, except that they've "had their differences." No details on that. But it's pretty crappy of Mom to leave me in a place that she hates with a person she's been determined to stay away from all these years. It really pisses me off.

Because we've always been a unit, the two of us, whether she's had a boyfriend or not. I'm not some little kid who needs a babysitter. I'm fifteen. And a *half*. But Mom left me here for the summer because she said she "needs some space." Apparently that means running off to California with her boyfriend, Ron, who has to "work up to the idea of fatherhood" before I move out there, too. I can't figure out anything good about "space" that includes Ron but not me. He's the kind of guy who tapes notes on his bottles of Pepsi and Snickers bars when he puts them in our fridge—in an apartment where it's just me and Mom—so no one else will take them. When she dropped me off, Mom said it might take a while for her and Ron to find the right place. Plus good jobs. But she loves me. And they'll send for me just as soon as they're all set up.

Yay.

The sun is shining onto my pillows now, making it tough to stay in bed. But I don't feel like going anywhere or doing anything. I don't know a soul in Possum Flats, Missouri, except Grandma. She says if I don't get out and do something, I'll be white as a sheet when school starts. Mom had better be back to get me by then, because I refuse to start school in this nothing place. In the meantime, I'll stay in my room and read. Write my letters. And draw the shades. Like some weird female Boo Radley.

I've already seen everything there is to see outside these windows. Flowers Funeral Home faces Main Street in downtown Possum Flats and my upstairs room overlooks the back alley, where Grandma takes her "deliveries" twenty-four hours a day. Not much there but dumpsters and stray cats, and, over the buildings, the tip-top of a church steeple. From the front sidewalk of the funeral home, you can see east down Main to the downtown square that has banks on opposite corners and a boring limestone courthouse in the center with a silver flagpole waving the U.S. and Missouri flags.

Possum Flats. Seriously? It sounds like road kill—and it's every bit as dead.

Just a few blocks west from us on Main is *The Possum Flats Picayune*, the daily newspaper, with the police station across the street. Beyond that, the library, the post office and the Dog 'N' Suds. Apparently, that's a drive-in restaurant for hot dogs and root beer, not a dog-grooming establishment, like I first thought. Even now, I can't help picturing soapy pink hot dogs.

All of a sudden, there's a scream from the basement, followed by a clanging sound, like something has fallen over. I should check on Grandma, but I hesitate a second. I've seen a couple of her "clients," and that was more than enough to make me want to keep my distance.

The steep stairway opens up into the dim viewing room, all deep burgundy carpet and velvet drapes. Then there's a narrow hallway with a bathroom on one side and the door to the basement at the far end. There, I practically collide with Roger. His thinning hair, combed into neat slick furrows with pomade, frames an expansive forehead shiny with sweat. He's in a big hurry to get to Grandma, too.

"What's going on?"

"Dunno."

Roger doesn't say much. Which is fine, given most of the people he works with are dead. Grandma says he needs to work on his social skills for the loved ones' families, who still require conversation, because she won't be around forever. But my opinion is that Roger is not going to change.

Roger leads the way, much to my relief, but I am hot on his heels on the rickety wooden staircase.

At the bottom, I peer around Roger and take in a gruesome sight: a naked senior citizen is laid out flat on one of the gurneys, the top of his head toward us. A hose dangling from his upper body is dripping fluid. Worse: my grandma is holding a crumpled sheet in her hands, sitting on the floor in a puddle of putrid ooze. She is laughing like a loon, an overturned folding chair beside her.

"Are you all right?"

Roger reaches out a hand and pulls Grandma vertical, all five feet of her. She's a little bit of a woman, but it's easy to forget how small she is since her personality is so big. I wasn't sure what to expect when Mom dropped me off. The only grandparents I knew were from books. And believe me, she's not your sugar-cookie-baking, warm-and-fuzzy classic. People around here seem intimidated by my grandma.

"Oh, yes. Damn the mess and everything, Roger. I needed to sit down all of a sudden and I missed the mark." She shakes her head. "After fifty years in the business, you would think I'd have lost my ability to be surprised."

She raises an eyebrow and gives Roger a stern look that would have withered a lesser man. "You could have warned me," she says. "That would have been the decent thing to do."

Roger's eyes bug out a bit and he swallows hard. His entire head is turning red, including his scalp, broken up by the tidy strips of hair. "Sorry 'bout that, Rose. But you know it was four in the morning when I rescued the Mayor."

Rescued? The *mayor*? How do you save a dead person?

I turn my attention to the body on the gurney and immediately understand what the excitement was about. Below the bald pate and the sunken, hairless chest and stomach, I see that the corpse is "excited," too. The Mayor has a boner.

Ugh.

Grandma shakes out the sheet in her hands with a snap and moves to cover the alarming appendage. When the Mayor is suitably hidden from the waist down, she turns to me, clearing her throat.

"Daisy, this is Bartholomew J. Watson, AKA 'the Mayor.' Lifelong resident of Possum Flats for the entirety of his ninety-five years and its mayor for close to forty. Not large in stature but a giant in terms of status and charm. Never met a stranger. Respected by his fellow men. And boy howdy, did he love the ladies."

"Loved 'em to death," chimes in Roger, deadpan.

"Apparently." Grandma pulls a face.

"What do you mean?" I ask. This is the most interesting thing I've seen or heard since I've been in Possum Flats.

"Well, we got a call this morning that the Mayor had died *in flagrante.*"

"In *what?*"

"In the act, as it were."

"Was he married?" I'm curious now.

"Yes, he has a darling wife, Ruby Rae." Grandma pauses. "They were married more than seventy-five years, I believe."

This is confusing. "Um. I guess I'm not sure why she would need to tell you exactly *how* he died?"

Grandma and Roger exchange a look. He shrugs. She does, too.

"Well, the thing is . . . she isn't the one who called."

Now she has my full attention.

"I don't want to get into details, but suffice it to say that Roger did a backdoor pickup at the pharmacy. Under cover of darkness."

"So . . . he was clearly with someone other than his wife."

Grandma and Roger neither confirm nor deny my theory.

"But did someone tell her?"

Roger busies himself by reinserting the end of the loose, dripping hose into a bucket. Grandma sighs. "Yes, that was my unfortunate lot a little while ago. Ruby Rae will be here with his burial suit later this morning, so we've got to get him in decent shape. And I do mean *decent.* Roger, can you hand me the duct tape, please?"

This is my cue to leave. I really don't want to know what she is going to do with that thick gray tape. But I can't let this go. "What did you say to her?"

Grandma puts her hands on her hips and frowns at me. "Why, absolutely nothing, Daisy. Except to give her my most sincere condolences. The dead share all sorts of secrets with me and it is my bounden duty to keep them. Like client privilege with a lawyer or a doctor. Or a priest.

"Believe me, Ruby Rae knows enough. Bless her heart."

I nod, but I'm still unsure. This is fascinating stuff. Maybe Possum Flats isn't quite as dead as it looks. Part of my present company excluded, of course.

"I will not—*we* will not—tell a soul," Grandma continues, raising a meaningful eyebrow at me and Roger. Mostly me, since Roger rarely opens his trap. She reaches up and tucks a long, stray hair behind her ear. I can see why she never cuts it. She has the most gorgeous long white hair that she wears in a single fat braid down her neck and back. I hope I got that hair gene. My own is boring, straight and dark.

"Alrighty, then." Grandma smooths her gray dress and the plastic apron she wears when the going gets messy. "Back to business."

ROSE

When it is just me and Mayor Watson again, I breathe a sigh of relief.

That was way too much action for this old lady.

Obviously, the Mayor had more action than he could handle, too.

I'd say that's what he gets for running around with younger women, but I'm not sure making whoopee with a seventy-something-year-old qualifies as "robbing the cradle." Normally, I wouldn't consider it any of my business. But since Roger had to actually pry old Barty here off of Ginger Morton this morning, it sort of became my business.

I'm not going to lie: I enjoyed her desperate plea for help at four a.m. No one loves being woken out of a dead sleep—ha! But when you discover your old archnemesis is stuck in a compromising position and you're the only one she can call for help? That's a delicious moment of schadenfreude.

After the Mayor took his last gasp, Ginger was stuck beneath him for about four hours until she wriggled one arm free and reached the bedside phone. Lucky for her, my number is easy to remember: 356-9377. FLO-WERS.

"Hello? Flowers Funeral Home." I had said it so often, I could do it in my sleep. Case in point.

"Rose?" Her voice was barely above a whisper. Little did I

know she had about a hundred and fifty pounds compressing her chest and lungs at that moment. "It's Ginger. I've got a . . . situation."

"At four a.m.? Must be a hell of a situation," I said. Like I said, Ginger isn't my favorite person and certainly not someone I'd choose to talk to at that ungodly hour.

She didn't waste any breath getting to the crux of it. For obvious reasons.

"And please, Rose," she said before hanging up. "Could you keep the details quiet? I'd appreciate it."

"You know me, Ginger. Silent as a tomb."

"Hmmm."

Then dial tone.

Of course, I rang up Roger immediately and sent him right over to her place, a spacious apartment above her pharmacy business. Not even a mortal enemy should be pinned to her bed by a dead body.

I give the Mayor the once-over. Where to begin?

Thankfully, Roger helped me with the deceased's most critical problem. There's a term for the Mayor's condition, of course: "angel lust." I've only seen it once before—many years ago—and that was a suicide. By hanging. A farmer who was about to lose his considerable acreage to the bank, property that had been in his family for a hundred years. Heartbreaking. I felt doubly sorry for his poor wife, who found him dangling in the barn that morning, neck snapped but somehow in a state of corporeal excitement. As if finding your husband swinging from the rafters isn't bad enough.

I'd venture to say the Mayor's issue is more a result of gravity than a trick of the central nervous system. Being dead facedown for a few hours pools the blood in all available nooks and crannies while rigor mortis set in. Unusual? Yes. Fitting? I would say so. Ginger Morton may have been the unlucky last, but she was by no means the first woman with whom Mayor Watson had a dalliance. It was no secret around Possum Flats that Barty could not "keep it in his pants."

Yet he and Ruby Rae stayed together. Despite losing a child. Despite his shenanigans. I marvel at that. There's a chance she didn't know what he was up to. I remind myself that no one really knows what goes on in a marriage except for the two people in it. I should know. But still: How could a person live with someone for three-quarters of a century and not know all of their secrets?

We had fewer than twenty years together, yet my sister and I knew everything about each other. But then, we were twins, and that is something special. I've read a lot about it, and the experts say that identical twins often know what the other is thinking or feeling or about to do without being told. That's how it was for us. Rose and Violet. Violet and Rose. The Flowers girls. The flower sisters.

How could a parent christen us with such unapologetically floral names given the verdant nature of our surname? My mother made no apologies. All she would say was that she couldn't help herself; we were such delicate beauties when we were born. We fit neatly in the palms of her hands, a veritable baby bouquet. And absolutely identical: same size, same coloring, same smile. The only difference was the minuscule bluish-purple birthmark at the top of one slender neck. Violet, of course. It was the only sure way our mother had of telling us apart before our hair grew in, dark and long. Then she tied a ribbon around my wrist, until our separate personalities began to emerge, just as one might predict: Violet, the adventurous, the secretive. A wild child who loved to be in a bunch, surrounded by friends and noise and fun. And Rose: prim and proper, stubbornly keeping to herself, and stuck on a single, thorny stem of her own making.

Ouch. It hurts sometimes when I think about all the ways I've made my life harder than it had to be. More complicated. Painful.

But clearly, I'm not alone in that. The Mayor here has made quite a mess of things, although he won't be the one to suffer the consequences. And when I get finished with him, he will look like the fine upstanding citizen and human being that he mostly was.

Upstanding. Ha!

After Roger and I finished up with the duct tape, he inserted the trocar near the Mayor's navel to get the insides punctured and liquids emptied out—stomach, bladder, large intestines. I can still stick that knifelike metal tube in and poke around if I have to, but it's more of a struggle than it used to be and Roger doesn't seem to mind. I'll fill the abdominal cavity back up with embalming fluid next. Then: bath time for Barty.

Meanwhile, I swipe a thick slick of Vicks VapoRub under my nostrils to kill the smells. And I wait.

The Mayor looks pretty peaceful. He died happy, I guess. This is my favorite kind of client—besides the matter of his unfortunate little surprise, I mean. I like the ones who die of "natural causes," who have lived to a ripe old age and then some. But no matter how many decades I do this work, I never get used to the ones who weren't ready or old enough to go. The car accidents. The heart attacks and strokes. The incurable disease. Suicides. And the babies; the children. Those still manage to break my heart, just chipping away at it. I wonder at the end of some days if I have anything left inside me. Anything besides a hard, black little heart-shaped stone. Obsidian, maybe. Something that has been through great fire and retained some strange vestige of beauty.

Of course, if you've already buried your twin sister and your husband, and as good as lost your only daughter . . . how could anything ever touch your heart again? Like that girl upstairs. What do I do with her? I'm nearly seventy years old, and I sure didn't get it right the first time.

Mayor Watson's hands are folded neatly across his heart, some-thing I took care to do right away, before he was completely cold. I want to work some lotion into the creases and lines around his large, knobby knuckles. I always use Jergens, not some off-brand or commercial grade stuff. Little details are what keep Possum Flats families coming back to Flowers Funeral Home. I'm a real stickler for getting everything just right with the dead. Sort of helps to make up for what I haven't been able to put right with the living.

Daisy. Maybe I could start there. Try to be a grandma to her. She's never had one. I've never been one.

I guess that makes us even.

I know she misses her mama. I've been biding my time, letting her be mad at Lettie for kicking her to the curb. Giving her a chance to get used to living here. Get used to me. But it's time for her to get out of the house.

Maybe after I meet with Ruby Rae, I'll take Daisy to lunch. I need to get the service info over to *The Picayune* this afternoon so they can run the obituary tomorrow. Not that everyone in town hasn't heard the news. But we love our obituaries in Possum Flats. Everyone reads them first, before the front page, sports or comics.

I like to think we have our priorities in order.

"Don't you agree, Barty?"

Still so much to do here. Shave. Shampoo. Trim the nails. Dress the Mayor in his suit, socks, shoes and trademark bow-tie. Makeup.

Some of this can wait until Saturday. Tomorrow. The makeup I will do Sunday morning, so he will look as "fresh" as possible before the funeral at two.

But what I can't put off much longer is my meeting with Ruby Rae. Despite what people might think, dealing with the living is the toughest part of my job.

"And you're making it even harder, Mayor," I say. I laugh, embarrassed, even though I'm essentially alone. "Oops. More *difficult*, I mean."

DAISY

When Grandma invited me to run errands and grab lunch, I jumped at the chance. But I had one condition.

"Anywhere but Dog 'N' Suds," I said.

"Good heavens." Grandma chuckled. "I agree. And after the morning I've had, I need somewhere with good atmosphere and an even better cheeseburger."

True to its name, the Sunnyside Diner is bright and cheerful inside, with egg-yolk-yellow walls, and a floor tiled in black and white squares. It's like a perfectly preserved slice of the 1950s, from tall sculpted milkshake glasses to the jukebox loaded with Elvis and the Everly Brothers. Every possible surface—from the shelves to the counter and each individual table or booth—is topped with unusual pairs of salt and pepper shakers. Grandma picks out a small table by the door that has dill pickle salt and pepper shakers.

I hope this is not a bad omen.

The smells coming out of the kitchen are amazing. Through the open window behind the counter I can see the one deviation from the '50s vibe: a stringy-haired old man with a tie-dye T-shirt and apron, at the grill, sweating as he turns translucent onions, hamburgers, and even a couple of late-breakfast pancakes. A cigarette hangs precariously out of the side of his mouth and I try not to think about the possibility of ashes in my food. My stomach is growling and I feel a deliciously naughty feeling inside because I know I am going to order a cheeseburger and that if my mom was here, she would completely freak out. She is a vegetarian, which means I've been one, too—mostly out of habit rather than philosophy—choking down tofu my whole life. I don't think I could find a single solitary chunk of the stuff in Possum Flats.

Grandma nods to people at other booths, and they return the greeting. A few say, "Hey, Ms. Flowers," and nod at me, too.

Elvis comes on with "All Shook Up," and somehow it feels right—although I'm not in love, just feeling the effects of living in Possum Flats. I am not used to everyone knowing who I am and it makes me feel off-balance, like they already have the upper hand and we haven't even met. I wonder if Grandma ever gets tired of everyone knowing every last thing about her.

Grandma waves over the waitress. There's only one for the whole restaurant, but she has a no-nonsense look that tells me she's got everything under control, from the hairnet to the apron with everything in it—order pad, pencil, pen, packets of sugar and Sweet'N Low, a handful of paper-wrapped straws—to the unglamorous white shoes with soles of chunky white streamlined foam.

"What'll it be, ladies?" The bored voice is part of her schtick, I think. Her eyes, enlarged by her bifocals, are kind.

"The usual," says Grandma, with a sly wink. "And Betty, this is my granddaughter, Daisy. She's staying with me for the summer."

"Is that right?" Betty laughs. "I may have heard something about that. How's our Lettie Steinkamp?" She is looking at me.

"Um. It's Flowers. And fine, I guess. She's in California."

"Flowers, eh? Just like her mom." Grandma flinches the slightest bit. "Married?"

"No." I find myself getting a little defensive. "But she's got a boyfriend."

"That's Lettie all over." Betty shakes her head. "Keeping those men on a string, never settling on just one. And who can blame her, right?"

"It's a woman's prerogative to change her mind," says Grandma.

And change it, and change it, and change it, I think. I have moved around a lot in my fifteen years: St. Louis, Denver, Houston, Chicago. When I was younger—like in elementary school—I used to write letters to the friends I left behind. I was the pen-pal-iest person ever. But they rarely wrote back and even if they did, it was only once or twice. By the time I was in junior high, I had decided it was easier to stop making friends. What was the point? I knew where things were headed.

"And what would you like, Daisy?" Grandma asks, deftly moving off the topic of my mom. She seems to understand that I'm a little prickly on the subject.

"A cheeseburger, please." My heart is beating fast, like I'm committing a crime.

"And what would you like on it?" Betty asks.

"Um . . ." What does she mean? "A bun?"

"Ha! I see she's got your sense of humor." Betty shakes her head at Grandma and reels off my choices: tomato, lettuce, onions, pickles, mayo, mustard, ketchup.

"I want everything," I say. "But please hold the pickles."

The front of the newspaper building is all plate glass, painted with gold scrolly letters that read THE POSSUM FLATS PICAYUNE: WE "NOSE" OUR NEWS.

Oh, brother.

As soon as Grandma opens the door for us, the dark metallic smell of newspaper ink hits my nose and I can hear the presses running in the back room, a thundery rolling, galloping sound that is muffled by the doors into the front office. There is a reception desk occupied by a plain-looking girl in long braids and even longer denim skirt who waves us past with a shy smile. She ducks her head to some task before her, peeking up at me as I go by.

There are no offices, just lots of desks turned this way and that in clusters. The people are just as casual. One man in jeans and a short-sleeved button-up shirt is propped on the edge of his desk, talking on the phone; two others stand nearby, chatting and drinking coffee. A thin old man hunches over a stack of black-and-white photographs on his desk. As we pass, he raises his white head to reveal a beakish nose and a strange, black-ringed magnifying lens over one eye. The enlarged blue eye makes him look what Mom would call "batshit crazy."

Grandma makes her way through the maze of desks to a fifty-something woman with platinum-blond hair framing her face in a heart shape. Up close, all I can see are the big black cat-eye glasses and the bright red lipstick. She is extending a manicured hand, nails the same shade of red.

"You must be Daisy." Her smile reveals teeth with the slight brown tinge of a serious coffee habit. "Another gorgeous bloom in a long line of Flowers girls. Sorry, I just can't help saying that. Right?" Here she nods at Grandma. "Tell her, hon. For someone who calls herself a newspaper reporter, I tend to go through my days completely unedited."

I take her hand, but squeezing it is like holding a kitten too tightly—I feel a bunch of tiny bones barely covered with skin. "Hi."

"Don't be fooled," says Grandma with a wink. "Myra here is the society page editor and has been practically forever. She's trying to get you to let down your guard. Before you know it, you'll be sharing your deepest, darkest secrets."

She and Myra laugh, then turn to Grandma's notes for Mayor Watson's obituary. Soon they are onto other topics: the weather, Grandma's recipe for Watergate salad and how the irises are blooming late this year.

My mind wanders. My eyes, too.

The back wall of the newsroom is lined with large, framed black-and-white photographs. I am fascinated by what I see. The first shows a farmer standing close to the camera, while in the background an entire herd of spotted cattle lies dead and bloated beneath a giant oak, stiff-legged, bellies stretched to the bursting point.

The farmer's sun-darkened face reminds me of a raisin. It's

hard to see where the worry lines end and the frown begins. In the corner of the photo is a handwritten title in quotation marks: "Lightning Strike, 1949." The farmer looks beaten down and his black eyes seem to say, "Well, what did I expect, anyway?"

The adjacent photo shows a man with his head lying on a bar, his face turned toward the camera with his outstretched arm clutching a drink. It takes a minute to register the small bullet hole between his curling bangs, with one drip of blood halfway down his forehead. "Payback at the Elk's Lodge, 1957."

Next is a shack with fire blazing out of both small windows on either side of the door, making it look like an angry face. A man and woman stand with their backs to the camera; his arms grip her blanket-wrapped shoulders. She obviously wants to run back into the house, and her head is thrown back in grief. This one is called "Fire at the Burgess Place, 1961."

"You like these?" A deep voice at my elbow nearly sends me through the roof. "Guess your grandma's business can't help but harden you up a bit."

I feel insulted, yet somehow pleased. "And what's your excuse?"

"Fence McMillan the Fourth, editor and publisher." An unlit pipe protrudes from one side of his mouth, and he is wearing a long-sleeved dress shirt and sweater vest, even at the end of May. He is slight and imposing, all at the same time.

"Daisy Flowers. But I'm sure you already knew that."

"Well, I *do* consider it my business to 'knows the news' in Possum Flats, Missouri." He gives me a mischievous look. "All the news that's fit to print."

"Were these pictures fit to print?"

He switches his gaze to the photographs and slowly shakes his head. "No. Not in *The Picayune*, anyway."

"Why not?"

"This is a family paper. A small-town community paper. People want to check the weather forecast, keep up on the high school football team, read the funny page. Life is hard here. They don't need their news hard, too."

"So then these are . . . ?"

"Oh, I suppose they're just my way of telling myself that the journalism degree from the university wasn't for nothing." He looks thoughtful now, as if he had not considered the "why" of these photographs for a while. "I love these pictures. Even if they never saw print. They still tell a hell of a story."

I consider this, my hands stuffed into the floral-patched pockets of my bell-bottom jeans. I love stories; always have. There is something magical about escaping into another world for a few minutes or hours or days. Even from the inside of a cramped, crappy apartment in St. Louis that looked essentially the same as one in Chicago or anywhere else, USA, I could live life through the eyes of someone else, someone other. Without ever leaving my couch.

Maybe I could tell stories, too. *Write* them. About real people who are happy or sad or strange or beautiful or afraid. *Hell-of-a-story* stories.

Before I can stop myself, I'm babbling away, as if slowing down would cause me to lose courage: "Do you need any help around here? I'm a great writer. With *tons* of experience."

Fence is caught off guard. He raises an eyebrow. "You don't say?"

"Yeah, sure, I've done lots of big profiles and interviews," I say. Where is this coming from? It's like I've tapped a vein of self-confidence I didn't know I had. I actually sound *cocky*.

Fence doesn't need to know that during my one year on the school paper I was relegated to interviewing and writing up blurbs on the new kids. Because I was new myself since Mom moved us around so much. Plus no one else wanted to do it.

"Let me guess. School newspaper?" Fence is clearly amused. It galls me that he isn't taking me seriously. Which prompts me to kick into overdrive, desperate to impress him. My mind scrabbles, seizes on a tiny kernel of possibility, even though I experience a sharp pang that must be my conscience. Didn't Grandma just tell me in no uncertain terms to keep my mouth shut?

"Actually, I know a pretty shocking story about one of Possum Flats' most famous citizens," I say.

"Do you now?" Fence's tone is still playful, but I can tell he's curious.

"Yes. It's top secret."

I have Fence's complete attention now. He adjusts his pipe thoughtfully. "Tell me more."

"Well, I'd love to. But a story like this is valuable. *Extremely* valuable," I add. "I would guess it's worth at least a summer internship."

I don't know where this new ballsy version of Daisy has come from. All I know is that I am sick of being quiet. Of nodding my head and going along with other people's ideas of what's best for me, even when I hate it. Like my mom's latest and greatest scheme.

I got out of school one day and there was Mom in her poop-brown Dodge Dart, idling curbside. Ron was hanging one heavily tattooed arm out the window, cigarette dangling from his fingers. I saw myself grow larger in the gold reflective mirrors of his sunglasses as I neared the passenger side while a cement block of fear formed in my stomach, getting bigger by the minute, too.

The rear dash of the car was crammed to bursting with grocery bags, shoe boxes, a toaster, a rolled-up rug. Opening the door, I discovered I would be sharing the back seat with my suitcase and—among other things—a lamp shaped like a woman's calf in fishnet stockings and high heel, topped with a gold tasseled shade. We were moving. Again.

"*California, here we come*," sang Mom, smiling at me in the rearview mirror.

"Can't I go home first? Make sure you got everything?"

"I don't really want to run into the landlord," she said. "Rent was due last week."

No, she explained, it was best to skedaddle. Ron had heard jobs were plentiful out in California. Paid better, too. And there was the beach; the sunshine.

"Better vibes," she said, looking at Ron. He stared straight ahead, thrumming his fingers on the outside of the car door. It was about a hundred miles further down the road when she broke it to me that I was going to Possum Flats instead. To live with someone she—by all prior accounts—couldn't wait to get away from when she was my age.

I couldn't help but notice Ron's mood brightened considerably at hearing this addendum, while mine plummeted.

I hated Ron. And I hated how my mom did whatever he wanted her to. What about *me*?

I *need* this job. This chance to do something *I* want to do for a change. To get out of my head, my books, my room.

"Let's talk about this in my office."

Fence gestures toward a short hallway lined with more grim photographs, with a break room on one side and an office on the other. His huge gunmetal-gray desk occupies most of the space in the room and is piled high with newspapers: *The New York Times, The Springfield News & Leader, The Kansas City Star, The St. Louis Globe-Democrat.* There is a nearly empty mug of cold coffee with a series of brown rings inside that make me wonder if it's ever been washed.

"Have a seat."

I back uneasily into the stiff, low chair he offers across from his own imposing leather office chair. When he sits, I see how strategic the setup is. I am looking up at him as he rests his elbows on the one cleared-off area directly in front of him, his hands forming a sharp steeple in front of his mustached mouth.

"Well, Daisy. Shoot."

I take a deep breath and squeeze the arms of my chair before plunging ahead. "You know Bartholomew J. Watson, right?"

"Of course. The Mayor. Your Grandma is likely giving the funeral details to Myra as we speak," Fence says. "A delightful man. An upright leader in our community forever and sharp as a tack right up to the end. God rest his soul."

"That's the thing. He's not an upright citizen." I pause, wishing I could unremember what I'd seen on Grandma's gurney this morning. "Well, not in the way he should be, anyway."

"What are you getting at, Daisy?"

This is getting awkward, but I soldier on. "Well, he wasn't with his wife when he died."

"Really?" It doesn't sound like a question. Fence's face isn't showing any emotion. He actually looks bored. I need to up the ante.

"He died . . . with another woman."

Fence still says nothing, waiting me out. But I can tell he's intrigued. Whether by the Mayor or me, I can't tell.

"He was . . ." Language is failing me. I'm not sure how to communicate the next part. "The Mayor was *doing it* with someone else."

Fence's eyes show real alarm, his eyebrows briefly disappearing beneath his sideswept bushy, gray-brown bangs.

"My word," Fence says. "With whom?" He is leaning forward now. He wants the rest of the story and I take my time giving it to him, enjoying the heady rush of power.

"Well . . . let's just say he died at the pharmacy."

"Ah." Fence smiles. "Ginger Morton. An interesting prescription, indeed. Certainly not everyone's drug of choice."

I nod, though I hadn't known her name before now.

"Plus, the Mayor died in an extremely embarrassing position." I'm unstoppable now. "Roger had t—"

"Whoa. Stop right there, Daisy."

I've gone too far. I may be in trouble. Big trouble. Fence stares at me for a long moment, sizing me up. Then he pounds his fist on the desk with a bang and hoots with laughter.

"I'll be damned," he says. He picks up the phone, punches a square button that lights up and proceeds to shout into the receiver: "Smiley, get back here. You're not going to believe this."

I am nervous about what comes next.

"Listen, Daisy. I'm sure you're telling the truth. I mean, I think I can figure out your sources." Fence's voice is a combination of awe and gentle reprimand. "The thing is, even if it's true . . . well, it's not a story. At least, not a story we can tell. What the Mayor did outside of city business isn't really *news*. I mean, everyone knew the Mayor was a little too—let's say 'outgoing'—for his own good. Maybe it wasn't right, but it wasn't against the law, either."

All my hope sinks in my gut like a chunk of concrete.

"But."

But?

"But, hell! I could use a gal who's not afraid to dig around for an interesting angle on our local news. An outsider's perspective, if you will."

The old pointy-nosed man is in the office now—but without the crazy eye, thank God—followed closely by Grandma and Myra. The room seems even smaller than it was before. I'm afraid I'm going to throw up, feeling riotously happy and nauseated at the same time.

"What's going on in here?" Grandma asks.

"Beats me," says the frowning old guy who must be Smiley. "You rang, boss?"

"Meet our new summer intern, Daisy Flowers. See if you can rustle up that old Olympus camera for her to take home. We'll see you Monday morning, Daisy, eight thirty sharp."

Grandma and Myra look at me and then each other with no small amount of amazement.

"Sure thing." I shake Fence's hand over the messy desk. "I'll be here."

DASH

It is a beautiful day for a funeral, praise the Lord.

Of course, I would tell members of my congregation that any day is a beautiful day to die in the Lord Jesus. No more pain and earthly strife. No more suffering and grief. Just the warm embrace of our Savior, welcoming us home at last.

But this is an exceptional day on top of all of that. Not a cloud in the sky. Still a little snap to the air. The kind of spring weather that makes you want to go for a stroll, put your hands in the dirt, let the too-bright sun warm your closed eyelids from the comfort of your front porch rocking chair. From my office here on the second floor of the Assemblies of God Church, just up the hill from the square, I can see downtown in its entirety. God forgive me, I feel a little like the Almighty Himself, surveying my kingdom from on high.

Most days, I can watch the members of my flock coming and going, like ants, single-minded in their tasks. Picking up mail. Shopping for groceries. Stopping in for a fountain soda at Morton's Pharmacy. Getting a bag of fertilizer and a good piece of gossip at Plunk's Hardware. I know what goes on, way in the back where there's still a wood stove in the winter and a coffeemaker that gives off a pleasant dark scorchy smell by midafternoon when the pot of regular gets low. I've been a preacher in this town for nearly fifty years now, and I have duly noted the pall that falls across a group of men sharing a chuckle or story whenever I appear. Ah, well. If my presence is a force for good and a little less evil in the world, then I am glad of it. But I am tempted sometimes to suggest that a clerical collar does not choke off one's sense of humor.

My father was a preacher before me. In the blood, you might say, though I had never intended to dedicate my life to the Lord's service. Far from it. But I believe my father christened me "Paul" for a reason. I have been on the road to Damascus. I have had the conversion experience. I was blind, but now I see.

Back in my salad days, no one called me Paul. I was Dash, always on the move—running toward the next shiny object or scheme or high-tailing it away from trouble. But these days, I'm neither one. I'm typically "Pastor Emmonds" to the larger Possum Flats community, and the more egalitarian "Brother" to the members of my flock. I've heard one cheeky teenager—my own grandson— casually refer to me as "Bro" when he thought I wasn't within earshot. I let him know in no uncertain terms that was inappropriate, although secretly I was touched he felt warmly enough toward me to give me a nickname. Even in my own household, my two daughters and wife opted for "Pastor," which seems odd now that I think of it. But those were early days in my ministry when I felt keenly the mantle of responsibility to my Lord. To be a "pastor" or faithful shepherd required a constant vigilance, for who knew when evil would rear its ugly head? As it says in Acts: *For I know this, that after my departing shall grievous wolves enter in among you, not sparing the flock.*

Today my view affords no peeks at my sheep. It could almost be a painting, everything is so still. The fresh soft greens of the maple trees around the square look like a moss bed I could jump into, if I weren't so old and brittle. Beds of oversized white irises line the courthouse lawn, nodding like nuns in wimples. I have already preached this morning—as have my cohorts at the Baptist, Methodist and Episcopal churches—so the streets are empty, everyone having had their fill of the word of God and hustling home to their more tangible meals of fried chicken or overdone pot roast. Usually one of my parishioners will approach me after the service, shake my hand and offer a tentative invitation to join his or her family for Sunday dinner. I can tell the invitation is more of a perfunctory it's-time-we-had-the-old-pastor-over-for-a-bite than a true desire to share time and table with me. I do not blame them. Yet neither do I let them off the hook: A man's got to eat, after all, and this man is short on the comforts of mashed potatoes and gravy. I lost my dear wife Susan just a year and a half ago, after forty-five years of marriage. It pains me that already I cannot recall the exact color of her eyes, and yet her peach pie's perfectly latticed crust, golden brown and laced with sweet, hot ooze, is as clear in my mind as a photograph. And the taste! Like late summer sunshine distilled down to its resplendent syrupy essence.

As if on cue, my stomach rumbles. The persistent cravings of the earthly flesh, even on this holy Lord's day, a funeral day. Mayor Bartholomew J. Watson, civic legend and man-about-town. A piece of Possum Flats history, passing into the next realm. I would be lying if I said it does not give me pause, here in my seventy-fourth year of life. When we bury our town fathers and mothers, we find our past does not reach back nearly so far, and that we ourselves are now the "elders" on the precipice. The view, no matter how secure one is in one's salvation, is a bit unsettling.

I am pondering how to fit this thought into my funeral sermon when there is a loud knock.

"Come in, Joe," I say. Only one person pounds my door as though I am deaf, and I prepare myself for the sight of my only grandson.

"How did you know it was me?" Joe's grin takes up his entire face, much like his frame fills up the open doorway now, a tinfoil-covered dinner plate looking rather minute in his football-player hands. His mother has sent him on this errand. His antsiness is palpable.

"A premonition," I say. "A vision. A cloud in the wilderness."

"Whatever you say, Brother," Joe says, setting the plate down on my desk with a flourish.

"That's Grandfather to you, son. And truth be told, my intuition had more to do with the heavenly smell of your mother's meatloaf than divine prophecy," I say, pulling back an edge of foil and breathing in a wisp of escaping steam.

Joe belongs to my youngest daughter, Marilyn. She married a local boy. John manages the Ford dealership. He's a good man, honest as the day is long. And he has provided Marilyn everything a woman and wife could ask for—except children of their own. That has been the one deep sadness of their marriage, although you'd never know it to look at them, all hustle-bustle and bursting with pride in their golden-haired champion of a boy. When they adopted Joe fifteen years ago, they opened up their arms to that week-old baby and shut the door on that subject for good. Sometimes I wish for Joe's sake that they had seen fit to take in another. I know the loneliness of being an "only," although under different circumstances. The spotlight burns a little too brightly on us singletons—and it can be a heavy burden, all those parental hopes and dreams piled upon one pair of young shoulders. I have felt the stifling weight of expectation and borne my parents' disappointments in bitter solitude as well.

My older daughter, Janie, married a Kansas wheat farmer and works herself to death raising the crops and five daughters. They kept trying for a boy—her husband Don would have given anything for a son—until, Janie said, it got to be embarrassing. And a little sinful, in my opinion. As Susan used to say to the girls when they were little: "You get what you get, and you don't throw a fit."

My plastic fork sinks deep into the velvety pile of potatoes. "Is everything ready downstairs?"

Joe helps me out for a few extra dollars. We have a part-time sexton during the week, so for a Sunday funeral like Mayor Watson's, I need someone to check the pews for leftover service bulletins—riddled with children's scribbles or stuck together with chewing gum—and put away the hymnals, Bibles and, on warm days, the cardboard fans that have been left out.

"Yep. Ms. Flowers has old Bart set up and ready to roll," Joe says, with the casual callousness of the young. For them, death is still a spectator sport.

"Respect, Joe. That's Mayor Watson you are talking about."

"Yes, sir." Unrepentant rascal.

"Did you put the lights on dim?"

"I did."

"Then I expect your work here is done."

"Thanks, Bro, I mean, Brother. Oops." The devil. He makes to leave, only the slightest bit sheepish, but then stops. "You've got mashed potato in your mustache."

"Bless you, my boy," I say. "And thank your mother for the meatloaf."

ROSE

I love Sundays. The Biblical "day of rest." Even though I'm not religious. I can't quite label myself an atheist, but on the God-fearing spectrum in "Flat Possums"—as the more fatalistic refer to our town—I'm probably somewhere left of center.

Philosophy aside, I won't be taking it easy since this isn't a regular Sunday morning. Today is Mayor Watson's funeral and it starts at two o'clock sharp. I've got to put his face on because, as I like to say, "When makeup is last, it makes the makeup last!" Roger will load him up for his final ride to church around twelve thirty or so, after the morning service crowd has gone home.

Ruby Rae decided she will get to the church early for her good-byes. She didn't want to see the Mayor at the funeral home. I don't blame her.

"And I don't want to know where you picked him up either, Rose," she said when she dropped off his suit. "I just need to know you'll have him looking like himself on Sunday."

Unlike the Mayor, I'm not wearing my "Sunday best," but my cotton turquoise housedress and George's old slippers—and I'm on the front lawn, waiting for *The Springfield News-Leader*. Of course, it's late the one Sunday I'd like it early. I look forward to catching up on the world outside of Possum Flats. Our own little paper comes out just five days a week, and honestly, I don't know how it manufactures that much news. Because despite his posturing as a serious newspaper man, Fence McMillan is more of a cheerleader for our town than a watchdog. There's a reason everyone calls him "Fence" instead of Frederick, like his father and grandfather and great-grandfather before him. He straddles every potentially divisive issue so neatly that it takes all the starch out of the editorials and the rest of the reporting, too—from zoning commission kerfuffles to school board elections. You won't see him come down on one side or the other.

As irritating as that is, I do like the man. We've worked closely together for years now. He was in high school with Lettie, and I imagine he had a crush on her. Most boys did. But she never went in for the studious, awkward types. She always liked the bad boys. Still does. This last one seems the worst of all, only wanting Lettie if she's free and easy. No teenage daughter, in other words. Lettie told me my new arrangement with my granddaughter is "just for the summer," while Ron warms up to fatherhood. We'll see.

But as much as I love staying in my housecoat till noon, drinking Folgers and reading the paper, my favorite part of Sunday is invisible.

It's the quiet.

A place called "Possum Flats" sounds like a serene, peaceful place. Far from it. Real possums are nocturnal—and that's when the human citizens of our fair town are raising a ruckus, too. By Sunday morning, though, the drinking and carousing and socializing of Friday and Saturday night are through. The hung over are squarely divided into two camps, those who take a couple of aspirin and struggle greenly into their hard wooden church pews and the rest who stay cocooned in bed, blinds drawn. Churches are the only places open; our blue laws prevent the sale of pretty much everything on Sunday, so it's a much-needed collective deep breath.

And then, there's me: friend of the God-fearing and the godless alike. I try to keep my judgments—like my eccentricities—

to myself. People had a hard enough time coming around to the idea of a woman-owned-and-operated funeral business. So I zip my lips and let them go about their living—and dying—and I go about my business, too. I like to think of myself as a gatekeeper for both the body and spirit, even though I am not convinced of exactly what the spirit is or where it goes.

Whump!

My newspaper has arrived at last.

"Morning, Ms. Flowers!" A young man's voice rings out in the still morning and I am aware of being caught bare-legged in a pair of too-big wool-lined slippers, standing like a statue in my dewy grass. I pull my faded housecoat around me a bit more snugly.

"Morning, Joe."

Joe Nichols is a beautiful specimen of a boy. He's been my paperboy for five years now, since he was ten years old. He is riding the same bicycle he has had forever, his hulking body precarious on the little banana-shaped seat. A large canvas bag of newspapers hangs beneath his left arm so he can throw with his right, while still pedaling and balancing the handlebars.

"Looks like you'll be ready for football season," I say.

"That's the plan."

"See you up at the church later?"

"Yes, ma'am," he calls over his shoulder. "Bro has me working today."

As I stoop to pick up the newspaper, my old back lets me know with a crack and a pop that it wasn't ready to do that so early in the day. But it's not nearly as early as it was. News of the outside world may have to wait.

If I'm going to get Barty made up in time, I'm going to have to shake my tail feathers.

Now there's something I haven't said or done in about five decades. The thought of this old lady hitting the dance floor again is ridiculous. And I lost my love of dancing when my sister died. I probably wouldn't even remember how to do it.

*   *   *

We got the Mayor delivered to the Assemblies of God right at half past noon. Roger backed the hearse up to the front steps, with me directing. Not that he needed it. He has done this hundreds of times, and knows the parking lots, entrances, exits and layouts of every church in Possum Flats like the back of his hand.

Joe was just arriving with a foil-covered plate and let us in. Delivering Sunday sustenance for the good pastor, I'm sure, as part of his duties today. Marilyn is a terrific cook. She tries to take care of her dad, especially since her mom passed. But it's a tall order since he's stubborn and convinced he knows what is best for himself and everyone else on God's green earth.

Roger and I set up the Mayor in front of the simple altar of honey-colored oak lacquered to a warm shine. Behind the altar, it's another story. The high-arching brick wall is adorned with a giant brass cross that is radiating gaudy concentric circles that make it look as though Christ is more of a radio tower than a savior: "You're listening to the Jesus network."

Roger raised the lid of the casket for me and is now off in the hearse, picking up Ruby Rae ahead of the crowd. And there will be a crowd. Even though the Mayor hasn't been in office for a decade or more, he made his mark. He's the reason we have a wonderful town park with a swimming pool and why the courthouse square always has banners and Christmas lights. Things we take for granted now but didn't exist before Barty was mayor.

I decide to wait outside for Ruby Rae on the steps to escape the low lights and the sickeningly sweet lilies. Probably hundreds of them in the church right now, between all the bouquets and sprays and wreaths. Those awful flowers are still a funeral favorite, even though we don't need them to cover up the smell of death and decay anymore. Give me a bunch of wildflowers in a mason jar any day.

Ruby Rae chose a gorgeous casket. Solid cherry. Top-of-the-line. And she insisted on a full couch, too. It's a little old-fashioned, showing the entire body of the deceased instead of just the top half. And it's more work for me, too, making doubly sure that socks match and shoes are polished to a high gleam. But she said it was what he would have wanted. A little more drama, more "wow" factor. That's the Mayor all over.

He looks good, if I do say so myself. I take pride in my ability to make most every corpse look "natural." That's different from "asleep" or "resting." Anyone who says my clients look as if they are taking a nap is sporting for a punch in the nose. If that's what I was aiming for, I'd pull their necks back, drop their mouths open and put a drop of glycerin at one corner to simulate drool. *Please.*

My watch says straight up one o'clock. Sure enough, here's Roger pulling to the curb and helping Ruby Rae out of the back seat. He gives me a nod before he reaches for her door handle. Roger cleans up pretty well. He's freshly shaven, wearing a pressed black suit complete with pocket square. What hair he has is slicked back so carefully you can see the comb lines. Neat as a pin.

There's the creak of the heavy sanctuary door opening and Dash Emmonds is beside me.

"Brother Emmonds."

"Rose."

We have a civil working relationship, but beyond that, there's not a lot of love lost between me and the good pastor. He can't hide his disdain for me. It's partly that I remind him of his "bad old days," which he would just as soon everyone forget. But he also seems to smell my unadvertised and inviolable agnosticism a mile away. And I'm not afraid to call a spade a spade, which really unnerves him.

Plus, if I'm being honest, I love getting under his skin.

"Hello, Ruby Rae." The petite widow is dazzling in a tailored black dress and pillbox hat complete with a sheer black polka-dotted fascinator that covers most of her face. Her dark eyes and crimson lipstick are luminous behind the netting. She is not a weepy widow. She is a rock—a well-put-together rock. I won't be dealing with hysterics or histrionics today.

"Good afternoon, Rose. Brother Emmonds."

Dash nods and puts a hand lightly on her shoulder, for a beat or

THE FLOWER SISTERS 43

two. He's unsteady on that bad ankle of his, but manages to open the wooden door and usher us in. I let Ruby Rae lead the way, clicking by stoically on her black kitten-heel pumps.

After the door sighs closed, the pastor and I stay back. One thing Dash and I likely agree on is the importance of giving Ruby Rae space to view the body of her husband of seventy-five years, maybe even touch him, say a few quiet words. My role is to be available for support or assistance, but to otherwise aim for invisibility. I expect Dash feels the same way—except for the invisibility part. He has always been a showman.

Ruby Rae is in front of the casket now. She bows her head, as if in prayer. The only noise in the church is the slight squeaking complaint of the ceiling fans, spinning lazily on their long dowels from the arched ceiling.

Until Ruby Rae gasps and lurches backwards. Her arms flail as if she is trying to find a perch or something to steady her.

I waste no time racing to the front of the church, Dash limping along behind.

It could be grief, of course. Or just shock at seeing Barty dead. But I don't think that is the cause of our unflappable widow's distress.

There must be something wrong with the corpse.

My skin prickles. I'm not real big on surprises. Most of what I have always liked about this job is its predictability, the amount of control I have over my clients. These people never backtalk or second-guess me.

Somehow, I guide Ruby Rae to a seat in the front-most pew where she collapses in a neat black heap. Then I assess Mayor Watson, my eyes automatically going first to his face. I assume there is a makeup problem, or the corpse has experienced an involuntary unpleasantness like a half-open eye. That doesn't happen often these days, thanks to the new-fangled spiky eye caps—a porcupine version of contact lenses that keep the lid in place. But no, everything looks good. His face is lightly powdered and rouged, with just the subtlest bit of color.

Then something lower down catches my eye. Much lower down. Dash, beside me now, sees it, too. It's like we're in a Mae West movie: *Is that a pistol in your pocket or are you just glad to see me?*

This can't be. Roger and I took care of Barty's little problem with close to a full roll of duct tape. Something else or *someone* else has interfered.

Dash gives me a look that can only be described as murderous before joining Ruby Rae in the pew to console her.

So much for my "no drama" expectations.

"My dear Mrs. Watson," Dash begins. "I cannot—"

"Please, Pastor," Ruby Rae interrupts. She is blotting her eyes carefully and precisely beneath the netting of her hat, so as not to disturb her makeup. "I wish I had the capacity to be truly shocked or horrified by Bartholomew's antics. But I'm afraid I lost that decades ago."

"This is an outrage!" Dash says, pointing at me. "How did you let this happen?"

"Me? I assure you I didn't 'let' this happen. I never leave anything up to chance. Even"—I pause, unsure how to phrase this delicately—"*private* things."

Ruby Rae has her compact out now, patting her cheeks with powder and applying a fresh coat of lipstick. She looks strangely calm, considering the circumstances. "Well, Bartholomew was a public figure. And unfortunately for our marriage, I'm afraid that his private parts were none too private.

"Honestly, I should leave him this way for the service."

"Now, Ruby Rae, I'm not sure what that would accomplish . . ." Dash is scrambling to regain some modicum of decency here in the church sanctuary.

Meanwhile, Roger is striding toward the front of the church, too, sensing something is amiss. I tilt my head slightly to the right and he joins me at mid-casket to cover for me. I can't believe I am doing this in church, right in front of God—if She exists!—and everyone. Silently asking the Mayor's forgiveness, I slide my hand slowly over the edge of the casket and deep down into his protruding front pocket until I reach something . . . stiff. And *papery?*

I give a slight tug and the whole thing comes free. It's a crumpled Assemblies of God hand fan, cheap cardboard on a thin wooden handle, with a painted picture of a serene Jesus surrounded by fluffy white sheep on one side and Psalm 23 on the other: *The Lord is my shepherd; I shall not want.* Beneath that, in small cursive type, it reads, *Courtesy of Morton's Pharmacy.*

If I weren't about to have a conniption fit, I'd laugh.

I smooth the fan out and impulsively stuff it between the satin coffin lining and Mayor Watson's backside. He might actually need it where he's going.

The funeral service itself is a relief. Roger, finished with his ushering duties, sits beside me in the back pew. This calms me. The dirge-like "Amazing Grace," on the other hand, which the organist is plodding through at a painful pace, does not. I hate that song, with its emphasis on how wretched, lost and blind I am.

Scanning the crowd, I see Myra up near the front with one of her giant hats, likely taking notes for the society page. Fence and Smiley are beside her. There's Betty, who has switched out her waitress apron for a dark blue shirtwaist. Up front, of course, is Dash Emmonds, wearing his best dark suit.

With a jolt of surprise, I spot Ginger Morton. She has every right to be here, I suppose. She's not a murderer, after all, although she technically killed Barty off with their extra-marital frolicking. Maybe more of an "accessory" to the crime. But it would be more noticeable if she *weren't* here, wearing her fur stole in the middle of May to remind everyone that she's loaded. If every woman who had a "thing" with the Mayor boycotted the service, there would be a lot of empty seats. And the Assemblies of God is jam-packed.

Possum Flats has turned out in force, which is quite a testament to Mayor Watson, since most everyone just got out of morning services a couple of hours ago. How much church can a person take?

When the organ music finally stops, Dash rises slowly from his chair to the right side of the altar and makes his way to the lectern.

"My brothers and sisters in Christ, I welcome you as we celebrate Mayor Bartholomew J. Watson's coming into the Lord's kingdom. Praise God!"

The pastor seems a little shaky. Probably the stress before the service, and, frankly, old age. He's only a half dozen years older than I am, but they show. Yet I can see faint traces of the gorgeous heartbreaker he was back in his prime. He can still pull himself up to an imposing height. And that hair—a thick white mane of it, with that one vain curl that yet graces his lined forehead. It makes me happy, that little curl. Otherwise I might not believe Dash was ever really human.

"'For God so loved the world that He gave his only begotten Son, that he who believeth in him, though he perish, he will have eternal life.' John 3:16. *Though he perish!* Our dear Brother Watson lived on this earth for ninety-five years. But it was only several days ago that his real life, his eternal life in Christ, truly began! He has moved beyond Possum Flats to the Glorious Heights that is life in our Lord Jesus."

"Amen, amen," a few in the crowd murmur. "Praise God!"

"Mayor Watson was a true gentleman. He worshipped and obeyed the Lord with every fiber of his being. He lived a godly life, spreading the Good News while he made Possum Flats a town we can be proud of, bringing others to Christ through his example, praise the Lord . . ."

I find myself starting to drift. *A gentleman.* I wonder what this man of the cloth would say about Mayor Watson's more adulterous side? Fornication was still against the Ten Commandments, last I checked.

Dash's voice still contains that velvety deep beckoning tone that I remember from way back when. But the words that come out of his mouth now! It is hard for me to listen. I feel certain that he believes them, but give me the unrepentant scoundrel he used to be, the young man who used to sweet-talk the girls into the back seat, not the front pew.

He drones on and on, delivering more of a sermon than a eulogy, as though the death of Mayor Watson is a jumping-off point to remind the rest of us it's not too late to avoid eternal hellfire and give our lives to the Lord. I hope he doesn't ask anyone to come down front and accept Jesus as his or her personal savior. I don't think Mayor Watson would want to share his big day.

A booming "amen" brings me back to the moment. Dash has finally turned off the faucet. It's time for everyone to pay their last respects.

A long line forms down the aisle between the pews. The organist does a depressing version of "What a Friend We Have in Jesus" in a minor chord as the line begins to snake its way in front of the casket and curve back and around to the pews. The light filtering through the modern, colored blocks of stained glass makes a rainbow in the middle aisle, giving everyone a strange hue as they pass through green, blue, red and yellow patches.

Ruby Rae is alone in the front pew, the Watsons having lost their only daughter tragically many years ago. The widow's shrunken spine is upright as she faces forward, taking in the somber parade. I wonder what she is thinking. I'm sure she loved him. To all outward appearances, he adored her, escorting her around town as if she were a queen. But what we see from the outside is rarely the uncomplicated truth.

Roger elbows me gently. The line has dwindled to the final few mourners. We always head up last so that we can close the casket in a quick but reverent manner after the final farewells.

I never cry at funerals. Call it stoicism or professionalism or even a callousness that comes with having so many of the dead pass through my doors. But I find myself tearing up as Roger and I take our separate places at the head and foot of the coffin. There is something so sad about living nearly a century and having two such disparate halves to your life. And doing irreparable harm to another in the process. Someone you love.

Maybe we can't always be the person we want to be. Maybe not even most of the time.

See you on the other side, Mr. Mayor.

Roger is trying to catch my eye. I don't know how long I have been standing like this, but the congregation is no longer singing and it feels as if the organist is trying to buy time. I nod at him and we reach at the same time for the lid of the casket and close it gently. I fasten the two golden latches on the side with a sigh.

I don't like what is coming next. And I don't mean the graveside service or the reception afterwards. What happened this morning with the Mayor tells me that someone has shared the unfortunate circumstances of his death. It wasn't me or Roger. I'm one hundred-and-ten percent certain it wasn't Ginger Morton, either.

I'm going to have to deal with that someone when I get home.

Daisy

Today is my first day at *The Picayune* and I woke up smiling in the dark, long before sunup. I haven't felt this way since before Mom and Ron dropped me off. Somehow it makes me miss her even more. She would think it was cool that I am going to be a real reporter. That's something that might hold her attention for more than a minute or two.

Okay. That was harsh. But it's true that the same things that make Mom so fun—her sense of adventure, love of new places and people—also make her quick to abandon the old or the boring. She's like a raccoon, drawn from one bright, sparkly thing to the next.

And she's good at avoiding the hard stuff altogether. There's that saying, "When the going gets tough, the tough get going." Mom takes that literally: She doesn't tap into some deep, inner strength in adversity; she just hits the road. And . . . it works for her. But sometimes I wish I could have a real house. A *home*. With a yard. Two parents. Friendships that lasted longer than one school year.

But that's not part of the package with my mom.

After I turn on the lights, I sit down at Mom's old desk, painted a princessy mix of white and gold, and start another letter. I scrawl two full pages in my steno pad without even trying. There is so much going on!

I do *not* ask about Ron. Ugh. He's lucky I even know his name. I learned early on not to get too attached or comfortable with Mom's love interests, even though—unlike this current disaster of a boyfriend—I actually liked a few of them. But she changes them out as regularly as she does her purses, so why bother?

When I tear out the pages, the frayed bits near the wire rings litter my desk. I pull out an envelope, slide in my letter and lick the sweetish glue on the flap before sealing it tight. Then I address the front in care of the post office in Petaluma, California. Mom told me she would pick up her mail there until she had a real address. *Petaluma.* A flowery-sounding place for my flowery-sounding mom: Violet Flowers. "Lettie" for short. She took her mom's maiden name after she left home—the *only* thing she took, she said: "I never really felt like a Steinkamp."

Anyway, I looked up Petaluma in Grandma's encyclopedia and apparently the name means "hill backside." Mountain butt.

Still beats the hell out of Flat Possums. I mean, *Possum Flats.*

Before I tuck the letter in my book bag, I bring it to my lips, just a sweet little smack on the front where I've written her name. I feel silly, because it's something a little kid might do. I mean, I don't put on Bonne Bell lip gloss or anything first. My kisses are completely invisible. But for some reason, I am superstitious about it. Like if I don't do it, Mom might not feel my love. And that kiss is the best I can do from here.

I will drop my letter off at the post office on my way to the paper. The old lady behind the counter probably knows me by now. Grandma grumbles every time we go about how stamps are up to thirteen cents this year. That's a whole extra nickel, she says. And up more than a dime from when she was my age. I think it is amazing that you can drop a piece of mail in a box with just a few words and numbers on it and it gets to a house or apartment a hundred or even a thousand miles away. But Grandma thinks everything was better in "the old days," which is a funny way to phrase it, because I think she is actually in her old days now. I wonder if I will ever look back on the time I am living right now as the best days of my life.

I doubt it.

In my letter, I left out the part where Grandma freaked out about the internship. Not that she wasn't excited about me getting out of the house, but she had a major bone to pick about how I got the job.

"Daisy May Flowers!"

I was propped up on my bed reading Kurt Vonnegut late yesterday afternoon when I heard the front door open and Grandma already yelling before it slammed closed. She was all decked out in her black dress that's too tight around the midsection and an old-fashioned black hat with a button on top. I think of it as her "funeiform." But I would never say that out loud, and especially not at that moment. Grandma's eyes were bulging out of their sockets and her neck was stretched tight so that all the cords showed beneath the skin. Instinctively, I pulled my knees up toward my chest.

"Did you or did you not tell someone where and how the Mayor expired?"

Uh-oh. I am getting a strange visual of the Mayor as a jug of milk past his prime. But I don't think that's what Grandma means.

"Why?"

"Because *something* came up at the funeral is why," Grandma snapped. "And I don't mean in conversation."

I had no idea what she was talking about, so I decided to try the honesty route.

"I may have said something at the newspaper the other day."

"You *may* have said something at *The Picayune*? Oh, that's just peachy." Grandma flounced down at my desk. "Why not just announce it on the radio or broadcast it on TV while you're at it? Or how about I wear it on a sandwich board, for Christ's sake?"

I didn't know what to say—or what a sandwich board was—but that didn't keep Grandma from continuing her extremely animated one-sided conversation. Soon she was up again, pacing my floor.

"Let me guess: Fence McMillan."

I nodded glumly. She hit one clenched fist into the palm of her other hand.

"Damn it. And he told Myra or Smiley or both and then . . . well, take it from there. The whole town knows now."

She sighed as if the starch had gone completely out of her, sinking down on the foot of my bed like so much black laundry.

"Listen, Daisy. I know you don't know this town or these people or even me, if we're being completely honest. But I do. For good or bad or otherwise, I've watched them live their lives and helped them bury their dead.

"There are some secrets you just don't tell. And if, God forbid, you do, you most surely don't tell them to Fence. That man is a complete chickenshit when it comes to publishing the real news. But he'll gossip till the cows come home. And that's how people really get hurt. Believe me, I should know."

I tried to imagine what secrets my grandma might have as she sat there pulling up the elastic of her ugly beige knee-highs and absent-mindedly rubbing one calf.

"I'm sorry," I said.

Grandma reached toward my hunched-up knees and gave me a pat.

"I know, honey," she said. "You just be careful around old Fence, all right? Write the truth, but make sure the truths you write are yours to tell."

"Okay." I wasn't sure exactly what she was getting at, but I knew I'd been warned.

Then Grandma lay back across my bed and began to laugh. At first it was sort of a cough, and I thought maybe she was choking on something. But after a minute, she was practically having a seizure she was laughing so hard. Tears leaked out of the corners of both eyes and she swiped at them with the lace handkerchief she had pulled from one pocket.

"Lord, but the old man gave a hell of a last salute, if you know what I mean."

I didn't, but Grandma was happy to explain.

"Courtesy of Morton's Pharmacy. Whoo boy." She shook her head, trying to regain her composure.

"But who did that? The thing with the fan?"

"I'm sure I don't know," said Grandma, her face clouding over. "But I'd love to find out. Someone out there has a twisted sense of humor. Or justice."

Maybe I'd find out. I was going to be a crack reporter, wasn't I?

I couldn't wait for my first assignment.

June 5, 1978

Dear Mom

How is Petaluma? Do you have a place yet? Please make sure that my new room has a window. Sometimes I sit at your old desk and think about you looking out of this window when you were my age. I'm sitting here right now, as a matter of fact.

I bet things looked pretty much the same. Boring. I can see why you wanted to leave. And didn't it creep you out to have dead people in the house all the time? Grandma acts like it's no big deal. Sometimes I think she likes them better than people who are alive. I hear her talking to them. It's weird.

But guess what? Next time you see something written from me, it might be in print. For real! I talked my way into a summer job at *The Possum Flats Picayune*. Fence McMillan is the editor. He says he knows you from "way back." He's a little obsessed with death (what is it with everyone around here?) and destruction. But other than that, he seems okay.

Actually, today's my first day, so I've got to get ready. I don't know what to wear. People dress different here. Kind of boring, honestly.

Anyway, I'm gonna drop this at the post office on my way to the newspaper so you get my big news ASAP. I hope you found a job, too, and that you and Ron will be ready for me to come out there soon. Love you/miss you/bye!

xoxoxo
Daisy

Hazel

There is a face smashed up against the glass door of my post office.

I see a flattened nose, the side of a hand pressed into the glass above a forehead, shading the eyes so the creature can see inside. I guess I'll be wiping away the oily smudges with some Windex after the "morning rush."

Typically, when I reach the heavy glass doors to flip the CLOSED sign to OPEN and twist the thick key in the lock, there is always a line—although in Possum Flats, the definition of a line can be two people. Lots of regulars come in early on their way to work or other errands, to check their boxes, mail a letter or birthday card or buy some extra stamps.

I marvel at people who buy a particular number of stamps—two or three or seven—instead of a sheet or a multiple of ten. Stamps aren't expensive, after all. But no, they force me to crease a perforated line from the large square sheet to tear off the requested number without damaging any. Buying just one or a few is a way of ensuring that a person will need to come back, maybe even as soon as the next day—when there's another bill or card to mail. If I have learned anything from my years as postmistress of Possum Flats, it's that we love our routines and rituals, large and small.

The impatient face peering through my front door is no exception. It has appeared there every Monday morning like clockwork for the past four weeks—and sometimes other mornings, too—and belongs to Daisy Flowers. And she belongs to Rose, of course. With that dark straight hair and matching eyes, she could *be* Rose . . . from fifty years ago. But she favors bell bottoms over drop-waist dresses. I'm sure being Lettie's child has something to do with that.

"Good morning," I say, holding open the door.

She mumbles something and slips by me, heading toward the counter.

Daisy makes me uncomfortable. It's not her impatience or her clothes. Or the fact that she hasn't bothered to learn my name, even though she's what I'd call a regular, too. Always posting letters to her mom in care of a post office box in California.

No, what makes me uneasy is the fact that, beneath my beautiful wooden countertop, varnished by decades of money and postage exchanging hands, is a growing stack of envelopes addressed to Lettie Flowers in Petaluma. Every single one is stamped RETURN TO SENDER—NOT AT THIS ADDRESS. I believe there are five of them now. And I've mailed a couple more that haven't returned yet, bent at the corners from their thousand-mile journeys and marked as rejected. I haven't opened them. I think it would break my heart to read what's inside. What I imagine is sad enough—loneliness, being a stranger in a small town, desperately wanting some news from her mom, who has left her high and dry. I've had too much grief of my own to take on more. Not to mention that opening those letters is against the law. Keeping this stash of un-opened letters from her probably is, too. But I'm going with the lesser of two evils.

I keep imagining that the moment will come when she will show up at my service window and I'll say, "I think I have something of yours," and set before her that bundle of . . . what? Pain and suffering? Rejection? Even worse: worry. She will think something is terribly wrong. An accident or maybe drugs or a controlling man. Her mind will go to the worst first. And who could blame her? We all know Lettie. Her moods run hot and cold—nothing in-between. Smart as a whip but short on common sense. Terrible taste in men. And I hate to use the word "selfish," but she has been in the "me decade" for about forty years.

And no one knows her better than Rose. She would not bat an eyelash to discover that Lettie has fallen off the face of God's green earth without a thought for her own daughter. I've thought about giving Rose the letters, but the idea makes me anxious. And not just because it's against the rules.

Rose Flowers is a good woman. She does her work in Possum Flats with decency and her own strange brand of kindness. But I find myself trying to avoid her, because when I see her, I see Violet. She was one of my good-time girlfriends, back when I enjoyed dancing and boys and carrying on. Rose reminds me that although I escaped death once, fifty years ago, the next time it comes will be for keeps.

It's better to let the letters be.

"Need a stamp today, hon?"

Daisy nods and pushes a dime and three pennies across the counter.

Daisy

"Obits," Fence says when Myra presents me at his door. "Teach this girl to write a proper obituary."

My heart sinks to my knees. I was thinking police beat, city hall, politics. Not dead people. Again. My life in Possum Flats has a theme—and I don't like it.

Fence sees my face. "Come on, now. Everybody learns on obits. Even Woodward and Bernstein started with obits. It's the best way to learn to write a news story. It uses the inverted pyramid and everything. Right, Myra?"

"That's right, sugar. You've got your big lead up top and it all ends in a point at the bottom, so you can relax and have a good time in the middle. I'll show you. It's fun."

Myra gives a little nod to Fence to let him know she's got everything under control.

Before I walked through the front door of *The Picayune* today, I was psyching myself up, trying on different attitudes as I made my way down the sidewalk. First I put a little swagger into my step, my bell-bottoms swishing along the ground as I walked. Too much for a rookie, I thought, especially one who has never written a real news article before. So I put a somber look on my face and tucked a No. 2 pencil behind one ear. Serious. I was going to be a serious journalist.

And now this: obituaries.

"C'mon, sweetie pie. I'll get you set up over here."

Myra weaves her way through the maze-like aisles in the news-room. Every desk is topped with an Underwood typewriter and scarred with coffee cup rings. There are lots of curious faces, and Myra uses her social editor skills to introduce me around.

"This is Patty, our receptionist," says Myra, when we reach the front of the maze. It's the girl with the extremely long hair and denim skirt. "Patty, Daisy here is going to be at extension five. So you can put all those hot news tips through, okay?"

Patty nods vigorously. "I've never met a hippie before." Gravely, she holds up a hand with two of her fingers forming a V.

"Peace."

I am dumbstruck. "Um . . . okay? Cool."

Myra looks amused at my obvious discomfort but spares me further interrogation. She takes one arm gently and pulls me toward the center of the newsroom.

"Daisy, I know you got a gander at him the other day, but I'd like you to *officially* meet Smiley, photographer extraordinaire and head of the photo desk."

I stick out my hand. I can't help but note Smiley's unsmiling demeanor, lips a thin line beneath a beaky nose. But as soon as he opens his mouth, I understand that Smiley is just the quiet type, not a grouch or curmudgeon.

"I'm the *only* photographer," he admits with a shy shrug.

"Now, Smiley. Don't be so humble," Myra chides in a flirty tone. She is older, but I've noticed she's still got some sway in those hips. She's decked out in a smart red suit with a ruffled blouse peeking out from the top as if she is going to a meeting or business dinner. But I have the feeling she dresses like this every day.

I meet Bill, a grizzled World War II veteran with one functional arm who manages the backroom presses and barely acknowledges me. Myra tells me afterwards that he is hard of hearing and doesn't like conversation—but a real "teddy bear" when you get to know him. Last is Sedalia, a bespectacled cylinder of a woman who is in charge of circulation—which I find out has to do with subscriptions and deliveries, not blood flow. She gives me a long up-and-down before pushing her glasses back on her nose and getting back to her paperwork.

"Nice to meet you, too," I say.

Myra's laugh comes out like she is choking, and she quickly steers me away from Sedalia and toward a small school desk piled with old newspapers, empty film canisters and a half-full cup of coffee with a layer of clumped creamer floating uneasily in the center.

"I meant to have this all cleaned off for you," she says, grabbing the coffee and papers. "For now you can use my typewriter. Do you type?"

"Hunt and peck."

"That's fine. You can even write longhand and type it later if you like. I'll be right back."

Myra disappears down the hallway toward Fence's office and I take a minute to survey my surroundings. Through the front wall of windows, it is a sparkling June day. The maple trees in front of the drive-through bank across the street are turning from neon green to the more lush greens of summer. A blond boy who is too big for his bicycle rolls by on the sidewalk, a canvas newspaper bag over his shoulder.

"Caught you looking," says Myra, giving me a little nudge. "No fraternizing with the paperboys," she says playfully.

I feel my cheeks heat up.

"Here's a legal pad, a couple of steno pads and pens and pencils. Smiley will get you some film for your camera." She pulls up two rolling chairs and holds one out for me, a manila folder tucked under one arm. "Now let's get started on this obituary."

She opens the folder and pulls out a sheet of paper with the Flowers Funeral Home logo. I can't escape who I am for a single moment in this town. I feel like everyone and everything in Possum Flats have their eyes on me. Suddenly, the macramé vest over my T-shirt and the blue jeans sprinkled with appliqués, which seemed so right this morning, make me feel hot and itchy and obvious. I glance up just in time to see other people look down at their desks, pretending not to have been staring.

"So. Here's the thing. We usually start with the full name, then the age the person was when he or she kicked the bucket. That means a bit of math. And remember that the person may not have had their birthday yet this year, so you may need to take one more off your total.

"Like Mr. Buck here. Born June 24, 1902 and here we are in early June. Poor old guy didn't quite make it to seventy-six. See what I mean?"

Myra pauses to look at me over the top of her cat-eye glasses. I am miserable. Why did I ever think this would be a good idea? *Mr. Buck kicked the bucket.* I want to be a writer. But I can't see how cobbling together a few paragraphs about a dead person is going to help me with that.

"Now listen, sugar. I know you're disappointed. You want to write big stories, right? The kind people can't wait to get their hands on, that tell them something they didn't already know? Stories that *matter*."

I nod, but keep my head low, unable to look her in the eyes.

"That's what obituaries are, don't you see?" She reaches her hand over and pulls my chin from my chest. "These are stories about a life. What could be bigger than that? And in Possum Flats or any other town, small or large, these are the stories that people are anxious to read.

"And maybe they learn something, too, about a person they thought they knew. About a neighbor or friend or someone who worked down at Plunk's. It makes them think about themselves and how they want to live. How they want to be remembered. I know that's true for me."

I feel hot shame creep into my face. Myra pats my knee. I have been forgiven.

"So back to Mr. Buck here," she says. "After the age, we usually write that he 'passed away' or 'went to be with the Lord' or 'received his heavenly reward' or something to that effect. And then the day of passing."

"Passing? That sounds like changing lanes on a highway. Why not just say he *died*?"

Myra looks thoughtful for a moment. "Well," she says, "*died* just sounds so, you know . . . final. Sort of like, *boom*, that's it."

"But it *is* final."

"Yes, but life is . . . difficult. In Possum Flats, we like our obituaries with a little optimism. The possibility of eternal salvation is our escape hatch. Our ace in the hole," Myra says. "Thank God for Jesus, right?"

I don't know what to say. To me, Jesus is something in between George Washington and Superman, kind of historical but with superpowers that make Him not quite real. My mom never took me to church. Sundays for her were for sleeping in after a hard night of partying. Sometimes a boyfriend or a date stayed over, emerging from her room hungover and blinking in the light, wearing a pair of faded boxer shorts or yesterday's rumpled shirt and jeans. He would always look surprised to see me, curled up on the couch in my footie pajamas eating cold cereal. As if he had forgotten—or maybe never knew—that I was part of the package. I'd just nod politely and return to my cartoons. I never saw most of them again.

I shrug at Myra. "So what's next?"

"Well, this is the juicy part. You'll want to mention when and where they were born and to whom. Then what their schooling was, high school or college or both. Their jobs. The groups they were active in, like the sewing circle at church or the Elks Lodge. Church membership is big. That should be the grand finale on that paragraph."

That's the juicy part? Kill me now. Myra is oblivious to my despair, chattering away and—like most people who love gossip or make a living at gossiping—reveling in the chance to tell someone something they don't know. I get bits and pieces of what she is explaining now: survivor lists, those who preceded the deceased in death, funeral arrangements, where to send donations. My mind wanders.

Suddenly, Myra is putting her hand on top of mine and leaning in so close I can smell her face powder.

"And one more thing, Daisy." Her voice lowers to nearly a whisper. "You might lose the hippie outfits."

She smiles apologetically.

"You sort of make people nervous," she says. "And I know you don't want to be that kind of girl."

As she stands up, she smooths her already wrinkle-free skirt. Then she's off to her own desk and phone and whatever news the day brings her.

What kind of girl am I?

I'm quiet. A little shy. I haven't ever had close friends—which goes back to the quiet and shy part. Compounded by the fact that I've never been at the same school for more than a year or two, since my mother wanders wherever the next boyfriend or perfect job takes her (declaring that this time, he—or the job—is "the one"). Ha. My mom can quit a job *or* a man faster than you can blink an eye. Which is why I've always tried to be invisible, to cause my mom the least amount of trouble that I can. So she won't quit me.

Maybe in Possum Flats I can be someone different. Someone who isn't quiet or afraid. Someone who takes charge. Who speaks up. And tells the truth, no matter what. It could be my chance to finally be *seen*. To no longer be invisible, but to be the person I've always been on the inside. After all, that's what got me this internship.

But I'll stay with my hippie chick chic, thank you very much.

I reach for one of the dozen pristine yellow pencils in the coffee mug on my desk.

Okay, Mr. Buck. I guess this is your first obit, too. Maybe we can figure this thing out together.

The morning flies by. I struggle to piece together Mr. Buck's life story. I can see the arc of it, the way the birth and death make bookends that include an eighth-grade education, decades of dairy farming, marriage, three daughters and a son, nine grandchildren, being an elder in the Church of Christ. I feel a twinge of genuine sadness as I type up the names of those who preceded him in death: his son as an infant; his wife of forty-nine years. Which hole was bigger? The wife who had always been there and then wasn't, or the baby boy whose birth likely came with so many hopes and expectations as the only male heir on a dairy farm? Nibbling the soft pink flesh of my pencil eraser, I decide that a hole is a hole—it is defined by the absence of something, small or large—and that it is the gone-ness that matters.

"Penny for your thoughts," says a quiet, gravelly voice just over my left shoulder.

Smiley.

"I might let them go for a dime," I say. "Inflation, you know."

Smiley finds this amusing. "Fence said you drive a hard bargain. What've you got planned for lunch?" He ducks his head down so that for a few seconds, I can't see his bright blue eyes, pools of calm in his massively wrinkled face.

"My grandma sent me a sandwich," I say. "Peanut butter with homemade blackberry jam. But I'm not really hungry yet."

"Could have fooled me," he says slyly, and I am suddenly aware of the cushiony pink eraser that sits brutally perforated atop my pencil.

"Just teasing. I brought a sandwich, too. Egg salad. I always bring egg salad. With pickles."

I cringe.

"Not a fan, eh? Well, what do you say you stick with what you like and I'll stick with what I like. We can eat separately . . . together. But I need to develop a few photos first. Want to see how it works?"

"Sure. I've got the camera Fence gave me," I say. "But I have no idea how to use it or anything that goes in it. I guess I'm an Instamatic kind of a girl."

"That is not photography." Smiley frowns. "That's like calling paint-by-number, art."

"Paint-by-number?"

"Never mind," he says. "But I hold that you can't be much of a reporter if you can't get the pictures right."

"I know. A picture's worth a thousand words and all of that."

"Yes, Ms. Smarty, that's true. You might think I would say you don't even need words if you have a good photograph, but you'd be wrong."

"I would? Well, that would not be the first time today," I say drily, thinking of Myra's attempts to educate me about the vocabulary of death and dying.

"Both," Smiley says simply. "You gotta have both. The picture gives depth to the words and the words give specificity to the photo."

"Specificity?"

"Identity," Smiley says, rubbing the faint gray stubble of his pointy chin. "Singularity. Uniqueness. It's like putting together the story with the picture makes us more likely to feel a connection to them both, you know? Something more than what each could accomplish on its own."

"Smiley," I say, "you're quite the philosopher."

"That's the polite term, Daisy," he says, the lines around his mouth deepening into a wry smile. "Most would call me a bullshitter. And I don't entirely disagree with that assessment, either."

"I guess I can make up my own mind about that," I say. "Let's see that dark room."

When Smiley closes the door, it is as if we have entered another world. It takes my eyes a moment to adjust to the dimness, the only light coming from a glowing purply bulb that makes everything white look electrified, bright and rimmed with lilac neon. The smell is chemical, not like cleaning products or my grandma's disturbing basement, but more like a lab experiment, where some amazing reaction or new element might be created. I shudder, but I'm unsure whether it's from the cool, still air in the tiny room or all the possibilities. I know already that I will love photography.

"Wow."

Smiley grins at me, his teeth brilliant white in the black light. "I know. Pretty great, isn't it?"

He shuffles into one corner in his unnaturally white tennis shoes. "This is my little hideout," he says. "Sorry there's not much room. I made it out of a storage closet thirty years back or so. It was supposed to be temporary. But now I wouldn't change it for anything."

There is so much to look at: every wall filled with a collage of black-and-white photographs, the small table topped with a line of silvery aluminum pans full of clear liquid, the fuzzy white rope bisecting the room with intermittent clothespins perched on it like birds on a telephone wire.

"Laundry?" I say, puzzled.

"Sort of," Smiley says. "Watch this."

He reaches for a rectangular sheet of pristine paper from beneath a large microscope-looking machine and places it gently into the first of the three trays. With a small pair of tongs, he submerges the paper completely, carefully pushing down each corner. His face, in profile, is even more intense in concentration: his wrinkles have wrinkles.

After the paper is completely wet, he sets the timer on a clock, round and black-faced with large white numbers. Then he grabs hold of one corner of the tray holding the paper and begins gently rocking it back and forth, like a mother with a bassinet. His look is expectant, too, so I fix my eyes where his are and am thrilled as ghost-like shapes take form. As the liquid ripples back and forth, I can see thick layers of light-colored flower petals clustered around a dark center. Soon another flower appears, smashed so closely against the first that it is as if there are two centers for one flower, the outer petals of both forming not a circle, but a figure eight. Two ordinary flowers creating something strange and stunning. Holding this odd double bloom is an angelic little kid with dark hair and eyes whose cheeks are nearly as full as the flowers. His expression is not one of joy.

"Who's that?" I ask, mesmerized by the weird contrast of off-kilter beauty and obvious distress.

"Oh, that's Hazel Hodges' grandson, Will," he says. "The old gal behind the counter at the post office? She's got an amazing flower garden out in back. She likes to dig in the dirt when things get a little slow."

"No kidding." Although I know that my regular dispatches to Petaluma have increased her workload.

"This first pan is full of developer fluid," he explains. "Next up is what we call the stop bath, because it stops the developing process. Thirty seconds is all it takes."

The image of the put-upon Will and the double-bloom flower seems to shiver slightly in its bath. Then Smiley moves it to the final tray.

"This is the 'fixer,'" he says, settling the photo comfortably at the bottom of the pan, fully submersed. "Takes just a little longer."

I am fascinated by the photo as much as the process. "Why is he holding that bizarre flower? He looks so miserable."

"Well, you might as well get used to it, because I'll bet you dollars to donuts that you'll be taking quite a few just like it yourself this summer."

"Pictures of Will?" I ask, confused.

"No, pictures of flowers. The strange and the beautiful. Like these Siamese twin black-eyed Susans, which Hazel found 'extraordinary.' But she wanted Will in the photo with them, not her 'scarred-up, dried-up old self,' as she so eloquently put it."

"Wait. I'm going to be taking flower pictures all summer?" This was not the accident scene or the courtroom criminal of my fantasies.

"No, of course not," he says kindly. I sigh with relief. Which lasts about fifteen seconds. "There's much, much more to it than flowers. Why, you'll have the chance to get up close and personal with a whole cornucopia of vegetables and fruits, too. And let me tell you, the fruits and veggies bring out the wackos, if you know what I mean."

"I do *not* know what you mean," I say, becoming more despondent by the second. I am thinking of my summer, stretching out before me as a long, hideous trail of obituaries and photographic documentation of oddities from the plant world.

"Well, it's kind of like those people who see an image of Jesus or the Virgin Mary in their toast," he says, removing the dripping photo from the tray. He edges by me to a small sink and begins running water over the surface of the photo. Then he grabs a couple of clothespins from the white rope and fastens the photo to it to dry, like a tiny, doll-sized sheet on the clothesline. "People see weird things in their produce. And they want nothing more than to share it with their neighbors in *The Possum Flats Picayune.* Last summer I photographed a man who swore his summer squash looked just like President Carter. I didn't really see the resemblance, but . . . anyway, there was a woman with a tomato that she called 'Dolly Parton,' for obvious reasons." Here Smiley chuckles, a little embarrassed.

"Such as?"

Smiley looked up at me in alarm. "You don't know Dolly Parton?"

"Never heard of her."

"Country music star? A little . . ." Smiley seems to be struggling for the right words. "Top heavy? Got her start on *The Porter Wagoner Show?*"

"Porter who?"

"Dear Lord, you've got a lot to learn," Smiley says. "He's a country music star, born right here. The main drag into town is named after him."

"Oh. Right," I say. Porter Wagoner Boulevard. I know I have a lot to learn, but I hope it's not all small-town trivia. "I'm ready for that sandwich now. But keep those pickles as far away as possible."

"Speaking of pickles, cucumbers are the worst," Smiley says, reaching for the light switch. The photography lesson is over. "Those suckers can contort themselves something awful. Don't say I didn't warn you."

ROSE

It's quiet this morning. A couple of boisterous cardinals treated me to some early musical repartee, but they've broken up the party now and are likely hunkered down somewhere in cool shade. A bright white cue ball of sun is promising to heat things up quickly. Sometimes I think spring lasts about fifteen minutes around here and then we're all sitting on Hell's front porch.

No new clients thus far today, although I heard at the funeral reception yesterday that old Mr. Morton—of Morton's Pharmacy—was on his last leg up at the nursing home. He's close to ninety-eight and weighs about the same. I saw him in the front lobby in a wheelchair a few months ago, when I was picking up a death certificate. He had shrunken in on himself like a baby bird just hatched out of the egg, limbs drawn up in the shape of its former container, head smooth but for the softest, feathery down.

Before the Mayor died, I would have said there is no way I would get the business when Mort's time comes. Ginger would have likely gone with an out-of-town funeral home. Springfield or somewhere even more big city. Because she can afford it. And she's never cared much for me. But now that I've saved her bacon? Maybe Morty will end up at Flowers after all.

I'll likely spend the morning tidying things up around here. For all the certainty of my means of making a living—since death, like taxes, is still very much inevitable—there is a real randomness to the timing. I may go several weeks without a customer and then—in a flurry of grim reaping—I'll get two or three in as many days, which has me and Roger working around the clock. So I don't waste a down moment when I get one. I inventory my chemicals and place a few orders. Organize the cleansing products and makeup bins. Dust the showroom hung like a macabre art gallery with all the sample coffin pieces—from pinewood and mahogany to polished chrome and everything in-between—and the small but tasteful selection of graceful double-handled urns. The citizens of Possum Flats have not yet embraced cremation. It's just a little too close to the concepts of hellfire and damnation. And for those who believe that the physical body will be raised up on the Last Day, keeping theirs as intact as possible is a priority. I'm more of an ashes-to-ashes type, myself. But the customer is always right. I've got the scars on my tongue—from biting it all these years—to prove it.

Speaking of keeping my mouth shut, I had to exercise some self-control when Daisy walked out the door this morning in that weirdo getup. It was Lettie all over again. I know how people think around here. I'm not saying it's right, I'm just saying how it is. I have raised plenty of eyebrows in my nearly seventy years in this small corner of the planet, whether it's what I've worn or sworn or done for a living. I don't regret my nonconformity. But I would like to spare my grandchild the hurt and pain of being different.

I know my life experience is fairly unusual. To be one half of a pair of identical twins would seem to be an exercise in similarity rather than difference. And it was, in many ways, a symmetrical life. To look into another's eyes that are your own eyes, but not; to think your own thoughts and realize them wordlessly understood in the mind of another. Which is not quite the same as thinking alike . . . for heaven knows my sister and I did not.

And yet it was our uncanny likeness to each other that made us so different from everyone else, the singletons. This was a couple of decades before the Dionne quintuplets up in Iowa, when twins were still a novelty. People stared when we ventured out. They saw two girls indistinguishable from each other on the outside, from the matching headbands to our patent leather Mary Janes— and they presumed a sameness of spirit or character. It was that expectation that caused me to push back, to fight to be my own person. Ironically, now I *am* my own person . . . because she is gone.

But Daisy.

My sense is that she is someone who can't help being different— no need for the funny clothes to make the point. And why wouldn't she be a bit odd, given her upbringing? That poor child. Of course, I don't know the whole story because Lettie left Possum Flats as quickly as she could and then stayed away for most of three decades. Never married. Never wanted children, or, at least, that was what I gathered. But maybe I'm crediting her for more control in her life and decision-making than she deserves. My Lettie has always been consumed with some man—bending her life into the shape of her current love. A chameleon, taking on the colors and feelings and desires of her surroundings, motivated—as the amphibian is—more by survival than self-fulfillment. And then, just when she is fully disappeared into that background, that other life, she shifts and changes all over again.

I remember when she called me from a pay phone somewhere in the California desert, eight months pregnant and crying. I was elated. Not that she was pregnant or crying, of course. Just to hear her voice. It had been eighteen years since she set foot in Possum Flats. And the sound of your child's voice is as visceral as a nursing mother's response to a baby's cry, no matter how old you are.

"Mama?"

"Lettie? Is that you?"

"Do you have any other children?"

All those years away didn't seem to lessen her need to deliver a jab to my gut. But I tried to ignore that.

"Are you okay?"

"Yes. No. I've somehow gotten myself knocked up."

"You're thirty-five years old. Seems like you'd have figured out how these things work by now."

"Ha. Was there a ring on your finger when Dad got you pregnant?"

She had a point, of course. And she didn't know the half of it.

"Didn't think so," she sniffled. I could hear traffic sounds, as if she were close to an interstate. For a moment, I thought she had just dropped the receiver, walked away. "I don't know why I'm even calling you."

"Is there a father in the picture?"

"Not anymore. Son of a bitch left yesterday. He's not dad material, he says."

"Lettie. Let me help."

"There's nothing to be done. I'm way too far along for that."

"That's not what I meant. Come home. I could help you take care of the baby."

"Mother." Even through the ether of the phone line, I could feel the eye roll, hear the suppressed sigh. "I wouldn't go back to Possum Flats if it was the last place on earth."

"I'm not saying it would be perfect . . ."

"No. It would be the opposite of perfect. It would be hell."

"Lettie."

There was just highway noise. Had I lost her? Again?

Then: "There's only one way you can help. Why do you always make me beg?"

Money. Of course. The only reason I had ever gotten a letter from my daughter since she left. And then only after George was gone. Going through the funeral-home ledgers after he died, I discovered he had been sending her money every month—checks made out to Lettie *Flowers*, not Steinkamp. Her decision? Or was he making a statement? Anyway, it wasn't a lot of money. But it added up over the years. And knowing George, she probably never even had to ask. He was a gentle, generous spirit. When Lettie ran away, it nearly broke his heart. And he blamed me, of course, although he never said so out loud. His eyes—on the rare occasion he looked at me—were full of disappointment. But then, that was the story of our marriage. Seemed there was no end to the ways I let him down, start to finish.

I took down the address. I wrote the check and put it in a funeral-home envelope without a note.

I regret that.

I didn't hear from her again until a month ago, when she showed up one rainy spring night with her latest boyfriend. And Daisy. Barely stayed long enough to unload the child's suitcase.

A couple of car-door slams later, there we were: this dripping wet, terrified girl—an eerie, granola-muncher version of me in my youth—staring at this strange old woman who was supposedly her grandma, and who lived not in some picket-fenced brick bungalow but in the upstairs of a funeral home, where the prevailing smells were embalming fluid and scented candles rather than fresh chocolate chip cookies.

Who could blame her if she looked like a death-row inmate resigned to her fate? I probably looked a little skeptical myself.

DASH

I wish I did not have to do my job today.

Contrary to what others in Possum Flats might believe, I do not relish every moment of tending to my parishioners. Surely I appear engaged at every juncture when they need me—the minor illnesses, the loss of a baby, the loss of a job, a closeted drinking problem—because I *am* interested. Even though I have heard every sad story in all its permutations, I always remind myself that however predictable or shopworn the tale, it is a fresh hell for the person living it.

But perhaps they do not think about whether or not their pastor is enjoying his vocation, which is the more likely scenario. People tend to think mainly of themselves, despite their best intentions and my repeated exhortations from the pulpit. A voice crying in the wilderness, that is what I am.

Today, I must address the near disaster of Mayor Bartholomew J. Watson's funeral with Rose Flowers, who is *not* a parishioner (dare I say it? Praise the Lord!). Nor, if the murmurings are true, a believer. But her unique line of work makes it necessary for us to cooperate when one of my congregants transitions to glory. She handles the unpleasantness of the earthly shell, so the grieving family can focus on the more important concerns of the soul. That helps me perform my own duties well, which I appreciate.

But now she breezes into my office as though she owns it. This

is both unnerving and irritating. Rose Flowers is a queen bee, a
gadfly, and a know-it-all of epic proportions. But it is more than
her unwavering self-assuredness that bothers me. It is the fact
that—despite the gray hair and thickened waistline—she is still
the after-image of her twin sister whom I took to the dance at
Lamb's that hot August night half a century ago. I do not like to be
reminded of that terrible time, or of my wild and unwisely spent
youth, and she is one of only a handful of people in Possum Flats
who can take me back there in an instant. In her presence, a range
of emotions—longing, pleasure, grief, guilt, shame—run through
me in an instant. There is a knowing look in her eye that cuts me
clean through. How much did her sister share with her? I have told
myself over the years that Violet would not have whispered a word
of our intimacy to anyone. Especially to her sister, who was her
polar opposite in temperament and tastes. I would have thought
Rose to be quite disapproving and judgmental. And yet: there is
an eerie quality to Rose. That strange twin aura of not quite being
a distinct person, sharing her sister's memories, thoughts, experi-
ences. Even though that sister has been dead and gone so long.
But then I decide I am overthinking, that my own survivor's guilt
has me imbuing this person with mystical qualities she does not
possess.

   And did I mention how irritating she is?

   "Pastor Emmonds." Her tone is mocking, I swear.

   "Mrs. Flowers." I've never approved of the woman relinquishing her husband's last name after his death, not to mention erasing
it entirely from his business.

   "*Ms.*" She flounces down in the chair across from me and the
old upholstered seat releases an audible sigh. Rose follows suit.

   "I guess we both know why you called this meeting." Her eyes
give nothing away.

   "Well—"

   "No, now, let me finish. I know we had a little problem with the
Mayor the other day."

   "A *little* problem?" I feel my blood begin a slow, bubbling boil.

"All right. A big problem."

"It was shameful what happened to that poor man. A respected public servant and congregant for nearly a century and he is made into some kind of dirty joke? And his widow has to endure that on top of her grief? Completely unacceptable!"

Here, Rose's face takes on a puzzled expression. Which I had not expected.

"Oh, dear." She leans back in the chair and stares at me with open dismay. Her silence is infuriating, but I try to keep my look one of calm expectancy.

"I'm afraid I don't understand. I presumed you would be showing up with an apology and an explanation for the circus that preceded Mayor Watson's funeral," I begin. "Is that not that case?"

"I am sorry," Rose says. "I am unbelievably, terribly sorry about what happened to Bartholomew. But I guess I just assumed that you knew it was an inside job."

An inside job? I have no idea what she is talking about. Inside what? The casket? The Mayor's underdrawers?

"What exactly are you saying?"

"Forgive me, Pastor," Rose says in a tone that decidedly does not seek forgiveness, "but Roger and I delivered the body in absolutely pristine condition—and position—in that casket at twelve thirty. Joe let us in and locked the doors behind us."

"So?"

"So no one else was able to get in the church before Ruby Rae's arrival, without being let in by someone."

Rose pauses, as if to allow me to draw what apparently to her were some fairly obvious conclusions. My mind scrambles around to glean the importance of this to the topic at hand. I am the only person I entrust with a key to the church—keys to my kingdom, as my namesake Paul might say—although I let a deacon or Sunday school teacher borrow one if I absolutely must.

"Are you implying that I had something to do with Mayor Watson's state of corporeal excitement?" What would Rose come up with next? "I was working in my office from after Sunday service until I went down to let you and Ruby Rae in. I am frankly insulted."

Instead of the smart aleck response that I expect, Rose explodes with laughter, nearly doubling over in her seat. It is difficult to maintain my sharp look of disapproval for the full three minutes it takes for her to stop chuckling. When she does finally trail off and wipe her eyes, I meet her gaze with a countenance I reserve for only the most hopeless and incorrigible of sinners, one that bespeaks both utter disdain and naked curiosity—how could one slip so far off God's righteous path? Of course, I realize I have never understood women in general, and this woman in particular I find a bewildering bundle of unpredictable incongruities.

"Pardon my frankness, Pastor, and I hope you will not be offended by my admission. But I wouldn't even *consider* the possibility of you getting in between someone's legs, dead or alive. You may have had that reputation in your youth, but it's a tough image to conjure in the present."

She slaps her leg and chortles another minute. I am not amused.

"And the thought of you grabbing another man in the crotch! Whoo boy! I can't get my brain around that one. Not a snowball's chance!"

I am confounded. "I'm sorry I don't see the humor in the behavior of sodomites, nor do I wish to be mentioned in the same breath. Whether I would or would not engage in that bestial behavior is a moot point."

Rose immediately stops laughing.

"Oh, dear. Again."

"What now?"

Rose grows serious. "Wait. You *did* know that Mayor Watson was a notorious adulterer, right?"

I feel as if someone has turned the room upside down. The world is making about that much sense. Of course, I'd heard whispers over the years. Nothing concrete. But what did that have to do with the disturbing display put on by the corpse?

When I do not respond—how could I?—she sighs again.

"Lord, forgive my indiscretion." She shifts in her chair. "You see, Pastor, I found out through my . . . *ahem*, professional relationship with the deceased that he was cheating on Ruby Rae. With Ginger Morton.

"I was willing to let the secret go to *all* of our graves, but unfortunately for me, my granddaughter spilled the proverbial beans at *The Picayune*, no less! And, well, you know how people will talk. Especially Fence.

"I'm afraid your grandson may have gotten the word, seeing how much time he spends at the paper and all . . ."

Here her voice begins to trail off as she watches me finally put two and two together.

"Joe."

"Mm-hm."

"But . . . how could Joe have anything to do with this?" I do not like the turn this conversation is taking. I am nearing my limits on my ability and willingness to picture much more of the proceedings she is gleefully describing.

Rose reaches into her oversized purse made of denim and quilt squares, and pulls out a crumpled hand fan, even though it is not at all hot in my office. Then I recognize the printed cardboard item as one from our own Assemblies of God pews. *Courtesy of Morton's Pharmacy.*

"Well, the Mayor's perpetual state of readiness was apparent when he arrived at the funeral home. But I took all the necessary precautions to keep things down. I won't give away any secrets, but let's just say that duct tape is a funeral director's friend."

I really, really want this woman to stop talking. My head hurts.

"But someone slipped one of these babies in his front pocket with the handle sticking up . . . and, well, we all saw the results."

I put my elbows on the desk and place my face in my hands, the manufactured darkness a welcome retreat from my obnoxious visitor and her unsavory news. Could I just remain like this for a couple more hours? Would she disappear? I know this is not a miracle I should pray for, but dear God, I am only human.

"Hello? Pastor?"

I rub my face once more before removing my hands and setting them on the desk in front of me, fingers laced in a feeble effort to contain myself and my emotions. I look at Rose and she stares back. Neither of us blinks.

"Now, I don't want you to be too hard on Joe," Rose began. Then she slaps her leg again and guffaws. "Did I really just say 'hard on'? Forgive the Freudian slip, Pastor."

"Rose, I am going to do us both the favor of pretending you did not just say that," I say sternly. "We're both too old for talk like that. It's not . . . dignified. It's actually obscene."

"Sorry, Pastor. I forgot that the Mayor wasn't the only one with a stick up his . . . oh, never mind. Anyway. I was saying: Joe is a good kid. Don't punish him too severely."

"It will be an appropriate sentence, don't worry."

"I'm worried about your definition of 'appropriate,'" Rose says, standing up and putting her purse strap on her shoulder. "Remember, Possum Flats needs its star QB. Practice starts in August."

"Plenty of time between now and then for a little attitudinal adjustment."

She is nearly out the door when she stops and turns to face me, slowly.

"You know, just because you found Jesus doesn't mean you have to lose your sense of humor."

"I'm praying for you," I say.

"Don't bother."

DAISY

Fence stops by my desk later in the week, stepping in front of the large plate glass window that forms the only "wall" of my office. He stares at me for what seems like forever, arms crossed, without saying a word. Fence can't be more than five-foot-six in his stocking feet, but somehow, he's still intimidating.

"Nice job on the Buck obit," he says finally.

"Oh," I say, relieved. "I actually kind of enjoyed it, once I got started. Like an archaeologic dig, sifting through the layers of his life and putting them in order."

Fence likes my answer. The sides of his mouth, barely visible through the mustache and beard, turn up slightly.

"Interesting you should mention archaeology. Because I have something else that requires some digging. Got a minute?"

My heart skips a beat. My first real assignment!

"Sure," I say, trying to sound nonchalant. But I nearly trip over my bellbottoms getting to my feet.

"Slow down," Fence says. "Don't get *too* excited. But I've got an idea for a regular column I think might be perfect for you."

A regular column!

Fence leads the way past his office and the dark room and opens a door at the end of the hallway to reveal a steep staircase into the basement of the building.

"We'll need to go to the morgue," he says, holding the door for me. "Ladies first."

I nearly fall down the stairs. The morgue! I hadn't considered that a town the size of Possum Flats would have a morgue, but of course it must. I feel a combination of dread at seeing another dead body—is this to be my lot in life here?—and a dark thrill at the story possibilities that body might represent. A murder victim? An unidentified transient? My heart is racing as fast as my thoughts. At the bottom of the staircase, a cool, dank smell of cement creeps up from the darkness. Fence reaches around the door frame and flips the light switch on. The room is large, the size of the viewing parlor at the funeral home, and it has a giant wooden table topped with a green-shaded brass lamp. A single matching chair is pulled up at its center. Three of the walls are lined with tall golden oak cases with tiny little drawers, like the card catalog in a library. I have watched enough episodes of Jack Klugman as forensic pathologist *Quincy, M.E.* to know that a dead person would not even come close to fitting in one of those drawers. Maybe a forearm or a foot, but certainly not a whole person.

"Where do you keep the bodies?" I ask, businesslike, trying to seem like an old hand at this death thing. The expression on Fence's face evolves from a slightly puzzled frown to eyebrow-raised disbelief and then, finally, mirth.

"Oh, my dear." He laughs, a deep belly laugh, reaching for the wall to steady himself. I have never actually seen someone shed tears of laughter before, but Fence is mopping at his eyes with his handkerchief, gasping between chuckles.

"We call this the morgue," he says. "But it's only the place where old stories go to die. Not people."

I feel embarrassed and stupid. This is not Los Angeles. Of course there would not be the steel drawers like Quincy yanks out of the wall each week, pulling back the sheets to reveal someone's dead son, daughter, friend, husband, whatever. Not at the newspaper building! Probably not anywhere in this tiny, stupid town. I want to sink into the cold cement floor, disappear. Die. The irony of that is not lost on me, either.

After Fence recovers, he walks to the nearest oak cabinet and slides out one of the long drawers. Inside, folded carefully to fit in the narrow space, are dozens of newspaper clippings. In between clippings are miniature dividers and tabs, organized alphabetically with typed labels showing dates and subjects. This was the "C" drawer, with "city council" and "courthouse" tabs, along with "Church of Christ" and "Current River."

"Most every local topic of interest you can think of here," says Fence, his manicured fingers reaching into the file and removing a yellowed clipping, which he unfolds carefully to reveal an article about a church fire back in 1956. "Along with the news-generating citizens of Possum Flats, past and present, both the famous and the infamous, listed by last name. Plus cross-referencing, of course."

He refolds the article, slipping it into place before closing the drawer gently. I see by his reverent movements that he is proud of this, all of this: the sum of his community, the highs and lows; its sheer ability to generate all of this paper. It had to mean something, right?

"Who *does* all this?" I ask, struck suddenly by the fact that the contents of this room did not organize themselves. I imagine a pale, hunch-shouldered man with his eyes magnified by thick black-framed glasses, blinking like a cold toad as he perused the day's paper. He would mark the articles painstakingly with a stubby, eraserless pencil before cutting them out and filing them in the correct drawer.

"Myra," Fence says. His face registers my shock. "I know. It doesn't seem like her sort of thing, does it? But she says she likes getting away from the hubbub now and again. Gives her time to think, she says. But maybe it just gives her the last word on what's really important in this town. And who wouldn't want the chance to play God, at least on a small scale?"

He adjusts his glasses and gazes at the far wall. "Now there's what I really want to show you," he says. The entire wall is a floor-to-ceiling grid of cubbyholes, each space filled almost to bursting with newspapers and labeled with dates and years. There are at least twenty-five years' worth of papers here. "And there's more in the room in back of this one. We've got old copies going back to the beginning, ninety years ago. We were just a weekly then, of course. That didn't change until the 1940s."

I am vaguely impressed, although I still do not see what all this old history has to do with me. Fence seems to read my mind.

"I thought you might start a column with old news," he says, crossing his arms with a satisfied air, obviously pleased with himself. "You know, an On-This-Date-in-History kind of thing."

He strolls in front of the cubbies and stops in front of 1963. "See? You could pull the date from fifteen years ago and see if anything interesting was going on. It could be a wedding, a new city ordinance being enacted, someone returning from combat. I'm picturing lots of names, something people will get a kick out of. You know, thinking back to themselves years ago or friends and relatives from even further back than that."

Fence reaches into one of the dividers and flips through the corners, reading the dates before sliding a newspaper out. He takes it to the table in the middle of the room and opens it, smoothing the spine of the open paper against the surface of the desk to flatten it. I join him at the table. As we start reading, I notice the type is small and dense on the yellowed pages.

"There!" he says after a moment, pointing to a sizable article on the inside front cover. "'Plunk's Hardware Displays First Color Television.' Perfect."

As I scan the article, Fence begins to read out loud:

"'Mr. Robert ("Pup") Sealey, Jr., second-generation owner/manager of Plunk's Hardware on Main Street, announced today that a new RCA color television set will be on display in the front window from now until Christmas. "Once you see it, you'll never want to watch black and white again," Sealey said. "It's like candy for the eyeballs." Despite the higher price tag, Sealey says he expects orders for the new technology to be brisk through the holiday season.'

"What do you think?"

I realize that Fence is expecting an enthusiastic response. But all I can think of is that first night at my grandma's after my mom and Ron had zoomed off. We had eaten a hastily prepared dinner of fried tinned ham and a salad consisting of a single piece of iceberg lettuce topped by half a canned pear, a dollop of Miracle Whip, and a maraschino cherry. Then we settled on the couch together in an awkward silence before Grandma finally turned on the television set, which took a minute or two to warm up. When the images had finally appeared, I was shocked to see that they were colorless. Very pale women in white dresses and men with black hair in dark suits, against scenery in black and white and grays.

"Your television's broken," I said.

Grandma turned away from the screen, which was small compared with the heavy mahogany wooden box housing it. She blinked at me slowly, like an annoyed owl.

"Nope," she said. "That's the way TV is supposed to look."

I had cried then. Not big, heaving sobs. But I couldn't seem to stop the tears from spilling over. It was like I was seeing what my life was going to be without my mother here in Possum Flats: colorless, boring. Hopelessly stuck in the past. Grandma didn't say anything. We just sat side by side for about a half an hour, watching some dumb variety show featuring a big band playing in the midst of what seemed to be a soap bubble blizzard. Then she turned to me and said: "I think we need some popcorn." I watched her small blue-housecoated frame disappear into the kitchen, and I guessed she knew how I was feeling, even though she didn't know what to say.

"Well?" Fence sounds impatient.

"Well, I think it could be interesting."

What I want to say is: It's better than obituaries. But still lacking in the "cool" department.

"Look, Daisy," Fence says. "I don't want crack investigative reporting. I want a column that showcases our history. Makes people feel good, or proud, or maybe a little nostalgic for the old days."

"I get it," I say quickly. Because I do. I like people reading my words and feeling something. And I like feeling something, too. This job is the first thing I have enjoyed since Mom left, so I don't want to jeopardize that. Yet I can't resist pushing back. "But shouldn't a look at history include the good *and* the bad? Anyone can be a hero in good times. It's the way people handle the tough stuff that shows what they're really made of."

I have struck a nerve. Fence visibly draws himself up a little taller, his shoulders thrown back. Am I challenging *his* character?

"Just do the assignment, Watergate," he says. "Use your best judgment. And remember: The editor always has the final word."

I am thrilled to the bottoms of my toes. This could be fun after all. Surely there is a city council controversy or maybe a major bank robbery or election scandal hiding in the dry yellow pages of this room.

Fence shakes his head. "Let's try this again: The editor always has the last word."

Oops. Got it. "Right."

But I can't keep the smile off my face. I can't wait to get back to the funeral home and tell Grandma.

First, though, I need to help "put the paper to bed"—which means getting everything that goes in that day's edition of the paper edited, typeset, put into the layout and ready for the giant presses to roll and churn out the broadsheets. I have already fallen in love with that sound, late in the day at *The Picayune*, usually right around 3:30 or 4:00 p.m., as the presses begin to clank, then chatter and roll, the sound of tight tubes of paper uncoiling onto the large wheels of the press. It's mechanical and musical, all at once, and flavored with smells of ink and drying newsprint. The rhythmic roll of machinery is incredibly loud, like thunder. I've noticed several men wearing earplugs or headphones, but Bill, the plant manager, considers that a sign of weakness. Of course, he is deaf as a post.

It is close to six o'clock when I finally leave *The Picayune.* Grandma will already be fretting about dinner getting cold. I picture Campbell's tomato soup in a chipped mug and a grilled cheese, bread browned on both sides with butter and a touch of mayonnaise for an extra golden crunch. Grandma always cuts it on the slant to "class things up a bit."

I swing my bag over my shoulder, thinking about my new assignment. It's my chance to prove myself on something other than obits, so I've got to make it count.

"On your left," calls out a cheerful voice behind me. And me being me—the kid who struggled with the Hokey Pokey and Simon Says—I step left instead of right. There is the sound of squealing rubber and a thud in my lower back. I have the sensation of flying, briefly, before I hit the ground with an unattractive gasping sound. I am in someone's front yard, with cool blades of new-mown grass poking into my bare arms. Above me, the sky is an unblinking blue eye.

Then there is a face blocking the blue, with freckles showing through the tanned skin and a halo of blond hair glowing from the sunlight above it. The moment gives me pause: Am I dead? No, I hurt too much to be dead, I decide. And if there are such creatures as angels—which I highly doubt—I don't think muscle shirts would be their garb of choice. I blink but the face doesn't go away. It looks worried.

"Whoa," it says. He says. This is a boy. The paper boy I saw on my first day at *The Picayune.* I make a half effort to get up but am stopped by a sudden clench in my back muscles. I take another minute before marshaling my strength to sit up and formally meet my attacker. As if reading my mind, he holds out a hand and I take it, pulling myself up to a sitting position.

"I am so sorry," he says. He plops down beside me on the grass. There is no sound but the faint buzzing of insects. The street in front of us is empty, except for the upside-down banana-seat bicycle against one curb, its front wheel spinning lazily. The bag of tightly rolled newspapers has spilled across the sidewalk, their rubber-banded middles giving them the appearance of corseted old ladies.

I am just about to let him off the hook when he says, "Can't believe you don't know left from right. Don't they teach that in the big city?"

Now I want to punch him instead.

"In the big city, bikes are on the street where they belong, not on the sidewalks, you moron," I snap. "And where'd you get that bike anyway? Your little sister? All you need are a couple of streamers and a pretty pink basket and you'd be set."

"Hold on now. Don't be insulting my ride." He laughs, much to my surprise. "She's my girl and has been for years, obviously. I haven't saved up enough dough for a truck and besides, I'm not sixteen yet. Yet," he says again for emphasis. "Counting the days, though. Why do you think I do this stupid paper route in the first place?"

"How do you know I'm from the city?" Realizing that he knows more about me than I do about him further infuriates me. "And who the hell are you, anyway?"

"Joe," he says. "I guess I figured everybody knows me. I'm the quarterback." He leans back on his arms in the grass with a self-satisfied grin.

"The what?"

"Oh," he says. "Wow. You *are* big city. Ever heard of the game of football?"

"Have you ever heard of being a jackass?"

Joe's cool blue eyes register shock, which gives me a deliciously righteous feeling. He sits up straight. But I am just getting started. "Have you heard of T-shirts with actual sleeves? Big-boy bikes? Or of minding your own freaking business?"

I pull myself up painfully to standing. By this time I am breathing hard and have a stabbing pain in my lower back. But I am not going to let that stop me from making a dramatic exit. I take a tentative step toward the sidewalk, followed by another. God, it hurts. And the funeral home is still two-and-a-half blocks away.

"Aw, c'mon. You can't seriously be walking off mad."

I don't turn around. It will hurt too much to twist my back, but that isn't the main reason. I have something to prove, although I can't put a name to it exactly. It is as if all the me-against-the-world—or the me-against-the-world-that-is-Possum-Flats—feelings have been building over the past six weeks and are finally boiling over.

It is extremely difficult to limp quickly and angrily, but I clench my teeth against the pain and do just that.

"C'mon, now. Daisy, right?"

I don't answer.

"Daisy. Please." Joe's cajoling becomes fainter as I put another half block between us. "Don't be mad."

I drag myself along, determined to remain vertical until I am safely inside the funeral home. I hear the click and hum of slowly turning bicycle spokes bearing down on me from behind. Then Joe is beside me, walking the bike between us. His canvas bag is jammed with hastily packed newspapers and slaps against his leg with every step.

"I'm not a bad guy. Really. Won't you forgive me?"

I pause on the front steps of the funeral home. Even though the sun is headed toward the western horizon, it is still beating hot and makes me dizzy.

"For running me over or for being a jackass?"

"Both." Joe laughs. "I'm sorry. But you gotta give me a chance. Your grandma loves me, you know."

"My grandma spends ninety-five percent of her time with dead people," I snap. "Of course you look sparkling by comparison."

Joe's eyes widen as he appears to look over my shoulder. That's when I realize the door is open.

"Hey, Ms. Flowers."

I turn to see Grandma, her expression mercifully muted by the mesh of the screen door.

"Joe. Since when are you walking my granddaughter home?" There is a hint of amusement in her tone and I am relieved she has not heard—or, at least, has chosen not to respond to—my insult of her choice of companionship. But as the full meaning of her words soaks in, I find myself blushing. And then: I'm pissed.

"Walking me home? Are you kidding me? He nearly killed me with his stupid bike! It's a miracle I am walking at all."

A sheepish look crosses Joe's face before he hangs his head for effect. For the first time, I recognize in him that ability that really attractive people have to be forgiven—just for being beautiful. There is almost a physical light that they give off that makes the rest of us want to do anything to be invited in, to stay in the glow of that circle no matter what, reflecting it back like a grateful moon.

My mom is like that, too. The beauty of her free spirit, her refusal to owe anything to anyone, makes people want grab on, to immerse themselves in her—and hope a little of that aura or magic will rub off on them, too.

When we lived in Houston, Mom and I went on a hike where I saw my first pitcher plants. They were weirdly gorgeous, vertical green blooms veined with red and containing a sweet, sticky juice to attract insects. I've read that the tropical ones even trap tree frogs. When an unsuspecting visitor falls into the pitcher, it can't escape and is slowly digested.

That's Mom. Uncommonly beautiful. A little bit sticky. And at times—I hate to say it—toxic. She hasn't just kissed a bunch of frogs in her time; she's eaten them alive and left only the undigestible parts of their webbed feet behind. To love her is to live dangerously.

And yet I—like countless unfortunate boyfriends—am happy to hang on for dear life, forgiving her for uprooting me or putting me in the back seat behind the latest love interest more times than I can count on both hands. She is and always has been my everything. She is worth the ride.

I am just about to let bygones be bygones with Joe, too, when Grandma pipes up: "Well, all the same, I appreciate you getting Daisy home, Joe." And then she winks. *Winks!* I feel ganged up against, enraged. But also too exhausted to fight back. I push by

Grandma and into the cool burgundy dark of the funeral home foyer, thinking only of my mom's old bed with its cool white sheets.

Halfway up, Joe's voice reaches me: "See you around, Daisy."

It is not a question.

I have to hand it to him: He's got some nerve.

Rose

Daisy pushes past me, clearly annoyed.

And yes, I know it's partly about Joe. But I also heard what she said—and clearly hadn't intended me to. She thinks I'm more suited for company and conversation with the dead rather than the living.

Maybe she's right. Honestly, it's a hell of a lot easier.

Living with me, living here. I understand it's not what she signed up for. And she wouldn't be the first teenage girl to find the situation unappealing. Unsustainable.

Growing up at Steinkamp & Son Funeral Home was a fate worse than death, Lettie would say, with absolutely no irony.

This is something I understood to a degree. After all, I would not have chosen it for myself, either. Until it became my only choice. I remember how my sister and I had laughed mercilessly about "that funeral home kid," calling George a "lucky stiff" and telling her I would "play dead" if he tried anything on me. "I bet that's a real turn-on for him," I'd chortle, dodging as she tried to whack me with my own hairbrush (she didn't want hers damaged, of course!).

Maybe it's macabre, living above a place where the dead are delivered, dolled up and dispatched to their final resting places. But Lettie had it good here, whether or not she would admit it now. There were four adults around who adored her—and two, in particular, who indulged her. Both George and his father, Hermann, were weak when it came to that girl. They spoiled her terribly, whether it was with a small bag of hard candies from Morton's or a dime slipped into her palm so that she could see a matinee, complete with a striped bag of greasy popcorn, while the rest of us did the oftentimes back-breaking work the business required. And even though her grandmother Gladys and I were stern with her—for her own good!—she meant everything to us, too.

She was the playful beam of sunlight in a still, dark place; the gust of fresh air in a musty room. Lettie enabled the rest of us to exist in a semi-harmonious state. She was the one thing that we could all agree on, that we all wanted to care for and entertain. We were like four suitors, vying for her fickle affections in our own ways and yet not begrudging any of the others their rarified moments of being the "favorite." By talking to her, we were able to communicate indirectly with each other. By all of us loving her so intensely, we were able to push down the hates and hurts we had all caused each other—even if some of us could never forgive them.

Even now, decades removed from her childhood, I can sometimes hear her giggles and shrieks bouncing off these old walls. Or I think I catch the barest glimpse of her white-blond hair disappearing around a corner, hear her patent leather shoes pounding down the varnished stairs. I see the teenaged girl, too, draped haphazardly over a sitting room couch, crunching into a Golden Delicious as she reads a Nancy Drew book or that new *Seventeen* magazine. That habit nearly drove Gladys to distraction, the way she would so cavalierly use the formal parlor as a lounge, and leave the barest skeletons of her fruit laid out on a mahogany tabletop— just the stem up top, the calyx at the bottom, and a few tough sinews connecting them both, embracing a core that was eviscerated but for the seeds. She did not so much eat apples as devour them; I should have taken that as a clue to how she would live her life, too.

She nearly ate me alive, I know that. Lettie was smart and headstrong and perpetually discontent, convinced that something better was out there—away from us, the funeral home, Possum Flats—and that we were the obstacles to happiness and adventure. She rebelled against the classes she was required to take in high school, things like sewing and cooking, when the boys were allowed to take PE and shop. The war further cramped her style and darkened her mood, forcing her to live without new stockings and to wear clothing made from decidedly dull fabrics and colors, so far away from the bright purples and greens and pinks she preferred. She refused to help with the Victory garden we put in the front yard of the funeral home (with a name like Steinkamp, it was crucial to put our patriotism on full display) and detested rationing in any form, decrying the fact that her butter was now a cube of yellow tinted vegetable fat—oleo!

"I would rather die than put this on my toast," she would declare as she aggressively kneaded the plastic bag the margarine came in, spreading the yellow dye spot in the middle throughout the white lard-like substance until it looked like over-enthusiastic butter. It was one of her few real assigned chores and she despised it.

I know she was a little spoiled. But I think mainly she was born in the wrong decade. She wanted more options, more excitement, more of everything than Possum Flats or being a young female in the 1940s could provide. Women were not allowed to be angry or disgruntled or worried about self-actualization. Simone de Beauvoir was just on the cusp of giving birth to *The Second Sex* and blowing some minds, but Gloria Steinem and Betty Friedan were still a decade or two away. Poor Lettie!

She wanted more power, more control. So she took it in the only way she felt was available: bringing boys to their knees. Lettie was a knockout and she knew it, with her green eyes and thick, long waves of hair that had gone from white blond to a rich golden brown, like sun-ripened wheat.

So much like her father.

Lettie was always looking for a good time, never thinking about consequences. She had a social life (by Possum Flats' standards) that could have put Lana Turner or Olivia de Havilland to shame! And yet there was such a restlessness to her, the way those emerald eyes would fall upon something or someone new and immediately narrow, catlike, assessing the object or person for potential amusement or worth. And how quickly those eyes could turn away, disdainful or bored, leaving more than one young man stranded in midsentence, heart unceremoniously yanked from his rib cage and casually discarded before he even knew he was in peril. Lettie was a violent storm that swallowed you up and spit you out, choking and gasping for air on some abandoned beach. Which is to say she left lots of heartbreak in her wake, like her dad had done in his time.

In *our* time.

It may seem harsh to assess my own daughter as so capricious and, well, *predatory*. But I am just being honest. I've spent the better part of five decades holding up the equivalent of a magnifying mirror to my own dark soul, the kind of mirror I use to make sure I've got a client as close to perfection as their genetics will allow. A mirror that not only reveals every bumpy mole, freckle, wrinkle and hair—but even the witchlike hair *inside* the mole! So I know that as much as Lettie is her father, she is her mother, too.

The poor thing was served up a double-dose of wild and selfish. And I knew her struggles and anguish like I knew my own. One would think that might make me more sympathetic, someone who could relate to being stuck in a small town when girls' dreams were given such strict boundaries. Hadn't I felt this myself?

But instead, her teenage years were a battle of wills. The tomb-like interior of Steinkamp & Son became a war zone, echoing with the rapid fire of harsh words, the pounding of angry feet, slamming doors. Any ensuing silence was anything but deathly; full, instead, of a sense of dread in anticipation of the next series of volleys and replies. Instead of sympathy, I operated from fear. Fear of all that could go wrong—that *had* gone wrong in my world—kept me trying to restrain and protect her.

During these outbursts, Hermann would disappear to the basement whether or not he had work to do. George would retreat to the office, where I knew he would have at least one drink—if not several—to get him through.

And Gladys?

The smuggest of front-row spectators, she would materialize seemingly out of nowhere when the fireworks began, suddenly in the parlor, plumping the stiff brocade pillows or sweeping away nonexistent dust on the landing of the stairs. I felt her eyes and ears on us—on *me*—every time Lettie threw one of her fits at the injustices of her small life. Gladys was a turkey vulture, circling on the hot updrafts of our skirmishes, waiting for first blood to swoop in with a raised eyebrow or acidic comment. Nothing escaped her sharp gaze, and she left nothing unsaid by her even sharper tongue.

"The apple doesn't fall far from the tree" was a favorite, although she took the most satisfaction from pointing out how she had never had such difficulties with her perfect son.

"I wonder where that girl gets her impertinence?" Gladys would muse darkly.

I hated it; every single minute of it. I was a reluctant black hole, pulling in every type of dark matter toward my core and swallowing it: Lettie's rage, George's sadness, Hermann's fear, Gladys' self-righteous indignation. It was a miserable way to live.

Of course, it couldn't last. But when the end came, it shocked me.

It was springtime, 1947. April. The forsythia had burst overnight into brilliant yellow fountains of spray, small floral suns dotting the yards and bordering the sidewalks of Possum Flats, which was still mostly cold, brown and hibernating. Lettie had just turned eighteen and was more consumed with her latest love—was it Bruce Foster or his younger brother Bobby?—than with finishing up high school. She and I had been round and round about anything and everything: her studies, her friends, her clothes, her boyfriends. Staying out too late. Every punishment that I meted out was met with complete ambivalence or open hostility, and seemed to push her to extend the seriousness and range of her transgressions.

When her grades slipped, I took away her telephone privileges.

When she didn't come straight home from school, I gave her an earlier curfew. When I caught her sneaking out of the funeral home at night, I grounded her for a month. Was it a bad decision during her last month of high school? Yes. But I was desperate.

Of course, it didn't help that I had no one backing me up. The grandparents stayed out of it, except for the sardonic commentary from Gladys. But George quietly undermined my authority by arbitrarily reducing or rescinding my pronouncements, the good cop to my bad. Lettie, when grievously misunderstood or maligned by me, would hightail it to her dad, who wanted only to be adored by his daughter and then left alone in peace with his flask.

"I'm telling Daddy!" a purple-faced Lettie would roar after one of our heated battles, when consequences had been decided.

"You do that," I would say, equally frustrated, and knowing that I had been one-upped in a situation that had no more possible "ups."

Late one night, about two weeks into Lettie's being "grounded for life" and a week away from her graduation, I was lying awake, alone as always in the double bed I'd had since my arrival at Steinkamp & Son. I was bone-tired, having had a funeral for a stillborn infant and a visitation for a downtown businessman who had died of a heart attack. And while the preparations for a miniature body by nature take less time, the emotional toll of handling a dead child was even more excruciating than the physical challenge of heaving around the two-hundred-and-fifty-pound hardware store owner, Plunk Sealey. But dealing with both in the span of a day had me exhausted yet stirred up, the steady ticking of the grandfather clock punctuating the agony of being unable to sleep, like tiny relentless punches to the brain.

That's when I heard it: a long, groaning creak, the reluctant sound of new hinges operating without lubrication. I stiffened in my bed, my ears on high alert for footsteps or the soft click of a doorknob. Instead, there was nothing. A pause. As though someone or something was taking a break, plotting the next move. We didn't need a cash register in our type of business, but we did have a wall safe for any large cash payments or for any jewelry that we needed to keep for our clients. We didn't like to leave any valuables on the body—a gold watch, say, or a diamond necklace—until time for viewing. They say you can't take it with you, but you can certainly make it difficult for anyone else to have it.

I got up from my bed and reached for the baseball bat I kept by my nightstand. A poor substitute for a man and the physical protection he offers. But there's something to be said for the strong, silent, wooden type. And I had no qualms about swinging freely. I was not a shy retiring flower, despite my name. Because I knew it would be up to me to handle the situation—if there was a situation. Hermann and Gladys were useless, as one was practically deaf and the other snored like a freight train. And I took no small amount of glee in the fact that it was Gladys who made sounds better suited to a fat, drunken sailor than a petite, persnickety grandmother! And George was generally three sheets to the wind by nine o'clock every night, flat on his back on the cot he set up years ago in the cramped office wedged between the chapel and the showroom.

I eased open my door and made my way to the carpeted stairs, descending stealthily, practiced in the art of going unseen and unheard in this place. I had learned that the easiest way to avoid Gladys' ridicule or rebuke was to stay out of her sight.

I padded down the hallway until I reached the open archway of the chapel, dark except for a sliver of moonlight that cut through the high window in the front of the room. The moon gave a peaceful glow to the polished mahogany casket in which old Plunk lay, where I couldn't help but imagine him critically inspecting the materials and craftsmanship of his new home.

A sudden rustling sound. Quiet again. I inched by the door of George's office/bedroom, which was uncharacteristically open. When I made it to the showroom, I lifted my bat up high. I could hear someone breathing, almost panting. More rustling. With my free hand, I reached around the edge of the archway and felt for the light switch.

"AUGGGGHHHH!" I screamed when my hand found—instead of the light panel—the warm flesh of another hand!

The lights came on as that hand flipped up the switches and it was as if a photographer's camera flash had gone off, freezing everything in mid-action. George was beside me, holding an empty whiskey bottle by the neck like a glass bludgeon, his shaking hand pointed straight ahead at the display casket on its wooden pedestal. And inside of it was the source of all the noise: our daughter Lettie scrambling up from beneath Bruce or Bobby, wearing just her lace camisole and clutching the casket's small cream satin head pillow to her chest to cover some extra real estate. Meanwhile, the terrified boy rolled unceremoniously onto the carpeted floor with a dull thud.

"You. Get the hell out of here," George commanded the young man, waving his bottle unsteadily. The boy needed no encouragement, snatching at his unbuttoned, unzipped pants flapping around his hips and attempting to gather his shoes in his one free hand before deciding to hightail it home sock-footed.

At this point, Lettie had calmly pulled on and buttoned her blouse, as if we were not there, as if she was casually getting ready for school, without a care in the world. In silence, George and I watched as she reached up to smooth her golden-brown mane and adjust her headband. Then, as easily as if she were hopping off a fence or one of those silver stools at Morton's, she swung her legs over the edge of the coffin, pausing to pull her twisted skirt around before dropping to the ground on both feet. She gathered her overturned saddle oxfords—clearly kicked off in haste—and started to walk right by us.

"Hold it right there, young lady," said George.

Lettie stopped in her tracks. Her father had never taken such a stern tone with her.

"Are you going to explain yourself?"

"What is there to explain?" She looked from George's face to mine and shrugged. "We were just having fun."

"Fun." The word sounded dead in his mouth. "Is that what you call this? Desecrating our home and our place of business with . . . these antics?"

Here, George paused to look at me.

"Did you know the kind of girl you were raising?"

"You mean *our* daughter?" My face colored with both shame and anger. I would not let him off the hook on this. Her boldness and contrary nature were as much his fault as mine, for giving in too easily and making her careless, reckless, in her behavior.

A long hard stare.

"She is yours, through and through," he said. "And I'll leave you to handle her."

Here, he placed the whiskey bottle on a slim table lined with sample urns and shuffled off to his cot. I could see the outline of a flask in his back pocket, the contents making it sag. I can't explain why that little droop made me feel suddenly so hopeless and sad. Then the office door closed firmly behind him.

When it was just the two of us, Lettie and I spent a good minute holding each other's gaze. I knew that her behavior was screaming for notice, for understanding, maybe even for everything to explode into nothing, which might allow us to start over somehow. But I could not back down. All I could see when I looked at her, defiant and hurting, was myself—and the choices I had made at her age that got me irrevocably into a life that didn't feel like my own. Wouldn't I have benefited from a little guidance, a mother who paid attention, who cared enough to rein me in? I could see in this angry teenager the small, willful toddler and headstrong child, and was torn between wanting to scoop her into my arms and turn her over my knee.

She was too big for either.

"You cannot behave like this and continue to live in this house," I said at last. "Your grandparents and parents cannot abide it. I will not stand by and watch you throw your life away."

Lettie pulled her shoulders back and looked back at me, appraising the situation. Then she sighed, a long, exasperated exhale that seemed to leave her smaller, more fragile.

"Okay," she said at last. "Okay."

I wish I had told her that I loved her. That I knew what she was feeling because I had felt it all, and more. I wish I had just reached out and touched her without saying anything at all.

Instead, I sent her to bed and told her that we would talk about consequences in the morning. Then I put the satin pillow in its place, smoothing the fabric lining the length of the casket and discovering a perfect kiss of lipstick on the side with the latches.

I bristled. I would try every possible means of stain removal, of course. But I would have to do it alone, unable to ask for help from Gladys. For her to see it would be blood in the water, and I couldn't bear the thought of what she would say in response to her granddaughter's transgressions this time. It was too much.

But I needn't have worried. The stain turned out to be the least of my problems.

The next morning, a Sunday, Gladys called everyone in for a hot breakfast of oatmeal and toast. Lettie didn't come down.

I remember stomping my feet extra loud on my way up the stairs, a warning to my daughter of the storm approaching. But I threw open her door to an empty bed, still made, and a dresser with its drawers thrown open and pillaged. The window was open, too, Lettie's white curtains fluttering in the hint of breeze.

We found out later that she had met up with the Foster boy and they drove a few towns away. But he was back within a day or two, unceremoniously dumped for someone else, was the story. She didn't call. She didn't write—at least not to me. Her father received intermittent requests for money, which he honored until the day he died. But I never heard her voice again until that day she called to tell me she was pregnant, nearly eighteen years later.

And I didn't see her until she brought me that all-grown-up baby girl last month.

DAISY

The next morning, I really want to head down to the morgue. But first, I check with Myra for any new obits—"Nobody kicked the bucket," she cheerfully reports—and stop by the darkroom to see if Smiley has a photo assignment.

"I've got a grip-and-grin at noon at the Lions Club," he says. "Want to cover it? Fence always picks up the tab," he adds, as if dining in the dark-paneled, windowless back room of the Wagon Wheel is a big draw. Even though I didn't love my years on the vegetarian straight-and-narrow—with the gross green shakes and probiotics—that place makes me shiver. Grandma took me for lunch once, and my "salad" was a wedge of pale iceberg drenched in buttermilk ranch with one hothouse cherry tomato for color.

"What's a grip-and-grin?"

He chuckles. "About what it sounds like: a couple guys shaking hands and smiling at the camera. Usually one of them is giving the other something quasi-important, like say a check for a couple hundred for a charity or a plaque for five years of service." He rolls his eyes. "Serious hard news. In terms of excitement, photographing deformed vegetables is a billion times more interesting than your standard grip-and-grin."

"Yikes," I say. "Well, I brought my lunch and I bet you didn't. So why don't you go ahead? I was going to spend the day in the morgue, anyway. Fence has me on a history assignment."

"All righty," says Smiley. "I was kind of looking forward to my country-fried steak anyhow."

My back is still tender from the run-in with Joe's bike, so I take the stairs slow and find the light switch. Where to begin? Five or ten years seems too recent, so I decide to jump right in to what was happening in Possum Flats fifty years ago, gently removing old papers from the large file drawers labeled 1928. Judging by the file's relative slimness, the newspaper was still a weekly then.

Each issue is filed flat, not folded like a newspaper in a newsstand, and I carefully remove one paper and place it on the large wooden table where I can open it fully. At first, the yellowed pages crammed with small, black type and few headlines or photos make my head hurt.

I take a deep breath, deciding to relax and take my time. Soon I am immersed in stories that aren't necessarily heavy at all. In fact, I find the voice of the narrator in each article to be a friendly one, as if the reporter were a true observer of—if not a direct participant in—the story. This is true whether the subject is national in scope—the invention of the iron lung, or the St. Francis Dam collapse that caused five hundred deaths in Southern California—or somewhere around Possum Flats. Like how Miss Myrtle Meyers hosted an afternoon bridge party with a theme of "spring flowers and showers" on each scorecard and centerpieces of small watering cans holding sprays of daffodils and tulips. Salted nuts and savory sandwiches were served along with pineapple punch, each cup garnished with a tiny umbrella.

Wow.

The morning flies by, and still I read on, making notes of potential "On this day in 1928" snippets and stories. I decide I will stop after August, since that's about the time I'll head to California. The lucky duck who inherits this job can take it from there. My fingertips are a satisfyingly smudgy black, having turned dozens of pages of newsprint; the cuffs of my white blouse are gray, too. My stomach rumbles so loud it echoes off the cement walls.

Grandma packed me a white bread sandwich slathered with Miracle Whip and layered with salami and a slice of American cheese (hold the pickle, I reminded her), all carefully folded in wax paper. Lunchtime. But as I refile the newspaper from the first week of August, the next week's paper catches my eye.

Unlike every other issue I had seen, this front page has a gigantic photograph that nearly swallows up the entire space. The headline is massive, too. A banner reads "Dance Hall Explosion!" and beneath that, "29 Dead; A Dozen Others Still Missing." I quickly scan the caption and to my horror, the photo is from Possum Flats. The backdrop is a brick two-story building with shattered windows. But the foreground—what should be the focal point, as Smiley taught me when we practiced with my camera—is . . . nothing. There is a large pile of rubble: ragged chunks of brick, rock and lumber, behind which is a smoldering black pit. There are lots of policemen, firemen and onlookers ringing the edge of the hole, gazing, it would seem, at the absence of something. It is impossible to read their expressions; the photo was taken too far away for that. But the slouch of their shoulders and the downward tilt of their heads say enough: Devastation. Disbelief.

At the edges of the photograph, I can begin to make out what must have been the skeletal remains of the destroyed building. Large charred beams and two-by-fours hang precariously from the adjacent buildings, which are also greatly damaged. A few broken-off sections of brick wall try to hold the contents of the explosion, like a broken teacup. A ghostly smoke rises from the pit, pure white in some places, transparent in others, giving the people and ruins behind it an otherworldly look.

I race through the article. I have to know what happened and how. I am struck as I read by the tone of the story. There is a hopelessness in the voice, a reluctant, regretful truth-telling. So many are dead, and so many are young people—a few high schoolers, many college age or in their late twenties or early thirties. Sons and daughters of Possum Flats' prominent business families and town leaders. The small town's population of three thousand meant that everyone was related to or knew someone who died or was injured. The entire town was shell-shocked and in mourning. And no one knew how or why the building exploded.

I turn the front page carefully, the aging newsprint filling my nose with the aroma of dried brown leaves. On the second page is a list of the dead, the injured and the missing. Even though I am new to this place, I am struck at once by all the familiar surnames, like "Morton" from the pharmacy on the injured list.

And then: my heart absolutely stops beating for a few counts. I feel a chill through my body like I have never experienced before or since. I heard once that a shudder like that means someone is walking over your grave—the place where you eventually end up planted for eternity. All I know is that the severity of this cold is so frightening that the newspaper quivers in my hands.

There, midway down the list of the dead is my own mother's name.

Violet Flowers.

For a few terrifying minutes—I can't say how long—the ceiling and walls of the morgue close in on me, the chilly cement blocks and aged bricks exuding a musty pull that feels like a tomb. As if a ghostly hand were reaching into my chest and clenching my heart with its translucent fingers. As I will my pulse to slow down, I am grateful for the wooden chair that I had been cursing for its lack of comfort earlier. I am sure its tall slatted back is the only thing that kept me from falling over.

Of course, it *couldn't* be my mother on the list. I know this. The date of the explosion was August 13, 1928. My mother wasn't born until the spring of 1929. And this Violet Flowers is listed as nineteen years old.

Nineteen years old. Fifty years ago. She would be nearly seventy now.

Just like Grandma.

As the math resolves itself, I feel sick inside. Grandma must have had a sister. A twin sister. Mom never mentioned having an aunt—but then, she wouldn't have ever met her. And my mother has always been evasive about her growing-up years in Possum Flats. "It took me eighteen years to get out of that shithole and I don't want to spend another minute there, not even in my mind," she would say when I asked for a bedtime story about her life. In between boyfriends, she would often fall asleep with me in my twin bed at night, her long wavy hair streaked with gray and smelling pleasantly of patchouli, sour sweat and weed. I would burrow into her, against her chest, soft and squishy under her T-shirt, feeling safe and loved, even as I knew it wouldn't last; that I would soon be displaced in that crazy cycle that was my mom's love life. But in those pauses, I was like a blackbird perched on one of the long, sagging wires stretched between electric poles along a small Missouri highway. Oblivious of everything to either side, what had been and what was to come—or of any potential shock—the warm sun soaking through my feathers, claws clenched around the wire, insides bursting with song.

Grandma was the one who had begun to fill in the gaps of my mother's childhood. But she had never mentioned a sister, either. Why would she? I was little more than a stranger to her when I arrived. Since then, we had been circling around like unfamiliar dogs, sniffing our way into an uneasy truce, getting used to the idea of each other.

Something inside me thrills: my grandma has a story! A past that includes a dead twin. And a giant explosion.

I have found my "scoop." I will retell this incredible event from fifty years ago from the "now." I'll talk to survivors, people who were there. People like Grandma, who lost family or friends. Maybe I can even figure out what happened, like on *The Rockford Files*, where James Garner gets onto a case, combing through evidence until he finds that one overlooked clue to unlock the mystery.

"*There* you are!" Myra's tone is both relieved and accusatory.

"Fence said he sent you to the morgue, but that was five hours ago. I've got an obit for you, and Smiley's developing photos from his luncheon that need captions.

"Wait . . . what's this?" Myra approaches the table, putting on the eyeglasses she keeps handy on a long, sparkly chain.

"It's my new story . . ." I begin. My mind is a kaleidoscope of brilliant, twirling colors, transforming before I can begin to describe what I see. There are so many angles, so many ways this story could spin out, all of them beautiful. I can't believe my good luck. *This* is my Watergate.

But Myra's face stops me cold. There are deep downward lines forming in her smoothly powdered forehead. Lines I had suspected where there, but that Myra hides by calking, painting and generally keeping a sunny outlook.

"Oh, no," she says, peering at me over the tops of those cat-eye glasses. "I'm not sure what you're thinking, sweet pea, but this . . ." She shakes her head. "This is off limits."

"What do you mean? Fence asked me to find some history to revisit, and I've discovered the perfect piece."

"No. This is a disaster." She begins folding up my newspapers, her irritation evident by the crinkling of the ancient newsprint under her efficient hands.

"Yes! It *is* a disaster! And how can I have lived in a town almost two months and not heard anything about it? No one has mentioned it, not even my grandma." I forge on. "Something this huge must have had an impact. So many people died! Shouldn't we remember them?"

"Honey, don't take this unkindly"—she pauses to look me directly in the eye—"but you aren't from here. You don't get it."

The way she tosses her head in a condescending dismissal infuriates me.

"You're just jealous." I snatch the folded newspaper from Myra's hand. "This is my big chance to do something besides obits and Lions Club luncheons and weirdo vegetables. You're only sorry you didn't think of it first."

Myra looks at me wearily. "No, doll. I decided a long time ago what I'd write and what I wouldn't, and I've stuck with it. What I'm sorry about is the people of Possum Flats who will have to relive this story. Fifty years might seem like a long time to you at your age, but I guarantee they are just a thin, raggedy Band-Aid over an ugly hole of loss. Are you sure you want to rip it off, expose everything to light and air?"

What *do* I want? To find out my grandmother's story? And the story of this great-aunt of whom I had known nothing until an hour ago? Yes. But maybe find out my *own* story, too. Where did I fit into this place, this town, which—although still like a foreign country to me—has more people who know my family and history than I have had in my entire fifteen years of moving from place to place?

I jut my chin out. "Yes," I say. "I'm the perfect person to tell this story. A few people might get upset, but most will feel better. Like after a good cry."

Myra sighs. But her frown has given way to something more like resignation.

"Does that mean that you'll help me?"

"Oh, honey. I don't know if I can help you," she says. "But I definitely won't hurt you."

"I guess I'll take that."

"But first, you'll have to go through Fence. No way over, under or around it."

DASH

Crime and punishment.

This is what I am contemplating over my cup of warmed-over coffee. Not Dostoevsky, but rather, the lesser—but not insignificant—transgressions of Joe Nichols. I have spent the last half hour authoring a fitting end to the sorry story of Mayor Watson's funeral wrought by my grandson.

Joe, for his part, has already been and gone. I had asked him to come into my office early and to be dressed for manual laboring. He showed up in jeans and an old T-shirt, carrying a pair of work gloves. Not exactly sackcloth and ashes, but he was appropriately penitent.

"I shouldn't have done it." He shook his head. "But I'd heard how he died. And where. I thought he was a hypocrite, you know?"

I fixed him with a stony stare and watched him squirm, twisting the mustard-colored gloves into a tight ball in his hands.

"I had the fan in my hand from cleaning up the pews. I didn't stop to think it through. Like about Ruby Rae." He looked pained. "I just did it."

I kept my silence. That and the unforgiving glare seemed to do more toward creating a clean and contrite heart in my grandson than any words I might have summoned.

"I really am sorry."

" 'Judge not, that ye be not judged,' it says in Matthew," I said. "Let's leave the Mayor to answer to his Lord."

With that, I gave him his penance, which was a hard day's work up at Ruby Rae's, cutting and hauling brush from the backyard along with some mowing and trimming. And anything else she might come up with. But I have a feeling the worst punishment is Ruby Rae knowing that he was the culprit. He will be eager to work off his transgressions and feel he has a clean slate. With her, with me and with the good Lord.

That pleases me. It feels right.

Because I know that sometimes a punishment does *not* fit the crime, the price too high for that one unthinking moment, one ill-advised decision. That hard and terrible consequences can ripple out from a split-second action for years.

For lifetimes.

My father, Henry Emmonds, was a man of no particular trade but unafraid of hard labor after years of moving around, tenant farming with his father from the hills of Kentucky to the open plains of Kansas and Nebraska and finally to Oklahoma.

There, Henry had his eye on a lanky auburn-haired girl whose family farmed about a dozen miles away. Her name was Rebecca and the first time he saw her was in the apple-picking season, the early fall when the hint of crisp air in the mornings was like the skin of the round orbs themselves, cool and tart with a sweet, juicy ripeness beneath. She was standing against the stone wall of the brightly lit church basement, and she met his eyes full on, without ducking her head or smiling nervously like other girls. It stopped him in his tracks, that look, her eyes so sharply blue and knowing that he felt exposed. There was nothing frivolous about her, from the faded but clean cotton print dress to the practical black boots peeking from beneath the hem. He took note of the tidy nails in her scrubbed red hands and understood that she knew how to work like he did.

But it was later that first night that he fell in love; after the warm fruit pies—gooseberry, rhubarb, wild cherry—had been cut into fat wedges and served, after the plates and forks were cleared and cleaned by the women, while the men loosened their belts a notch and began moving the tables out of the way and placing the chairs into a circle. A few with strong backs pushed the church's upright piano toward the center, while Rebecca's brother unpacked his fiddle and another slender, bow-legged young man got out a mandolin.

The lights were turned down, and when everyone was seated, the coughing and whispering stopped with the first notes of the piano, joined by the sweet notes of the fiddle starting low and climbing slowly higher. Then Rebecca opened her mouth and her clear alto voice began to sing. It was as if she had cast a spell instead. It seemed to Henry that there was nothing in that room but that voice, which reached out with the gentle, creeping fingers of a low-lying fog and wrapped around his heart: *"Lead, Kindly Light, amidst th'encircling gloom, Lead Thou me on! The night is dark, and I am far from home."*

My father often told that story, how that stolid girl sang in the way that pierced him, how that awkward, unlikely angel became his own kindly light. They were married in the spring, when those same apple trees that had been so heavy with fruit now were arrayed in the light, frilly finery of fragrant blossoms. This was in contrast with Henry's practical bride, who wore a dark gray dress and her bountiful blaze of brown-red hair bound up in intricate plaits on her head, save for a wisp at either ear, an attempt by the clutch of farm women who attended to her, perhaps, to soften the severity of her look. Her face was porcelain, smooth and translucent with just a hint of blue and dusted with freckles. But it was her smile that made her beautiful, that rare slight upturning at the sides of her mouth that portrayed innocence and wisdom all at once. My father could not believe that he was the inspiration for that happiness, that light.

"I am the most fortunate man on God's green earth," he said.

He vowed that he would make it his life's mission to keep Rebecca smiling.

But this turned out to be more difficult than my father, in his youthful exuberance, had bargained for. He found his own tenant-farming position about fifteen miles west of where he grew up and moved his bride into the one-room, dirt-floor shack that came with the job. He worked like a man driven, up before dawn and home at dark, tending to the animals and crops—corn, beans and both summer and winter wheat—of the hard German who owned the farm. He toiled and sweated and ached for that land, while Rebecca bought a couple of laying hens and coaxed a garden out of the dry red earth—tomatoes, lettuce, peppers, cucumbers, beans, beets, peas, potatoes and corn in exacting rows, punctuated by patches of lavender, summer savory, rosemary and lemon balm. She did not plant flowers that did not yield something beyond their beauty; she allowed a few roses for rose hips and a small patch of nasturtiums whose brilliant orange, red and yellow blooms could be fried in butter or eaten with salad greens. They never once did eat them, but knowing that they could allowed her to bask in their playful loveliness in a way she could never have enjoyed a zinnia or a trellis of morning glories.

At night, they would pray together, counting their blessings on their knees on the rough braided rug cleverly woven by Rebecca from strips of burlap feed sacks. Then they would fall into bed, bones aching inside their skins, and Rebecca would rub his shoulders with her large, strong hands before welcoming him into her arms. He could feel her smile, there in the dark, and for the first two years, it was more than enough.

Then I was born, spindly and weak. My father said I looked like a hairless, tail-less monkey, not at all like the fiery New Testament preacher Paul, for whom I was named. When my mother had exhausted her own knowledge of herbal remedies and concoctions—as well as that of her mother and the other women in the surrounding community—the doctor was finally called in.

My medicines were costly, and Henry had to put them on his

running tab with the farmer, along with the doctor visits that accompanied my first tenuous year. I eventually turned the corner, but our debts meant that my father had to redouble his efforts on the farm. He began loaning himself out to a man the next farm over on his Sunday off to make extra money, despite my mother's disapproval.

"On the seventh day, God rested," she said. "And so must you."

"God did not lack for land and a home to call his own," my father said.

His plan almost worked. After four years of relentless day-in, day-out exertion, we had our own horse and two spotted sows, and with Rebecca—hugely pregnant once again—selling her eggs and extra vegetables, the ledger was close to even. Henry went to his Sunday job one early spring day with the intention of finishing the plowing, but one of the farmer's mules wouldn't get up in its stall. Henry knew the work could not wait. The weather would not hold and the seeds needed to find their homes in the earth in time for the crucial spring rains. So he trudged back to his farm and—while it was still dark—borrowed a mule from the sleeping German farmer. He could get the plowing done while everyone was off at church; it would not even garner notice. The first streaks of light had just appeared in the east, pale cool gold that would soon turn to electric pink and orange, when Henry heard the pop of the bone. He knew before he looked what he would find: a half-hidden varmint hole and the unnatural crook of the mule's leg above the wide gray hoof. Henry sat on the hard unbroken ground, his back against the massive flank of the heavy-breathing animal, watching the indifferent sun rise over the flat, stubbly field and his future.

I was only five years old, but I remember when the farmer showed up at our door, his mouth in an unforgiving line. He and my father stood on the front porch, while my mother shooed me back inside and closed the door. The meeting did not take long.

The farmer pulled his horse and wagon next to our pig pen and
loaded the two sows, and he and my father chased the hens around
the front yard with a burlap sack until they had captured the full
dozen and put them in a large cage on the back of the wagon. My
mother stayed inside, crying over those hens she had named and
talked to every day as friends, fellow sisters toiling together under
the empty blue bowl of Oklahoma sky. I was frightened because
my mother so rarely shed tears.

"Please," my father said. "Can we keep the mare one more
day? My wife and boy would like to say a proper goodbye." He
held his hands out to the farmer, who looked toward me, my face
pressed against the single window in the front of the house. I saw
his shoulders relax, although the straight line of his mouth did not.

"You'll be bringing her to me first thing tomorrow then, along
with her tack," he said. "Then we'll tally how much you still owe."

"Thank you, sir. I know I don't deserve no favors."

"No. You've already taken a favor without asking, and it has
cost us both dearly."

My father hung his head.

"It also makes me wonder what else of mine you may have
borrowed or taken over these years, when I had counted you for
honest."

The German was not a tall man, but the seriousness with which
he carried himself made him seem much larger. He was immac-
ulately dressed, his work shirt clean and ironed, tucked evenly
into the waistband of his creased work pants, a brass belt buckle
perfectly centered on their front. The farmer did not look like he
had just exerted himself at all, as he brushed a hand down either
sleeve to make sure he was still as smooth as when he had arrived.
My father, in contrast, was red-faced, sweaty and disheveled.

"I been honest, sir," my father said, eyes downcast. "I'd ask
that you believe me. You seen the way I worked for you these long
years, bending my back over your land day and night."

The farmer gave him a hard look. "Even one drop of dishonesty is all it takes to poison the pot, I am afraid. But you are a hard worker, I give you that. And you're going to need that strong back for a few more years to make things right."

He climbed up into the wagon and rode off down the red dirt road without a backwards glance. I admired the stiff way he held his shoulders and the sure way he snapped his whip at the horse's flank. I wanted to be like him, confident and powerful. Righteous. I felt a twinge of shame that I did not want to be like my father, grateful that the farmer did not turn around to see him sitting hunched on the steps, holding both hands against his bowed forehead, his body trembling with tears and rage.

That night was the first time I saw my parents argue. My father believed that the events of the past day were God telling them that it was time to leave, to take a new path. "The prophet Isaiah tells us: 'And thine ears shall hear a word behind thee, saying, This is the way, walk ye in it,'" my father said. "That very voice is thundering in my head now. Would you ask me to turn away from God?"

"But leaving *is* turning against God," said my mother, who had known nothing but farm life. "'Thou shalt not steal.' It is one of the clearest commandments we are given. Would you condemn us to the fires of hell for your unwillingness to pay your debt, to work off what is owed?"

She rubbed her hard, swollen belly with the heels of her hands, as if to stave off the small contractions that so often beset her these days. When my father said nothing, she pressed her lips tightly together and never brought up the subject again.

We left in the dead of night. Mother had bundled up our clothes in feed sacks and used her one trunk—the large black steamer that had accompanied her on their wedding day—to put in our meager store of dishes and silverware, pots and pans, sheets and tablecloths, her homemade soaps, and as many jars of preserves and vegetables as she could. She swathed the glass jars against breakage like precious babies, in our sheets and clothes and rags.

She grabbed dried bundles of her medicinal herbs: rosehips, Echinacea, lavender, and envelopes of seeds. She stood in her herb garden near midnight in the light of my father's one good lantern, which I held with both hands, while she cut the herbs, which were just beginning to emerge from winter, down to their roots: rosemary, sage, thyme, mint. I was so frightened by the fierce look on her face, made ghostly white in the light, that I dropped the lantern, shattering the glass globe. My mother's arm shot out and I ducked, trying to avoid the blow that I knew was coming; the blow I deserved. But instead, her hand clutched my sleeve and pulled me to her, and she knelt there in the dark garden and held me tight against her for what seemed like an hour, my eyes closed and nostrils filled with the smell of cool, turned earth and the green pungency of the slashed herbs. Nearly three-quarters of a century later, fresh rosemary still smells like leaving to me; the sharp-edged woodsiness of goodbye.

My father hitched the bay mare to our small wagon and loaded our trunk and the few odd burlap bundles of food and clothing. My parents exchanged not a word as my father helped my mother onto the wooden seat beside him. I squeezed between, uncomfortably bound by the several layers of clothing I wore so that my mother could pack less. I was unable to turn around and take one last look at what had been the only home I had ever known. The picture in my mind was probably infinitely more cheery and warm than what would have greeted me had I turned—a darkened shamble of a house, with its unpainted gray boards warping in on themselves and one sad window eye watching us go.

I nodded off in the snug warm nest between my parents' bodies, lulled by the horse's rhythmic hoofbeats on the miles of clay road. When I awoke, hints of light were breaking through thick, purply clouds in the east. We had pulled up to the train station and a town beyond the tracks consisting of a general store, two bars, a farrier and a Methodist church. My father unloaded the trunk and the bags onto the deserted platform and told us to wait. My mother and I sat huddled on the trunk in the chilly spring morning, watching the sunrise take over the eastern sky, slicing the dark clouds with brilliant lines of magenta and fiery orange. For a while, I leaned against her chest while she absentmindedly played with my hair. This was one of the few rituals around grooming or what my father referred to as "vanity" that was somehow allowed in our no-nonsense home, a place that boasted not a single mirror, not even a powder mirror or the small, gilt dressing table variety many women owned. Mother would lick her index finger and wind the longest hair of my bangs tightly around it, repeating the action over and over until she had achieved a single spiraling curl that ended at my forehead. When she was satisfied, she reached into a scratchy feed sack and pulled out a hard biscuit for me to nibble while we waited. It was nothing like the steamy, soft butter biscuits I ate at home.

"Is this manna?" I remember asking. In my young head, I had equated our leaving with the Biblical exodus and the subsequent wanderings in the wilderness. It was the only story about uprooting that I knew, and I understood that leaving was hard.

"Don't be foolish," my mother snapped, impatient with my father, who had been gone nearly an hour by now. Her boots stuck out from beneath the hem of her long dress, and I could see how the laces had been loosened to accommodate her swollen ankles. Being pregnant seemed to make a woman bigger all over, not just in the belly. The mother I knew was disappearing in extra flesh, and yet her color was not one of plump contentment. She was a sickly white, even beneath her sun freckles, with dark, puffy pouches beneath her eyes. She sighed a lot, a sound that I don't think she realized that she was making.

When my father returned, he was free of horse and wagon, his step unburdened, too. When he reached us atop our humble pile of belongings, he pulled my mother to her feet, oblivious to her strained expression.

"We have enough for the tickets!" His sun-weathered face was practically glowing. He was pleased with himself, and it made me feel hopeful, too. "The train arrives in half an hour!"

But my mother looked stricken, not overjoyed as I had expected from my father's exuberant announcement. She reached frantically behind her with one hand to find the trunk so that she could sit once more. "Please tell me you got more money than that for the horse and wagon."

"Philippians 4:19. 'But my God shall supply all your need according to his riches in glory by Christ Jesus.'" My father's voice raised. "Do you doubt this?"

For a long moment, there was nothing but the sound of the wind from the west, blowing in the few oaks by the station steps, rippling through fields of clay and scrubby grass behind it that stretched as far as I could see.

"I do not doubt that I have married a fool."

On the train, I sat wedged in the space and silence between them, an ache in my empty stomach, as my father read and reread a dog-eared pamphlet about the imminent arrival of God's kingdom in Los Angeles. My mother was turned toward the window and the uneven, uncharitable landscape that could snap a mule's leg and a young couple's dreams with the remorseless alacrity of a summer lightning strike. Dry-eyed, she watched as the rough-hewn red rocks and slender snaking rivers of Oklahoma slowly disappeared.

Daisy

At *The Picayune* the next day, Patty waves me down with a pink paper.

"Fence wants to see you. ASAP." Patty smiles, a wide grin that reveals large, unevenly spaced teeth, but reminds me that behind the prim skirt, braids and glasses is a girl not much older than myself.

"Perfect," I say, trying to stay cool. "Because I want to see him, too."

A small pit of worry opens up in my stomach. I had planned on pitching him my story idea this morning. I didn't want to be ambushed with obits or derailed by some soft news item—someone's out-of-town visitors or recent trip to the Grand Canyon. I wanted nothing more than to head to the cool quiet of the morgue and read more about the dance hall explosion. Then I wanted to walk around downtown—see what buildings remained. I wanted to track down survivors, visit some victims' families. I didn't need Fence to slow me down.

I put my lunch in the fridge in the break room before heading down the hall that housed the nightmarish photo gallery. I take in the pictures with a new eye. The dance hall explosion would be perfectly suited to Fence's love of the macabre with multiple deaths, large-scale destruction and a giant fire.

Of course, the explosion happened before Fence was born. Did he only display photos from his own tenure as editor and publisher?

Or was this a family tradition? At the end of the hall, I see it in stark black and white: the smoldering pit of debris ringed by half walls of broken brick with two firefighters dragging a long black hose toward the ruins. But the focus of this picture is a single ragged beam sticking up from the bottom of the pit like a claw. There is something hanging from it, maybe a large charred piece of trash or clothing. No. Ugh. It is the blackened remains of a human being, impaled on the beam. The head droops onto the chest, which is made strange by the wood sticking through it. What remains is shiny, skinless muscle, cooked beyond recognition.

"Fascinating, right?" Fence.

"Pretty obvious why that one didn't make it into print, right?" He sighs. "People don't want to see their friends and neighbors barbecued. If this happened in the big city or in another country, anonymity would let us scrutinize the corpse with naked curiosity, and shiver safely with the knowledge that we somehow—by divine Providence, maybe—have been spared. And then turn away when we've seen enough, forgetting the whole thing in a matter of minutes."

I disagree. I am not from Possum Flats, but I could never forget this photograph. It occurs to me that Fence is a little twisted. Maybe more than a little. But wouldn't that make him open to revisiting the story? Before I can ask, he is pointing out the next photo.

"Unbelievably cool."

Reluctantly, I tear myself away from the distressing photo of the explosion to one that at first seems strangely serene and out of place in this dark, death-filled gallery. Taken from above, the photo is an odd composition of an upright piano lying prone—not "upright" at all—across a sidewalk.

Then I notice a single human forearm, extending out from beneath one side of the piano as if it caught the instrument as it fell. A woman's arm, with fingers curled into a soft, helpless fist. Then: something worse. My stomach lurches.

Peering over the top of the open piano lid is a face. In fact, most of a woman's head. I hadn't seen it at first because it is half in shadow. And it isn't exactly a normal face and head, outlined as it is in an inky black shadow that I thought must be hair, but upon closer inspection is a pool of dark blood. Her giant dark eyes are open wide, staring skyward. Her mouth appears to gasp as if from the crushing weight of the piano.

"That's Beebe Monroe," Fence says. "From what I've heard, she was the best piano player this town has ever known. She could do all the classical stuff. But she loved ragtime. 'Maple Leaf Rag,' 'Pineapple Rag,' 'The Cascades.' She made those Joplin rags sound better than even he would have imagined possible. And she could improvise like nobody's business, so she was ready-made for jazz, which was just getting popular."

"When was this photo taken?" I ask, my mouth dry from hanging open so long.

"This is from 1928, taken by a reporter from the Springfield paper. The Lamb's Dance Hall explosion. Beebe was killed by her own instrument at age twenty-nine."

How can he be so matter-of-fact about this young woman's death? "I've got to tell this story."

Fence is confused. "It's an old story," he says. "Do the math. This happened fifty years ago."

"Which is exactly why it is perfect," I say, talking faster. I don't want to give him an opening to shut me down.

"Remember your idea to look back on different dates in our history? Well, this is the story I want to write. I found some incredible articles about it yesterday. It will actually be fifty years this August. This is the perfect time to remember what was lost—*who* was lost.

"I can interview survivors, families of people who died. I think everyone would like a chance to—"

"To relive the most horrific event in Possum Flats' history?" Fence snorts. "You don't know what you're talking about. People want to forget it ever happened."

I hate being told I can't know or understand something. I've heard it way too much. Like when Mom didn't want to explain why she kept us moving from place to place, why this boyfriend or that didn't last, why I didn't know my grandparents. "You're too young," she would say. "You wouldn't understand."

"People don't want to forget what happened. That means forgetting about the people they loved who died. And no one wants to do that, even if remembering hurts."

Fence gives me a look somewhere between surprise and suspicion. "How do you know that at your tender age?" he asks.

He rubs his forehead like he has a headache while a long minute passes. "Okay, Daisy. But I don't want to hear from anyone—and I do mean *anyone*—that you're asking too many questions or stirring up unpleasantness. If the answer is 'I don't want to talk about it,' that means 'no,' not 'ask a different question.'"

"Of course," I say, slowly exhaling. *I get to write my story.* "Deal."

At my desk, there is a new obit request from Myra with a pastel blue note clipped to the top: *End of day, please.* It looks like pretty standard stuff. Old man, eighty-one years old, farmer. Nothing cool or noteworthy that might inspire a side story. Wow, I am getting callous. I remind myself that he is still someone's father or grandfather or friend, and they probably didn't think of him as "standard stuff."

I make quick work of the obit and spend the morning in the morgue, poring over the articles about the dance hall explosion, making a list of possible interview names to follow up on with Myra.

So much of what happened that night fifty years ago seems mysterious. The dance hall itself was located on the second story of a brick building that housed an automobile dealership and repair shop. Did some flammable liquid or a buildup of fumes in the shop spontaneously combust? The dealership was owned by a slippery character named Timothy Woodbin, known for his wheeling and dealing that had included several failed ventures before the automobile dealership. Was he in dire financial straits at the time of the blast, as a few people in follow-up articles believed? Could the whole operation have gone up in flames for insurance money? Yet Tim Woodbin was one of the victims of the blast, found about fifty yards from the building, third-degree burns on his front—not his back, as there might be if someone were turning and running away. And who would blow up a building with so many people in it? There's desperate or greedy—and then there's being a sociopath.

It's well past lunchtime when I fold the last of the yellowing pages. For the past few hours, I have felt as though I was alive during that crazy and horrible time in Possum Flats. I've read the testimonials of the survivors, awful descriptions of the destruction, tributes to the dead. There was a huge outpouring of both kindness and criticism from the townspeople—because for every person who felt the explosion was a terrible accident was another who saw a vengeful God.

At the top of the stairs, my morbid thoughts are jarred by the cheery bustle of the newsroom echoing down the hallway. Myra nearly runs me over coming from the break room, her coffee mug edged with one perfect red imprint of her bottom lip. Does she make it a point to drink from the same spot to avoid a mess all the way around the top? Somehow, I know the answer is yes.

"Saw your obit, hon, and you nailed it."

"Like a coffin," I say, enjoying Myra's brief look of horror.

"Well, someone's certainly feeling their Cheerios today," she says. "Researching your big story? I heard Fence gave it the a-okay. Or at least a lukewarm thumbs-up."

"Speaking of, I've got a list of names to run by you. It would save me time and energy to know who's alive, who's not, and who you think might be willing to talk."

"Sure thing, sweetie. Shoot."

I whip out my spiral notebook and a pencil like the seasoned professional I envision myself to be.

"Okay. How about Hazel Sampson?"

"Why, sure. Hazel Hodges now. She's the postmistress. You've surely met her."

I feel heat creeping into my cheeks. Of course, I know the post office lady . . . by sight. But I've never formally introduced myself. It's just not something we do in the city. But in Possum Flats, I am probably considered snooty or worse for trying to conduct my business anonymously. Hopefully Hazel will cut me some slack.

"Mo Wheeler, the sax player?"

"Well." Myra pauses. "That's a tough one. He's alive, but lost his eyesight in the explosion. Moved out of town. Last I heard, was in a nursing home in Sleepy Springs, about an hour from here." My face falls and she adds, "Worth a try, though."

"Jimmy Jeffers?"

"Oh, yes. Chief of police for decades."

"And a big hero that night, right?"

"Yes. But you won't get that from him."

"We'll see about that."

"Hmmmm," says Myra. "I like your moxie."

"Dash Emmonds?"

"That's *Pastor* Paul Emmonds, these days. Preacher at the Assemblies of God Church."

"What? Wow, that could be good."

Myra shakes her head as if she can't believe my ignorance. "Probably not great for business for the preacher to talk about sowing his wild oats."

"Charlie Walters."

"Passed away. There wasn't a whole lot left of him, I heard."

"Oh." That's grim.

"What about Ruby Rae Watson? She and the Mayor lost their only daughter, Fern, that night."

I feel doubly sorry for Ruby Rae now. As if being married to her cheating husband wasn't enough.

"And don't forget to ask your grandma. She's the right age."

"Top of my list. I saw that a Violet Flowers died that night."

"Violet? I've never heard her mention a sister. Now *that* would make a good story."

"A twin, I think. But she hasn't said anything, so I might have to work up to it."

Myra laughs. "Are you scared of your grandma like everyone else in this town?"

"No," I say. But when she raises a skeptical eyebrow, I laugh, too. "Maybe just a little."

JIMMY

One of the best things about being police chief is having an office. The other two best things are that the office comes with a door and blinds, both of which can be closed. It's not a *big* office, more like a glorified janitor's closet. And the way I let paperwork pile up on my desk and in every corner makes it even smaller. I have two walls of windows: one is a floor-to-ceiling number next to the door with sun-yellowed blinds that can be closed for meetings or my important post-lunch snooze. I don't know why I bother to close them; everyone knows what I'm doing in here. I guess it's a point of honor that they don't bother me until the shades reopen about forty-five minutes later.

When those blinds are open, I can look out on the hodgepodge of desks that form our squad room. There are usually two cops on duty at any given time and, during the day, we have a secretary. Mabel's been with us practically forever. My boys (and yeah, the bra-burners won't appreciate that it's men only, but an old dinosaur like me is *not* going to change) are a mix of young and middle-aged. Guys like me have all retired or keeled over from heart attacks or something else. I have been in law enforcement for nearly fifty years, since I was a kid of twenty.

"Mabel, where's my goddamn coffee?"

I poke my head out of my office. She usually has a steaming mug sitting on my desk when I get here in the morning. But I am early today. I have an interview at nine a.m. sharp and I couldn't sleep thinking about it. Decided I might as well come on in to work.

"It's in the goddamn pot," she says. Some of the guys have mentioned I should fire her for insubordination, but we understand each other, me and Mabel. We're about the same age and we speak the same language. "What are you doing here this time of the day? When I saw your office light on this morning, I had to go back outside just to make sure Hell hadn't frozen over."

"Did I forget to say please?"

Stony silence.

"Mabel, *please* bring me my goddamn coffee."

My other office windows face Main Street. Our squad is in a small, two-story brick building that somehow survived the 1928 explosion down the street. Downstairs is where the good guys take care of police business; upstairs is where we keep the bad guys. But honestly, the two cells upstairs are usually empty. Sometimes we get a belligerent drunk or a guy who gets a little carried away smacking the wife. But there isn't a lot of murder and mayhem here in Possum Flats. In the few homicides we've had, the perp might be taken into custody and housed here overnight. But we ship any *really* bad guys to a bigger, badder facility. Which is fine by me.

I like my view onto Main. I know all the routines, from early morning to suppertime. I watch *The Picayune* people come and go, the sweet smoke from Fence McMillan's pipe arriving just ahead of him around eight. Smiley, shortly afterwards, weighed down by all his cameras. Myra, striding down the sidewalk at an impressive pace in high heels.

Midday might give me a gander at Rose, bustling into the building with a funeral notice, while midafternoon it's the paperboys, arriving early enough on their bikes to stand around or pop a few wheelies before delivery time. The occasional idiot will light up a cigarette. But most are smart enough to realize that my office is right across the street and that I have no problem mentioning any bad behavior to a mom or dad or grandparent. That is small-town police work at its finest, nipping things in the bud. Some might say, "It's just a cigarette, for crying out loud." But I've seen how a cigarette can lead to a few beers, which leads to hard drinking (often accompanied by pranking and loitering), which slips pretty easily into petty crime or general no-good-laziness (which isn't a crime, but ought to be) and on down from there.

Joe is the paperboy all the others are trying to impress. It's obvious in how they circle him, showing off on a bike or bragging about a date with a pretty girl or bagging a ten-point buck. Something about him draws people—besides his status as an up-and-coming football star. He's a kid with good manners who is genuine and friendly to all.

Nothing like his grandpa.

Now there's another character who shows up outside my window. Old Pastor Emmonds, descending from his watchtower to limp to lunch or some coffee and awkward conversation at Plunk's. He's never fit in with his sheep. Too holier-than-thou. That wasn't always the case, as us old-timers could surely tell, but likely wouldn't. People around here generally prefer to wear their smug on the inside.

I still think of him as Dash, although the name and person I knew back then died in the explosion. His body survived intact except for a crushed ankle. But the person I pulled from that god-awful burning heap no longer exists.

To be fair, I'm not the same person, either. Back then, I was just a fat farm boy, fresh out of high school, who hadn't found his place. Some fellows in our gang had plans to head off to school, maybe the university in Columbia or the teacher's college in Springfield. A couple were going into the family business, like dry goods or banking. One had a summer job at the lumber yard that he thought might turn permanent. And then there was Dash, who had no plan except right now; he was all about the fun. He was crazy that way, and I guess that's what we liked about him. Wherever Dash was, that was where the party would be, whether he was at Lamb's or out at a country bonfire, drinking hard liquor and telling fantastic lies.

I knew what was ahead of me was a life of hard labor on our dairy farm. My parents were up at four thirty every morning, getting the milking and feeding done, and when I was old enough to help, that was my lot, too, before going off to school. Sometimes in class, I would fall asleep at my desk, especially in the winter, when the ancient radiators would ping and creak and thaw my frozen mass to a cozy warmth. I got a reputation for being lazy, which was about the furthest thing from the truth. But my teachers saw what they saw. Combine that with my lack of book smarts and, well . . . it looked like I would be heading to the farm after graduation. Which had me depressed. I was in denial that summer, going from party to party, drinking too much, trying to fit in with the smooth guys like Dash and his friends.

And then there was Nell.

Nell Peters was hands down the prettiest girl in the world. Long straight hair as gold and smooth as a field of freshly cured fescue; blue eyes like a winter sky. And built sturdy as a barn, not slim or willowy, like some popular girls. She looked like she'd been fed cream instead of milk. She had birthing hips, my dad might say, a real womanly shape. I was smitten with her.

I had chased her around all summer, wanting to get noticed, have a chance for a date and (in my stupid mind) possibly more. By August, she at least knew my name—thanks to me latching onto Dash. And that night, she had agreed to go to the dance with me. I could not believe my luck.

I haven't thought about her for years. Or any of this stuff.

I'm lying. I'd be a shitty policeman if I allowed otherwise. I think about Nell and lots of other folks who aren't around anymore because of what happened that night. Every day.

The worst part is how one of them will just pop up, unexpected, in my memory or even around town. Like when I patrol downtown and see old Mr. Walters. He has to be in his nineties now, shrunken and harmless, nothing like the man who made people sweat bullets sitting across from his big desk at the bank. He started closing in on himself when Charlie died, got even smaller after his wife gave up and died, too. Charlie was supposed to take over for him. God, good old Charlie. Good Time Charlie. He liked being where the action was and hung around with people who made things happen. He didn't have much imagination beyond dollars and cents, even seemed to be tallying his return on investment sometimes—whether that was in a bottle of whiskey for Dash or a hamburger for his arm hang, Hazel. I never really believed she liked him. But to her and a lot of others, he was a means of bankrolling their fun. But he was all right by me. Sure didn't deserve what he got.

Or maybe I'm talking to some young kid, making sure he's keeping his nose clean, and the way he shoves his hands in his pockets or stutters or looks at me out of the corner of his eye reminds me of someone. Maybe it's his great uncle, someone I had nearly forgotten about; someone who died that night fifty years ago. Then it hits me like a ton of bricks.

There is a knock on my door. Mabel. But she doesn't normally knock.

"Is it my goddamn coffee?"

"Ahem." Mabel clears her throat and I realize there is someone else at the door, too. "Your nine o'clock appointment is here. Early."

Jesus H. Christ.

"Well, for God's sake, send her in." I sound grouchier than I mean to, but hell, I haven't had coffee and I am not really up for this. For Daisy Flowers.

When Mabel closes the door—harder than she needs to—there is a girl left in front of it, dressed like she's straight from Woodstock.

Her hair is longer, but if you swapped out those crazy-looking blue jeans and shoes made out of baling twine for a smart dress and pumps, she would be the spitting image of Violet Flowers. Down to the smirk that said she knew more or better than you.

I motion to her to sit. She keeps her eyes on me, as if I'm going to cuff her. Mabel says I'm intimidating. But the old cop in me knows to use this to my advantage.

"So you're Daisy Flowers," I say, as if this were the first time I laid eyes on her. She doesn't need to know I've been tracking her comings and goings at *The Picayune*. I've seen the way she looks around as she walks. She's an observer, someone interested in Possum Flats the way other people visit a zoo. She doesn't think she belongs here, can't picture her mom or grandma living here when they were her age. But she's wrong. She is Possum Flats through and through. She just doesn't know it yet.

She reaches her hand across the desk for me to shake and I do, a forceful squeeze with an abrupt drop right after. Just reinforcing who is in charge, not that a skinny hippie is any real physical threat to me, even in my seventies. But in my career, it's good to let people know who is the boss without actually saying it.

"Nice to meet you," she says, and her voice surprises me. She doesn't sound afraid at all. She opens her notepad and leans forward in her chair. "I guess Mabel told you I was here to interview you about the dance hall explosion."

"Well, she may have—"

"Fence is letting me do a story—a retrospective, we decided to call it—on the events that happened that night fifty years ago this August. It's going to be big. I'm talking to survivors, to relatives and friends of people who died. And of course, the people who responded to the disaster. The heroes," she says. "Like you."

Heroes.

I feel my stomach clench. I take a breath and wait until the feeling passes. I am trying to keep my head.

I have never been a hero. I believe they exist, those selfless people who put themselves in harm's way to save another human life or lives. But I also believe those individuals make up a tiny percentage of so-called heroes. The rest are people like me who are scared shitless and act without thinking. I am not a saint. I wouldn't even call myself a good person.

This Daisy kid is looking at me with her big eyes, expecting me to "aw, shucks" or some such. She has no fucking idea.

"I am not a goddamn hero," I say, pushing back from my desk

with both hands and jumping to my feet. I lean toward her, both palms flat on the stacks of paper on my desk, and make my face as nasty as I can. My "bad cop" face. "So if that's what you want to talk about, this interview is over."

I am so close to her face that I must have spit on her—unintentional, but not a bad ploy to strike the fear of God into someone—because she calmly reaches up to wipe her left cheek.

"Okay," she says. She sets a tape recorder on my desk, inching it toward me so I have to back off. She pushes "record" and then leans back in her chair as cool as a cucumber. "So what would *you* like to talk about?"

I take my own index finger, so much bigger and clumsier than hers, and punch the "off" button before taking my seat. I cross my forearms on the edge of the desk.

Why did I agree to have this girl in my office? This girl who—if I forget where I am, the time that has passed—*is* Violet Flowers reincarnated. Poor Violet. It strikes me that what I really want to talk about is how tired I am, how tired I have been my entire adult life, from carrying the burden of all the people lost in that god-damn explosion. Wishing them back. Wishing myself back.

Not that I want to be the Jimmy Jeffers of that night, a selfish hothead full of himself and the false sense that he was made for better things than milk and manure. Who felt like he really could have the girl and the life he wanted—no, that he *deserved*, for some stupid-as-shit reason. I hate that kid. I don't pretend to like the grownup who has replaced him. But at least I can own who I am, with no illusions of grandeur. Or heroism, either.

That's what I want to talk about. But I don't know where to begin.

"I think it's best if we let sleeping dogs lie," I say. The girl's face registers shock. She thought she had me. But I can't do this. It's too hard.

"Now, if you don't mind? Get the hell out of my office."

Rose

I am in the bowels of the funeral home, trying my damnedest to give old Mort here one last close shave. But Daisy has me so upset I can't think straight, let alone hold a straight edge.

I don't want to talk about my sister.

I got so flustered when Daisy brought it up at breakfast that I spooned a pile of salt on my oatmeal from the saltcellar instead of the sugar bowl. Which thoroughly chapped my ass.

"But . . . she was your *twin*!"

"Goddamn it, Daisy," I shouted. "I'm well aware. But I don't want her life littered across the pages of *The Picayune*. Being a reporter doesn't give you a license for shit-disturbing. Stick with the prize veggies and leave us out of this."

I pushed away my chair, leaving my salty oatmeal untouched, and stomped downstairs. "I'll be in my office!" I slammed the door, a totally unnecessary but satisfying exclamation mark.

Now I'm alone with Mort and a razor blade, trying to collect myself. I know I overreacted. I should be happy that Daisy is taking an interest in the family. But it's complicated, the story of my twin sister and me. Certainly nothing I want printed in black and white when our relationship was anything but.

I hear Daisy on the steps, and in a minute, she's pulled up a cold metal folding chair opposite me. I've got to hand it to her: She's stubborn. And I don't have to wonder where that came from.

"So . . . *Mort*, huh? Is that your nickname for all the old dead guys?" she asks, trying to change the subject, reverse the bad mood she's put me in. "I guess that makes you a 'Mort-ician' then?"

"Haha. His name really is Mort. Well, actually Morton. Last name."

"As in 'Morton's Pharmacy'?"

"The very same," I say. "I never thought he'd end up here, to be honest. Old Ginger never cared for me. But she may have had a change of heart after the Mayor incident. I bet it was one of Mort's last requests, that I take care of him. He always was a little vain and he knew I'd make him look good."

I unwrap a hot, steaming towel from the gray face and begin patting shaving cream around his mouth, down his neck and up on his sunken cheeks. He looks like a shopworn Santa Claus, after twenty-four hours of Christmas globe-trotting.

Daisy scoots her chair closer. I refuse to make eye contact, but I can hear her take a deep breath, like she's about to jump in a swimming pool.

"Grandma, I don't see what it would hurt to talk about Violet. Don't I have a right to know what she was like?"

Like I said: stubborn.

"You've gotten along just fine for fifteen years without knowing you had a great-aunt. I'm not sure why you need to know now, other than to make newspaper hay with what's nearest and dearest to my heart."

The way her face crumples, I can tell I've landed a blow. She definitely wants a good scoop. But I've questioned her motives and she doesn't like it. I see her set her jaw.

"Doesn't Violet deserve to be remembered? Think of all the people who knew and loved her. You aren't the only one. Shouldn't they have the chance to get reacquainted?"

I don't answer, but she is wound up. The arguments just keep coming.

"And what about the other people in Possum Flats? Those who

never knew her? Keeping her story to yourself just makes her more dead. Do you want her memory to die with you? If you ask me, that's pretty darn selfish."

I keep my focus on Mort's neck whiskers, wielding my straight razor with the authority of a seasoned barber. Some might say knowing I can't hurt my customers gives me an edge, as it were. But honestly, I'm just that good. I'm concentrating so deeply that I almost forget about Daisy until I hear her foot tapping impatiently on the concrete floor.

"Listen, Daisy. I know I'm a selfish, cranky old woman. I've been on my own a long time now."

I pinch the razor blade between my fingers and wipe off the excess shaving cream. Then I take a damp towel and pat Mort's face to get any stray foam bits.

"I'm set in my ways. Including the ways I want to remember my sister. I loved her more than anyone else in the entire world. She *was* my world. And I was hers. Our appearances were so similar— except for a birthmark on the back of Violet's neck—that we could and *did* fool our own mother at times. But our personalities, interests, friends and behavior were nothing alike. Night and day, as they say. As different as the flowers we were named for."

I pause and fold the little towel into a neat rectangle. This next part is going to be tough to get out.

"The thing is, Violet was . . . how can I say this? Wild. Temperamental, experimental—even *detrimental*—to herself. She danced, she drank, she smoked, she was a huge flirt and a social butterfly. She even got herself knocked up, if you want to know the truth."

It was strangely satisfying to see Daisy's jaw drop.

"Yes. Knocked up. Bun in the oven. What do you kids call it these days? Anyway, she was pregnant. Unmarried. And let me tell you, back then, that was the end for girls like us. Our mother—had she been informed—wouldn't have had the money to send her off somewhere to have the baby and return, pretending it never happened, like the rich girls who got in trouble. Ending a pregnancy in those days took the help of a coat hanger or an abortionist, both terrifying options. Not everyone survived, whether she took things into her own hands or gambled with a back alley 'expert.'

"No one knew about the baby, of course. No one but me. But everyone knew Violet was a good-time girl. So when she died that night at Lamb's? Most people figured she got what was coming to her."

Daisy is stunned.

"Isn't that kind of harsh? Even if she raised a few eyebrows, do you really believe people in this town thought she deserved to die? Like *that*?"

I can't look at Daisy right now. I couldn't believe Possum Flats could rationalize the death of a nineteen-year-old girl by immolation as something that she had coming to her, either. But that was how it had felt. I try to snip a few curling hairs from the edges of Mort's cavernous nostrils with my pointy silver scissors. My hand is shaking.

"Grandma?" Daisy can't let it go. "What did *you* think?"

I let the scissors clatter onto my tool tray.

"I thought maybe they were right."

"*What?*"

"No, listen. Part of me could understand their thinking: Violet was pretty well up to no good. And when things happen that we can't explain—when the merciful God we believe in isn't anywhere to be found—we have to tell ourselves something. We make up a story or a rule so we can cope. 'If A, then B.' That sort of thing.

"We have to believe that nothing like that could happen to us. If we say our prayers, toe the line, do unto others . . . everything will be okay.

"It's not true, of course. But I understand it. How I felt, though, was that my sister absolutely should not have died that night. It was like having my beating heart ripped out of my body. And to hear the whispering, to see the approving nods when it was Rose that was spared, not Violet . . . it was devastating. Because I would have given anything, *anything*, to be in her shoes that night."

Daisy touches my shoulder. She is unsure about how to proceed. I don't know, either. How much of this story of mine can she handle?

"I still feel guilty, fifty years later. That I am here and she is gone. That I am gray and wrinkled, had a husband and child and . . . a *life*. Things that should have been hers."

Daisy looks at me expectantly. What else can she possibly need to understand about why I don't want to share my sister's life and loss with the entire town?

"So . . . you'll let me write Violet's story?"

"When pigs fly."

Her face falls flatter than a meringue in summertime.

"B-but," she stammers, "I *need* this. Chief Jeffers already said no—"

"Who else is on your list?"

Daisy is trying hard not to cry. She pushes that long stringy hair back behind her ears and starts naming names.

"Stop right there," I say. "That's the one. I'll drive you myself. I've got a few things I could tend to in Sleepy Springs. Does tomorrow work for you?"

It's not the interview she hoped for. And I can tell she hasn't given up on me yet. But she's smart enough to take the bone that I'm tossing her.

DAISY

Grandma pulls the hearse right up to the front of Sleepy Springs Nursing Home with a crunch of her tires, creating a dust storm on the circular gravel drive. There is a ragged boxwood on either side of the entrance to the squat rectangular brick building with a dozen identical windows. Each one has the blinds partway down, giving the whole place an exhausted look that matches its name.

"Hear that?" Grandma puts the gearshift in park, peering over the steering wheel. I am struck by how tiny she is, like a child playing at driving. It's an image reinforced by the thick foam cushion she puts under her backside so she can sit up high enough to see.

I strain my ears, but hear nothing. I crank the window down halfway.

"What is it?"

"The sound of all the old people wheeling over to the windows to see who's kicked the bucket." Grandma chuckles. "I really shouldn't have driven this, but Roger has the Cadillac in the shop. Hope I didn't give anyone in there a heart attack."

"That's a little dark."

"Indeed. But spoken by someone who realizes her own time to get carried out on a stretcher looms."

"Grandma!"

"Sorry, dear. The black attitude about death is just an occupational hazard. Just like my wardrobe. But I'm open-minded. Like Coco Chanel said: 'When they make a color darker than black, I'll wear it.'"

Someone is certainly full of beans today, as my mom used to say. I picture my grandma as a playful, freckly pinto bean to Mom's odd garbanzo. I wish I felt half as chipper. Instead, my anxiety about interviewing Mo Wheeler has got my legs leaden and my heart skittering crazy.

Before I can close the door, Grandma leans over. "Good luck in there," she says seriously. "You'll be fine. Mo's good people."

I nod, my throat too dry from gravel dust and nerves to speak.

"And Daisy? Give Mo and Julie my best."

Inside the nursing home, the smell of Pine-Sol is so strong, it makes my nose tingle. But I guess it's better than other smells that could be hanging around this place.

Following the signs, I take a right and with a few squeaks of my platform sandals, find myself in front of room number 8. A yellowed nameplate that slides into parallel tracks on the door reads MORRIS WHEELER, and I think how long this name must have been here . . . and yet how easily it could be removed. A quick swipe to the left or right and Mo would be gone. Replaced.

Myra had warned me that Mo might not be a good interview. Blinded in the dance hall explosion, his life had been a struggle, she said. "Sweet, sweet man. Couldn't ever do much more than blow on that horn after the blast and there wasn't a big demand for that. His wife was a saint. Worked herself right into an early grave, taking care of him and their three kids."

I knock and the door opens right away—but instead of an old man, I am greeted by a fifty-something Black woman with a head of tight gray-and-white curls who immediately grasps my hand.

"You must be Daisy," she says, her voice deeper than I expected. "I'm Julie, Mo's oldest. The nurse contacted me when you called about visiting."

"Nice to meet you."

"Daddy doesn't say too much these days," she says. "But he is always glad to have some company, even if he can't remember it the next day. Or even the next minute."

I follow her into the small cracker box that is Mo's room. There is nothing on the painted cement block walls. Mo's saxophone—highly polished and perched on a wooden pedestal—is the room's only art or decoration. Mo sits in a high-backed wooden rocker, gently moving to and fro. Dressed neat as a pin in pressed gray trousers, button-down shirt and cheerful red suspenders, Mo sports a tweed fedora with a small fan of colorful feathers tucked into the band. His eyes are hidden behind dark glasses, but his kind, expectant face is turned toward us.

"Daddy? This is Daisy. Daisy Flowers. From the newspaper in Possum Flats?"

Mo nods solemnly and extends his right hand. I'm surprised by the strength that quietly resides in his handshake.

"Pleased to meet you, Mr. Wheeler."

"Mo is just fine, honey," pipes up Julie, who has chosen to sit on the bed, motioning for me to take a chair by her father.

"Mr. Mo," I amend, taking a seat.

Julie laughs and I like the sound, sort of rumbly and musical all at once.

"I'm doing a story about the dance hall explosion," I start. I'm not nervous anymore, but I still feel awkward. I know Mo is blind because of the explosion and I don't know if he will want to talk about it.

"Could you tell me what you remember about that night?"

Mo grips both of the arms of his chair as though he were bracing himself for an onslaught of some type.

But he says nothing.

The rocker squeaks in excruciatingly slow four-four time.

I don't know what to do.

"Well, I figured this might happen," says Julie from her perch on the bed. "It's like he is shutting down, a little piece at a time. The saddest part is his saxophone." She crosses to where the gleaming brass instrument sits, runs her fingers along the smooth metal, tracing around the keys. "He hasn't played in months. Even when he wouldn't talk to me, he still picked up his 'pretty lady,' as he called her."

"That *is* sad," I say.

My palms begin to sweat, even in this air-conditioned room. What now?

"It's okay, Daisy. I'm getting used to this version of my daddy. It's like those nesting dolls, where there is a smaller one inside and then an even smaller one inside of that. I'm dreading the day when there's nothing left inside.

"He had a hard life, you know? You may have noticed, there aren't many people who look like us in Possum Flats."

I nod. I actually don't think I've seen a single African American. Not like the big cities where Mom and I have lived, with so many different types of people.

"That wasn't always the case. My daddy's family lived on the edge of town and there were several other Black families. There was hard work to be done on farms and at the sale barn or in the stockrooms of a few stores and businesses. Some custodial jobs. We got by. Separate but left alone.

"But then when Lamb's blew up, that was it. I mean, Daddy lost his sight, so he wasn't worth much to anyone needing a hand. But it went beyond that. Daddy and Dale Diggs—the drummer— were playing in the dance hall that night. There were people who felt like some of the music they played was 'devil music.' Jazz, you know?

"Seemed to them that the people that blew up had it coming. The musicians maybe most of all."

"But . . . that's crazy. It was a terrible accident."

"Yes, it was. Terrible. But not an accident, according to many. After Dale was buried in the big grave at Oak Lawn, Possum Flats let the Black families know that they weren't welcome anymore.

"Soon as my daddy got out of the hospital, we got out of there. A few small towns like Sleepy Springs took some of us in. Other families headed to the big city. But none of us been back to Possum Flats in fifty years."

I look at Julie and Mo, who is nodding as he rocks gently back and forth.

"I'm sorry," I say.

"Don't be, child. That was long before your time."

"Well, I appreciate you letting me come. My grandma said to say 'hey' to Mo."

"Your grandma is a good woman," Julie says. "She opens her doors to everyone, near and far, Black and white. I'm sure that hasn't made her popular sometimes."

"My grandma couldn't give a crap about popularity," I say. "You probably know that, though."

Julie laughs. "Mmm-hmm. You don't need to ask Rose Flowers what's on her mind. Just wait a hot minute and she'll let you know."

"That's my grandma," I say.

Rose Flowers. The woman. The myth. The legend.

June 19, 1978

Dear Mom

Are you okay? I am worried that my letters aren't getting to you. I want to think you are working hard and don't have time to write back or maybe you haven't quite found the job or home that you want for us and are holding out, wanting to give me all the good news at once? Is that it? It's okay if life isn't perfect out there. I mean, how could it be without me?!? Please let me know you are alive and kicking, okay?

To be honest, life isn't perfect here, either. In fact, it kind of stinks. I was SO excited because I discovered the Lamb's Dance Hall explosion in the old newspaper clips at *The Picayune*! Did you know Grandma had a twin sister who died in the blast? I couldn't believe it! The perfect "scoop." It took some fast-talking, but Fence agreed to let me write a series based on interviews with survivors and family members.

But . . . no one wants to talk to me. Not even my own grandma! Fence and Myra warned me about that, but I didn't believe them. I met Mo Wheeler, the band's saxophonist that night, but he's old and blind and doesn't talk anymore. And Ruby Rae Watson wouldn't let me in the door! You probably knew her. She was married to the Mayor, who died recently at ninety-five—although that was NOT the most interesting thing about him. But Grandma won't let me share any client secrets, even with you! Anyway, they lost their daughter Fern in the explosion, but Ruby Rae said it still hurt too much to talk about. She hoped I could understand.

It seems like everyone has a side they don't want to share. Sometimes I look around your old room and can't imagine you lived here or slept in this canopy bed with ruffly pillows the color of old teeth. Who were you? What did you think about, lying on this bed like I am now? Books? Boys? Or were you only plotting your escape?

I better stop for now. I gotta drop this at the post office on my way to *The Picayune,* and I like to be there when Hazel unlocks the door.

WRITE ME BACK!!

xox Daisy

P.S. I met our paper boy, Joe. He basically ran over me with his bike last week. I think he might be a self-centered jerk but the verdict is still out.

P.P.S. Yes, he is cute. I know you are wondering!

DAISY

After dropping off my letter, I spent the morning at *The Picayune* developing a roll of black-and-white film I'd taken at the 4-H cattle show. The pictures were like "grip-and-grins," but with a kid holding the halter of a dairy or beef animal instead of a check or plaque. A twelve-year-old boy in a black cowboy hat—and a can of Skoal in his back pocket—took great delight explaining that a steer was "a bull with his nuts cut off." He probably considered me a hopeless city slicker or an idiot. I'm not sure which is worse around here.

Smiley had offered to help me with the photos, but I'd decided to try doing it myself. Now, hanging up the finished products to dry, I feel a twinge of pride. Not bad.

There is a knock on the door.

"Don't come in!"

"I won't, sugar pie." Not Smiley, but Myra.

"But if you're at a stopping point, you've got someone waiting at your desk."

I put the last undeveloped roll of film back in its plastic canister. When I open the darkroom door, Myra looks about to pop with excitement.

"Hurry up now. He's been there about fifteen minutes. I wouldn't push my luck," Myra says with a wink.

For some reason, that wink makes my face feel hot. But I barely know anyone outside *The Picayune*. Who could it be?

It doesn't take long to find out. Emerging into the daylight of the newsroom, I see Joe. He is sitting in my chair, hands clasped behind his head and ankles crossed, as comfortable as if it were his own.

"Excuse me, did I die and make you intern?"

"What?" Joe's face goes dark for a second, like a cloud shadow scooting across a sunlit skyscraper. He lets loose an exaggerated sigh.

"I guess it would be too much to ask for you to be happy to see me." He gives me a goofy grin and shakes his head. "What is it with you, Flower Child?"

It takes a minute to register that he has given me a nickname. I should be flattered—he is the hometown hero, the star quarterback hopeful—but instead I am goaded by his brashness. Something in his tone feels like entitlement. Or worse: ownership. Maybe it's just confidence that comes from a life of winning. But it rubs me the wrong way.

This is not, however, the time or place for a showdown. The newsroom bustle has gone down a couple of notches. Make that a dozen notches. It's closing in on funeral-home quiet in here. The typical clicking of the typewriters and slicing of the paper cutters, the voices on the phones—everything has died to a hush. No one is looking at me or Joe directly—except Patty, who is staring at us with her mouth wide-open—but I sense that we are in the corner of every eye in the building. What do I expect? People are curious; newspaper people even more so. But I am wondering right along with them: What does Mr. Possum Flats Golden Boy see in the hippie bookworm?

I keep my voice frosty. "Are you here to see me on business?"

There is a crash and an accompanying shriek from Myra's desk. She was apparently paying too much attention to the drama at mine and has let go of her coffee cup, an oversized mug that reads: If You Can't Say Something Nice About Someone . . . Sit Next to Me. Pieces of ceramic litter the gray tiled floor, and her crisp white capris are completely spattered. There is an uncomfortable shifting as everyone in the newsroom who saw what happened pretends they didn't.

I guess no one talks to Joe like that.

Joe is quick on the uptake. "As a matter of fact, I *am*. Lunch business."

"I've got work to do."

"This is a working lunch. There's something you've got to see. For the story you're working on."

Jesus Christ Superstar! I can't believe he knows about that already. Which means everyone else in Possum Flats must know, too.

"I'm not sure I really need your help," I say.

"Really? From what I've heard, you're getting a lot of face time with closed doors."

"But—"

"Grab your lunch," Joe says. "We're going on a field trip."

When I return from the break room with my brown bag, the office has resumed its normal hum. Myra's stained capris are the only reminder that the entire newsroom just participated in a moment of shameless rubbernecking.

The show is over.

I sling the clunky Olympus camera over my shoulder and tuck a small notepad and pencil in my back pocket. Outside the building, the day is glorious. The noon air is warm and rich with early summer smells—from the catalpa trees, hung with their grapelike blossoms to the green scent of uncut grass and the damp, black dirt beneath it. Without speaking, Joe and I head to the shady side of the street lined with young maples. He is wheeling his bike, his own lunch bag crumpled at the top where he clutches it against one of the handlebars.

"So. Where are we going?"

"You'll see."

We walk by the post office, turn at the Dog 'N' Suds, and pass the Sunnyside Diner. The trees along Main Street are much larger, but further apart. I am sweating and conscious of the picture we make, not just two teenagers trudging purposefully along the sidewalk but Joe Nichols walking around with Daisy Flowers. Everyone will have us married by nightfall.

At a corner where railroad tracks cross the road, I see a large cemetery through an eight-foot wrought-iron fence held in place by aged cement corner pillars. The train tracks trace the eastern boundary of the cemetery before heading out of town. Joe props his bike up against the entrance gate with the words OAK LAWN CEMETERY, POSSUM FLATS, MO woven into the wrought-iron lattice work. What are we doing here?

"I guess this is how you impress all the girls," I say.

"What?" Joe's face looks genuinely confused. "Whoa. Wait. This isn't a date. Like I said, it's a field trip. A little background research." He shakes his head and I can almost hear the unspoken: *"Women."*

If I could claw my way under a nearby headstone, I would gladly do so. But instead, I am forced to stand here, mortified beyond words, awaiting further instruction. Somehow, I get the feeling that Joe is enjoying my discomfort.

"Follow me."

We wind our way through the cemetery on the unpaved road, a mix of packed red clay and small golden rocks. There's obviously enough traffic to keep the tire paths clear, but not to prevent clumps of grass from growing in between. The heavy camera bumps rhythmically against my rib cage with every step. Before long, the easy silence that Joe keeps as we walk, each in our own tire track, allows me to forget my embarrassment and enjoy my surroundings.

It is a gorgeous place, with the stately fenced boundaries that seem to both protect it and keep it in another time. Unlike the cookie-cutter rectangles that serve as grave markers in modern cemeteries—allowing only bouquets of artificial flowers on certain holidays—Oak Lawn has a random but pleasing variety of headstones, monuments, markers and tributes. There are tiny headstones embossed with angel heads for stillborn infants with just the single date of their birth/death juxtaposed with nearby obelisks proclaiming the leadership of a family patriarch. Some stones have labels like MOTHER or FATHER above the names and dates—and many couples share a headstone, oftentimes with children who died in childhood or infancy. There are chipped and crooked marble stones whose numbers and names are faint, but clearly from a prior century, alongside a freshly dug grave, the raw red clay heaped with wilted bouquets of gladiolas. I feel a jolt of recognition: Bartholomew J. Watson. I mentally apologize to him for so callously sharing his last secret with Fence and, ultimately, the wider world. I am sure he is well beyond caring, but a part of me feels sad that he had a secret—or somewhat secret—life. But how many people ever manage to be the same person on the outside that they are on the inside? I can't think of many, although my grandma seems pretty "self-actualized," a term my mom uses for people who are unapologetically true to themselves.

The other thing I love about Oak Lawn Cemetery is the trees. There is no rhyme or reason to the placement of this gathering of giant post oaks. It's more like the dead have arranged themselves around the trees, as if spreading cloths and blankets for a picnic. The feeling is friendly and welcoming. Comfortable. There are other trees, too, of course, as well as shrubs and flowers that add personality and homeyness. Grandma loves pointing out plants, and I am pleased that I can recognize the out-of-control sprawl of spent peony bushes, an oversized forsythia, and small glades of bladelike iris foliage hiding the headstones. As if people had transplanted pieces of their everyday lives here, to comfort themselves, as well as the dead.

I am conscious of the brightness of the day. Everything seems scrubbed clean, down to its essence: the deep greens of the oak leaves, broccoli-like in the way the branches mound and fill in the shapes of each tree; the white of the marble stones; the orange-red smears of exposed earth. There is no soft focus. Every edge is distinct.

Joe jars me out of my musings by stopping abruptly.

We are standing in front of a huge rectangular granite stone that must be ten feet across. It sits upon a base that is slightly longer and that forms two steps, flanked on either side by a large squarish end cap holding a shallow granite vase filled with a faded assortment of plastic flowers. IN MEMORY OF THE UNIDENTIFIED DEAD the slab reads, along with the date, AUGUST 13, 1928, simply and starkly in engraved block letters. Two rows of names run down each side of the giant grave marker, each one accompanied by a date of birth. Different beginnings, but one terrible end.

"Wow," I say, and mean it. I have never seen anything quite so grand in a cemetery that is not either a mausoleum or centuries old. I lift the camera to my eye and snap photos from a few angles, trying to capture the drama and scale of it. In a couple of snaps, I include an unsuspecting Joe at the edge of the frame.

"I know, right? This is my favorite lunch spot. You can sit on the steps here"—Joe nods for me to do just that—"and soak in the peace and quiet. You can even hear the 1:10 train blow by if you're on a late break.

"I've sort of enjoyed keeping it to myself. But since you're doing a story on the big explosion, I thought you'd want to see it."

Joe seems strangely awkward in a way he probably isn't on a football field.

"What do you do when you come here? Besides eat lunch, I mean."

"Think, mostly." He plops down beside me. "About how I can get out of this place."

"Out of Possum Flats?" I am surprised. "I would think you'd want to stay here. People love you here. I mean . . ." I instantly start rushing my words in case he is getting the idea that by "people," I mean me. "I've gotten the impression that everyone practically worships you around this town. You're like a hero or something."

Joe's face is solemn, an expression I have not seen before. It does something interesting to his features, making them less symmetrical, harder, and yet somehow more beautiful. I realize how much the rascally smile he generally sports softens him, makes him seem human.

"What happens after football? I mean, I love it. And I hope that I get to play my heart out these next four years. But then what? Do you know what happens to old jocks in this town?"

"No?"

"They stay. They're everywhere, as a matter of fact. I could give you the washed-up QB/point guard/pitcher tour anytime you like.

"They work at a gas station or garage. Maybe the furniture factory or the lumber yard. A few have better jobs, like a landscaping company or managing a bar. A few lucky SOBs with money might inherit the family business."

I'm not sure how to respond. Obviously, Joe must have aspirations beyond paperboy, but it hadn't occurred to me. I realize just how much I have been centered on myself since I arrived, struggling to find my own way to survive in Possum Flats for as long as I am stuck here. "Why do they stay?"

"For the love, of course. Possum Flats loves its heroes—but it's a love that keeps you stuck, so you can't grow or change. Or just be you."

"And just *who* exactly are you, Joe Nichols?" I am trying to lighten things up, but Joe doesn't get the memo. He is serious as a heart attack.

"Honestly? I don't know. But I know I don't want to be them.

"They only have the 'good old days' to talk about, because there are no good days for them now. I don't want this to be it, the peak of my existence. This town likes to put people in a box. And sometimes you don't even get to choose your box."

Joe stops to unroll the top of his lunch sack and I do the same. My grandma has packed a crustless PBJ wrapped in wax paper and dry around the edges, a freckly yellow apple and four Fig Newtons, still clinging together front to back in a tight hug that suggests they'd been pried unwillingly from their siblings in their plastic sleeve.

"I mean, I didn't really choose this town. Or my family," he says.

"No one gets to choose their family."

Joe starts to say something, but doesn't. Instead, he pops open a can of Pepsi and sets it beside him before reaching into his bag and removing a bologna sandwich, potato chips and Oreos. "Want a swig?" he asks, noting my lack of liquid refreshment. I usually get a cup of water at *The Picayune*, but in my haste had forgotten to bring anything to drink.

"No," I say. "Soda is terrible for you."

"Oh," he says, taking another long pull at his Pepsi before wiping his mouth with one tanned forearm. "I've heard Fig Newtons are super healthy."

Oops. Sometimes I forget how much of my new life I have adapted to, while stuck to the old in my mind. My mother didn't allow soft drinks, processed cookies or chips, so I ate carrots, hummus, granola bars, raisins, celery and nuts. Occasionally, I got natural peanut butter smeared on a slab of dense, whole grain bread. Just the thought of one of those "sandwiches" makes my jaws hurt.

"Sorry," I say. "That was my inner hippie talking. Actually my mother." I bite through the soft, buttery cookie crust before hitting the sweet, chewy fig nougat inside, both layers deliciously warmed through by the sun.

"Your mother is a hippie, too?"

I laugh. "*Too?* Is that how you see me?"

Joe grins back. " 'Fraid so, Flower Child. Your inner hippie has an outer hippie, too. But don't you want out of Possum Flats? I mean, you've seen other places. Cities? Different states? You don't want to be here forever, either, right?"

"Of course not. I'm just here until my mom and her boyfriend get things set up for us in California."

"So you've heard from her?"

How does he know I haven't? *Because it's Possum Flats.*

"Not yet," I say, more defensively than I mean to. There's a sick lurch in my stomach as it occurs to me as clear as the bright June sun that I have been here in Possum Flats for six weeks and have not had a single letter from my mother. I had put the silence down to her and Ron getting settled in. But I feel like a fool in front of Joe. The whole town! They probably feel sorry for me, kidding myself that my mother is actually going to come back and get me.

Only, she *is*. She *will*. I take a breath. My insecurity got the best of me for a moment, but I know my mom. She's a flake, but she loves me. She wouldn't leave me here.

She did leave me at a gas station once, though. I was five, just finished kindergarten. I don't remember the guy's name that Mom was with at the time, but we had pulled up stakes from Chicago and were heading to St. Louis. We'd stopped at a Sinclair station and Mom's boyfriend was saving a few nickels by doing self-serve at the pump. Mom and I went into the store to get a drink and the key to the restroom. She told me to pick out a pack of gum, which was a rare treat.

I was weighing my options: Juicy Fruit or Big Red? Or what about Beech-Nut, with Yipes the zebra on the front of the package, and each slender piece striped with a different color and flavor? Or maybe a pack of Trident. That meant going sugar-free—which I hated to do, given the rare option for something sugary—but the packs came with more pieces, even if they were smaller.

The next thing I knew, a lady with a long gray ponytail was squatting down beside me in the cramped aisle, peering at me over those gold wire glasses that are only half circles.

"You lost, hon?"

I remember looking around to make sure she was talking to me. Then panicking inside as I looked out the plate glass windows. No boyfriend. No car.

"My mom's in the bathroom," I explained.

"Oh. Dear. Well, she turned in the key ten minutes ago and drove off," the lady said. She must have seen the fear make its way across my face as I realized I had been forgotten, because she scooped me up in her thin arms and plopped me down on the red Coca-Cola chest by the register. She popped the top off of an ice-cold Fanta and handed the glass bottle to me while she seemed to consider what to do with me. I sipped it slowly, wanting to savor it, despite the anxiety in the pit of my stomach. Mom didn't allow me to have soda. The bubbly orange drink burned my throat slightly. I don't drink much soda these days, either, but I avoid Fanta. It tastes too much like loss.

She had just started to dial up the sheriff when Mom and her boyfriend pulled up to the station with a metallic squeal of worn brakes and a door slam.

"See?" I said to the lady. "She didn't forget me."

"My mom will be back. *Soon*," I snap at Joe, a little more harshly than I meant to. He looks concerned. As if I'm delusional. Or maybe it's just the sun making him squint.

"Well, anyway," he says, finally. "I come here to remind myself that I've got to find a way to get out. Look at the names on this stone. So many people close to our age. They went to a dance one night and *poof*, that was it. Game over. At age eighteen or nineteen, twenty-two. Life in this town killed them."

"It was an accident. Possum Flats didn't kill them."

"Maybe not. But my gut feeling is that sooner or later, this town will be the death of me. Not my body, but my soul—*if* I have one. Don't tell my grandfather I said that, by the way. You'll want to talk to him about the explosion, too. He was there. Bro Emmonds?"

"So your grandfather is . . . *Dash* Emmonds?" The cub reporter in me perks up her ears, recalling the list of the injured from *The Picayune* articles. Maybe Dash could be my first successful interview.

"*Dash?* No, Paul. A respectable biblical name for a respectable biblical man."

"So that makes you a 'PK'?"

"More like a *PGK*. Preacher's Grandkid. Not as rowdy and re-

bellious as the classic PK," he says sheepishly. "But I have my moments. Like my Mayor Watson moment. Which I mostly regret."

My jaw drops.

"You. Wait. Are you kidding me? *You* did that?" I don't know
whether to laugh or cry or punch him in the solar plexus. "I got in
so much trouble with my grandma over that . . . thing you did with
the hand fan."

"Yeah, that wasn't cool. It was a split-second decision made
out of boredom and a misplaced sense of justice. But hey, you
shouldn't have blabbed in the first place. I just took it the next
step too far. Which, you have to admit, was a little bit funny."

I don't want to admit it. But I remember how even my grandma
had enjoyed a somewhat reluctant laugh with me over the whole
thing.

"Touché. We were both assholes," I say. Yet I don't like how a
part of me enjoys being grouped together with Joe.

Time to change the subject.

"So does your grandfather ever talk about the explosion?" I ask.
"Would he talk about it with *me*?"

"Well, it wouldn't be easy. I wouldn't even know about it except
that one day when I was little, I was playing toy soldiers in his office. I asked him if he'd gotten his limp in the war. I loved the idea
of him in a foxhole or dragging a fellow soldier to safety when he
got hit by a shell."

Joe crumples up his lunch bag and passes it back and forth in
his hands, like a lumpy paper football, before leaning his back
against the rose granite. I follow his example, and the hard slab
immediately cools the skin beneath my sticky shirt. We are looking out over the cemetery, not at each other, and I sense it's easier
for Joe to talk this way.

"Anyway, he yanked me up by my shirt until my face was even
with his. I don't think I'd ever been that close to him and it scared
the heck out of me, his face was so purple and angry.

"'This God-blessed ankle is the reason I didn't get to be in the war,' he said, practically spitting on me. I started bawling, of course. He let go and apologized for taking the Lord's sacred name in vain, but not for scaring the shit out of me."

Joe laughs and I do, too, which is a relief. I am scared of Pastor Emmonds already and I haven't even met him. And I hate to think of five-year-old Joe being terrified of his own grandpa.

"Don't worry," Joe says, seeing my face. "I'm good with Bro Emmonds. Well, maybe *good* is a strong word. I respect him and try to toe the line so that he respects me. He's just not the warm, fuzzy type is all."

"Thanks for the warning."

"You're most welcome, Flower Child," he says. "I told my mom what happened and she explained about the dance hall explosion. She warned me to never bring it up again. But he's not the only one who feels that way. No one talks about it. When I found this giant headstone last summer, I was amazed. I hadn't known it was here. I didn't know *they* were here," he says, gesturing at the names behind us. "That's why I keep coming back, I guess. I hate that everyone has forgotten them."

"Well, maybe I'll get them remembered," I say. My prickly porcupine defensiveness at the start of our lunch adventure has disappeared. I might even call this a truce. "So, when can I talk to your grandpa? He's actually at the top of my list."

"I could get you in the door. But he's a hard-ass. I wouldn't put him first."

"Well, maybe not *first*," I allow. "But he sounds fascinating."

"Fascinating?" Joe laughs. "He's about as interesting as watching paint dry. He's got his Bible and he knows exactly what it says and exactly what he believes—and what you should believe, too. He's a lot like a newspaper. Black and white."

"Maybe there's more gray than you know."

Joe sighs. "I wish. Then maybe I wouldn't feel so much like a sinner."

For a moment, I consider what Joe might mean by that. He

doesn't strike me as a hopeless miscreant. The Mayor incident was bad, but not unforgivable. It's probably tough to live with someone who has all the answers *and* God on his side, if you're having doubts about both. Or maybe wanting more than Possum Flats has to offer feels like a sin to Joe? Either way, I don't think I can ask.

Joe looks at me for a long minute and seems to decide something. "Hand me a piece of paper. And your pencil."

Curious, I fold open my steno pad to a fresh sheet before passing it to him with my sharpened pencil stub.

He rests the pad on his knee and makes several quick swipes with the pencil. I watch, fascinated, as the lines—so random at first—quickly take on a human shape. Joe is frowning as he concentrates, the smallest bit of his tongue pressed in a triangle above his lips. He turns the pencil lead to one side and shades in a few places. A few little squiggles and he hands back the pad to me.

I am amazed. It's me. Or a caricature of me. I am a sticklike figure in some sort of woven tunic, bell bottoms and sandals, a steno pad in one hand and No. 2 pencil in the other. My dark hair is straight and slightly unruly, and my eyes take up half my face—while the other half is smirk. Tucked behind one ear is a giant daisy.

"Joe, wow. That's incredible."

The tips of his ears color. He is obviously pleased by my response.

"Yeah. Thanks." He abruptly stands up, dusting off his hands as if he had dirtied them. "Not a big market for cartoonists in Possum Flats, though."

"What about *The Picayune?*"

Joe's half smile is a rueful one. "I think everyone around here would prefer I use my arm for touchdown passes."

"But after football? You could go to school for that. You *should*."

"It's like I said about people putting you in a box around here. My parents—and grandfather—might understand me going away for college. But to make goofy little drawings?" He shakes his head. "That doesn't make sense."

I look at the goofy little drawing of myself, and carefully close the notepad. It makes sense to me. But I don't know Joe well enough to go all "rah-rah" cheerleader on him.

"Well, we better get back to work," I say instead.

"Yep."

"Thanks for bringing me here," I say, standing up to stretch. The sun has gone behind a cottony puff of cloud and the day feels delicious. Maybe because I actually have a friend here in Possum Flats, as unlikely as I would have guessed it to be. I close my eyes for a minute. I hate to leave.

I am not sure if it is vertigo from having my eyes closed, but I feel wobbly all of a sudden, as if the earth were rumbling beneath the steps where I stand with Joe. My eyes fly open in alarm, but Joe is there and he reaches for my arm to steady me.

"This is the best part!" he says, as the rumbling turns into a roar. It is not my imagination. Joe lets go of my arm, slipping his hand into mine, gripping me tightly while we both shiver and shake on our granite perch. Even the trees seem to be shuddering, as I hear a long, low horn and realize: The train is coming through. I had forgotten how close the tracks were to the cemetery wall. There are a few shrill blasts of the horn as the engine passes over the street we had followed on our way here, then the only noise is the steady throb and hum of the train cars as they pass, a rolling, wavelike rhythm that I can feel in my breastbone. It seems to last forever, or maybe just a minute or two. I can't really tell, because my mind is concentrating so hard on standing upright . . . and the feel of Joe's hand in mine. Not sweaty at all, but instead warm and comfortable, like a favorite glove. I can't differentiate the quick, hard heartbeat in my ears from the pounding of the passing train and I worry that Joe can hear my heart racing, too.

Then there is one last creak and gasp and the rumbling is past, just a disappearing hum, an echo of an echo . . . and the train is gone.

And just like that, Joe releases me to stand on my own two feet.

"Wasn't that cool?" he asks, clearly pleased with himself and the effect the surprise train has had.

All I can do is nod. I don't trust myself to say anything. It *was* cool.

"It's like everyone from Lamb's is out on the dance floor again, moving and shaking to the music."

"It's very cool," I say. My response feels inadequate, but Joe doesn't seem to care.

"Even cooler that you're going to write about them," Joe says. "It's like bringing them back to life, you know?"

I hope he isn't overestimating my abilities. At the same time, I am flattered that he thinks I can do these people—and this story—justice.

"Well, I guess we better get started," I say.

There is a silent beat between us as Joe takes in what I have just said.

"*We?*" Joe laughs. "Well, all right, Flower Child. I thought you'd never ask."

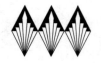

Hazel

I love how peaceful my post office is after lunch. The sunlight shines through the dust in the air and gives the wall of oaken post office boxes a golden glow. There's the scent of warm wood, clean tile and brown packaging paper—with a hint of mint adhesive. From about two to three thirty is a chance to catch my breath, the time when I sit on the three-legged stool behind the small worn service counter and think. Maybe daydream, too. In good weather, I'll slip out the back door, where I have a little flower garden.

But just as I put the RING BELL FOR SERVICE sign out so I can deadhead some zinnias, I see Joe Nichols and Daisy Flowers coming up the sidewalk.

I am immediately suspicious: Daisy mailed her letter this morning and Joe is missing his sack of the rolled and rubber-banded newspapers I slip into the mailboxes at four every weekday.

"Hello, Ms. Hazel." Joe holds open the door for Daisy. The rush of air is warm and rich with summer smells: fresh clipped grass, warm sidewalks, honeysuckle vine. Then Joe steps in, too, like the sunshine himself with that bright smile and self-confidence.

"Joe. You're early."

"Oh, I'm not delivering papers today, Ms. Hazel. Not yet anyway." He grins. "I brought you someone. I think you know Daisy Flowers?" He nudges the girl forward toward my counter.

"Hey," she says, holding on to a cassette player like a life preserver.

"Well now, I believe we've met a number of times, although I can't say we've been properly introduced." I let her off the hook. She is just a girl with the misfortune to be a familiar face in an extremely foreign land. We all know her family, her history. We can predict her smarts and behaviors, recognize family traits—from the way she walks to her blood type. But she doesn't know us. Poor thing!

"I'm Hazel," I say. "Pleased to officially meet you, Daisy."

"Me, too," she fumbles. "I mean, I'm glad to meet you as well."

"What can I do for you two today? Need a few stamps?"

"Um, well, I wanted to ask you about the Lamb's Dance Hall explosion."

The look on my face must be complete surprise. No one has asked me about that in decades. I answered a lot of questions early on, back when the police and firefighters and grieving families wanted to know "why?" or "how?" But eventually, everyone realized that "why" and "how" didn't change anything. Those who needed answers blamed God and the sinners who had brought down His wrath on us like a bolt of lightning. And none of us talked about it.

"Ms. Hazel?" Joe sounds worried.

I manage to find the support of the stool behind me, then place my hands flat on the counter to stop the shaking. I feel like I've been punched in the chest. Hard.

I wore my blue drop-waist dress. Clusters of rhinestones followed the curve of the neckline—which showed just the slightest cleft of my bosom—with single sparkles sprinkled throughout the rest of the crepe fabric. It was like wearing the night sky, so dark blue and scattered with stars, the filmy material falling against my body like a cloud.

I had been watching the sky from my front steps, having a quick cigarette while I waited for Charlie Walters. It was a double date, and Charlie was picking me up last since I lived just a few blocks from the dance hall.

It was shaping up to be a perfect night. Well, almost. I was crazy about dancing. I loved my friend Violet, the other female half of our two couples. And I adored being driven around in a fancy car with a handsome young man and treated to a hamburger and soda at the end of an adventurous evening.

There was only one problem: I longed to be in the back seat with Dash Emmonds rather than up front with Charlie.

Charlie was nice enough. He was a banker's son, a soft college boy. His looks—a lackluster combination of thinning brown hair and weak chin—certainly were not what made him attractive. It was more his sure confidence that good things would unquestionably come to him as a matter of course. That and his wallet.

My family had next to no money, my father's wages from the railroad stretched as far between paydays as the tracks themselves across southern Missouri on into Oklahoma. So I was surprised when Charlie asked me out for a phosphate at Morton's the summer after my sophomore year—and terrified that when he pulled up to our tumble-down shack he might turn around and never come back!

That first date, we sat side by side on red leatherette stools at the drugstore counter. I let Charlie buy me everything my heart desired—a greasy grilled cheese cut into fat, oozing triangles, french fries and a cherry vanilla soda. But the best thing he bought for me was something I couldn't eat or drink: the delicious feeling of having everyone's eyes on me. You could almost read the word bubbles coming from their open mouths, as if they were comic book cartoons: "What in the world is Hazel Sampson doing with Charlie Walters?" And when Ginger Morton spun around on her stool to take a look at me, she knocked a full glass of soda all over her smart crepe de chine skirt. The ensuing commotion was heaven because I knew I was the cause of it. I loved being envied; it was something brand-new to me. But I know what Charlie saw in me: I was a stunner. I know it now and I knew it in a vague way then. Boys could not keep their eyes off me.

But I was young, not quite sixteen. Charlie's money wasn't enough to keep me entertained forever. So that night at the dance hall, I was silently but bitterly enduring another one of his monologues about money and wishing I could just get out and kick up my heels. I ached to be watched. Appreciated.

"See that guy over there? His dad just came in to get a second mortgage on their farm. Poor schmuck. My father says that his land is as good as ours now."

Charlie leaned against the doorframe in the far corner of the dance hall, holding a glass of "hooch," as he liked to call it, even though it was probably bourbon nicked from his father's liquor cabinet. From there, he could see everyone coming and going. And it was as if he could see through them—but not their thoughts or souls or anything I would be interested in. He could only see through their wallets and pockets and handbags. He knew how much everyone was worth, their family's debt and savings account balances. And he did not possess the scruples to keep that information to himself.

"There's Jimmy Jeffers. And Nell Peters. I hope they don't get married. At least not to each other. Dad says neither has two nickels to rub together."

I craned my neck to get a look at Nell. I'd heard she had been trying to get rid of Jimmy for just that reason, but I didn't want to encourage Charlie further. Instead, I took in her not-new-but-nicely-pressed sailor blouse and navy skirt, the hat jauntily atop her straight blond hair. She looked ready for a good time, while Jimmy seemed nervous, fingering his tie over his tightly buttoned shirt. He was a big box of a boy with a slack mouth that was always slightly open. He scanned the room suspiciously, as if he knew he had rivals everywhere. Poor boy: He did!

But the person I couldn't stop watching was Dash. I had grown peevish with the financial analysis of Possum Flats' next generation. I did not give a fig who had a fat loan, a note due or a negative balance. I just wanted to dance and laugh. And judging by the way Dash moved through the crowd there at Lamb's, he felt the same way.

"Um-hm." Charlie didn't need real answers in order to keep talking. Just the occasional affirmative noise.

I watched Dash wind his way through the smoke and the dancers, skirting the edge of the dance floor. He stopped and gave a dramatic bow to the band itself, and was rewarded by a long low blast on the sax at close range, Mo Wheeler's cheeks puffed out like an adder. When Dash righted himself again, that blond curl across his forehead bounced with him and his smile was like a flashbulb going off, illuminating the crowd, freezing it in time. It was as though the whole gathering, the music, the hum of anticipation, was all for him—and he knew it. The crowd, in fact, broke out into applause at his antics.

I scanned the faces for Violet's and finally spied her hanging back, away from the band and the clapping crowd. She looked strangely out of her element, not a part of the goings-on at all—and as if Dash read my mind, he reached out a hand to her, pulled her toward him through the throng, which parted in her wake. He held her hand up high in his and suddenly took another bow, throwing Violet off kilter. She gave him a startled glance as she righted herself on her heels, Dash laughing the whole while. When he took one last bow, she was ready and synchronized herself perfectly with him, her face when it surfaced flushed with blood and searching his as if to see if she had gotten it right. It was strange to see her so reluctant to perform, when she was usually Dash's equal in the entertainment department. I had even seen her dance on top of tables at Lamb's before.

I had asked Violet to let me know when she wanted to take a cigarette break. Typically a bunch of us girls met up about halfway through the dance for a shared smoke and to gossip about the evening's happenings: who was on the outs, who was drinking too much, who was in the back seat with whom. Violet and I hadn't been friends before I went with Charlie, but we got along marvelously. I admired her brash, fun-loving ways and she basked in my adoration and delighted in "corrupting" me. I wanted to *be* Violet.

Especially where Dash was concerned, even though he had hardly said two words to me.

The band's next tune was the Charleston, and the downbeat put the dancers in a frenzy of pairing up. The women left without a man were undeterred, lining up in the front and kicking their heels to their hands in perfect time, the brass alternately blasting staccato then sliding into a rhythm that seemed to both push and pull the crowd. Yet across the room was Violet, clutching her purse and looking around frantically. She wasn't one to skip the Charleston, typically in the thick of things, knees knocking, hands spread and flashing around her face like those new neon signs. She must really need that smoke. Our eyes met and she waited a beat before nodding toward the exit and rushing out the door. I knew I should follow, but the music beckoned me and I didn't want to leave the beat behind. I wanted to crawl inside of it, to jump and hop and stamp the floor, to twirl my dress and feel the breeze swirl between my legs.

Instead, with one shiny pump, I kicked my purse back beneath the chairs lining the dance floor in the semidarkness, their backs draped with sweaters and jackets, a few giving some bowler hats a seat to themselves.

"Charlie," I said, interrupting him droning on about interest rates. "Would you be a dear and look for my purse? I left it in the coatroom with my sweater."

"What?"

"Navy blue, beaded, fringed at the bottom. Strap about this long?" I hold my hands apart to help him picture it, but I knew I had lost him at "purse." "Pretty please? I really need a cigarette."

"Purse? Sweater? Cigarette? Coatroom?" He was still processing as I gently pushed him toward the coat check near the entrance. I knew the search would befuddle him and that I had just bought myself at least ten minutes.

"Thanks, Charlie," I purred. I watched him bob through the crush of energetic kicking and shuffling. When he disappeared,

I took a deep breath and shimmied toward the dance floor. My heart hammered behind my breastbone, threatening to break it loose; my palms were damp. I felt as if I were about to commit a crime . . . which was just plain silly, I told myself. It's a dance. One dance.

I reached up to touch him on the back. He was talking to Jimmy Jeffers, who looked like he had been crying, which was hard to reconcile with his six-foot, two-hundred-fifty-pound frame and unsentimental farm boy personality. Maybe he was just mad. Or sweaty. Or both.

When Dash turned around, he didn't look at all surprised to see me. He reached for my hand and brought it to his mouth for an exaggerated kiss, which I felt all the way up my arm, like he had electrified me somehow. He was drunk; I saw it in the way his eyes were not quite focused when they looked into mine . . . and then when they dropped to fixate on my bosom. When he realized he was being indiscreet, he gave me one of those devilish grins that I always found so charming, but had never had the pleasure of having turned on just for my benefit. It completely undid me.

"Aw, Hazel," he said, still holding my hand near his face. "Would you dance with me?"

I nodded several times, relieved that I didn't have to articulate my desire. It was unlike me to be so forward, especially since he was Violet's date and Charlie's best friend. But Dash and the music were pulling me out there, and the beat took over. It was such a crazy dance anyway, with turns and spins, kicks and steps. And Dash had it down. He reeled me out and pulled me back in, and started side-kicking as we created our own little orbit—my left kicking out with his right, my right with his left. Soon the rest of the dancers parted, giving us the room we needed to really get in gear. I didn't think, I just followed Dash's lead, which was flawless even with all those drinks on board. He barely touched me and I knew what to do. We were moving so quickly and together, even with his improvisations. It was the best dance of my life. I felt fluid and flashy, my skin warm and my body taking control, moving confidently in the rhythm of the dance. My dress twirled as I kicked my legs out to the side and then behind me, never missing a beat. And though I'd never had more than a few nips on a flask, I was totally drunk—on the heat, the beat, the clapping around us. And the way Dash looked at me as he pulled me so close I could smell his skin, sour with sweat and smoke, and then released me.

And then it was over. Just like that, the music swelled and stopped and the two of us were no longer center stage. At least, not for anyone else. Some other dancers filled in the spaces around us, some breaking from their partners and drifting toward the edges of the room, wanting a drink or a break or someone new to dance with. But I was left in the middle with Dash, who was sloppily kissing my hand and looking up at me while he did. And whatever he must have seen in my face—shock? encouragement? desire?—caused him to kiss it again, then move his way up my forearm, trailing damp kisses up my shoulder until he was right against my neck.

"That was fun," he breathed through my hair, into my ear. "I didn't know you could move like that."

I didn't say anything. I couldn't.

"What other moves do you have, little Hazel?" He was whispering, but I felt like everyone must surely hear him. "Would you show them to me sometime?"

I yanked my arm away from Dash and turned, practically running off the dance floor. He had misunderstood me . . . or had he? I pushed my way through the crowd and out into the night, my skin immediately cooled by the air. I felt a strange combination of shame and longing. It was okay for me to want Dash, as long as he didn't realize it. But he had felt the same way as I did, wanting those kisses to keep going from my ear down my neck to . . . *Oh my God.* I had done something terrible, even though I didn't love Charlie. I didn't want to wreck my friendship with Violet. But now I knew that given the chance, I would have run off with Dash in that moment on the dance floor. That shook me.

I leaned against the cool brick of the building near the bottom of the fire escape, regretting kicking my handbag into a dark corner of the dance hall. No cigarettes. And no Violet, either. She had probably already gone in and reclaimed her partner. There were a few young men visiting through the window of a car by the courthouse square. Their collars were loosened beneath their ties, hats askew from their exertions on the dance floor or elsewhere. There was the flash of a silver flask as it passed between one of the young men and the driver of the car.

The music that streamed out from the doorways and open windows reached its velvety arms down and made me want to start swaying again, close to someone else. "At Sundown." I closed my eyes as Mo Wheeler gave a bluesy blow on his horn and I got caught up in that melancholy note that matched the dark inkiness of the night.

Then, in front of my closed lids, there was a brilliant flash. The bricks behind me gave a terrible shudder. The very ground gave way, rolling beneath my heels. But before I had time to reach back to steady myself, there was an awful explosion of sound and light and the wall behind me was gone and I was gone, too, rocketing over the alley, flying toward heaven with my eyes wide, too surprised to scream. I wanted to reach out and grab onto something—a tree limb, a street lamp, the moon?—but too soon I was falling back down, the earth rushing up to catch me.

I was found several hundred yards away from Lamb's, facedown in the grass of a vacant lot. My face was covered with blood from a large gash in my forehead. So much blood, in fact, that when Jimmy Jeffers rolled me over, he was sure I was dead. But then I called out for Dash and Violet. At least, that is what I am told. I don't remember anything beyond the explosion, not until days later, when I finally came awake in a hospital bed with my head wrapped like a swami.

I did not ask for Charlie.

But his parents asked for me.

John and Virginia Walters were my first visitors in the makeshift hospital the day I opened my eyes again. I didn't understand why

I was in a hospital, with nurses buzzing by and yanking the curtains between other beds in my row. It felt so strange, like being inside an almost-morning dream, when you are about to wake and can decide what is going to happen next. I remember wondering why in the world they would visit me. I had only met them once— Charlie and I bumped into them downtown after a movie when they were coming from church. I wasn't even sure they knew my name.

"Hazel." His father spoke first.

It was hard to focus on this solemn, perfectly dressed couple at my bedside.

"Hazel. It's good to see you awake," he continued. "How are you?"

I could not string words together. My head hurt and where there had just been my boyfriend's parents, I now saw them in duplicate. The two mothers opened their mouths at the same time.

"Please, Hazel. I . . ." The twin women faltered. I closed my eyes and reopened them to a single mother, one who was now dabbing at her red-rimmed eyes with one gloved hand and clutching her leather handbag on her lap with the other. "I know this is hard for you. But you are so lucky to be alive, Hazel."

I did not feel lucky. I did not remember anything that could explain how I had gotten here, and why my head was pounding beneath the tight bands of gauze.

"Mother?"

"She's here. We just sent her to get a cup of coffee, poor woman. She's been sitting here the past thirty-six hours, waiting for you to wake up," Charlie's mother said. "She'll be right back, dear."

"But Hazel. About the dance," his father continued. "You were with Charlie. And we were wondering . . ." His voice cracked, startling me, since his demeanor was usually as cool and flat as the freshly printed dollar bills in his bank.

My eyes traveled over to Charlie's mom, trying to understand what was going on. All at once, I flashed on the explosion, how I had flown among the chunks of brick and mortar, wood and broken pieces of glass. The realization of what had happened lay like one of those broken bricks on my chest.

"Charlie?" I could barely croak out the question.

"Charlie is missing, Hazel," his mother said, trying to pat her husband's heaving shoulders while she focused her eyes on mine. "We thought you might know where he was when . . . it happened. If you were together? Because right now we are still hoping . . ." She paused, twisting her handkerchief in her hands. "We are hoping Charlie is still alive, as slim as that hope may be. That maybe he went on a lark with a friend or . . . I don't know." She stopped, trying to gather herself. "It is probably insanity to hope, but right now, his body hasn't been found. It is as though he has disappeared into thin air. So we are hanging on, waiting for word—from the search team, from him, from you . . . anyone.

"We just want our boy home." She blotted her eyes again.

The awful reality of what she was saying hit me at once, harder than anything that had assaulted me in the blast. I understood that I was alive and that Charlie—and many others, I guessed—were likely not.

"I . . . had gone outside," I began, my voice a rough whisper. The crime of smoking seemed so insignificant at this point, but yet I didn't want them to think less of their son for going with a woman who did. "I wanted . . . some fresh air."

It all came back to me then: sending Charlie off on a wild-goose chase, my dance with Dash that had gotten me so worked up I had needed to collect myself before coming back down to earth and my boring boyfriend. Was I truly that shallow?

My boring boyfriend, apparently, was dead. And I had sent him to the coatroom, where he was instead of with me. The implications filled my mind and I felt sick, so sick that I began to vomit. I couldn't stop throwing up, even when the nurse came rushing in—my mother on her heels—at the Walters' anxious cries for help. Even when there could have been nothing left in my stomach. I was throwing up remorse, fear, guilt and even a strange sense of relief that I hadn't died like Charlie.

Those working on recovering bodies did eventually find him. Or at least what was left of him. Rose Flowers told me once that her mother-in-law's worst moment as a funeral home owner was the day Mr. Walters came and identified as his son's the fine leather shoe that was still attached to the charred chunk of flesh, the dark sock melted into the skin and muscle beneath. It had been wrapped in a swath of cotton sheet and delivered in a plain cloth bag—like many of the remnants of human remains—and labeled "J. Charles Walters III." Mr. Walters had watched Gladys Steinkamp carefully peel back the layers of material until the shoe and partial leg lay in front of him, displayed on the sheet like some precious artifact or strange piece of jewelry. He reached into his breast pocket for a handkerchief, a white one, starched and pressed into a white triangle with a "W" at the hem. But instead of wiping his eyes, he surprised Gladys by reaching for the shoe, cradling it in one hand, while rubbing at it tenderly with his hand-kerchief. She left him alone in the room with what was left of his son, and when she came back, the leather shoe shone like new, the ruined handkerchief folded neatly beside it like a discarded shroud.

"He must have polished that shoe with his own tears," she told Rose.

The Walters did not come to see me in the hospital again. Or at my home, where I recovered for several weeks. In fact, I never saw Mrs. Walters again. She rarely left the house after Charlie was confirmed dead. I ran into his father a few times on the square as he headed to or from the bank, looking so much older and striding less purposefully than he had before the blast. But as I faltered for something to say, he looked right through me, as though I weren't there. As if he knew how much I had wished that were the case.

It is hard to be a survivor.

At first, you feel grateful just to be alive. But it doesn't last.

You are soon eaten away by guilt because you lived while others, maybe more worthy, didn't. And there is the constant replay of events in your mind: What if one little thing had gone differently?

If you hadn't danced with Dash. What if you hadn't gone out for a cigarette and had looked for your date instead? Would Charlie be alive? Or would you both be dead? And, much later, as the weeks slowly wind up into months and then years and then decades: Would Dash be an Assemblies of God, holier-than-thou preacher? Would you have married the first enlisted man who danced with you before heading out to war because you were already twenty-eight with a huge scar on your forehead and no prospects? Would you have ended up a war widow with a son and a small pension and the necessity of finding work? Would you have spent nearly forty years behind the counter of this post office? Would the moan of a saxophone have the power to bring you to your knees?

How much of this did I share with the young woman sitting across from me? I don't even remember coming outside to this small wrought-iron table-for-two in the shade of my flower garden. Her cassette player is squeaking intermittently as the tape rolls, a sound magnified by its strangeness against the low hum of insects and bees. How long have I been talking? *Have* I been talking? Or just reliving everything inside my head? I haven't a clue. Joe is nowhere to be seen. My armpits are damp and cold, even on this warm June day.

She reaches over and presses "stop."

"Thank you," she says, "for telling me your story."

When I meet her eyes, it's like falling back into time and seeing my friend Violet. I have to stop myself from reaching out to touch her cheek. *I have so much to tell you, Violet! So much has happened that you wouldn't believe!*

But then I see my own reflection in her eyes. Who is that old, scarred woman? It is as if no time has passed and fifty years have blown by all at once.

"Thank you," I say, barely above a whisper. "I guess I needed to tell it. But please. Be gentle with all of us."

June 26, 1978

Hi Mom

How is life in Petaluma? I hope you and Ron have found a good home for us. I am secretly hoping (well, I guess not so secretly, since I am telling you right now!) that I will have a view of the Golden Gate Bridge. Can you see something that big from thirty miles away? I have seen it in Grandma's *Encyclopedia Britannica*. I keep that volume (No. 8) in my room just so I can look at it whenever I want.

I guess you must be busy settling in and that is why I STILL have not heard from you. I have been pretty busy myself at *The Picayune*. I am interviewing people for that big story about the 1928 Lamb's Dance Hall explosion. When Fence sees the amazing stories I am getting from survivors and family members, he'll have to finally admit what a great idea this is.

Like last week, I talked to Hazel the post office lady. Do you remember her? Frankenstein-y scar on her forehead? She still feels terrible about the explosion. She cried, telling me how she went outside to smoke after dancing with someone other than her date and then the whole place blew up. Her date died; her dance partner didn't. What if she hadn't danced with someone else? She still thinks about that.

It made me think, too. How little things become big. Or how bad things actually turn into something good. Like if I hadn't told that secret that I knew about one of Grandma's clients, I wouldn't have this job! I *definitely* shouldn't have done that. Grandma was P.O.'d!! But this job is the best thing that has happened since you dropped me off. I've met some cool people and working makes the time go faster. Otherwise, I would just be stuck in your old room, reading everything I can get my hands on from the library. Which isn't much. I've probably checked out the same books you did. They look that old.

Anyway, love you, miss you, write back ASAP! The next thing you'll be getting from me is my article about Hazel. My first "byline"!

XOX

Daisy

P.S. Remember Joe, the guy who ran over me? He's actually been helping introduce me to interview subjects and Possum Flats landmarks. Maybe not as much of an arrogant ass as I thought?!

P.P.S. Hazel's dance partner that night was Joe's grandfather! The Assemblies of God preacher? I can't imagine him dancing. Joe is lining him up for my next interview!

Fifty Years Ago in Possum Flats:
Remembering the Lamb's Dance Hall Explosion
Part I: Hazel [Sampson] Hodges

by Daisy Flowers

June 30, 1978

She had just stepped outside the dance hall to cool off when the brick wall she was leaning against shuddered. In a blinding flash, Hazel [Sampson] Hodges was launched into that starry August sky back in 1928.

She was told Jimmy Jeffers found her "flopped facedown like a Raggedy Ann doll." He thought she was dead, her face so covered in blood that she was almost unrecognizable. But he scooped her up and carried her to safety, away from the ring of burning rubble where the dance hall had stood.

"I'd seen Jimmy leave the dance earlier in a huff," she said. "So I'm not sure where he came from, but thank God he was there. He saved my life."

Hazel remembers the strange feeling of flying that night, but has no memory of hitting the ground.

But her body remembers. Hazel still can't move her left shoulder without pain. Most noticeable, however, is the jagged, lumpy scar across her forehead. She could cover it with bangs, but chooses instead to keep her hair pulled back in a proper bun. She doesn't feel it would be right to hide her scar.

"The Lamb's Dance Hall explosion marked me," she said. "It marked all of us."

JIMMY

There is a pink note taped to yesterday's *Picayune* on top of the pile that is on my desk. I figure it's a phone message, because it's the size Mabel usually uses—with all those black preprinted boxes to fill with the name and the time someone called. She says they're a big timesaver.

But this is a handwritten note on the plain backside of one of those phone slips and it's obvious that Mabel is the culprit:

> *Didn't know I was working for one of Possum Flats' biggest heroes.*
> *—M*

I rip into the rolled, folded newspaper. What in the Sam Hill is she talking about? I just know it has something to do with Daisy Flowers.

There it is, front and center: Hazel Hodges.

It feels like the earth is opening under my feet to swallow me up. Everything is off kilter and I end plopping onto my cheap rolling chair so hard that I feel the shock all the way up my spine.

I saw him leave the dance earlier in a huff.

What else did she say? What else did she *see*?

There's a knock and suddenly a big black beehive is poking around the half-open door, followed shortly by Mabel's smirking face. "So, I was thinking about ordering in lunch today in your honor," she says. "Maybe a 'hero sandwich'?"

"Jesus H. Christ, Mabel. Cut the shit. Seriously. This—" Here, I throw my arms up somewhere between confusion and surrender. "I don't know what this is. But don't believe everything you read."

She nods exaggeratedly, making big knowing eyes at me. I honestly would love to strangle her.

"Well, at least now I know what you're doing when you've got the blinds closed in here." She winks. "Putting on your Superman getup, right?"

She laughs like a maniac before she disappears back to her desk.

"Mabel, shut the fucking door!"

The door shuts with a bang, but I can still hear her out there. Laughing.

Hell, yes, I was angry that night. Irate. Furious.

But that's not how it began.

When I picked up Nell that night, I was embarrassed. For starters, I was driving my father's farm truck. Second, and even worse, I had exerted myself so much cleaning up the inside—removing straw and clods of dirt from the floorboard, plus a halter, milk bucket and work gloves from the seat—that I had sweated big stains in the underarms of my clean shirt. Then, having rolled down my window to dry off before I got to Nell's, I had taken the full force of the breeze through my carefully combed hair and looked—I saw in my rearview mirror—like a crazy rooster.

At Nell's, I did my best to fix the damage, spitting into my palms and smoothing my hair back before I got out of the truck. I hitched my pants up under the ledge of my belly and glanced at my armpits. Not quite dry, but better, at least.

I hadn't even made it to the front stoop when Nell appeared, pulling a navy sweater around her shoulders and closing the door behind her. It was barely more than a shed in the worst part of Possum Flats, across the tracks from the colored neighborhood. But it was painted and the yard was tidy and full of those purply-red crepe myrtles. Was Nell sneaking out? Or maybe she didn't want me to meet her family. A child's face peeked through the curtain panels and disappeared so quickly I thought I might have imagined it. But then it happened again, this time with two little towheads instead of one.

Nell took her handbag and swung it with gusto at the window, scaring the faces back behind the curtains. "Get yourselves out of here," she hollered. I was surprised such a rough, angry voice could come out of that peachy face.

"Little sisters are so annoying," she said. Surveying me head to toe, she took everything in at once: the hair, the sweat, the rumpled shirt over my thick middle and, over my shoulder, the beat-up truck. I swear she looked around before taking the arm I offered—like someone might be watching? or maybe there was a better option?—and walking all businesslike to the truck.

"Well, I hope there's less manure on the inside than out." She sighed, as if I weren't there or didn't have feelings. I thought I'd cleaned the old thing up pretty good.

I don't remember exactly what we talked about, or what *she* talked about. Mostly who might be at the dance—would Dash be there? Charlie and Hazel? What would that Fern Watson be wearing this time? While she chattered away, I was having a hard time keeping my eyes on the road. Her profile was captivating, her skin the creamy blue-white of freshly skimmed milk with a perfect spot of color high on her cheek. She wore a touch of lipstick, but there was nothing else added to her beauty—it was effortless, something that probably made girls like Ginger Morton envious, as they plucked and powdered and drew in the brows they wish they'd been born with. The wind from her half-open window meant to keep us cool had Nell removing her sailor hat, then constantly retucking her wind-whipped hair behind her ears. I barely noted her irritation, enjoying the smell of intertwined seasons on that breeze—the bleached pasture grass and sunbaked clay of late summer laced with Nell's own spring-fresh smell, like lilacs and line-dried sheets.

I couldn't believe that a girl who looked and smelled so lovely had agreed to go out with me.

But Nell was not as satisfied with her natural good looks that evening as I was. When we got to Lamb's, she tugged at the side mirror until she could see herself, and scowled. Then pulled a small hairbrush through her tangled hair until it fell into a smooth blond curtain again and reattached her hat. She frowned into a little compact mirror before snapping it closed and throwing open her door. I realized that I should have been there to help her out instead of staring openmouthed and practically drooling. I scrambled out my door, jogging to catch up.

"Hello, Violet. Hello, Dash." Nell was a step ahead of me, waving and nodding to everyone she saw on our way up the stairs to Lamb's. I barely had time to pull open the heavy wooden door at the top so she could walk in without breaking stride.

The band was already at full tilt, and it wasn't even nine. I nodded at Beebe, pounding away at the piano, her back as straight as the music was meandering, almost begging. Like a dog at the door, scratching to get out. Or in. Which was it? The music was all around us, but it got inside of us, too.

I was still on Nell's heels when we reached a corner table and two empty chairs. Nell turned to check out the dance floor before choosing one of them, draping her sweater on the back with a fuss. I pulled the chair out for her and started to sit in the other when she reached her hand up to stop me.

"I'm thirsty," she said. "The hot drive in that old stinky truck took every bit of water out of me."

That irritated me. Hadn't I driven her to the dance? It was better than hoofing it. And I didn't like her criticizing the old jalopy. But I also felt caught out. Shouldn't I have thought of getting her a drink in the first place? I felt like a big country clod.

"Want some water?"

Her blue eyes blinked slowly closed and then opened again. She was aggravated.

"I was hoping for something a little stronger, James," she said.

I had never been anything but Jimmy my whole life. Maybe she was trying to fancy me up, scrub off the farm, hide the fat beneath a more polished sounding name. Just hearing her say it made me wonder if I could live into it, some better version of me.

Then she winked and suddenly everything I had been feeling—the irritation, the inadequacy—was forgotten. I would crawl through the desert to get Nell a cup of water or anything else she wanted, if I had to wring it bare-handed out of a cactus or rattlesnake myself.

I left her at the table and began to navigate the dance floor and its dark edges for a likely source of "something stronger." I had no flask of my own, generally content to mooch off my richer, more liquid friends like Charlie or Dash. I kicked myself for being so stupid. My idea for the evening had been the two of us sitting in a romantic corner, talking. And dancing. I wanted every dance of the night with Nell, especially the slow ones, where I'd have a chance to put a hand on that waist and pull her close to me. My palms got sweaty just thinking about it.

There was also the problem of Prohibition. Which, best I could tell, stopped no one from drinking. It just made it a hell of a lot more inconvenient. And created more dirty, untaxed money for those who didn't mind profiting on the wrong side of the law.

Lamb's wasn't a speakeasy, though. It was just a dance hall, and the bar along one wall was just another place to sit. There was nothing to drink there but a trickle of rusty water from a bathroom sink. I looked around for Dash and found him already drunk and dancing, loose-limbed and leering; Charlie was nowhere in sight. I pushed my way through the crowd in front of the door and burst back into the August night, which—while dry as toast and just as warm—felt like a relief from the sweaty hot box that was Lamb's on a Friday night.

"Hey, Jimmy." I'd recognize that voice-crack anywhere. Smiley. He was a few years younger than me, still in high school. Skinny kid, with a big beak and an Adam's apple that yo-yoed when he was nervous. He was smart—a genius, I'd heard—but not too slick otherwise. I don't remember which one of us started calling him Smiley in honor of that big, shit-eating grin. Never a sign of happiness, that smile. He was just uncomfortable in his own skin, protecting himself from whatever came next. Smiley was always on the outside, wanting to break in. He tried to talk to me, but my own standing in popularity was too shaky to give him a hand up. I was polite, but never friendly.

Until now. Smiley might have an "in" to a source of bathtub gin.

"Hey, Smiley." His look of surprise at my familiarity erased that goofy smile. "Can you do me a favor?"

Smiley's face went back to anxious smiling. He nodded, in direct opposition to that crazy Adam's apple. I was afraid his head might pop off. "Sure thing, Jimmy," he said, sounding anything but.

"I need something to drink," I said. "For my girl."

Smiley still nodded, like one of those weird glass woodpeckers that keeps dipping its head in a cup of water.

"I don't touch the stuff myself," he said, finally. "But I might know where you could find it."

I followed Smiley around the corner of the building and into the alley where the streetlight didn't make much headway in the dark. It took my eyes time to adjust as I kept them on the white patch that was Smiley's starched shirt. Then we were at the back stoop of a run-down apartment where some guys were shooting dice against the steps, whooping or grunting, depending on the results. They were country boys like me, but without the means or ambition to clean up. Patched shirts, pants an inch or two short, scuffed boots instead of shoes.

The thinner of the bunch unfolded himself from a squat and took me in, top to bottom. I felt he could see through my shirt and tie to my farmer's tan; the forearms that were almost one continuous freckle against the pasty white of my chest and biceps. As if he knew I was rejecting our heritage. His hair was a brown scrub brush above a pair of squinting eyes and facial hair that looked like it had never been groomed since sprouting a year or two earlier. When his eyes reached my two feet in their shiny cheap loafers, he spit a stream of tobacco juice between them.

"Who we got here?" he asked Smiley, while looking at me instead.

"This here's Jimmy Jeffers. I reckon you know him. His family's got that dairy farm south a town." Smiley cleared his throat when the young ruffian didn't respond. "He's kinda thirsty. I thought you boys might know where he could get something to drink."

"It's for my girl," I said, not sure my own currency would be enough with this crowd.

"You don't look like no dairyman," he said, a slow grin taking over the space between mustache and scraggle of beard. His teeth were uneven and brown from tobacco. "But I reckon your money's the same whether you are or you ain't."

"You bet," said Smiley, looking at me with raised eyebrows. As if I might have been expecting free booze. I knew better than that. I didn't have a lot of cash—I'd been thinking of a late-night stop at the diner after the dance, before I took Nell home on a long, looping drive that I hoped would include a stop for making out. This would be a better use of my dough. Maybe I wasn't the smartest guy, but I figured a girl with a couple of drinks in her might be a little more open to that plan than one with a belly full of burger and fries. So if a drink was what Nell wanted, by God, she would have one. And maybe I would have one, too. A little "liquid courage" to kiss that sweet red mouth.

My pockets were lighter, but I felt full of hope for the evening. My purpose accomplished, I left the men to their dice. Smiley tried to keep up with me, but he was like a puppy I no longer had use for. When I pushed my way back in the door, the music and heat hit me like a wall. It was hard for a big boy like me to thread my way through the crowd holding a couple of pint glass canning jars filled to the tip-top with booze, but I managed.

When I reached the far side of the dance floor, panting from the effort, our table was empty. Nell's sweater still clung to the back of her chair, so I figured she was taking a powder break like girls do—usually in a herd. I set down our drinks and pulled up a chair facing the band and the dance floor. The writhing mass of sweaty flesh and stomping feet reminded me of cattle in a corral, moving everywhere but going nowhere. The Charleston. A line of girls popped out from the throng, touching their heels with their hands before stepping them back down to the floor, then quickly repeating the motion. Each moved in a small circle with their hands pushing up and down in the air. I had to hand it to them: The dresses they wore swirled just right with those dance moves, revealing a number of knees and sometimes more before the material came to rest. I could watch those girls bouncing up and down all night, particularly the ones with the bigger . . . assets. The slimmer girls seemed to have strapped everything down on top, making themselves nearly as straight as a piece of pine lumber. With girls like Nell, those curves could be fenced in but not contained; there was still a pleasing jiggle that held me—and, if I were a betting man, most of the guys in the room—spellbound. The dairy farmer in me couldn't help picturing my hands on them.

The band shifted to a Bessie Smith piano tune, "Lock and Key," and the throng of dancers doing the Charleston as a group splintered into couples. And to my surprise, there was Nell, front and center. She was staring up at some slick guy I didn't know, with her hands on top of his shoulders; his were resting on her lower back. My heart lurched and I felt hot all over. I reached for my glass and took a giant gulp of the gin, which burned so much on the way down that I could picture the contents of my stomach igniting. I shoved my chair back, stood up and strode toward Nell, vaguely aware I was bumping into other dancers. I must have looked scary, because the dancers parted like I was Moses and they were the Red Sea. I was seeing red, that's for sure.

I tapped the guy hard on the back.

"Hey, buddy. That's my date."

He turned his head toward me, revealing Nell's surprised expression as she saw who was cutting in. He took in my hot, messy bulk and my angry face.

"No law against dancing, is there?"

"No, but I . . ."

"Relax, friend. The night is young. You can get in line like the rest of us." He turned his head of sandy-blond curls back to Nell, who seemed embarrassed by the attention we were drawing to our little triangle on the dance floor.

And then they were gone, shoved off like a rowboat onto the smooth surface of a pond. I was left to make my way back to our table alone. I sat down in a huff, taking another fiery swig of gin and glaring at the dance floor.

The night didn't get any better. Nell never took a break from the dancing, making the rounds with what seemed like every single guy there. Meanwhile, I kept drinking—I was well into her glass of gin after draining my own—and alternating between steaming and wanting to bawl like a baby. When she finally sashayed over to wet her whistle, I grabbed her wrist. She tried to pull away, eyes flitting around to see if anyone was noticing how she was being strong-armed.

"What's wrong with you?" she hissed.

"What's wrong with me? I brought a girl to a dance and haven't had a single turn with her yet," I said, my voice angrier than I intended.

Nell rolled her eyes and allowed me to lead her into the throng. It felt like dragging a reluctant dog on a leash. Everything in the dance hall was starting to tilt. The voices seemed louder and the music strangely sharper, as if each note on the trumpet or piano chord was assaulting my body. By now, many had given up the pretense of going outside to smoke, lighting up at their tables or at the edge of the dance floor. The smoke softened the room into a hazy fun house, where people seemed to come in and out of view with no rhyme or reason. Here was Dash, slapping me on the back; there was Charlie's girl, Hazel, making moon eyes at Dash instead.

It was the worst dance of my young life. Nell held me at arm's distance, as if I smelled bad or might rub off on her dress. I tried to focus on her face, but my vision was blurry and she was looking everywhere but at me.

As the music wound down, she tried to make an early exit, but I wouldn't let go of her hand.

"What's going on with you?" I was shouting to be heard over the band. Her face showed embarrassment as the music abruptly stopped and I went on yelling in that uncomfortable pause between songs. "I feel more like your chauffeur than your date."

The other dancers turned to watch, clearing a pocket of space around us.

The cherry spots on Nell's cheeks were scarlet. She pulled her captive hand, moving backwards. I knew I should let her go, but I couldn't. I held her hand tighter. It was strange, feeling the smooth hand that I had been wanting to hold all night twisting in my larger one, like a trapped quail. Feeling resistance where I wanted so much to feel give made me even madder. I wanted to crush those birdlike bones into powder, to feel each finger bone and knuckle and grind them together until there was nothing but loose, flapping skin at the end of her perfect arm.

"Well, thanks for the ride," she said.

There were a couple of gasps. A hoot of laughter.

And just like that, I let her go. It was as if all the rage that I had felt in my hand suddenly left, racing up my arm and into my chest until I felt I would explode.

I was not in control of myself. I rode my anger like a wild wave, totally at its mercy. I felt I might say or do anything, words rising in my throat that I knew I should keep back. And also—if I am being honest—tears. That shocked me. Forcing my fury down squeezed it out through my pores, my eyes, my nose and throat. I hadn't cried since I was a little boy; my father didn't tolerate weakness. I swiped at my face with my sleeve as I pushed through the dancers that had once again swallowed up the floor. I grabbed at the tie around my collar, tight as a tourniquet. I pictured my head bulging with blood, my eyes popping and bleeding.

Outside, I gulped in great lungfuls of air, ripping the top button off my shirt in my hurry to free my swollen, choking neck. I found myself at the side of the dance hall that shared a dark alley with an apartment house. The large brick wall was broken up by the employee entrance to the auto repair shop under Lamb's, a ramshackle door with a glass panel and a drawn shade. Alone at last, I fought to pull myself together.

I wanted to hurt someone. Maybe Nell. My father never raised a hand to my mother and that kind of violence was foreign to me. But my hands prickled with the need to break someone or something.

Before I knew it, my right hand had curled into a tight, merciless fist and I was punching through the door's glass window, bits of wooden frame and shards of glass tinkling onto the ground at my feet. I punched again; more glass and wood. I reached my hand—it was bleeding like crazy, but I don't remember it hurting at all—into the hole where the window had been and ripped down the shade, which I promptly tore in half. I could not stop my rage.

I grabbed for the inside knob through the broken window, flicked the lock and threw open the worthless door. Inside, I breathed in the chemical smells of black grease and oil, fresh paint and tire rubber. Gasoline.

As my eyes adjusted, I saw the hulking forms of a heavily laden Ford farm truck and some type of roadster. I was breathing heavily, my heart and head pounding. If I could have found a crowbar or hammer, I would have whaled away on the vehicles in front of me. But I didn't see anything; tools and parts had probably been hung up or returned to a toolbox for the weekend. As the anger began to drain out of me, I could hear the band upstairs and the rhythmic pounding of feet on the dance floor. I backed up to the wall near the door until I touched it, sliding slowly down the rough bricks until I found myself sitting on cool, damp cement. I dug out my handkerchief and mopped my forehead and face, wet with tears and sweat. I hated Nell, how low she had brought me. I hated all of them, dancing without a care in the world, thinking only of the beautiful gal or guy they were partnered with. Not worried where their next dance, drink or smoke would come from.

Suddenly the tempo of the music changed, the saxophone moaning low and mournful as the feet above me stilled. A slow dance.

I kicked my legs out hard in front of me, bumping a metallic-sounding can that sloshed heavily before it overturned. I could make out the shape of a gas can with its handle and screw cap.

This is the part that I always go back to when I lie awake at night. The whole evening at Lamb's plays on a continuous loop, but it is this moment that seems to slow down, so that every action seems more magnified. More deliberate. Something inside of me switched off and I began watching someone—not myself, but someone in my body—take over. My hands right the can, and I can see the pale flash of my fingers, unscrewing the lid, the fumes that escape so strong, they sting my nostrils. I watch my hands dousing my crumpled handkerchief with gasoline and wadding it back into the nearly full can so that it sticks out like a wick. It is terrible, what I watch myself do. And every time, I will it to unfold differently.

It never does.

I find myself standing, feet shuffling the can across the floor until it reaches the grill of the pickup truck. I feel a hand in my front pocket, digging around until it closes on a book of matches.

The second that a single match grits across the folded cover, that quick poof of sound turned to flame: It is like a halo of light that touches everything in its immediate circle—the front of the truck, my bloody hand, the gas can—and it could so easily have ended up as just a flash, like a photo or a memory, if I had stopped there. Returned to the safety of darkness.

But of course, I didn't. My hands didn't.

What happened next wasn't what I wanted. I was enraged, yes.

Out of my mind with jealousy and rage. I wanted to burn something, make some fire, some noise, a distraction. Make Nell notice
me, maybe ruin her night.

God, just so fucking stupid. So fucking young and stupid.

Never, ever did I want to kill her or any other human being.
Thirty-nine other human beings. My friends. People I had grown
up with, seen on the streets, in school, stores. Church. I didn't
mean for the entire building to explode and leave a hole that
looked like a living hell.

And the screams. Worse than a baby rabbit.

Most people don't even know that bunnies make noises. But
on the farm, I had been awoken by a young rabbit getting its guts
torn out by a cat. It sounded like a human baby being murdered, a
piercing, desperate scream that echoed in my head for hours and
made me sick inside. It was that visceral.

But I would gladly listen to the sound of a thousand dying rab-
bits in exchange for the memories of the sounds that came from
that burning hell hole that August night. There were men and
women shrieking in horrible pain, calling out desperately for help.
For God. People were on fire, trapped and burning where they
had fallen.

The screams of those people on fire haunt me.

I wake up shuddering in the night in a cold sweat because of
those screams, my nose filled again with the chemical smoke and
stench of cooked human flesh.

Those sounds and smells brought me to my knees more than
once that night. I threw up between efforts to drag people out of
harm's way, to rescue anyone that I could get to. Dash, for one. With
what could only have been adrenaline and desperation, I loosened
the beam that had him trapped. Hazel. Others burned so badly
that they died in the hours and days afterwards. Like Fern. Some
were already dead when I got to them: Beebe, crushed by her
piano. Dale Diggs. And the pieces; the parts. Sickening chunks of
human bodies—arms, legs, hands, feet, faceless heads and head-

less torsos—littered in and around the rubble like so many bricks. I remember one female hand with polished pale pink nails, like the inside of a puppy's ear, still gripping a round purse.

The strangest part was being called a hero, when I knew I had brought this hell down on everyone with my anger and a single match. But I didn't set anyone straight. Even with my insides sick and rotten with the knowledge of what I had done. There were lots of chances. The newspaper reporters, dark circles beneath their eyes, looking for a hero to offset the awfulness of that night with something shining and good. The firefighters and cops that clapped me on the back and called me brave, encouraging me to join their ranks. And the families of the people I'd rescued spoke to me as if I were the Savior Himself. I remember Hazel's dirt-poor parents pressing a twenty into my hand, probably several months' worth of groceries and rent, when I saw them on the street.

I kept my mouth shut. I didn't want them to hate me. I hated myself enough already. I didn't want to ruin the one good thing they had to hold on to. Without my efforts, there would have been more death, more heartache. Of course, what they didn't know was that without me, there wouldn't have been an explosion in the first place.

Jesus Christ? More like Judas Iscariot. Except I skipped the hanging and held on to the silver pieces.

I feel like shit about it, like the lowest life form on the planet. Every goddamn day.

I've tried to make up for my sorry life. To be one of the good guys. I've made it this long, so long that some days I can almost forget how I got into this line of work and what it's cost me. An honest existence. A wife. A family. I knew I didn't deserve a life like everyone else's. But I thought, somehow, if I did enough of the right things, I could live with myself.

It hasn't been easy.

Early on, when I was new to the force, hell, even a couple years in, I'd look at that gun they'd entrusted me with and imagine putting its dark barrel into my mouth. I could almost taste the cold metal, having touched the gun enough to know that smell—like a pocketful of dirty nickels—from the palms of my hands.

Part of me wanted that so bad, that release from my secret and the suffering I'd caused. But the part that always won out said I didn't deserve the easy way out. I had too much to make right. And that's what kept me going, even in those moments. What still keeps me going. What keeps me holstering that gun night after night, when I'd love nothing more than to swallow it up and get on my way to eternal damnation.

That and the fact that I'm scared shitless. Of dying *and* of hell.

What a goddamn coward.

Dash

I do not want to talk to her.

Period.

"Come on, Bro. *Ther*," he amends quickly, catching himself. "Grandfather, I mean. *Please?*" My grandson continues to wheedle. Joe has come over to the rectory to mow my grass, which has nearly reached crisis length, enough to start tongues wagging about the sad state of my life. I used to take care of my own yard, even with my bad ankle, but lately Marilyn has insisted that Joe do it. I get winded so quickly these days.

"It keeps him out of trouble," she said. Of course, the incident with Mayor Watson could serve as Exhibit A on how that plan is *not* working. But I didn't argue. I was grateful for the help.

"I don't see why the girl needs to talk to me," I say. I gave Joe a glass of lemonade for his efforts and the ingrate is now badgering me about an interview. "She talked to Hazel already. And that story she wrote—it's not news! Isn't she with the *newspaper?*"

"Well, for starters, you're a surviving eyewitness." Joe hesitates. We haven't really talked about Lamb's. He wasn't alive and for all intents and purposes, the man I was when it exploded is dead. "You were there. Reporters like to talk to survivors."

"Ha!" I scoff. "Besides, she's not even a real reporter. Just a nosy intern. Rose's granddaughter, right? Probably inherited her busybody ways. Well, we can't expect an outsider to understand, anyway."

"Understand what?" Joe is genuinely curious.

"That what happened fifty years ago was the unwavering wrath of God. 'Vengeance is mine, I will repay, saith the Lord,' and He had His on Possum Flats. That's over and done with, and no one wants to revisit it. Especially me."

"Do you really believe that?"

"Believe what? That no one wants to wallow in pain and suffering for some misguided girl's little reporting project? I feel a hundred percent confident on that count, Grandson."

"No. I mean, do you really believe that God caused all of those young people to die? Because they were sinners?"

"I do not pretend to understand the mysterious ways of God. But he has given us guidance on right and wrong in the Good Book—guidance that many of those young people chose to ignore. Did they deserve to die? I have spent many an hour contemplating that very question and I cannot answer it."

"Dancing? That's a sin in your book?"

Dancing. Drinking. Gambling. Carousing. Lusting. Fornicating. I do not want to go into the full list of sins that were part of that night and many others at Lamb's. I do not want to talk about this at all, not with Daisy Flowers and not with my grandson. I reach up to loosen the clerical collar that's asphyxiating me. Assemblies of God pastors don't typically wear one, but I've always felt it was a good reminder of my role—both to me and my flock. But I am regretting my choice in this moment.

"Second Timothy tells us 'Flee also youthful lusts: but follow righteousness, faith, charity, peace, with them that call on the Lord out of a pure heart,'" I say. "It is not that dancing is wrong, Grandson. Dancing in the Bible was part of 'making a joyful noise unto the Lord.' But it is more what it can lead to, especially a man and woman dancing close together. Impurity.

"God tells us to 'Abstain from all appearance of evil,'" I say. "I was a young man once, and I know the siren song of the womanly flesh. Purposely putting oneself in a position where sin may occur is inviting the sinful behavior."

"But . . ." His handsome face takes on some furrows. "I can't believe God or Jesus or whoever is supposed to love me would blow up a hall full of people who were just having fun."

"You yourself have said it: I was an eyewitness," I said. "Suffice it to say that what I saw that night would have brought the Lord no pleasure. Not a single iota."

"Aren't you being a little hard on everyone?"

I can feel my blood pressure—for which I grudgingly ingest a pill twice daily—rising. The ignorance, the conceit of youth!

I raise my voice. " 'Every tree that bringeth not forth good fruit is hewn down, and cast into the fire.' "

"But . . ."

"Enough with your impudence, Joseph. Your grandfather has seen a great deal more of life than you have and I know, as Scripture says, 'For the Lord your God is a consuming fire, even a jealous God.' "

"So those people, those kids, had it coming?" Joe is incredulous. "And what were you doing there that night? Warning them to mend their ways?"

There is a knock at my open front door.

It is Violet Flowers. *Violet!* Here to expose me as the hypocrite and sinner that I am. God have mercy on me, a poor sinful being!

Only . . . it's not her. It's that Daisy. Violet Flowers—even her ghost—would not dress like such a mangy hippie. Weird flared jeans with patches, T-shirt and stringy long hair.

"According to Hazel, your grandfather was out on the dance floor at Lamb's that night, boogieing down with the best of them."

After this, the little imp has the nerve to smile.

"Um. This is Daisy. Daisy, Pastor Emmonds, AKA, my grandfather."

"AKA, *Dash* Emmonds, correct?" The devil is coming for me, hand extended. Before I know it, she is yanking it up and down like a pump handle. But she'll get nothing from this well, this deep black hole of forgetting. I promise myself this, yet I feel unsettled, as though that dark place is being dredged. The modicum of pure sweet peace I had achieved after so many years is in danger of being swirled up again, the waters clouded, clarity destroyed.

I pull my hand away as if I've been burned, as if I have been shaking hands with Lucifer himself.

"And I believe—tell me if I'm wrong here, but this is what I've got so far—that even though you danced with Hazel, you actually came to the dance with Violet Flowers?" She looks so pleased with herself, I feel an un-Christian urge to choke her hippie neck. "The great-aunt I never knew I had . . . until recently."

It is hard to explain what I am experiencing in this moment, an old man with strong beliefs, but no longer much call for strong emotions. I am woefully unprepared for the eddying currents of rage, fear and disbelief. And all channeled through this girl who looks uncannily like the one I held during that last dance at Lamb's, the flesh-and-blood beauty I saw suspended from that beam as I lay trapped and helpless to save her. Begging for my own life like a coward.

It was too much.

" 'Get thee behind me, Satan,' " I thunder, raising my fist to the heavens. " 'Thou art an offense unto me: for thou savorest not the things that be of God, but those that be of men.' "

"Bro, what is going on?" Joe steps between me and the girl and not a moment too soon. I put my arm down, my heart hammering. I am sorely in need of a chair.

Before I can verbalize that thought, Joe has me by the arm. He lowers me into the oversized recliner that my wife referred to as my "throne," one of her few expressions of humor and sedition in the household that I ruled like—or so I believed at the time— a benevolent dictator. But truthfully, I was just a dictator.

"Uh, what . . . is . . . happening?" Daisy seems shell-shocked.

"I think you upset him," Joe says. He is making certain I will not get up again, holding me down with his throwing arm. Which enrages me further.

"Get. Out. Of my house," I say in a low, terse voice. "And stop doing the devil's work. You are out of line, stirring this pot, and I, for one, will not allow it to continue!"

"You've got to get a grip," Joe says.

"And you need to let go of yours," I reply. "I will not rest until this girl, this she-devil, is quieted. And if you have any sway with her at all, I strongly suggest you use it. Now: go!"

But the girl has already taken off, her hair streaming behind her as she runs down the sidewalk and out of my vision at last.

Joe is at the door, watching her disappear. He shakes his head.

"Wow, Bro. You really know how to make people feel at ease," he says. He does not correct himself. And he is not smiling, for once. "If you've gone and ruined things for me with Daisy, I don't think I can forgive you."

Just like that, the door slams and Joe has disappeared, too.

Sweaty and discombobulated, I sit back in my chair and get out my handkerchief.

Forgiveness.

It's something I've been in search of my entire life.

Daisy

The low hum and random flicker of the overhead fluorescent lights are my only company. I have been at *The Picayune* since six this Tuesday morning and the regulars won't be here for another hour. I wanted to get started on my next piece about the dance hall explosion.

My first article on Hazel came out Friday, and the response has been amazing. Patty said there were seventeen calls for Fence yesterday, none of them irate. I'll call that a win. But I sold Fence on a four-part series in the month leading up to the fiftieth anniversary on August 13th. So I've got three more articles to write at the pace of one a week—and no one lined up to write about.

I'm feeling the pressure.

I really want Jimmy Jeffers for the "hero" angle, even though he was a terrible interview. I will have to use what other people say or remember about him. But along with Hazel, Jimmy rescued Dash Emmonds—and he made it crystal clear he doesn't want to talk, either. Joe thinks he can soften him up with time, but I don't have that.

Of course, I am still hoping that Grandma will change her mind and talk to me about her twin sister. That would make three.

So . . . since I can't have Dash—and I've struck out with Mo and Ruby Rae—who could be my fourth? There's Ginger Morton from the pharmacy. She's never been a big Flowers fan. And now she probably thinks Grandma blabbed her secret about the Mayor. Of course, that was me.

I am so deep in thought that I don't realize someone has slipped up behind me.

"Boo."

I rocket right out of my rolling chair. "Smiley!"

"Did I scare you?" He laughs, since it is obvious what the answer is. "Got a big scoop? Is Possum Flats getting a Walmart or McDonald's? Can't figure why else you'd be at it so early. Unless somebody important kicked the bucket." He pauses, his face turning serious. "No one died, did they?"

"No, but you're in danger of it if you do that to me again," I say, trying to act like his interruption was a minor inconvenience, not a shocker that nearly made me pee my pants.

"Occupational hazard," he says, grinning. He is wearing his usual one-pocket T-shirt and jeans. He dresses the same whether he's going to a city council meeting or covering a car wreck.

Smiley.

Of course! He must have been around for the explosion!

"Smiley, *you're* my big scoop! I swear to God, you are exactly one-hundred-percent perfect."

Smiley's Adam's apple starts bobbing. He's not used to being anyone's perfect anything.

"Now, Daisy. I don't know what you've got in mind, but I've spent the better part of a pretty long life trying to stay out of the news while keeping my finger on the pulse of it. I'm the behind-the-camera guy, not the in-front-of-the-camera guy."

"No, Smiley. I mean . . . well, this big story I'm doing. The one about the explosion at Lamb's? It's like a big anniversary or remembrance kind of deal."

"Yes, I've heard Fence muttering," he says. "I can't believe he's letting you do it. He doesn't like to cause a kerfuffle."

"Do I look like a troublemaker to you?" Here, I watch with dismay as his eyes drop and he doesn't answer right away.

"Well, now, you don't exactly *look* like a troublemaker," he begins, "but you don't look like the girl-next-door, either. I mean, unless you live in Berkeley." He looks sheepish, as if he hates to be the one to break this news to me. "I mean, I think you're a pretty neat kid. But I'm not your typical Possum Flats citizen, either. So . . . I guess I'm in your corner on this."

"Thanks?" Should I be grateful that he is rooting for me or disturbed because he thinks—along with everyone else—that I'm a Flower Power outsider determined to drag their sweet town through the mud? "So, I'm taking that as a yes."

"Yes?"

"Yes, you'll be the fourth profile for my four-part series." I am almost giddy.

"Oh, no. No, Daisy. That's a negatory."

"But . . . you said you were on my side! That this story needs to see the light of day! You're *part* of the story!" I begin to panic. I have as good as cemented his presence in my pages already. Everyone in Possum Flats loves and respects Smiley. He is one of their town "characters," with his wild white hair and his bachelor status—although a few have said he's married to his camera. His version of the night at Lamb's would be a coup for me and would make great reading for everybody else.

But wait. Was Smiley there the night the dance hall blew up? He may not be as old as I think he is.

"I'm sorry, Smiley. I got ahead of myself," I say. "What I meant is . . . *were* you around for the explosion and if so, would you consider being interviewed? I think people would love to hear your version of that night's events."

"Now, Daisy, don't go feeling bad," Smiley says, as if he can read my mind. "I'm an old fart, that's for sure. So yes, I was alive back when it happened. But I was about the same age you are right now, and I didn't know my ass from a hole in the ground.

"Actually, my ass was practically *in* a hole in the ground that night. If I hadn't stayed out in the back alley with some hooligans after rustling up some hooch for Jimmy Jeffers . . ."

"Wait a minute. Jimmy Jeffers, the police captain? Drinking . . . *hooch*? Whatever that is—and I'm going to guess it wasn't Kool-Aid."

"Aw, shit, Daisy. I mean . . . crap. Pardon my French," Smiley says ruefully. "This is exactly why I don't want to talk to you for your story. I'm going to open my gosh-darn mouth and light up the whole town of Possum Flats. I don't want anything I say to be used against anyone—"

"In a court of law." I finish his sentence. Grandma and I have been watching a lot of *Dragnet* reruns in the evenings and I have the opening monologue down cold.

"What? No, I don't want anything I say to hurt anyone—dead or alive," he says. "I wouldn't want people to know that Jimmy Jeffers was trying to score a little bathtub gin to impress a girl and get a good buzz on. Just like I wouldn't want to name the ruffians in that back alley who were gambling away their Friday pay.

"So much of what was going on that night is the exact oppo-site of what many folks around here considered 'moral.' Danc-ing, drinking, gambling, jazz music, short dresses." He pauses. "I could go on."

"Please do," I say in my most serious reporter voice. "This is great background. None of the articles I read in *The Picayune* men-tioned anything about that. I mean, besides the fact it was a dance hall and people were dancing."

"Well, it shouldn't have been in the paper," Smiley says. "None of those things had anything at all to do with what happened that night. The explosion was the worst sort of accident. Just plain bad luck.

"But after it happened, lots of people thought it was those very things that brought hellfire and destruction to the sinners of this town. That God had looked at us and seen the modern-day Sodom or Gomorrah.

"And they weren't the only ones," Smiley went on. "Our explo-sion made the news overseas. Letters to the editor poured in from all over the world, equal parts condolences and condemnations."

"But . . . why? I thought God was love and all of that," I say, summoning my meager working knowledge of a Supreme Being.

"God's love is for those who stay on the right path, Daisy. Not for those who frequent a den of iniquity like Lamb's," he says. "I've never been religious, but even I had to wonder—at the tender age of fifteen—what kind of unforgivable things I must have done to have witnessed the wholesale human suffering I did that night.

"It was awful, what I saw," he says. "But it was also the beginning of my photography career."

"Hold on." I pull my cassette recorder out of my book bag and clunk it onto my desk. Smiley looks at it, then at me, for a long minute.

I push "record."

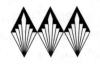

SMILEY

What I remember was how normal everything was at Lamb's that night. I was scrubbed clean raw with a bar of my mother's cracked lye soap and wearing my one good white shirt, frayed at the cuffs, but ironed crisp and neat. I didn't expect to get close enough to anyone that my hygiene or outfit would matter. But hope rose like a phoenix in my teenage heart.

I wasn't good-looking; that much is obvious. At school, people liked to say that if I turned sideways, I'd disappear. I was that thin, a stick figure of a boy. Couple that with a big honker and an Adam's apple like a goddamned yo-yo and you've got the picture. My nickname was slapped on me by those who figured out that I smiled when I was nervous. Which was practically all the time. But as nicknames, I've heard worse. Grin and bear it, right?

Everyone liked me, but I wasn't really friends with anyone. The "Smiley" moniker meant that at least I wasn't invisible (whether I stood sideways or not). I liked hanging around on the fringe of ball games and get-togethers, watching the guys with the athletic skills or smooth talk or dance moves. Guys like Dash Emmonds and his gang—Charlie Walters and old Jimmy Jeffers. Even the guys that threw dice in the alley and bartered and sold their illicit hooch. I knew people in both high and low places.

That August night was roasting hot, but after any time at all inside Lamb's, it felt good to be outside. It was the typical evening for me, nervous hands hidden in my pants pockets, hovering around the outskirts of the dance floor, hoping against hope that some very forward gal would ask me to dance with her. God only knows what I would have done if she did! I didn't really know how to dance, but decided I'd just cross that bridge when I had to.

The only thing different about that night was that Jimmy Jeffers needed a favor. No one noticed my existence unless I could be of use; I accepted that. Jimmy needed something to drink for his thirsty date, Nell, and I managed to hook him up. Not that it helped. I'm pretty sure he ended up drinking his hooch *and* Nell's after she dumped him on the dance floor. Was he ever pissed!

But that was it. Like I said, nothing exceptional about that night.

Until it happened.

One minute, I was standing in the alley behind Lamb's, watching a dispute brewing between two dice players. The loser had questioned the authenticity of the dice and the winner, jacked up on cheap drink, had started rolling up his sleeves.

But instead of a fist fight, I saw a flash and then the brick building behind the potential brawlers seemed to inhale, sucking in on itself before completely coming apart.

That's all I remember of the actual explosion. I honestly do not know how I survived it. I must have been hit upside the noggin by some debris or else my mind simply shut down. Because everything after my memory of Lamb's last breath is completely blank, like when a movie reel runs out, leaving a white screen and flapping piece of film.

The next thing I knew I was standing on the sidewalk, blocks away from the square, with Rose Flowers putting a blanket around me. It must have been wool, because it was scratchy and rough against the bare skin of my back and legs. I remember thinking that was odd, and looked down to find myself as naked as the day I came into this world, my underwear in filthy shreds around one ankle. Ordinarily, I would have been mortified to see my hairless chest and other parts exposed. But it was like looking at someone else. I just knew I was alive and that seemed like a miracle.

I know I must have said something, because Rose ran off, headed toward downtown. Worried about her sister, of course. And then old Mrs. Flowers, in her robe and nightcap, was steering me toward home, as gentle and patient as if guiding a small child. She didn't know yet that she had lost a daughter; that sad news would come soon enough.

When we arrived at my matchbox of a house, there were no lights on, as you might guess at nearly midnight. Mrs. Flowers saw me up the two crooked steps to the front door and knocked, quietly at first, then with more oomph. I heard a stop-and-start strangled sound, and realized with no shortage of amazement that it was me, crying.

"Goddamn it to hell!" My father's voice growled through the thin wood veneer. When the door finally jerked open and he took in the sight on his steps, he really let it fly.

"What in the name of Christ is this?" he raged, his thinning hair in wild disarray. "What kind of no-good business have you been up to?"

He poked me in the chest, but when I nearly fell over, his eyes widened and he peered at me more closely.

"What's wrong with him?" he sputtered. "And why in holy hell is he naked as a jaybird?"

Mrs. Flowers, God bless her, wasn't used to such a foul display of temperament or language. She put her arm protectively about my shivering body, even though she was a foot shorter than me.

"There's been some sort of accident downtown," she said, her voice soft but sure. "We found him wandering the sidewalk like this and thought we should get him home."

"Accident? Giant boom woke me up but . . ."

"Yes, there was an explosion and now there's a huge fire," she began.

"Lamb's," I interrupted. "Lamb's blowed up. And everybody with it."

It was her turn to be in shock. She looked at me as if I were some alien creature, and frankly, I fit the bill—naked, grimy and wrapped up like a pig in a blanket.

"Lamb's?" It was just a whisper, the smallest bit of breath making the word for her. Then, in the next instant, she let me go and collapsed on the porch.

My father pushed past the screen door and scooped her up, that wisp of a woman who probably didn't weigh more than eighty-five pounds sopping wet.

"Pull yourself together and get some clothes on," he snapped at me. "We've got to get her home. And then we better go help."

I don't remember how, but I managed to get dressed and put on a pair of tight shoes. I'd lost my only pair that fit in the blast. Dad carried Mrs. Flowers to her place like a baby, setting her on the couch with surprising tenderness. He took the woolen blanket that had so recently covered my own thin shoulders and poked it awkwardly around the edges of her limp body. He seemed embarrassed, caught at something he shouldn't have been doing.

"What are you staring at?" he said gruffly. I didn't answer. I just wanted to keep this facet of my father—this small sliver of kindness in a forest of loud-mouthed, mostly drunken bluster—perfect in my memory.

Then we were out of the apartment, following the smoke and flames against the night sky and the piercing sounds of sirens and human wailing.

I can't talk about what we saw there. I just can't. My dad jumped right into the fray, helping to look for survivors and carry the dead or fragments of the dead to the makeshift morgue on the courthouse lawn.

But I had nothing to offer in brute strength, and my stomach wasn't strong enough to deal with the carnage, either. Especially since the dead and wounded were almost all people I knew.

What caught my eye was a man dressed in a suit with a camera around his neck, a tripod under one arm and a suitcase in the other hand. He clearly was not from around here. I watched as he surveyed the smoking, burning hell in front of him and then got to work, setting down his case and assembling the tripod. Before I knew it, I was introducing myself and asking how I could help.

"Reginald Woods, *The Springfield Daily News*," he said, ignoring my outstretched hand and removing the blocky black camera from around his neck. "I sure picked a helluva night to be passing through. Can you open that box and find me a light?"

And so, even though I had no earthly idea what I was doing, I became a photographer's apprentice that night. It was truly a trial by fire—as we made our way around the smoking, burning remains of Lamb's and the maimed and broken buildings down Main Street and on the square. We stepped over bricks and bodies and so many other things that were out of place: a single red satin high heel standing on the sidewalk, a snare drum in a tree. The scene was surreal. I focused my attention on Reginald Woods, lugging his equipment around and holding his flash. It kept me from thinking about the death all around me in such personal terms. So when we ran into Beebe, flattened beneath her piano, I ignored the hand that stuck out from the side of the instrument. Instead, I ran to find Reginald something to stand on so that he could take the photo from above, marveling at the way his eye took in his subject and surroundings. He was an artist, I could see that— although I don't know if he would have thought of himself that way.

And the way he took the photos of the survivors, the grieving friends and family, catching them unaware in their most naked, honest expressions of despair. He asked their names afterwards, removing a stubby yellow pencil from behind his ear and flipping open the slim notebook he kept in his breast pocket. He wasn't coarse or unfeeling. But he had a job to do, and he did it, despite the hysteria, despite the smell of burnt human flesh.

Through those long hours, I led Reginald from place to place, person to person. By the time he was wrapping up his last photos and an interview with our distraught mayor—whose teenage daughter was unaccounted for—I found I could anticipate which camera he would want and where to stand to hold the flash. He never acknowledged this, but simply took what I handed to him as no less than what he expected.

Dawn finally came. We sat bone-tired on the steps of the Victorian courthouse, with its shattered windows and large cracks running top to bottom. And that's when he thanked me.

He didn't actually use the words "thank you," but instead reached into his suitcase and rummaged around until his hand latched on to a chunky black Leica with an old shoulder strap.

"This is for you."

"What? I couldn't take your camera," I stammered. "I wouldn't even know what to do with it."

"Actually, I think you would," he said, matter-of-factly. "I think maybe you've got a knack for it. I can tell you're interested, and that's half of it, right there."

I was so surprised that I couldn't do anything but nod. I was afraid I might cry if I opened my mouth. Sometimes after you've been through something horrific, a simple kindness can do more to unleash the floodgates than anything.

On Sunday, it took a while to find the newspaper boy, a kid younger than me and dressed worse. Usually he was outside the bank at Main and First, but that corner was roped off, still full of debris and broken glass. But at the opposite corner, I found him on a pile of *The Springfield Daily News*, eating a bread-and-butter sandwich.

Normally, I would have chewed the fat with him: local sports, the weather. But that day, I placed my precious dime across his dirty palm and impatiently waited for him to put his sandwich down, and peel a copy off the top of his makeshift seat.

"Thanks," I said, avoiding his curious eyes as I held the paper to my chest, my heart pounding in my ears.

I ran all the way home. As soon as I was sure that I was alone on the front steps, unlikely to be disturbed by my exhausted father or timid mother, I unfolded the paper to its full length. I remember the way the newsprint hit my nose first, and then the image came into focus. The entire front page was the burning hole where Lamb's had been—ringed with survivors and family members and firefighters—and the jagged remains of the buildings on either side. Gray curls of smoke and hands of flames rose to meet the headline topping the photograph: JUDGMENT DAY: DANCE HALL EXPLOSION KILLS 29!

It took my breath away, what one man had done with a camera. And although I was not the best reader, I devoured every word of the story, too. All of the scenes Reginald had photographed—*we* had photographed—somehow made sense of the chaos. The close-ups of the panicky faces searching for loved ones. The blackened body stuck through a beam, dangling above the fiery hole. The satin shoe alone on the sidewalk. The drum nestled in the branches of a redbud like a songbird. The Lamb's Dance Hall sign broken neatly in half and propped against a mound of bricks.

All the mayhem and madness of that night had been boxed up, held inside the borders of these photos—yet it did not make them less powerful, but more so. Instead of the acres of devastation and clusters of crying people and all the pieces of lives littered across the landscape, the photos made me focus. I saw the small details that told the larger story and made it more moving. Like the unbearable grief in the face of a mother kneeling over the body of her grown child.

When I was finally done poring over every inch of each photograph, I understood. My experience and the experience of Possum Flats had been not only captured, but illuminated. That night could not be explained; it could never make sense. But those pictures and the words of those who were there . . . they told the truth. And that resonated. What happened to me, to us, was real. And terrible. Yet in its telling, our story became something we could begin to grapple with, each in our own way. But also together.

Words and pictures. Pictures and words. Each can pack a wallop on its own, but the combination? I hadn't come across anything like it for making a person think and feel.

I did not finish my last two years of high school. Why would I? I knew what I wanted to do. What I *had* to do.

I took that Leica on its worn leather strap and headed to *The Picayune*, looking a lot more knowledgeable and experienced than I was. I did not ask for a position from Frederick McMillan III—Fence's father—as much as I just started doing the job.

Fifty years later, I'm still at it.

Fifty Years Ago in Possum Flats:
Remembering the Lamb's Dance Hall Explosion
Part II: Smiley Barnes

by Daisy Flowers

July 7, 1978

Few around Possum Flats can remember him without a camera strap around his neck, but fifty years ago, Smiley Barnes was just another poor kid going to high school, not sure what was next.

At age fifteen, he wasn't popular. But he loved being around people, figuring out their stories and watching their hijinks—mostly from the outside.

That night at Lamb's Dance Hall on August 13, 1928, was no different. Smiley had been on the edge of the dance floor half the night, hoping for an invitation to dance, although he says "the chances were slim and none—and Slim left town." The other half of the evening was spent in the back alley, taking in a hot dice game and tracking down some "hooch" for none other than one of Possum Flats' heroes from that night (who, he insists, must remain nameless).

When the dance hall blew sky-high, Smiley was initially knocked senseless and naked by the explosion. But he made his way home, got dressed and headed back downtown to the disaster, with his father, to help. There, he quickly found himself in the service of a big-city photographer from *The Springfield Daily News*. Smiley's genuine relationships with everyone from farmhands to banking heirs made him the ideal guide to Possum Flats. He hauled the man's camera, lights and equipment all over town those next eight hours, helping him capture the photos and interviews that would bring our community's horrific tale to the wider world—even as he mourned the loss of so many of its citizens.

"I can still see the bodies, people we all knew and loved," he says. "It's been fifty years. But that never goes away."

As thanks, the photographer gave Smiley his first camera. But more importantly, he showed him the power of pictures to tell a story . . . something he's been doing for Possum Flats ever since.

DASH

A slash of morning sunlight cuts across my desk, illuminating the newspaper I have spread out before me.

Likewise, I am having my own small epiphany.

What strikes me, reading about Smiley Barnes, is that the dance hall explosion determined his career. It is incredible to consider, how one night, even a few dark hours, could shape the trajectory of a life. Of a life's work.

But what is truly remarkable to me is that Smiley's story is not unique.

I found my calling that terrible night, too.

It was not so much a discovery of a talent or interest as it was an eleventh-hour bargain with God for my life and soul. The fact that I survived meant I would take up the cross and follow Jesus, without question or complaint.

This was difficult. Not because it is hard to live a godly life or to pastor a flock of broken humanity through life's trials and tribulations. Although I would hold that those are both impossible tasks.

It was excruciatingly difficult for me to turn to God because I had watched my father do so with unwavering trust—only to be brutally and bitterly rewarded. My family suffered mightily and irreparably from his faith.

I did not want to be anything like him.

* * *

When we arrived in Southern California, we had scarcely any money left for an apartment or even a room, not to mention furniture or food. But Father was, as always, optimistic—almost dangerously so—preferring to put our fate in the hands of the Almighty rather than be bothered by the nitty gritty of our regrettable human needs. My father asked around until he got directions to the First Testament Church, where he figured we would get help and guidance, prayers and possibly a warm meal. We must have looked like something from Luke's Gospel, trudging along the run-down streets of Los Angeles—near Azusa Street where the Pentecostal movement had been born. My ragged father, dragging our trunk of worldly belongings on a makeshift dolly; my heaving mother, so large with child, looking for a place at the inn or anywhere else that would have us. Plus me, of course. I don't believe Jesus had a big brother, but I was a reluctant participant in our ragtag nativity scene.

My memories of those months in California are like a series of sepia-toned photos, stark and mostly devoid of color. There was lots of moving around, from shabby room to run-down boarding house to a few frightening nights in a make-do tent in an encampment of other penniless God-seekers. We had so little—any stick of furniture that my father might bring home after a payday from odd jobs could be gone the next week to buy groceries. The emptiness of those rooms echoed like the hollow pit in my stomach. I had never gone hungry on the farm, even if I had had to eat a few suppers of mealy potatoes or suffered an overabundance of mustard greens.

My father's inability to provide was not due to any work shortage. There were jobs to be had—perhaps not regular or well paying, but jobs, nonetheless. The problem was God.

"Today I spoke the Gospel of Truth at a meeting of brethren down on Main Street," he would report, returning to our room late in the evening after being gone since sunup, his hands empty, eyes bright and fevered. "We saved seven for the Lord's kingdom."

When my mother would ask how we would eat that night, he

would become agitated and command us all on our knees to pray. He would remind us that when we had needed wood last week, we had prayed and a bundle had appeared at our door the next day. And that the prior month, when rent was due, a brother from the church had written out a check for us, unsolicited.

"God will wonderfully pour out his spirit upon us, if we but have faith," he said.

But the "miracles" my father spoke of were far outstripped by the times we found ourselves without flour for hard biscuits, or even a couple of potatoes. All the carefully preserved fruits and vegetables we had brought with us from our Oklahoma garden were long gone. And by this time, my sister Ruth had arrived and my mother—she with the broad, strong back and boundless energy for work—had been reduced to translucent skin stretched over bones from nursing this mewling, uneasy baby who was rarely comfortable or satisfied. My mother resembled an Indian tipi, with the faded fabric of her loose dress billowing around the thin struts of her legs and arms. She had sold nearly everything of value from the trunk—pots, pans, linens, extra clothing—and then, eventually, the trunk itself.

We were destitute.

I remember my stomach rumbling over my father's humble supplications as we prayed, the knobs of our knees aching on the hard floor. I almost preferred nights when he didn't come home, swept up in a revival in a small church or tent or warehouse somewhere. We were still hungry, but at least we didn't have to spend hours praying. The three of us would huddle together on a pallet under one of my mother's few remaining patchwork quilts, a wedding gift pieced and stitched by the women of her rural church.

Mother would tuck my sister in the crook of one arm and worry that lock of hair into a spiraling curl on my forehead, singing hymns in her clear alto. She favored "Shall We Gather at the River" and "The Old Rugged Cross," singing them slowly, mournfully. But the peace would not last. My sister, fussy and hungry, would inevitably interrupt with shrieks and tears from which not even my mother could calm her.

One November morning, my mother woke me in a panic.

"Your sister is burning with fever," she said. "I need to find your father. She needs medicine or a doctor or both, and I have no money."

I rarely needed to be woken up. Ruth's wailing was usually our alarm clock. As I shook the dreams from my head, I realized how strangely quiet it was. My father had not come home again last night. My mother clutched the baby to her breast, trying to interest her in nursing. But Ruth's wary blue eyes were closed for once, mouth a tight line. Her skin was yellow and transparent as an onion's, scorching to the touch.

My mother instructed me to sit up on our pallet with my back against the wall. She placed Ruth in my outstretched arms. My sister was light as air, a soft little cloud, and so still, her own arms swaddled against her sides with a flannel blanket to keep her from flailing and fussing.

"Just hold her and try to soothe her if she screams," my mother said, pulling on her black boots. Through dollar-sized holes in the soles, I could see the thin gray layer of cardboard she had used to reline them. I nodded, though I had no idea what I was doing. My mother, sensing this, paused in her efforts to tie her boots.

"Sing to her. Rock her in your arms," my mother said, and I moved my sister back and forth until she gave a terse nod. She brought me some water in our lone tin cup, bending down to set it on the floor beside me. Then she reached into a pocket, removing a small drawstring bag. I recognized it as our sugar sack, but it was woefully flat. Mother placed it on the pallet as if it were a precious gem.

"If she seems hungry or won't stop crying, dip your finger in the water and then the sugar. Just a bit. Then stick your finger in her mouth for her to suck. It should help you by."

My mother gave me a distracted pat on the head and was

quickly out the crooked screen door, which groaned open and came to rest again with a slam.

I looked down at my baby sister, her face wrinkled up in pain, the heat from her fevered body warming me through the blanket and my own thin shirt. Then I looked through our one window, which from the floor only afforded me a sliver of sky. I watched that sky turn from the pinky rose and pale yellow of dawn into a robin's egg cloudless blue as the sun climbed. I was terrified to move, and sweat began to build up on my forearms and chest where I held Ruth so carefully. She would occasionally squirm unsuccessfully against her swaddling, but mostly she was still.

After what felt like hours, but could have been ten minutes or half a day, I felt my stomach clench as though it had been punched. I was starving. Mother had not thought to feed me anything—if there was anything—before she left in search of my father. I was used to a low-grade gnawing in my belly, but sitting with my sister in this quiet room made it difficult to distract myself from my hunger.

I balanced Ruth onto one arm, while I reached for the cup of water. I wet my index finger and then pulled open the sugar bag, bunching it up as my finger felt for the meager granules at the bottom. When I felt them stick to my finger, I withdrew it carefully and placed it gently on my sister's mouth.

Ruth would not open her lips, but flinched at my touch, her brow briefly wrinkling into a grimace.

I made another half-hearted attempt to break the tight seal of her lips, but she turned her face away and I worried that she would start screaming.

But she stayed silent.

The heat radiating from the little bundle reminded me of how my mother would ease my stomachaches with a hot water bottle and it comforted me, making me feel less frightened and alone.

I stared at my finger, covered with crystals of our precious sugar and watched as that finger came slowly to my own lips. Before I knew it, I had licked off every tiny speck. The sweetness caused me to salivate, and I swallowed. The sugar made a warm, delicious trail down the back of my throat.

The minutes and hours crept by, and after waiting as long as I possibly could, I again dipped my finger in water and the sugar. I would touch my sister's mouth, and when she made no attempt to take the sugar, I would put it in my own. The mixture of shame and elation I felt was nearly unbearable, and I each time I did it, I would tell myself it was the last time.

But soon, both water cup and sugar bag were depleted. I became terrified of what my mother would say when she found I had eaten all our sugar—and yet also scared she would never come back. My sister cried only once, but I sang "Jesus Loves Me," over and over, even though I wasn't convinced that He did. Ruth quieted again, her face relaxing for the first time all day. Her fever seemed to have broken at last, and she began to cool perceptibly in my arms. The light in the room faded as evening approached, my sliver of sky turning a dusky blue. I could hear the *clip, clop* of horses and the occasional motorcar, as people made their way home for supper. I needed to relieve myself, the sugar water having made its way through my system, but still I sat on the pallet, holding my sister and waiting for Mother to return.

I must have fallen asleep. The next thing I knew, the door was creaking open and my mother was jostling me awake, reaching for Ruth. Close behind her were my father and a mustached man in a dark coat and hat, clutching a black-handled bag. The doctor.

"Here she is," my mother said, extracting Ruth from my arms. "That's a good girl now, Ruthie."

What followed was a great commotion, as my mother screamed and the doctor intervened to ascertain the cause. He swiftly unwrapped the baby, peeling the layers away until there was only her pale, bloodless body exposed.

"Start up a fire!" my mother commanded my father, although we had maybe two small sticks in the kindling box. "She needs to warm up. Give her to me!"

But the doctor, cradling all of my baby sister in his open palm, shook his head. "I'm sorry," he said. He wrapped Ruth back up loosely in her blanket and made as if to hand her to my mother.

"No." Her voice was gritty with determination, only a hair away from breaking as she reached toward a kitchen shelf. "She just needs a hot water bottle and a little fire. Her fever's broken."

My father stood in the middle of the room, paralyzed. He did not know whether to follow his wife's orders or to go toward Ruth and the doctor. I had not seen this version of my father in California, indecisive and weak.

"She is gone," the doctor said.

My mother turned from her task, her face torn ragged with the understanding she had fought so fiercely against. Still, she shook her head no, but stretched out her arms for her daughter.

Gone.

But *where* had she gone? I could see her so clearly in front of me, pallid and still. As a child raised on a farm, I knew that death came to living things, whether chickens or pigs fed and slaughtered for our own use or the golden wheat or hay of the pastures that met the threshing machine or the sharp, arced blade of a scythe. To me, it was simply the opposite side of the coin to the eggs that I gathered every day or the newborn calf that caused her mother's udder to swell and harden with enough milk for the both of us.

Yet I had never seen or experienced a human death before. My five-year-old heart was torn to pieces. Surely this was not the normal way of things, that an infant could die. But I knew with sick certainty that it must be my fault. I could feel my tongue in my mouth, roughened from those hard crystals of sugar over the course of the day. Why hadn't I tried harder to get my sister to take even the smallest taste, the tiniest bit of sustenance? Shamefaced, I knew the answer: I had selfishly wanted that sweet luxury to myself.

I burst into tears, burying my face in my mother's skirts, even as I feared her wrath for my part in this tragedy.

I felt myself torn away by two strong arms. My father held me tightly as the doctor reached a cool, smooth hand to my forehead.

He turned my face from side to side, peering deep into my eyes where I felt sure he could see my guilt. But he seemed grimly pleased with whatever he saw or didn't see there.

"The boy is fine," he said. "But see he doesn't miss his meals."

My father turned an awful shade of scarlet, embarrassed by the doctor's implication.

"Of course," he stammered. "And here's something for your trouble, Doctor," he said, digging deep into his trouser pocket for money that we all knew wasn't there. The doctor seemed to understand this was just for show, and cut him off before he could come up empty.

"That's not necessary," the doctor said briskly. He tipped his cap to my mother and father before turning to take his leave. "I wish I could have been more of a help. God bless you."

There was an awful silence as my parents looked long and hard at each other. I don't remember what was said, if anything. But I believe in that moment that my mother made clear that she would not abide this place—California—or this life. I don't know how my father managed to come up with the money for train tickets. I'm sure there must have been an outpouring of sympathy from the church brethren, that they likely passed the hat at the devastating news about Ruth. I imagine that their generosity was both a means of protesting the unfairness of an infant's death while also attempting to somehow ward off this bad fortune from infiltrating their own homes and families, secretly uncertain that prayers alone would be enough to keep them safe.

All I recall was an endless train ride through the dry, barren deserts of Arizona and New Mexico and the way the rolling rhythm of the wheels on the track comforted me and put me to sleep in a way that sitting between two stiff, silent parents could not. And the other thing I remember was the damning bundle that was my sister's body, the awful evidence of our failure—mine and my father's—wrapped up tightly in several small cloths and her baby quilt and held on my mother's lap like a loaf of bread. The binding layers were not enough to completely stem the sickening stench of death, and although other passengers held their noses and gave us wide berth, my father and I sat uncomplaining with my mother and Ruth as our well-deserved penance. Mother had insisted that her baby not be left behind, buried in a hateful place with no one to remember her or visit her grave. I could not bear to look at the lump that was Ruth, and I'm sure her still presence, permeating the stifling hot air on that train, ripped the heart out of my father as well.

It took most of a grim week to make it back to the middle of the country, to southern Missouri, where my father had been advised of a small rural congregation in sore need of a preacher. My mother had only agreed to a church post because it came with a house and a small plot of land, which would provide both a resting place for Ruth and a ready-made second job for my father as a farmer. She knew that with their work ethic, our family would never need to go hungry again. And my mother believed in the generosity of the land—subject as it was to drought or heavy rains or insect infestations—more than she did the power of a fickle God to provide.

This is how we came to live a dozen miles or so outside of Possum Flats, where I grew up determined never to be a farmer or a preacher like my father.

I avoided the first fate—but I could not escape God's plan that I become a man of the cloth and His Word. I saw the light, as they say, and it came in the form of a hideous explosion and fire that consumed many of my friends and every bit of the dandy I had believed myself to be.

July 10, 1978

Dear Mom

Are you okay? I still haven't gotten any mail from you! I keep going back and forth between worried and kind of mad, to be honest. Wouldn't take much to write a postcard or drop a few lines in an envelope. Stamps are thirteen cents!

Did you like my article about Hazel? I'm enclosing the second piece—it's about my newspaper buddy, Smiley. Do you remember him at all? I had to really dig for this story; he would have never spilled it on his own. He's sort of the shy, humble type. But quite a talker when you get him going!

Anyway, I hope you and Ron are settling in and making a good life for us. I think I am going to love California. Grandma and I have been watching CHiPs at night—do you like Ponch or Jon?—even though she mostly just shakes her head at what she calls all the "shenanigans." The people seem laid-back and casual. And beautiful. Cities on the water, beaches everywhere and palm trees and sun, sun, sun. But not too hot: just perfect. It doesn't look like people sweat out there. Am I right?

Here it is sun, sun, sun, too. But it's too hot. And humid. The only reasonable thing to wear right now is a bikini or just your underwear. But this isn't California. People are not laid-back and casual here. But you know that.

Last week we went to the Fourth of July fireworks show at the fairgrounds. Meaning me and Grandma, of course, but also Joe and Patty from work. While we waited for the sun to go down, Joe drew funny pictures of everyone and Patty and I wrote their dialogue bubbles, which was hilarious. We also brought fried chicken and watermelon—and Grandma brought a jar of her homemade bread-and-butter pickles. You know how I feel about pickles . . . but these are actually sweet and tangy. Surprisingly good!

Which is what I would say about the fireworks, too. The official name of the show is "Fire in the Sky," but Grandma calls it "Flash in the Pan." For the Bicentennial two years ago, the town raised like twenty thousand dollars for some big, fancy fireworks. Everyone set up blankets, lawn chairs and coolers and passed the time till dusk eating, playing Frisbee or listening to Cardinals baseball on the radio. But when the sun finally went down, they were treated to a spectacle that lasted exactly two-and-a-half minutes. Talk about hot! People still get riled up about it. Grandma says they go for quantity over quality now, so I was expecting something like amped-up sparklers. But the display was actually pretty cool. Mostly it was nice to hang out with Joe and Patty and feel like I finally have a few friends.

Speaking of fireworks, Grandma really blew up the other day. I wanted to interview her for my series. But when I asked about Violet, she got defensive. Pissed, actually.

I guess Violet was pretty wild and Grandma says people felt her sister got what was coming to her that night. And that it was better that the "good twin" survived. Meaning her. But she would have given anything to be in her sister's place that night . . . even though her sister was apparently pregnant, with no plans. Guess being unmarried and pregnant is a thing for the Flowers women? Don't worry; I'm not about to be next.

Gotta go. I'm working on my third article. It's on

Jimmy Jeffers, the police chief, the big hero of the night. The problem is, he threw me out of his office! But luckily I've got some other people for quotes.

Your Ace Reporter & Daughter,
Daisy

P.S. The Fourth of July is halfway through summer. See you in a month or so!? XOX

Fifty Years Ago in Possum Flats:
Remembering the Lamb's Dance Hall Explosion
Part III: Jimmy Jeffers

by Daisy Flowers

July 14, 1978

You can call him Chief. Or you can call him Jimmy. The name plate on his office says James Jeffers.

Just don't call him a hero.

"I am not a goddamn hero," he says, glaring from behind the daunting stacks of paperwork on his desk at the police station.

But many in Possum Flats would disagree. In fact, they can vouch for his heroism firsthand. Because Police Chief James Jeffers is the reason they are alive after the devastating explosion of Lamb's Dance Hall back in August of 1928.

"Jimmy found me thrown a hundred yards away, knocked out cold," says Hazel Hodges. "He said I looked so bad when he rolled me over that he almost puked. He had just decided to leave me for dead, because the fire was spreading, and people were trapped in the building rubble. It was a triage situation. He had to act fast to save those who were still alive."

Fortunately for Hazel, she chose to cough at that precise moment. Jimmy, startled to see she was alive, gathered her up and carried her to safety.

According to Joe Nichols, his grandfather—Pastor Paul "Dash" Emmonds—was also one of Jimmy's rescues that night. "My grandfather's ankle was wedged under a heavy beam and he couldn't pull it free. If Jimmy hadn't saved him, the fire would have burned him alive."

The list goes on: Mo Wheeler, the sax player in the band that was playing that night. Ginger Morton of the Morton's Pharmacy family. According to survivors, Jimmy Jeffers was everywhere that night, risking his own skin to save his friends and neighbors from the flames and wreckage.

"We were all just so lucky Jimmy was around," Hazel says. "He had been upset at the dance earlier and left in a terrible huff. Thank goodness he hadn't gotten too far before the building exploded. Because he single-handedly saved a dozen or more of us. He was our big burly angel."

Not surprisingly, Chief Jeffers refused to be interviewed for this story.

Fortunately, there is no shortage of Possum Flats citizens who are happy to recall his heroics of that long-ago night.

DAISY

When I get to the paper Monday morning, Patty is waiting for me, pink-faced with excitement.

"Good morning," she says, stepping out from behind a tall stack of yesterday's newspapers. "I read your article on Chief Jeffers. It was really, really good."

"Thanks, Patty. He wasn't what you'd call cooperative. I had to fill in some holes."

Patty nods and then slyly adds: "Speaking of holes, Smiley brought donuts."

Somehow, we've become friends, even though all we have in common are our ages and place of employment. Honestly, we're both a couple of oddballs.

Her typical outfit is a long, faded denim skirt with a plain uni-sex T-shirt and scuffed black Mary Janes that reveal the two innocent half-moons of her white tube socks. I've glimpsed the tops of those socks and they don't even have the double or triple stripe that make a tube sock worth wearing. She is plain vanilla to my rainbow sherbet. Maybe that's why we like each other.

"Hold on a minute," I say. "Myra already tipped me off about your big day." I dig around in my sling bag. "I brought you something. Happy birthday."

I had stopped at Morton's on my way home yesterday and wandered the aisles until I felt inspired. It took a while. What do you get a girl who has the opposite of everything?

I settled on the palest pink fingernail polish and a bottle of polish remover. The old lady behind the counter puckered her lips disapprovingly. Judging by the depth of her mouth wrinkles, she disapproves of everything. This must be Ginger Morton. The Mayor's side chick.

"You're that newspaper girl, Daisy Flowers," she said sourly. Not a question.

I nodded. I was used to this now.

"Writing those stories on the explosion, right? Sort of missing someone, aren't you?" Her eyebrow quirked up.

"You mean *you*? You were there, right?"

The shock on her face nearly cracked the foundation on her forehead.

"No. I mean, yes. I was there." Ginger's face was hard to read. "But I don't remember much. I was knocked unconscious and when I came to a week later, most of that night was just . . . *gone*. I mean your grandma. I'm sure she knows something more about what happened that night. To Violet and the rest."

"Why would you say that?" My hackles had gone up. The old witch had better not slander my grandma. I hadn't known her as long as Ginger Morton had, but I knew she was a good person. Decent. Loyal. Honest. *Too* honest, maybe.

"I mean, I ran with Violet, not Rose." Ginger paused. "But still. She was never the same afterwards."

"I'm sorry. Did *you* lose your twin sister in a tragic accident? Because you might not be the same, either."

"I lost my best friend. Fern."

There was an uncomfortable silence as we stared at each other over the nail polish on the counter between us. Finally, she blinked.

"Not really your color, if you want my expert opinion," she said primly, ringing up my purchases on an old-fashioned, push-button register that caused numbers to appear in the clear window at the top with a loud *ding*.

"I don't." I heard how rude I sounded and didn't care. Who was she to be all righteous? "But it's not actually for me."

"Hmmmf."

Now here I am, second-guessing myself as Patty opens the gift box and fumbles with all the layers of tissue paper. Either I've overdone it, or else she is not used to opening presents. I realize it's the latter.

Patty's eyes widen when she reaches the bottles. "Oh!" she says, holding the black lid of the polish between her forefinger and thumb as if it smelled a bit off. "Oh," she says again. "Thank you, Daisy."

She quickly wads the tissue paper around the bottles and jams them back in the box as if she has been caught committing a crime.

"You can take them back . . ." Something is wrong.

Patty gives me a weak smile. "No, it's fine. It's really, really nice of you. I can use it for labeling things and stuff."

"It's *nail* polish. Not paint." Now I am getting a funhouse mirror feeling, like what should be normal is distorted somehow.

Patty weaves her fingers together and looks down at her shoes.

"It's just . . . well, I can't wear nail polish," she says. "It's . . . against my religion."

I've heard lots of people say things are "against their religion," and it's usually because they don't want to do them. But the look of Patty's face, like a deflated balloon, tells me she means it.

Sometimes I think I will never understand this town. Or the people in it.

"Don't worry," she says, grabbing me by the elbow and steering me toward the break room. "I'm not supposed to celebrate birthdays, either . . . but I guess I can't help it if Smiley happens to bring in two dozen donuts on the seventeenth of July, can I?"

Her happiness is contagious and I totally get it. I didn't have a lot of extras, but one thing Mom made a big deal about was my birthday. No matter where we lived, we ordered my favorite takeout—usually pad thai—and my mom would splurge on a perfectly frosted chocolate cake for two from a fancy bakery. Then we would paint each other's toenails and stay up late watching old movies. Like *Breakfast at Tiffany's* ("Never love a wild thing, Mr. Bell") or *Seven Brides for Seven Brothers* ("You can't make no vows to a herd of cows").

It was never about presents, but *presence*, Mom liked to say. Being together. And I loved being the full focus of her attention. No boyfriends or work shift taking priority. I guess that's why the nail polish seemed like a perfect gift, even though I realize it wasn't. At least for Patty.

It's crowded in the break room: No Fence, but Myra and Smiley are here, along with Bill, the press foreman, and Sedalia from circulation—who Joe says keeps all the paper boys in line. On the table, there is a Day-Lite Donuts box with an oval plastic window showing two neat rows of glazed: half chocolate, half regular. Plus a greasy wax bag of donut holes. Everyone scooches in to make room, and Myra leads us in *The Picayune*'s birthday ditty, sung to "Ta-Ra-Ra Boom-De-Ay."

"This is your birthday song/It isn't very long."

That's it. A perfect piece of editing. Everyone laughs at the abbreviated ending, just like they always do, before wishing Patty a happy day. I am surprised to learn she is actually two years older than me. It's probably the Pentecostal thing that makes her look more like a girl than a young woman—with no makeup and simple clothes that hang straight instead of collecting on any curves. She is grinning from ear to ear, her face glowing. She really is beautiful. I don't know how I had missed that before.

I am eyeing a third donut when Fence appears in the break room doorway. His face is gray, which makes the worry lines more noticeable. It is the first time I have thought of him as old. He frantically scans the curious faces around the table before settling on Smiley.

"Grab your camera," he says, clearly flustered, since Smiley always has his camera around his neck. I've often wondered if he sleeps with it, too. "Next door. The police station. Jimmy Jeffers has been shot."

It's like a giant vacuum sucks all the air out of the room. There's a gasp from Sedalia, and Myra puts her hands to her mouth as if to stifle a scream. The two donuts in my stomach suddenly feel like a couple of hard fists.

"Shot?" My voice comes out as a croak. I just sat across a desk from him two weeks ago. "Is he going to be okay?"

Smiley is already out the door, but Fence turns at my question before following him. I'll never forget the look he gives me, a weird mix of pity and disgust.

"He's dead," Fence says. "You might as well have pulled the trigger yourself."

What? Now it is everyone's turn to look at me. *Why would he say that?* The skin on the back of my neck prickles and I start to shiver, uncontrollably, like I'm freezing cold. I feel my outsider status more sharply than I have in weeks. There is an uncomfortable minute of shocked silence that finally ends when Patty breaks into sobs. As Myra and Sedalia turn to comfort her, I bolt.

I've got to find out what's going on. And since death's involved, I know there's one person who will surely know the how and the why. Trying my hardest not to ugly cry, I run, lungs burning, camera thumping against my chest. All the way to Flowers Funeral Home and my grandma.

ROSE

I didn't believe it when I got the call at the crack of dawn.

I didn't believe it, even when the ambulance backed up into my driveway just as everyone else in Possum Flats was drinking coffee and thinking about heading to work. No flashing lights; no need. This person's emergency had already come and gone.

Even when the two young paramedics brought him out on a stretcher, his bulk covered in a white sheet with blood spots blooming from the lump that should be his head . . . I still couldn't believe it.

Jimmy Jeffers is dead.

Our chief of police, who had brought us through so much since he joined the force nearly fifty years ago. Who had gone from hometown hero to community guardian, never taking time out for a real life. Our safety and well-being *were* his life. And now it's over. Just like that.

"Mornin', Ms. Flowers," says the short, balding paramedic. "Sorry to start your day like this. Mabel called from the station as soon as she found him, but there wasn't anything we could do for the poor guy."

"Been dead for hours," agrees the thinner one with a face full of acne that makes him look no older than fourteen or fifteen. "But he probably died right away. By the looks of things."

They wheel him in, unload his considerable heft onto my table and leave. I pull up a chair beside him, listening as the ambulance doors close and the engine starts to life, motoring off to the next crisis. Then there's nothing but my own breathing. Roger's off today and Daisy's left for the newspaper already. She'll get the news soon enough.

I'm looking at Jimmy, and I still can't believe it.

"Well, Chief," I say. "What happened?"

Part of me wants to leave him covered up, pretend he's asleep. Or imagine that a man his age—who weighs two-fifty and whose only exercise is lifting an eight-ounce mug of coffee to his face a couple hundred times a day—could easily fall over dead from a heart attack.

Yes. That's it. He was sitting at his desk, looking over yesterday's *Picayune* or finishing up a crime report when his chest seized up. And before he could put his arms out to stop himself, he was listing to one side, falling from the chair. He was probably already dead when his forehead hit the sharp corner of his metal desk on his way to the floor. That's what caused all the blood.

So much blood.

I sigh. "But that's not what happened, now is it, Chief?"

Gingerly, I turn back the edge of the sheet near his feet, carefully rolling it up as I go. Slowly, he is revealed: the black polyester pants with the crop of pilling white balls at the hem and pockets; the stretched-out leather belt on its very last notch, one that had clearly been made by the chief himself to accommodate his expanding waistline. For some reason, this extra hole makes me tear up.

I purposely stop rolling up the sheet when I reach his neck, and tuck the gathered thickness behind it, leaving the head covered for now. There are large spatters of blood on his white, no-iron short-sleeved shirt, and he isn't wearing his badge. His thick forearms, covered with curls of black hair, are laid out neatly at his sides.

I don't need to see his face, or what's left of it. Not yet. I know what happens when a .38 Special is discharged into the roof of the mouth. There won't be anything that resembles Jimmy when I pull back that sheet.

I had dialed the police station as soon as I'd gotten the call about Chief. I had to talk to Mabel. Maybe she knew something, saw this coming. But she had gone home for the day, one of the young cops told me. Too upset after finding Jimmy that way. She was the closest thing he had to family in this town. She'll probably be in charge of the arrangements, once she pulls herself together.

There's no one else.

I'll wait for Roger to get the chief rolled side to side and dressed in whatever Mabel thinks best. Not that it matters. This is definitely a closed-casket situation. But I can get this outer layer of clothes off and give him a last bath. Get rid of the spray of blood on his arms and neck, clean and trim his nails and get him set in a peaceful pose before he stiffens up. I hated interrupting Roger's plans for fishing Bryant Creek today, but he knows how unpredictable our business is. I told him to go ahead and catch a few rainbows for me—what my father-in-law liked to call "speckled beauties"—and come in this afternoon.

"Best fishing is early anyways," he said. "But are you sure? Maybe I better come on in." He paused before hanging up, giving an uncharacteristic postscript to our typically no-frills conversations: "Jimmy Jeffers. Who would have thought it?"

"I know," I said. "But you never really know what people are going through."

I grab a pair of shears to begin the careful work of cutting the chief out of his shirt. Not just any shears, either. These are the long, silver-bladed scissors that I "inherited" from my mother-in-law. Meaning they came with the business. She wouldn't have purposely left me anything special. In fact, I refer to them as "Gladys" when I use them, talking to inanimate objects—including dead people—like I do. They are pointy and sharp and extremely good at what they do, just like she was.

Lord, she could cut you!

First I undo his shirt front, no easy task given the strain on each translucent button and its thinning threads. His big body pulls the material beyond taut over his midsection. I am slicing along the seam that goes from underneath his arm and down his side when I see it: There is something in his breast pocket. Right over his heart.

I probably should call the police department, have someone come up and take a look. Then listen to that person "aw, shucks" his way through an explanation of why someone missed it before dropping Chief off. How upset everyone was, how they checked his desk and, well . . . it just didn't occur to them to check his pockets, what with all the blood and gore, you know?

But since I've never been one to go by the rule books, I don't pick up the phone. Instead, I set old Gladys down on my silver tray and reach for a pair of tweezers. I slide the tips into Chief's blood-soaked pocket and pinch down, grabbing on to a slim, folded piece of paper that was not completely spared, despite the layer of fabric protection. It is a blue-lined piece of paper, with one fringed edge where it was torn from a spiral notebook, folded to fit his pocket. Do I dare open it?

What if it is just a grocery list or a reminder to stop in at Sears for a new refrigerator filter? Or a note from Mabel, with the name of someone he needs to call back? But I have a sick feeling that the note is for me. For Possum Flats.

My hands are shaking. Under the fluorescent light of my workroom, words in blue ballpoint begin to take shape on the dampened, creased page:

> *I can't be the hero you thought I was anymore.*
> *I've never been one. I'm the exact opposite of what a hero is.*
> *I am sorry. For everything. I should have taken responsibility fifty years ago, but I was too chickenshit.*
> *Guess I still am.*
> *I don't deserve your forgiveness. I know that. But Christ, I loved this goddamned town.*
> *—Jimmy*

My vision blurs. Am I having some sort of heart attack or stroke? But, no. It is just tears. Tears for Jimmy. For whatever impossibly heavy burden he had been lugging around by himself all of these years. How much of it was true and how much imagined? Whatever he had done or not done back then, couldn't he see the worth in what he *had* done for all of us?

Of course, I am also crying for myself, for the young, carefree me I'd lost those many years ago. And for my sister, the other half of me whose life I had scorned—until she was gone. How unsettling to discover yet another person living a completely different life than what others saw or believed. Bartholomew Watson. Jimmy Jeffers. How many others of us are living a lie, too?

Gently, I slide the note back into Chief's chest pocket and try to stand. I feel woozy, but I've got to call someone. Who? Should I share the note or let Jimmy go to his grave amid rumor and speculation? All the *whys*? Is that better than the truth of what he is implying?

Roger will be here soon. He'll know what to do.

I steady myself with both hands on the work table that holds Jimmy Jeffers. I can't believe how hard this has hit me, this death—in its suddenness and its violence—and everything said and unsaid in that note.

So I shouldn't be surprised that when I let go of the table, there is nothing to hold me up. I fall face forward, see the cold cement coming so quickly that I can't even close my eyes. Or maybe I do.

All I know is that everything goes dark.

DAISY

"Grandma!"

I am yelling before the screen door even slams behind me. I throw my camera on a chair and rush to the basement, nearly colliding with Roger. He has apparently come in through the back with the same destination in mind. And he's in a hurry, too.

"Whoa, Daisy. What's your rush?"

We both stop at the top of the stairs, panting.

"I could ask you the same question, Roger." I start to push past him but he puts an arm across my path, bracing it against the wall.

"You don't want to go down there, Daisy," he says. There is both warning and kindness in his voice.

"I've got to talk to Grandma. Jimmy Jeffers is dead."

Roger's face registers relief that I don't need to be told that unfortunate bit of news. But he still won't move his arm.

"That's the thing, Daisy. Jimmy's down there. And I don't think you want to see him the way he looks now."

My heart flips over in my chest. I look Roger straight in the eyes as we stand there unmoving, stubborn in our resolve as to what will happen next.

"Okay," I say at last, shrugging my shoulders as if giving up. Roger slowly lowers his arm. But then, like a shot, I'm past him and down the steep stairs.

"Daisy!"

Roger's feet are pounding down the stairs behind me. When I reach the bottom I twist the door knob and shove open the beveled wooden door. The sight that greets me pulls me up short. Surprised by my sudden stop, Roger bumps into me and would have knocked me over had I not been still holding on to the doorknob.

Blood. There is blood everywhere I look. On Grandma's worktable, there is the hulking remains of what surely must be Jimmy Jeffers, uncovered but for the bloody mound of sheet that hides his head and face. His shirt is splattered with blood and other bits that I don't want to even think about identifying.

"Grandma!"

"Rose!"

Roger and I see her at the same time, facedown in a darkening puddle of her own blood. Unmoving. I can't understand what is happening, my mind trying to make connections. Is she dead? Has she been shot? Did Jimmy Jeffers shoot her and then himself? Where's the gun?

My brain races while my body remains totally paralyzed. I'm as helpful to Roger as the average corpse that arrives at our back door. He's clearly used to it. He has left me in the doorway gaping like a perch on a riverbank and is kneeling beside Grandma, grabbing one of her sharp shoulders to turn her faceup.

That's when I scream. Her nose is completely flattened and shoved to one side of her face, mouth hanging open to reveal a bloody tongue and a missing front tooth. Her entire face is smeared with her own blood and the tip of her beautiful white braid is an iron-red, too, resting in the puddle by her head.

"C'mon, Rose, old girl. Talk to me." Roger is gentle as he lowers Grandma onto her back. To my massive relief, she moans like a set of old pipes.

She is alive.

"Daisy, grab a towel. Maybe some warm water? We've got to see what's going on here," Roger says. "You've really done a number on yourself this time, Rose. Haven't you?"

Grandma answers with another long groan. I scramble around for a towel and run water in the industrial-sized sink, waiting impatiently for it to turn warm. Meanwhile, Roger takes the cushion from her work chair and places it beneath her head. He stands, hands on hips, satisfied that she is going to survive. Then he reaches for the phone mounted on one of the support beams, spinning the rotary dial with a bloody forefinger.

"Hello? Yeah, this is Roger down at Flowers. I need an ambulance. ASAP."

There is a pause. Roger's typically calm face darkens. There seems to be some confusion on the other end. "I know you just dropped off. Tell the guys to turn their butts around and get back over here. I've got a real emergency . . . a *live* one."

He slams the handset down onto the receiver so hard that the bell dings.

"Goddamn nosy Nellies in this town."

Roger wrings out the towel I've brought him, in a galvanized pail of warm water. Thankfully, the bucket was empty when I found it, not full of something disgusting.

Roger is surprisingly tender as he dabs at the blood on Grandma's face, especially around the wreck that was her nose. He sticks a corner of the towel in her purpling, swollen mouth and swipes around slowly, removing the better part of the missing front tooth. I want to vomit. She looks so broken and old. I realize how her spirit and personality somehow double her size and without them, she is positively petite, frail. It's like a trial run for her funeral. I try to push that thought out of my mind by finding something useful to do.

I reach for her hair, that gorgeous white braid as thick and perfect as one of the challah loaves at the bakery by our old Chicago apartment. The heft of it surprises me and I wonder how Grandma supports the weight of it on her birdlike neck.

I take out the loop that holds the braid together, recognizing it as one of the thick, flesh-colored bands that come around *The Picayune* every day. Practical. A rubber band that was likely rolled on our paper by Joe. My face heats; I'm ashamed for thinking about Joe when Grandma is laid out like this.

The bottom of the braid loosens in my hand and I pull apart the three entwined chunks of hair until I get to the tighter French braid that runs from the base of her skull to the top of the back of her head. I reach for the pail and cup some water in my hand, soaking the hair gummed with Grandma's blood. I work the hair between my fingers, loosening the places where the blood has thickened.

"Need a brush?" Roger hands me one from Grandma's work-table. He has gotten the worst of the mess from her face. Yes, her nose is all wrong and her mouth looks like a window with a pane broken out. But she is at least recognizable. She is going to be okay.

I place the hairbrush in my lap, and reach beneath Grandma's head with both hands and ease it to one side, so that I can easily reach the rest of her braid. I run my splayed fingers through the braid, loosening it until the hair all falls free. Starting at her crown, I bring the brush all the way through the tips of the hair, which are wet and still a little pink.

Roger has moved on to Jimmy Jeffers. I am grateful that I can't see what Roger does when he raises that sheet. Fence's words return, echo inside my head like a siren: *You might as well have pulled the trigger yourself.*

I am pulling the brush through the layers of Grandma's hair eas-ily now, but my head is pounding, that siren sound that had started as a low, deep wail now increasing in intensity and volume. Then I realize it is not in my head at all.

It's the ambulance, of course.

As the doors slam, I decide to take one last sweep from under-neath, to make sure there are no tangles before I send Grandma on her way to the hospital. I'm not sure why I feel that's important; maybe just to finish what I've started. From the base of her skull, I bring the brush bristle-side up through her hair, which pulls away to reveal—for a split second—the knobby white neck beneath.

Roger is holding the back door open for the paramedics, who rush toward me and Grandma with a stretcher. The one with a face full of zits looks my age, but thankfully, the older bald one is in charge. I want Grandma to be well taken care of, not someone's first emergency. I want to tell them to stop, to wait for just a minute before they load her up and take her away.

I need to take one more swipe through that hair, that amazing hair Grandma has maintained all these years without anything more than a trim. Because now I understand why she wears it the way she does. Why she hasn't cut it and never will.

That incredible hair has been hiding a secret. And in an instant, the hairbrush had revealed it to me. I want to make doubly sure I haven't imagined it.

Grandma has a violet birthmark on the back of her neck, right beneath the base of her skull. *Violet.*

But . . . her name is Rose.

Isn't it?

DASH

Jimmy Jeffers is dead. By his own hand.

Dear Christ, what a waste of a life. Of a man! When I think of what he has meant to this town. And to me, of course. I wouldn't be here if it weren't for him. Literally pulled me from the mouth of hell, Jimmy did. And not just the raging pit of fire that was Lamb's Dance Hall, but the hell of my young sinful life.

If I had died that night, it would have devastated my parents. My mother—who had already seen one beloved child put in the ground—might not have survived a second.

And my father.

The deep shame and embarrassment I caused him with my wayward life were a source of extreme friction between us. He heard the rumblings, the whispers around Possum Flats. He knew I was not living anything remotely resembling a godly life. And living it unapologetically, not even attempting restraint or a modicum of discretion, extending to him the figurative middle finger, a slap in his pious face. I was his cross to bear.

But my survival and complete about-face changed all of that. I was Lazarus, resurrected from the grave; the lost sheep in whose discovery the shepherd rejoices; the Prodigal Son come home at last.

My father never said he was proud of me. Pride is one of the seven deadly sins. But he took my newly reclaimed life as an af-

238 Michelle Collins Anderson

firmation of him and of his chosen path. No doubt he used it as a means of recruiting other lost souls for the Lord: For "with God all things are possible," says the Gospel of Matthew.

Yet Jimmy Jeffers obviously did not find all things possible with God, namely continued life on this planet. I do not presume to know the burdens on his heart or the claims on his soul, but I find myself casting about for a way to understand. To reconcile Jimmy Jeffers to the eternal damnation I know awaits those who take their own life.

He and I never spoke of the night Lamb's blew up. I sensed he didn't want my thanks—nor the continued gratefulness of others whom he pulled from certain death. It appeared enough for him to know he had done what he could to serve his community. His town. I felt he would happily—or at least grudgingly—continue to watch over the people of Possum Flats until he was unable. And that day, when it came, would be a day of sadness for us all. I'm certain there would never have been a retirement party. I believe he would have simply drawn his last breath in his office, maybe stopped breathing during one of his famous post-prandial naps behind those blinds.

He never would have shot himself. I feel in the very marrow of my bones it is that girl who has done this to him.

This whole unearthing of our past and our ghosts. It's too much.

The girl has gone too far.

Daisy

I'm at Grandma's bedside. It's late afternoon and the window is open because the August heat is ferocious and she doesn't "believe" in air conditioning. The Swiss-dot sheers on either side of the window frame hang still as death. There is no breeze. Nothing moves in the yard except the occasional bee, droning in the dark pink clusters of the crepe myrtle. Everything else has long since bloomed. A few plants might think about a second flush of flowers when it cools off. But right now, most are just bent on survival.

Sort of like Grandma.

She's not at her prettiest, either. But she's alive, biding her time and healing up for another good run, I hope. Roger and I have her propped up on pillows so that it's easier for her to breathe. She's sleeping peacefully at the moment, except for the ragged intake of air through the square where her front tooth used to be. She sounds like Darth Vader. Like any minute, she might open her eyes and say in that deep, heavy-breather voice: "Daisy . . . 'I find your lack of faith disturbing.'"

I have to be honest: I find it disturbing, too.

I mean, I know she's my grandma. But my faith in everything else I thought I knew about her has gone out the window the last two weeks.

Instead of Grandma Rose, she's apparently Grandma Violet. Rose is dead and has been for fifty years. And my mom's dad is not, apparently, George Steinkamp, the man I assumed was my grandpa.

I've got a lot of questions. But Grandma hasn't been in any shape to answer them. She's been out of the hospital for a week, but the pain meds that keep her from crying out also keep her from talking or doing anything. Sometimes her eyes will come open and dart around, wild, until she settles on me. Looking at me seems to give her some relief before she disappears again back down the rabbit hole of sleep.

Meanwhile, I'm living life as an outcast. Or at least I will be if I ever leave the house.

Apparently on Sunday, Dash blasted me from the pulpit. Said I was basically Satan incarnate for the trouble I was stirring up. That I caused Jimmy Jeffers to take his own life by digging up the past. He stopped just short of saying I should be run out of Possum Flats, but I think that was the message.

Patty came by Monday, the day after Brother Emmonds rained hellfire and brimstone onto my head. When I answered the door, she looked around first, as if she would hate to be caught at the home of such a notorious sinner. She wouldn't come inside, hoping to say her piece and run.

"That's okay, Daisy. I don't want to bother you and Miss Rose." She reached into the pocket of her long denim jumper. "I brought you this."

She shoved a folded white program into my hands. It was the Assemblies of God service leaflet from Sunday, full of mimeographed purple verses from Proverbs 6:

These six things doth the LORD hate: yea, seven are an
    abomination unto him:
A proud look, a lying tongue, and hands that shed innocent
    blood,
An heart that deviseth wicked imaginations, feet that be
    swift in running to mischief,

A false witness that speaketh lies, and he that soweth
   discord among brethren.

When I finished reading, the only sound was the pulsating metallic buzz of cicadas. Patty was looking at her feet.

"Brother Emmonds said you are everything the Lord hates,"
she said, apologetically. "That you are . . . well, you know, sowing
discord among brethren here."

"Is that what you think, too?"

Here she raised her pink blotchy face and met my eyes at last.

"I don't know what to think," she said. "Anyway. I just wanted
you to have that. To know what's out there."

"Thanks, I guess." I tried for a brave smile but my voice wa-
vered.

Patty grabbed my hand and gave it a squeeze.

"It will be okay," she whispered, then turned and fled, her long
heavy skirt flapping and showing more ankle than I am sure she
would have liked.

I feel like I've been attending my own funeral. Patty was the
first in a parade of people in and out of here. Glum faces, awkward
silences, words that are meant to comfort me but don't. Not about
Grandma; I won't let anyone see her the way she is right now.
Roger and I have an understanding about that.

No. Everyone's trying to make me feel better about the mess
I've made for myself in this town. Smiley. Myra. Joe. "It's not your
fault," they say. "Come back as soon as you can. We miss you."

But they look so miserable.

All of them are caught in the middle. On the one hand, there's
Possum Flats and Fence and the newspaper that's employed them
and given everyone their news for years and years . . . and on the
other hand, there's me. It was easy to be my friend when we were
on the same team at *The Picayune*. But now it feels like I'm on the
wrong team, somehow. Even though I didn't want to be.

Smiley was especially valiant. "I've photographed one potato that looked like the Pope and Hazel found a two-headed garter snake in her garden," he said. "You really missed out."

When I wasn't able to crack a smile, he gave me a half-punch on the arm. "We need you, kid. I've gotten used to having you around."

Myra complained about having to do obits by herself. "You had the touch, honey pie. Even if you do prefer your citizens dead as doornails as opposed to 'passed away.'"

I was just glad I hadn't had to write Jimmy's obituary. I read it, though, and Myra did a great job skirting over the truth of how he had "gone to his heavenly reward."

And Joe? That was the worst.

I heard the knock on the door two nights ago, while Grandma was snoozing. Bounding out of the floral upholstered wing chair, I felt guilt at my excitement to break up the monotony of spending nearly every waking hour (and sleeping hour, too) at her side. But once at the front door, I found myself irritated at how little protection a screen door provides. There was nowhere for me to hide from the blond boy on our front steps.

And I desperately wanted to hide.

"Hey, Flower Child?" Joe's words were more of a question than a greeting. I didn't respond, which made him fidgety. It was weird seeing Joe unsure of himself.

The small squares of the screen door both darkened and blurred him, taking the edges off, making him seem unreal, like a dream. Why was he here? After his grandfather had ripped me, he was about the last person—besides Dash himself—that I had expected on my doorstep.

"Well, are you going to invite me in or just stare at me all day?"

"Unlike other females in Possum Flats, I have more important things to do than make moon eyes at you, Joe. Believe it or not."

Joe's laugh was a relief to us both.

"Well, I'm glad to hear that you're okay," he said. "I was worried all the drama might have gotten to you. Or are you just acting tough?"

He shaded his face with his hand and leaned nearer the screen to see better. For some reason, the small gesture totally undid me. I threw the door open, and pulled him inside, the screen door slamming behind us like an exclamation point.

I don't know who was more shocked when I reached my arms around him and started crying. I like to think I'm strong in the face of adversity, but show me a little sympathy and I exhibit all the backbone and mental toughness of a jellyfish. I was grateful Joe was there; that he cared how I was doing.

"Um . . . Daisy?" It sounded strange to hear him use my real name. When he realized I couldn't say anything back, his body relaxed and he wrapped me awkwardly against his chest. He smelled nice, like hot sun, soap and something else good. Green grass, maybe.

"I'm sorry," I said, through snot and tears. I was embarrassed. But I didn't back away.

"For what?" His voice near my ear was kind; his breath warm in my hair.

I made myself pull back then, although he wouldn't quite let me go. I was forced to look him in the eyes, their usual cool blue a couple of shades darker, troubled. Was he worried about me? Or maybe it was just a trick of the twilight.

"I never even wanted to be here in this stupid shit town in the first place, with all these people I don't know but who think they know everything there is to know about me. But I *tried*! I got the newspaper job and started to find out more about this place and its history and *my* history and I felt like Possum Flats was starting to be my town, too—"

Before I could finish my sentence, Joe's mouth was on mine. And instantly, every single thought in my head just evaporated . . . *Poof!* Joe was kissing me, rough-tender, a slight brush of whiskers before his lips touched mine. Warm but a little unsure. As if his mouth was wondering if this was okay, or if he had done the wrong thing. But my own mouth was light years ahead of my brain at that point: I kissed him back.

When he finally pulled away, we looked at each other with disbelief for a second. Then the shit-eating-grins took over.

"Wow, Flower Child."

Wow was right.

"This *is* your town," Joe began. He had released me from his arms, but somehow ended up with both my hands in his. "And I'm happy you're in it. Everything's going to be okay."

"No, it's not!" I shouted and yanked my hands from his, romance completely forgotten, reality setting back in. "You don't understand. If I hadn't come here and started digging around, everything would be fine. But I did and it's not."

"Come on," Joe said. "You can't believe that. What Chief Jeffers did was his own decision. You brought up the story, but his response is out of your control. And the Bro? Well . . ." Here, he just shook his head woefully. "He's just freaking out because he's an old man who wants the past to stay in the past. You've upset his applecart, that's all. He'll come around."

"He won't. And Jimmy Jeffers can't. But that's not even the worst of it."

I wiped my nose and face with my arm, which was super gross. Joe actually walked away from me at that point. Who could blame him? I slid down to the linoleum floor, defeated.

But then Joe came back. With a box of Kleenex. I took one, grateful that he hadn't left me after all. He knelt down beside me on the floor and watched worriedly as I rubbed at my face, then blew my nose with a loud honk.

When I had pulled myself together, he reached for my hand—the one without the crumpled-up Kleenex.

"Okay. So what's the worst of it?"

"My grandma isn't who she says she is," I said. "Apparently she's been impersonating her dead sister for the past fifty years."

Joe's eyes got big. But he managed to stay cool.

"Um . . . *what*?"

I poured out the story. About Grandma's twin sister, the other

Flowers girl. About the birthmark that made Violet distinct from Rose. And the explosion, which left only one of them alive.

"Yes. Rose," he said. "That's your grandma, Daisy."

"That's what she told me," I said. "That's what everyone in Possum Flats believed. But the birthmark I found on her neck last week told me something else."

Joe nodded. He was with me.

"*Violet*," I said. The word feels foreign, almost violent, in my mouth.

"Your grandma's name is Violet." Joe spoke slowly, as if he needed to give the words time to soak in.

"And that's not all," I said, trying to rush his thought process along.

"I can't imagine what else you could add to this," Joe said warily. "Go on."

"Are you sure you want to know? Because this has everything to do with you."

"Me?" Joe's eyebrows went up. Oh my God, I really liked this boy. That kiss. If I kept going with this conversation, I could lose it all. Lose him. But I had to tell him what I knew. I owed him that much. And, well . . . he asked.

"Yes," I held my breath for a moment. "I think you just kissed your cousin."

It is evening. The cicadas are buzzing in the trees outside, weirdly symphonic in the way their scratchy rhythm ebbs and flows. I'm still at Grandma's side, watching the backyard sky glow fiery red and brilliant, dripping orange before fading to a deep plum laced with the palest rose.

Rose. And violet.

Seeing those colors together makes me wonder where my grandma is right now. She goes in and out of consciousness, never clear long enough to talk. Is she with Rose? Twins are supposed to have a special connection. Does it go beyond the boundaries of this life? Are their spirits hanging out with each other right now?

Looking at Grandma's bruised and bandaged face, the lines on her forehead and the puckering around her mouth, it isn't too hard to imagine her slipping permanently to whatever waits on the other side. If Rose is there, that might just pull her over the edge on which she is balancing so precariously.

No, I say to Rose. *You can't have her. Not yet.*

There is so much I want to ask Grandma. Until two weeks ago, I didn't know *what* to ask. Since she wasn't who I thought she was. Who *anyone* thought she was.

I have to hand it to you, Violet. You took advantage of a bad situation. But was she just a selfish opportunist? I don't know everything about her, but I know her heart. There has to be more to the story.

The light is nearly gone. And with it, all the colors. Purples replaced by black; pinks muted into gray. The insects and tree frogs are in full throat, but will soon tamp it down, lending the night a comforting hum.

Like the backyard, I have been slowly blanketed by the dusk, my outline softened and indistinct in the half light. I reach one of my hands to my face, tracing my lips with an index finger. I am thinking about Joe. And that kiss. Did he feel something?

I did.

But what I feel now is a deep, painful regret. What if he kissed me for the wrong reason, like pity? Or maybe that kiss was my only chance with him. My first kiss . . . and I didn't take one extra minute to enjoy it. I had to immediately open my big, stupid mouth and wreck everything.

As soon as I saw that birthmark, everything began falling into place. Joe hasn't had the time I've had to puzzle it out. As soon as I'd finished spewing out all of my facts and theories, he went dark, closed up like a Possum Flats store on Sunday. He shook his head repeatedly, as though he couldn't make the necessary leaps and assumptions. It did not compute. Then he took off, the screen door banging like a thunder clap behind him. Gone for good, I imagined. His own good.

I feel very alone. Deserted by people I've come to feel something for these past months. Everyone at *The Picayune*—Patty, Smiley, Myra . . . even Fence. Joe. Grandma. And of course, my mom is nowhere to be found when I need her the most. As usual.

Tears start to fill my eyes and I realize that sitting in the dark is not helping my frame of mind. I fumble for the switch on the bedside lamp, and just like that, light disappears the dark. And while it doesn't change anything about my situation, I immediately feel better. Less alone somehow.

That's when I see that Grandma is awake. Really awake. Not panicked or confused. She is just taking everything in, as if she is inventorying her room, her life, and finding things more or less as she expected. Her eyes finally rest on me.

"Welcome back, Grandma," I say, with more spunk than I feel.

She is studying my face, looking for clues as to what has gone on, what she has missed.

"Daisy."

Her voice is the barest whisper, rough, like a low tire on a gravel road. I have to lean in to make out what she says next, and take one of her hands.

"Tell me . . . everything."

So I do. Well, *almost* everything.

How Roger and I found her facedown in her own blood, sure she was dead. About Jimmy Jeffers' funeral, featuring the old pastor's fiery eulogy that basically labeled me the spawn of Satan. How Fence told me Jimmy Jeffers' death was my fault. And that I hadn't been back to *The Picayune* since, despite Smiley and Myra and Patty's encouragement. That they—and so many other Possum Flats citizens—had dropped by the house with cards, a mason jar of fresh-cut zinnias, casseroles or a crumb cake.

At this, Grandma interrupts: "I hope to hell you didn't let them see me like this. I may be old, but I'm still a little vain," she says, touching her bandaged face gingerly.

"Of course not," I say. "Not even Joe."

"Joe?" There is a pause, a single beat. My cheeks burn and I hate that I'm powerless to stop them.

"Well, I guess I missed out on quite a bit while I was . . . gone," she says. I am so relieved to hear that note of sarcasm in her voice that I don't even care that it's directed my way. Everything I've been holding back these last ten days surges inside me, like the swell of a wave. Tears slide down my cheeks and I do nothing to stop them.

"Daisy?" Grandma tries to pull herself up from her pillows. I've managed to surprise her. We have lived together for three months and she's never seen me like this.

She presses my hand in hers. "You haven't been worrying about me now, have you, child? My time will inevitably come, probably sooner than I'd like. But for now, I'm not going anywhere. You know I'm a tough old bird."

"Okay," I manage, reaching for another Kleenex. "But I'm not sure that I *do* actually know you that well. *Violet.*"

For the second time in as many minutes, I've managed to befuddle my grandma.

"Oh," is all she says. She sinks back into the pillows, lets go of my hand. "I see."

Grandma sighs deeply. Resignation? Relief? I inch forward on my chair, unsure of what's coming next. Whatever it is, I don't want to miss a word.

"Well, you better grab your notepad and a couple of sharp pencils." She smiles weakly. "It's a long, complicated story. But it's time to tell it." Another sigh. "To you *and* to Possum Flats."

Wait. She wants me to write this for *The Picayune*?

"Um . . . are you sure about this?"

"Never been more certain. I'm going to be your final installment, Daisy," she says calmly. "I owe you that. But I owe it to myself, too. And Rose."

I am out of my chair, stumbling toward my backpack, which has lain untouched for weeks. I dig around frantically for my notepad and pencils.

I've got to hurry before she changes her mind.

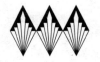

Violet-Rose

I fell asleep fully dressed on the couch, covered with a crocheted afghan, waiting for my twin sister to come home from the dance.

Mother had gone to bed long before, after brushing her waist-length silver hair the requisite one hundred strokes and meticulously tucking every last strand beneath her nightcap. Before heading to her room, she had touched my own dark glossy bob with wonder. "Now you've gone and made yourselves impossible to tell apart again, haven't you?" She sighed. "Even for your poor old mother."

If she only knew.

"Won't you go to bed then, Rose?" she said. "You look so pale. And you barely ate a bite of dinner."

I didn't want to think about that paltry portion of pot roast and potatoes I had forced down. Dinner had been just Mother and me, the only sounds the scraping of silverware on our chipped porcelain plates. I had to excuse myself from the table, barely making it to the bathroom. I retched until there was nothing left, then retched some more, the toilet water yellow-green with bile. When I couldn't stand any longer, I knelt. The dry heaving hurt my midsection most of all.

I was ignorant enough about my own body to wonder if I could actually throw up a baby. It felt possible. But I was getting used to it, having spent every morning and evening of the past week close to our bathroom.

If my mother suspected anything, she was either too polite to mention it, or simply refusing to acknowledge what might be going on. So I was left to my own dark thoughts. I didn't want to admit to myself what I knew to be true: There were the beginnings of a baby inside of me. A baby I neither wanted nor—if the way it made me feel was any measure—wanted to be with me.

I remember clearly what I was dreaming that night on the couch. I was alone in a gorgeous green park. It was not dry, dusty August but the height of spring. There were spectacular flowerbeds everywhere I looked—a formal rose garden with tea roses in every imaginable color; another with orange-red geraniums set off in a border of spiky purple salvia; a bed with a mix of maroon foxglove, coral bells, blue bellflowers and purple-y campanula, rallying around the taller rich blue of staked delphinium. But it was a single red daylily that caught my eye, growing right in the middle of the perfectly mowed grass. It was surely a volunteer, a mistake—and yet it was so gorgeous. The red was almost carmine, set against the brilliant orange stamen that sprang from filaments deep within the bloom, covered with a rich dusting of yellow pollen. I reached to pick the flower—for what harm was it, to pick something that obviously doesn't belong? Something that would be destroyed with the next mowing? But just as my hand reached for the stem, the flower closed up, tight as an umbrella, slipped through my fingers and disappeared down into the ground. Then the strange lily popped up a few feet away, stems and all, pushing itself up through the grass as if it were growing in seconds rather than days. Again, I grabbed for the slender stem, only to have it fold in upon itself and disappear. My frustration grew as the flower teased me, disappearing and reappearing, taking me further into the park, deeper into the shadowy trees that formed a dark forest at its edge.

The red lily had just reappeared in the dim light when I heard my sister's voice: "Violet!"

But she was nowhere to be seen. I hurried toward the lily and into the forest—where the darkness now felt menacing, rather than cool and welcoming. I extended my hand once more toward the flower before I was close enough to reach it, my fingers spread and ready to yank the wily stem.

"Help me!" My sister's voice was frightened, pleading. I spun around but saw no one, just the subtle movement of wind through the shadowy boughs. When I turned back around, I just caught sight of the lily's pointed red tips, tight as a robin's beak, retreating into the earth.

"Violet!"

This last cry of distress finally woke me. I sat up, disoriented, my heart racing, the fine hairs prickling on the back of my neck. The room glowed amber from the table lamp beside the couch. The mantel clock showed a few minutes after eleven. I willed myself to calm down, to scatter the upsetting dream from my mind like dust from a beaten rug.

But then it was as if all of the air in the front parlor was suddenly sucked out, gone. There was a flash of light outside the windows and then an earth-shattering boom. The floor rumbled beneath the couch, I rolled and pitched as if I were on a small damask boat. The windows rattled in their frames. What was happening? An earthquake? I had never felt one, although our closeness to the New Madrid fault in the Missouri Bootheel made everyone wary. There were rumors that an 1812 earthquake centered there had rung church bells in Boston.

But the flash? It didn't make sense. And as suddenly as the rumbling and rattling had begun, it was over. At the front windows, I stared at the penumbra of orange-gold light around downtown five blocks away, a strange and wondrous halo.

That time had an odd, stretched-out feeling. Mother joined me at the window, her sleeping cap at a rakish angle, grinding the sleep from her eyes with her fists like a child.

"What has happened?" Her whisper held only a hint of alarm. Neither of us understood yet that something in our small, safe universe had shifted radically, irrevocably, and that our very hearts would soon feel torn from our bodies. We were still in that blissful state of unknowing, unaffected by whatever was going on downtown—and only mildly curious, at that late hour, what it might be.

But then came the sound of someone running hard down the sidewalk from the direction of downtown. In the streetlight, we saw a young man come to a halt right in front of our apartment building. He wasn't wearing a stitch of clothing. My mother turned away, whether in horror or modesty, I can't say. But I was mesmerized by this naked envoy from the square, watching him turn in circles on the sidewalk in a daze. He was flapping his arms, bringing one, then the other, up to his face. I thought maybe he was drunk or disturbed, but his gestures were more desperate than that. He was sobbing.

"Rose, don't you dare go out there!"

But I ignored my mother—and not just because she called me the wrong name—drawn to this naked boy bawling on our sidewalk. He didn't seem to see me, even though I was right in front of him, unwinding the afghan from my own shoulders and draping it around him. His face was scraped and bleeding, one eye bruised and nearly swollen shut; his chest and legs had a scalded look. The remnants of his underwear looped loosely around one ankle as he shivered in the hot night.

"Are you all right?" I asked. I recognized him then: Smiley Barnes. Not much more than a boy, fifteen or sixteen at most, his face still smooth.

"The dance hall blowed up," he said.

"What?" I understood the words, but my mind could not take in their meaning.

"The dance hall blowed up," he said again, simply. He swiped at his eyes with the afghan, smearing blood and tears across his cheek.

"Lamb's?"

"It blowed up and everyone with it. Then the fire came and there ain't hardly nothing or no one left." He covered his face with both hands. "My friends was with me. And now they ain't. Blowed sky-high with the rest of 'em dancing."

But I wasn't really listening anymore. A cavernous pit had stretched open in my stomach. *Rose.* My sweet Rose.

Nothing mattered but finding her, reconnecting with my other half. I began to run barefoot toward downtown.

"Rose! Where are you going?" I stopped briefly and turned to see my mother on the stoop, pulling a shawl around her nightdress.

"Something's happened downtown," I said. "Get that boy home. I've got to find my sister."

Damn you, Dash Emmonds. I harbored a strange hope that he had somehow talked my innocent sister off the dance floor and into his back seat—a thought that I had banished from my mind earlier in the evening, when I had wished jealously, desperately, to be in her shoes. To be on his arm. Maybe they were somewhere else, in another, much tamer kind of trouble—outside Lamb's for a smoke or a couple of snorts of gin. Or, even better, at Morton's for an ice cream soda.

These were my thoughts as I ran toward downtown and the flames that flickered in my view. Later I would find that I had savaged my feet by running so recklessly down that rough sidewalk, littered with broken glass from the businesses lining the downtown square and even those blocks away from Lamb's.

But at that moment, I felt nothing but the overwhelming need to get to Rose. I ignored the fear that had lain heavy on my heart since waking from that terrifying dream, when I heard my sister call my name for the last time.

I put my head down and ran.

I remember teaching my sister to dance. We waited until Mother was out delivering all the laundry and mending she had done, then rolled up the floral rug on the living room floor and pushed the creaky velvet armchair and old damask sofa against one wall. Then we put on our pumps, just for the flirty feel of it. There's nothing like a little heel for sex appeal. Especially for the Charleston.

"You can't dance like that." I was exasperated by my sister's timidity. Rose had blushed her way through the Lindy and was now attempting the Charleston. She bent her knees stiffly, wiping her arms in front of them as she opened and closed her legs. The timing was all wrong. "No! Your arms cross the opposite way of your knees. So it looks sharp, like this."

I started the record player over, dropping the needle at just the right groove. The Victrola was our one luxury, and our mother would kill us if she knew we were using it without supervision.

I bent my own knees, slashing my arms in front of them, my knees opening and closing in time to the beat.

"I can't!" she cried. "Besides, it looks so . . . naughty."

"Oh, it's naughty all right," I said with a flip of my bob. "But it wouldn't hurt for you to open your legs now and again."

"Violet!"

"You might find out it's fun. Just another thing Mother has been lying to us about."

"What do you mean?"

"She says good girls don't do that. Or anything! But what are we saving ourselves for, anyway? Husbands who don't dance and get fat and gray? And give you a houseful of children? Not this gal."

Rose considered this. She thought she knew everything about her sister. "Have you really done it then, Violet?"

I made a little circle on the floor, both hands up and sashaying side to side with each step. I stopped when the music ended, looked up through my lashes and held my mouth in an O.

"Not yet, Sis, but I will. I want to see what all the fuss is about."

Rose reflexively closed her thighs beneath her tweed skirt. "But . . . what if something, you know, happens?"

"Don't worry about me, Sis. Worry about yourself. You're going to dry up down there if you don't have some fun once in a while. George try anything yet?" I raised my eyebrows up and down a couple of times. "If you know what I mean?"

"*Violet!*" Blood flamed her face up to her hairline. "George is a gentleman. Maybe you should try one sometime."

"Has he kissed you yet?"

"Just once," she whispered. "On the cheek."

"Rose! And did you feel his hard . . . *salami* when he pressed up against you?"

Rose's eyes grew large. She took a pillow from the sofa and threw it at me, as I ducked and chortled. At the sound of a key in the entrance, we scrambled to put the room back together, falling over each other in our haste. I smoothed the rug; Rose nearly dropped the record as she slid it back in its sleeve. We had both flounced down onto the repositioned sofa when our mother breezed in, removing her worn white gloves one finger at a time.

"Dancing again, girls?" she said, giving the room a once-over before heading to the kitchen to start supper.

We looked at each other and laughed so hard it felt like we would never catch our breath. I leaned in to whisper in Rose's ear: "Salami!"

The giggling fit began all over again. I wanted that feeling to last forever, to stay inside that laughter with my sister. Just the two of us, always.

The square was thronged with people—officials like firemen, policemen, a sheriff's deputy, a night watchman from one of the banks, a doctor—and then regular people like me, arriving by the minute. We converged on the four streets that formed the square and pushed and shoved our way east toward Lamb's like a herd of spooked cattle. There was shouting and warnings to look out for the fallen bricks and shattered glass. An alarm sounded at one of the banks, its large plate-glass windows completely blown out. In the middle of the square, the grand Gothic courthouse sat sad and crooked, windows destroyed and frames hanging askew.

I was frantic to find my twin. The people I jostled against must have felt the same way. There were desperate calls of mothers and fathers for their children, people yelling for spouses, siblings, friends. I searched for my own face, my own mirror image, in every passing profile.

But I didn't need to call her name like these wide-eyed, shell-shocked others shouting out hoarsely, hopelessly, all around me. If she were close by, I knew she would feel my presence as surely as I would hers. It was like a sixth sense; a connectedness that often meant we read each other's thoughts, but sometimes was viscerally physical as well. As small children, when one of us would fall down, the other one cried.

Which was why I felt so terrified.

I didn't have that low hum of connection, that invisible filament that had bound us together our whole lives. I hadn't even understood that it existed, before it didn't anymore. I had thought that what we had was normal, the way everyone felt.

The crowd had grown now into a tide of dazed humanity, pushing its way past Possum Flats Savings & Loan and onto East Main. But then the people in front of me stopped short and I nearly lost my balance. I was shoved from behind, as the momentum that had built up in our forward progress halted abruptly.

Impatiently, I waded my way through, using my small size to advantage, bobbing and weaving into every sliver of space that opened up. When I reached the front of the crowd, there was a terrible, awful silence as each person took in the scene before us. It became quickly apparent why we had all stopped: There was no place to go.

The building that housed the grocery next to the bank was gone—as were the next two buildings down, including Lamb's. Instead, there was an enormous, yawning pit full of broken bricks, concrete and fallen beams that covered nearly a full block. And in that pit were fierce orange-blue flames so bright that I wanted to turn away, to shield my eyes from what looked like the entrance to hell. But I couldn't, numbly taking in the massive hole piled with heaps upon heaps of glowing embers.

The heat was so intense, it felt as if we were baking in a cruel midday August sun even though it was midnight. The firemen ringing the pit directed woefully inadequate streams of water toward the raging flames. Smoke and steam wafted from the debris, choking us where we stood in that slender slice of silence, the downbeat before understanding took over—and from there, hysteria.

Policemen attempted to hold back the weeping, raging mob from the wreckage—frantic in our helplessness, our disbelief. Where was everyone who had been at the dance? The musicians, the dancers, the coat-check girl inside? The drinkers, smokers and gossipers who hung out idly on the balcony, the side alley or the front sidewalk?

Rose wasn't here. She couldn't be here.

"What the hell, woman? Watch where you're going!"

I began to back away from the perimeter of the pit, while being elbowed, shoved, and cursed by those who hadn't yet made it to the edge. I became aware of my bare feet, the consistency of raw hamburger on the bottom, while the tops got crushed by the heels of boots and shoes. But the pain didn't fully register. I didn't have room for it alongside the jagged fear that had taken over my entire body, making it feel as though all my nerves and blood vessels and organs were on the outside of my skin, screaming for relief.

When I finally made it to the back of the crowd, I paused, turning in a slow circle. I was still trying to figure out where everyone at Lamb's had gone. They had to be somewhere. People didn't just disappear.

Eventually, I ended up near the broken courthouse, the lawn filled with people scurrying like ants at a picnic. There was a dapper young man dragging another, zombie-like, by the hand; a man in his nightclothes heaving a limp young woman in a scorched sequined gown over his shoulder. Voices barked instructions, called out desperately for the missing.

That was when I saw the bodies.

They were lined up along the sidewalk and draped in whole or part by blankets, jackets and suit coats, tarps and even burlap feed sacks. There must have been a dozen of them, at least. I could see a man's forearm with a wristwatch sticking out from beneath a spread overcoat, a bare foot from beneath a blanket.

I turned my head to the side and vomited.

"Jesus!" said the unfortunate recipient beside me. I looked up to apologize to the man but then I was collapsing away from him, the frantic crowd, and the vulnerable-looking row of the newly dead.

When I came to, I was in a hospital bed. But not in Possum Flats Hospital, the quaint, one-story cottage just north of the city park that had been added to over the years until it resembled a failed experiment with children's blocks. This was one massive, high-ceilinged room where I lay in a low cot in a long row of similar cots filled with patients in various states of sleeping and waking. Many were swathed in bandages like mummies, or had an arm or leg in a cast. A long clothesline ran the length of the room near the foot of the beds and was clothespinned with bedsheets, a makeshift divider of sorts. From the moans of pain, I realized there must be more beds on the other side. On the cot next to me, a completely bandaged body cried out through the single mouth hole in the gauze wrapped around its face and eyes.

The smell of antiseptic was strong but tinged with the odor of urine. Where was I? My feet burned and throbbed with every beat of my heart, sticking out at the bottom of my bed and swaddled like newborns. It looked like a hospital on the front lines. The Great War was not that far removed from my consciousness, even though I had been just a child then. I remembered the fear that colored those years, although my mother had reassured us that the war was far away. And the deprivation, the coupons and rations and Rose and I never being able to have new dresses. When one is already poor, it is hard to do with even less.

Suddenly the divider sheet at the foot of my bed was yanked aside to reveal my mother in her Sunday dress, a brown jersey shirtwaist with darker brown belt and her round-toed pumps, re-heeled and polished to a reluctant shine. But whose large male hand was holding open the sheet for her?

"Oh, my dear! You're awake."

I didn't have the strength or the clarity to respond. But she didn't need encouragement. She pulled open a squeaky metal folding chair there in the narrow space between my cot and my neighbor's. But I was fixated on the pale, freckly boy behind her who couldn't meet my eyes. I probably looked frightening. Or maybe he wasn't made of very sturdy stuff.

He stood against the sheet, his overlarge hands stuffed into his tan twill pants. George Steinkamp. From the funeral home. I couldn't figure out why he would be there. I wasn't dead. At least, I didn't think I was.

He started fidgeting and I realized I was staring. I turned toward my mother, small and weary, her flesh as thin and translucent as an onion skin. She shrank further under my scrutiny.

"You gave us a fright," she said, reaching for my hand. I saw a nurse attending to a poor bandaged lump at the end of my row. A visitor sat nearby, speaking in soothing tones.

"The armory is being put to good use," she said at last.

The armory. Of course. I was in the armory. But why?

My mother reached over to smooth my hair away from my face and it released a smell of smoke, not cigarette or wood smoke, but something more chemical. I shuddered as the night before came back to me.

The explosion. The fire. The bodies. My anguished search for my twin.

"Rose?"

My mother's loud whisper pulled me back to the gray high-ceilinged armory, where every footstep, cough and moan echoed like a pronouncement from on high. I noted the dark, crepey half-moons under her bloodshot eyes, and this gawky stranger who couldn't string two words together for his own girlfriend's sister.

And why was she asking about Rose? I tried to speak, but I couldn't make any sounds, my throat rough as a washboard. Of course, I already knew the answer to her question, to the only question that I might have asked, too: Is my sister all right? The stark absence of that thin, buzzing thread connecting us was all the proof I needed. The silencing of her voice had silenced my own, whether in sympathy or simply because alone, I had nothing worth saying. I began taking the measure of a life without her, wondering if it were even worth living.

"They found her at least," my mother said. She let go of my hand long enough to press a perfectly ironed handkerchief to her eyes. "There's so many they haven't found. All burned up or blown to bits . . ." Her voice broke. She nodded to George and he stepped closer to me. The look on his face was both apologetic and pained; this was not where he wanted to be or what he wanted to be doing. I pitied him.

He dug into a pocket and removed a handkerchief, too. But this one was not pristine with crisp seams like my mother's. It was a black-smudged, crumpled affair with blue trim. A man's handkerchief. He unwrapped the small bundle in his palm with the freckled finger of the other hand, pulling back each edge as though it were a delicate flower petal.

It was my locket. The golden heart with the tiny diamond at its center. The fragile chain was blackened with soot and the heart itself smudgy. But it was my locket, no doubt, the one that Dash had given me just two short months ago. A lifetime ago.

With great effort, I held out my hand to receive what he offered with wonder—like a communion wafer or holy relic. I thought about the brutal fire that had desecrated this necklace, and the slender white throat it once encircled. A throat identical to my own. It *should* have been my own! I closed my eyes, sinking back into the thin hospital pillows. But I didn't cry. I didn't say a word.

I just wanted to die.

"Rose."

Rose was dead. And I couldn't begin to imagine those horrific moments when she may have suffered so greatly, broken or crushed by debris. How she might have watched her death approaching in the monstrous tongues of the flames. I said a silent prayer that she had not known any of it, that she had been spared that suffering.

But from that agonizing plea I had heard in my head, I knew

that wasn't the reality. She had been conscious at the last. It was a burden I would never be able to shed, nor share with anyone else.

"Rose?"

Why did she keep repeating her name? There was anguish in my mother's voice. Couldn't she understand what I was feeling? How this new, ugly hole in my center could never scab over? Briefly, I wondered at her fixation on the dead, when she still had one treasured daughter in front of her. Injured, yes, but alive. *What of Violet?* I wanted to say, but could not. *What about Violet?*

My eyes flew open. I stared at my mother and then at George. Of course! It became clear in that moment that they still believed that I was Rose and that it was Violet—poor Violet!—who was gone.

My mother mumbled something about giving us a minute, rising with great effort and disappearing behind the thin sheet. George gave me a shy, embarrassed look and edged nearer. He patted my shoulder in a completely inadequate gesture of sympathy.

I barely noticed. My thoughts were tumbling over themselves in a race to make sense of this strange world I had opened my eyes to. In this world, I was no longer who people thought I was. Instead, I was someone I knew as well as I knew myself, of course, but who was unlike me in so many ways.

I thought of the life that I had ahead of me and involuntarily, I winced. I was pregnant. Before that, I had had few real prospects for employment—I was just a good-time girl living off her mother—and now I had none. Dash would have no interest in fatherhood. Or marriage. I had already felt his eye beginning to wander after he fastened that necklace around my throat and made off with my virginity. Not that I had minded. I knew what I was getting into when I fell for Dash Emmonds. The sum total of his ambition could fit on the head of a pin. But I was young and having fun, not worried about my future.

But now it wasn't just me. It was "us," this baby and I.

I closed my eyes again and let go of a sigh so deep that it seemed

to contain not just my breath, but my spirit, too. It was as though I
were taking my last breath as Violet . . . and when my eyes finally
opened back up, I was Rose.

The decision was that quick. It was that easy. Everything that
would come afterwards?

Not so much.

I looked with renewed interest at this overgrown boy who hov-
ered uncomfortably at my bedside. Could I like him? I mean,
really like him? Enough to make a life with him? He returned my
gaze and his blue eyes were warm and honest. I could see clearly
that he adored me—or, at least, the person he believed me to be.
Nice guys held no charm for me. But if Rose had found him worthy of her affection, I knew without a doubt that he was a better
man than I deserved.

I said nothing. I didn't trust myself to speak.

Instead, I reached for one of those large freckly hands with one
of my small, white ones. It was warm and dry, not the funereal
chill and clamminess I'd expected.

George blushed again, deeply, but held my eyes.

"Rose . . ." he began, as if he needed to ask me something.

But I just shook my head. I wasn't yet ready to speak for my
sister. For my new self. I needed a little more time to get used to
the new person in my old skin.

My feet began throbbing more painfully. It had been too long
since my last dose of morphine. All I wanted to do was sleep, a
deep healing sleep with no pain or dreams or sounds. And when I
woke up, I would feel like a whole new person. I would be a whole
new person.

I would be Rose.

After a week in the infirmary, it was time to go home. Mother
had brought me a prim gray shirtwaist for the occasion and it
matched my mood: colorless, patternless, revealing nothing that
wasn't absolutely necessary. I had put it on and was lying in my
cot, contemplating my feet. They were still painful, but the nurses

who changed the dressings told me the blisters were no longer oozing and the jagged cuts from the glass and gravel had mostly scabbed over. I hadn't seen my damaged feet for myself. From the vantage point of my pillows, they seemed unconnected to me, so heavily swathed in bandages that they looked like two large profiteroles.

There was a sudden screech of metal as an ancient nurse named Maxine yanked my curtain back and rolled in a wooden wheelchair.

"Your young man is here to take you home," she said. "What a nice boy," she added, appearing to search my face for some evidence of worthiness. She didn't seem convinced that I had any redeeming qualities. It was no secret that she and the other nurses felt that I had landed in their care due to my overly dramatic antics. I was taking up precious hours of bedside care that should be distributed among the truly needy, those injured in the explosion. Not some hysterical teenager. After all, practically everyone in Possum Flats had lost a family member, friend or neighbor. What made me so special?

None of this was ever said aloud. But I could feel it in their cool, quick movements as they unwound my bandages and how they looked through me instead of at me. I know now it was just their means of coping, like the rest of Possum Flats, trying to categorize and make sense of the awful loss. *Why that person and not this one?*

I was waiting in the wheelchair on the sidewalk, where Maxine had abandoned me, when George pulled up to the curb in the hearse. The sun glinted off the shiny black paint of the long, box-like car, an ironic play between light and dark. George got out of the driver's side and opened the passenger door.

"Sorry about the ride," he said. "Dad needed the other car for a business call this morning, so that left me with the Grim Reaper. I hope you don't mind."

"No, it's absolutely perfect," I said. I could feel him looking at me oddly. But I couldn't put into words the way I felt right then, as if my old life—my mortal remains—truly were being hauled off.

I was leaving the last of my old self behind, being drawn into this new life with George and dead people. Not to mention the life inside me, growing and asserting itself more forcefully each day. I wanted to crawl back into the cool, starched sheets of my make-shift hospital room and the unconsciousness of pain medicine.

"Rose?"

George looked unsure what to do next. I stretched my arms up to him and in the next instant, he lifted me up under my gray-skirted knees and carried me to the car. I buried my face in his neck, inhaling the faint smell of formaldehyde that I would soon grow to detest and then, over time—was it months or years?—did not smell at all.

Back in our little apartment, everything reminded me of Rose. My mother had done her best to put away the evidence of her last hours here: scarves and belts and slips and shoes that had been tried on, scrutinized and discarded, strewn haphazardly across our twin beds and the floor of our room as we had dressed her for the dance. But now her dresses and skirts hung like ghosts in our closet; her tops and underthings neatly stacked in two of the four bureau drawers. Mine were the top two, of course, since she always let me choose first. Why did that make me feel like crying?

But the bathroom was the worst. My mother had done what she knew how to do: clean and launder. There were no stockings drying on the edge of the bathtub, slightly crisp in the toes and smelling faintly of feet; no undergarments hanging damply and demurely over the dark wooden towel rack.

"Mother!" I cried out when I saw the starkness of the tiled bathroom, my nostrils filling with the bleach that meant spotless floors, white sink and tub; the vinegar that allowed the mirror to provide a perfect reflection of my distress. But as bad as it was not to smell her face powder—our face powder—and the lilac water that we favored, that was nothing compared to the heartbreaking absence of the ordinary, functional tools of our daily lives: my toothbrush and hairbrush were gone!

"Mother, what have you done with my brushes?" Two tiny nails in the wall right above the sink; only one pink toothbrush. Beside the mirror was a white wooden shelf which held our toiletries: there was our lilac water, our tin of Glossine, the shared arnica toothpaste. But only Rose's hairbrush remained, gold plated with a delicate pink rose on its ceramic oval back.

I heard my mother's hurried footsteps, then her gray head peeked around the door. "Why, Rose. Those *are* yours. I thought I should put Violet's away, you know . . ." Her voice trailed off. "But now I see I've done the wrong thing." Her eyes began to glisten. She put the toilet lid down and sat down beside where I perched on the edge of the claw-foot tub. I could not look at her face, afraid of the grief I would see there—strangely, grief for *me*. For Violet.

I had forgotten who I was. Who I had chosen to be.

I had not realized, when I made the decision in the hospital bed, how confusing this would be. I had no doubt I could be a convincing Rose—we did look so very much alike. But in my fevered state of suffering and grieving, I had not considered all the little things that make up a life, a person.

Just seeing a single dark hair sticking out from the head of the brush made me panicked and weepy. Her hairbrush was the one item that Rose absolutely would not share with me and that I didn't dare co-opt with my communist leanings.

"I don't want your cooties," she always said, half teasing, half serious. "And you never clean out your brush!" This pronouncement was made with a pointed glance at my own hairbrush, a purple-flowered version of her own, but with the look of a dark furry animal where the bristles hid beneath a thick, matted collection of my hair. How could I brush my hair with her hairbrush? Or more impossibly, how could I keep it pristine, as Rose always had? The overwhelming burden of adopting not only my sister's physical being, but her habits and worldview, made me feel like giving up. I could confess my dishonesty to my mother right here, right now in this bathroom. And while it would be a terrible thing to admit to having put her through—the loss of a daughter, just not the one she had thought!—I felt sure she would forgive me. I could blame the whole thing on the explosion, the emotional wreckage from the loss of my best friend and twin sister; my inability to separate myself from her mentally or physically. It sounded a little crazy, but I knew it fit Violet to a T. It was just the kind of reckless, selfish stunt I would pull, with total disregard for others. More material with which the town gossips would feather my nest as the out-of-control, thoughtless, zany twin to my sister's Pollyanna goodness. A goodness that, while real—I could admit without grudge—would rise to mythical status if everyone knew Rose died in that dance hall instead of me.

"Mother," I began.

And then I felt it. A twinge down deep in the center of my body that I understood as "quickening," the slight bubble-burst in the womb when life asserts itself, moving perceptibly for the first time. I almost fell backwards into the bathtub.

My mother's thin arm shot out to steady me. "Rose? Are you all right?"

I felt awful watching her face, etched with lines and curves like a thick, hand-stitched quilt, and so much deeper than before the explosion. Her dark eyes flitted over me, searching anxiously for whatever had caused me distress. A strange sadness washed over me, something like the pity one feels for the very young—an ache for all they don't yet know, along with a yearning for one's own lost innocence. I couldn't take away her pain, but I had to protect her as best I could from additional suffering.

I couldn't come clean.

For her sake *and* my baby's. I needed Rose's life to give order to everyone's world. Violet was dead. *I* was dead. Which was—as terrible as it sounded—the right choice. Like the Old Testament, vengeful-God stories of Noah or Sodom and Gomorrah: the wicked had perished; the sinner had reaped the reward of her sins. And meanwhile, the good, dutiful daughter was left to live out her remaining days. There was a terrible beauty in the justice of it all. Only I would know the truth: God did not care a speck.

And I desperately needed Rose's good life, the kind, dependable heart she had found in George. In that life, with that man, my baby could grow up without the stigma of an unwed mother. We could avoid the disapproving looks and the whispers that would follow almost imperceptibly in our wake, like a soft spring wind in new grass, gone when you turn to look, everything still and perfect. As if you had just imagined it.

"I'm fine," I finally said. My mother patted my knee, relieved.

"I know it looks like I tried to clean Violet out of the house. I thought it would help to get rid of the little reminders." She sighed. "I should have known that the absence of those things would make you think of her, too, which is even worse. I'm sorry."

She was close to tears. It was my turn to reassure her. "No, Mother. I understand what you were trying to do. I appreciate it."

How could I say that every missing item was like an open window, a tiny portal into a vaster, darker emptiness that was life without my twin?

"I kept something for you," she said, rising from the toilet seat and smoothing her skirt. "It was yours, actually."

While I waited on the edge of the tub for her to return, I cupped my soft belly with one hand. Nothing. *You chose the right time to say hello.* Clever baby.

When I heard my mother coming, I took my hand away. What something of mine had I lost or misplaced that she would have found and kept for me? I couldn't think of a solitary thing.

"Here," she said with a pleased look, thrusting a satin drawstring bag onto my lap. It had heft for its size, which was about that of a kitten. I slowly untied the pale purple cords, a darker shade than the bag itself. When I pulled the bag open, I gasped.

"I thought you'd be surprised," my mother said, satisfied. "I found it that night, after you had gone to bed and Violet was off with Dash. You two girls had gone crazy, by the looks of the place, all those skirts and dresses and shoes all over your bedroom. And then that left by the sink."

I pulled out a long coil of dark, painstakingly braided hair. My mother had gone to great efforts to gather Rose's hair from her im-promptu bob that night, putting the ragged lengths together, trim-ming them evenly and intertwining them into one glossy whole. Each end of the braid was secured with one of Rose's pink hair ribbons.

I dropped the hair as if it were a snake. My mother, seeing my agitation, tried to smooth the coil in my lap.

"I don't know what got into you that night," she said. "I would have never thought you would part with that hair of yours. It was beautiful," she said, stroking the hair with a hand reddened from bleach and suds. "*Is* beautiful."

I couldn't believe Rose had let me cut her hair, either. Neither of us were acting like ourselves that night. But I had wheedled and cajoled and finally overcome her uncertainty with big sisterly authority—those seventeen minutes of seniority that I always had on her—and my inability to take no for an answer. She had agreed to be me for a night, not realizing she would end up being me for eternity. And I wielded the scissors quickly and decisively, Rose's locks falling like dark rain onto the tile floor.

"I feel so . . . light," she had exclaimed, shaking her shorn head and laughing. "And wild!"

"Be careful," I had chided her. "Dash likes his women a little wild. If you want my two cents, I would stay on the dance floor and out of the back seat."

"Hmmm, like you always do?" Rose gave a devilish laugh, and I had to join in. After all, who was I to give advice? And yet, part of my laughter was rueful. She had no idea how much trouble I had gotten myself into, my morning sickness something that she, in her innocence, would not recognize for what it was.

"Thank you," I managed at last. My mother patted my hand, turning it over and pressing the braid into my open palm. She had no idea the gift she had given me.

"I guess you just wanted to be a little more like Violet," she said. "I can't blame you. You've always been a good girl, Rose. But

I've often wondered if you know how to have a good time. Violet had that in spades." She turned to leave. "I'd never have said that to her, though. She didn't need any more encouragement."

Alone in the bathroom at last, I reached out one of my bandaged feet to close the door and finally allowed myself to have a good cry, clutching my sister's hair in my hands like an amulet, like a desperate prayer. I felt the hole in my heart of two lives lost, my sister's and my own.

It would be the only time I allowed myself that luxury.

I did not see much of George the entire next week. He had dropped by a couple of times, but always stood awkwardly, refusing a chair, until my mother told him to "skedaddle" and get back to helping his family. Scores of dead all at once meant big business for Steinkamp & Son. George and his father Hermann and mother Gladys—the unnamed but essential partner in that family funeral business—were working nearly twenty-four hours a day.

There were thirty-nine dead in all by the time some of the injured succumbed to their wounds. That created a demand for caskets that far outstripped the Steinkamp inventory. Hermann Steinkamp had to make a desperate phone call to a maker of simple raw pine coffins in the small town of Houston, nearly an hour away—and the tiny operation worked all through the weekend, including twenty-four hours on Sunday—to create the burial boxes. And, of course, other unmentionables. The additional embalming fluid for the few open-casket funerals. The supply of large rubber bags that would hold the remains of those whose caskets would be mercifully sealed, protecting their friends and loved ones from viewing their disturbing leftovers.

And the bodies! *If* you could call them bodies. So many bore little resemblance to human beings. George never spoke of what he saw during those terrible weeks after the blast. But I knew he had gone to the high school gym, where the victims were taken and laid out in rows on pieces of canvas. He had offered to identify my twin sister for my mother and take care of the body. I was in the hospital, drifting in and out of a morphine haze, and my mother had been hysterical at the idea of having to see her daughter burned to a crisp. "Violet" had been found dangling from a beam above the smoldering pit, with the necklace from Dash—*my* necklace—as the only means of identifying her.

But far worse than the charred or broken bodies that came through the back door of Steinkamp & Son were the remains. The non-bodies. The burned bits and ragged pieces, embedded or fused with hair or a torn bit of fabric or clothing. So many fragments of so many lives; so much meat and bone. George's mother was a stoic, unflappable Welsh woman, but she would surprise me years later over an embalming by sharing how awful that time had been for her.

"A father would come in clutching a small bag that contained nothing more than a finger with a ring on it," she would say, shaking her head. "Or a blackened foot pried from a familiar shoe. It made me ill. I still cannot stomach the smell of barbecued meat."

Of course, she would not consider the impact of sharing her memories with me. And I did not want to discourage her confidences, as they were few and far between. I never had to see my sister's blackened body, thanks to George. But I imagined and felt the excruciatingly painful way she died, every single day of my life. I could not tell my mother-in-law about the way my entire body had burned in that hospital bed with a fever that the doctors could not readily explain or remedy. Only I knew, from the strange, frightening depths of my fevered dream-state, that I was burning along in sympathy with my twin. After nineteen years of being able to weirdly tune in to my sister's headaches, menstrual cramps and other aches and illnesses—as she did for mine—that was the last time I ever felt that strange connection. When my fever broke at last—a sudden, final surge and sweat-filled finale—I was completely alone with my own pain.

For Gladys and Hermann, the weeks immediately after the dance hall explosion were simultaneously the darkest times in their lives and the most wildly prosperous, as the business made money hand over fist.

"But it felt like blood money," she would say. "There was no joy in that work. We simply did what we knew how to do, easing the suffering of the families as best we could. I saved my tears for the viewing room late at night, as I placed bags of remains the size of a feed sack into the satin lining of a casket. I wouldn't wish that on anyone."

Back then, there was no real means of identifying fragments of bone and pieces of human tissue. The Steinkamps' funeral business became a repository for all of the bits and chunks and slivers that could not be given a definitive name. Gladys found herself putting bags and boxes into the icebox. Soon the basement became the overflow space.

"We have to do something," she told Hermann on the third morning after the explosion. "It's going to start to smell."

Hermann called the mayor, who in turn called the cemetery. With donations from the city and downtown churches, a large burial plot edged with oak trees on a knoll overlooking the rest of the cemetery was purchased at a steep discount. For those families whose loved ones were not among the positively identified— and there were twenty of these, half of the dead—Hermann arranged for twenty identical coffins at cost. The Steinkamps also donated the memorial stone, the granite behemoth set upon two graduated steps that ran the length of the slab.

Later on, I would think about the unlikeliness of the buried intermingling. Would a banker's daughter sit at the same drugstore counter with one of the working boys from the auto repair or—even more unimaginable—someone like Dale Diggs, one of Possum Flats' handful of Blacks? I recognized death as the great equalizer, an idea that would surface over and over again during my years as a funeral director. No one is special; no one is spared. It was a concept that was both infuriating and comforting, depending on my mood or on the client beneath my careful fingers any given day.

* * *

After a few days at home, I began to realize that I had some real time pressures; mainly my midsection. I could feel the slight distended roundness of my belly and knew it was only weeks or maybe a month before my secret wasn't my own anymore.

George and I needed to get married. Fast. That much was clear. But how to move this plodding, methodical, well-mannered boy off the slow track and down the aisle? I barely knew him, and at the rate things were going, I would be twenty-five and well on my way to old-maid-hood before he proposed. Worse, I would be twenty-five with a five-year-old child.

After things settled down at Steinkamp & Son, George began showing up at our door every evening at eight p.m. sharp, freshly bathed and smelling only slightly of chemicals. At that time of the night, my mother was always ironing someone's laundry in the front room. She could see his shadowy form through the screen door, hat in hand, poised to knock but never quite making the motion. She would set down her iron and wipe her rough hands on her apron, then tuck in any stray hairs that had fallen from her practical bun. It was almost as if he were her suitor or beau; his presence put a spring in her step that had been noticeably absent since the explosion.

"Ro-ose!" my mother would call out playfully, as if each night were an unexpected surprise. "Rose, your friend George is here!" She'd let him in and I would finish my preparations in the hand mirror that had been my sister's.

"Rose," I repeated to the mirror, closing my eyes and summoning my twin's spirit. I opened them to find Violet staring back, a bitter look in her dark eyes. She would not go quietly into this good night, nor any other. There was defiance there; an unwillingness to put on this new life. *Why should I have to be the one to die when Rose is the one who went up in flames?*

"Because you had your chance and you made a hash of it," I said to the mirror. "That's why."

If Rose had been in the back seat of that Plymouth with Dash, this never would have happened, Violet retorted. *Goody-Two-shoes. You can see where that got her. Please! Let's live a real life.*

"But your real life is completely ruined. You don't get a second chance."

You call George Steinkamp a second chance? Violet's eyes flashed in the mirror. *You are one sorry sister.*

"I *am* sorry. Sorry about everything I've done that's led to this," I whispered. "But you're dead. That's final. I will not let you mess things up with George."

You better start messing things up with George, if you know what I mean.

"Don't."

How do you think he's going to like finding out you're pregnant with someone else's baby? He's not going to take it as well as Joseph did from Mary. Catholics believe in immaculate conception, but I'm pretty sure that was on a one-time-only basis.

"Stop it."

All I'm saying is you better move fast, or we're both dead. Or as good as. Think about it. And get busy.

I swear Violet winked at me. My hands were shaking as I turned the mirror facedown on our dressing table with a clatter.

"I'm coming!"

I tried to make my face into the calm collected one that George would recognize before opening my bedroom door for another evening of couch- or porch-sitting in virtual silence with the man I intended to marry.

As was his way, George stood when I entered the room, still limping slightly on my tender feet. His ears—sticking out like jug handles from the sides of his head—were already crimson.

"I'll just leave you young people to visit," Mother said, forcing a lightness into her voice. She folded up her wooden ironing board, carefully wrapped the cord around her precious electric iron—a luxury she had scrimped and saved for—and ran a glass of water for herself before retreating into her small bedroom for the night. What did she think about there? That she was nurturing romance, watching a love story develop between George and her daughter? I felt a sudden rush of shame that I had never wondered before if she had romantic hopes of her own. She had been my mother, my caretaker and breadwinner, since I could remember. I had no memories of my father, a man she never talked about. I knew he had abandoned her—and us. I didn't even know whether they had been married. I had assumed so, in that way that children do, filling in the gaps of narratives with what is familiar. I had a brief sense of feeling untethered, wondering what I knew at all about the secret hopes and dreams of my mother, my sister, this earnest young man sitting uncomfortably on our worn floral-patterned sofa, hands clasped in his lap as though he were praying mightily for something. I felt the strange urge to reach out and pinch his cheek as hard as I could, just to feel something solid between my thumb and forefinger; to get a reaction, any human response, that could make me understand that this was real. That we were connected by more than a shared memory of my sister—whether we were aware it was only a memory or not—and who we expected her to be. I was going to have to make her life my own, not just guessing or assuming how to proceed, but living into it. And I might as well start now.

I reached a hand up to George's face, but didn't pinch him. Instead, I placed it carefully along his cheek and jaw.

"Georgie," I said. He looked startled, and blinked quickly a couple of times.

"What is it?" I asked. "Something wrong?"

What had I done? I started to take my hand away, but he caught it and put it back, holding it there with one of his own.

"No," he said, after what seemed like a long minute. "It's just that, well, you haven't called me that since . . ." His voice trailed off, and he closed his eyes. When he opened them again, he was looking at me intently.

"I've missed you," he said, voice croaky with emotion.

"And I've missed you," I said, and it almost felt true. "Can we go for a drive? Please? I'm so tired of this couch and this house and this town."

"I'm in the Grim Reaper tonight."

"Please, Georgie." I felt both manipulative and absolutely at his mercy, all at once. "You know I don't care about that."

"But your mom . . ."

"I think she would be glad for me to get out. She adores you, you know." I knew as I said them that the words were true and that she wouldn't care if I drove to Boston with him. I rose from the couch too quickly, unsteady on the sore feet that I'd forced into a pair of pumps. Like one of Cinderella's nasty stepsisters, jamming a maimed, bloody foot into a shoe that was not her own, angling to marry the prince. George caught my arm and I let myself fall into him, against his chest. I could feel his heart pounding beneath his jacket.

"Well, if you're sure it's okay. We could go for a little drive, I suppose."

"I'll tell Mother," I said, pulling away from him and straightening my dress. "You start the car."

I watched him practically skip out of the front door. At my mother's room, I raised my hand to knock, then thought the better of it. "Goodnight, Mother," I said.

I heard shuffling. "Are you going to bed already?" she asked. "George gone? Is everything okay?"

"He just left. He has an early morning at the funeral home," I lied. *Sorry, Rose. Things are going to be lot more interesting for you from now on.*

"Oh. Well, all right. Goodnight, Rose."

I heard my mother's voice so close that she must have been standing right on the other side of the door: "You're a good girl, Rosie."

I didn't answer. Instead, I tiptoed toward the front door and everything beyond it, George waiting in his car alone, the indigo sky held up by little pricks of white like my mother's pincushion.

On the front steps, I breathed in the sweet rotting smell of plants past their prime and the first frail fans of yellowed leaves fallen from walnut trees. From a porch a few buildings down came the sound of a woman's laughter, smoky and sly. It was just early September, still technically summer, but it felt like the world was getting ready for the next season—for cold nights, fallow fields stiff with the remaining cut brown corn and bean stalks. The miniature secrets inside seeds held close and blanketed in the dark frozen earth.

I headed toward the long black car, humming low and steady in the dark street.

The first thing I did was to scoot as close to George as I could. His body stiffened as our sides touched, but I ignored that and lay my head against his shoulder like it was the most natural thing in the world. I knew nothing, I realized, about his and Rose's romantic life. I had taken cruel delight in teasing her for the things that they most certainly had *not* done, but I hadn't the slightest idea about their actual shows of affection.

"Where should we go?" George asked, clearing his throat before putting his hand on the gearshift.

"I don't care," I said. "Wherever you want. Away from here."

Away from downtown. The giant crater where Lamb's had been had smoked for a solid week. A month later, many businesses still had knotty plywood boards where their plate-glass windows had been—1st Community Bank, Morton's, the police station, a small apartment building—and only a few were open. I had avoided the scene of the explosion, but Mother faithfully reported the progress of Possum Flats' cleanup efforts.

"The buildings look surprised, as if they don't know what hit them," she remarked once. "The broken windows are like empty eyes, missing noses, open mouths. Like human skulls."

Her eyes had gotten watery then, and I knew she was thinking of Violet. Of *me.*

George pulled the purring black car onto the subdued evening streets. The dark road illuminated by the golden beams of our headlights seemed to move toward and then beneath the hearse as if it were being devoured. Near the outskirts of Possum Flats, we paused at one of the town's only stop signs, at a junction that offered the option of heading further south, toward Arkansas just ten miles away, or west toward the Jacks Fork of the White River. The car made no movement either way.

"Well?"

"Well," George said, an apologetic note in his voice. "I'm not sure where to go."

"Just go where you usually go," I offered.

He looked puzzled. "We've never gone for a drive, just the two of us, Rose. And I don't think you want a ride to the cemetery or the funeral home, which are my usual routes."

No cemetery. I still hadn't gotten used to the idea that my sister was there. And the funeral home? I had only vaguely considered that it would be my home if I married George. It was probably spooky that time of night. Maybe all the time. I couldn't imagine living a normal life—sleeping, eating, arguing, crying, laughing, listening to the radio—while below you a cold, lifeless body or two awaited your attentions. It gave me chills.

"Let's go to the river. To the bluff."

"The bluff?" George sounded distressed. "What do you know about the bluff?"

"I know people go there for fun," I said. "What's wrong with that?"

"That's not the kind of fun a girl like you should be having, Rose."

Christ. This was harder than I ever had expected it to be. I suddenly felt exhausted beyond words.

In the end, though, George was a man. And while Dash Emmonds was the only man I had had sex with, I had plenty of experience taking the boys I dated and danced with to the brink. I stayed barely on this side of safe and—while I wasn't close to what I would classify as a "good girl"—virtuous. I had discovered a lot in the dark corners of dance halls, in the backs of coat closets and cars, even up against the rough grooves of an old oak tree on a midnight walk. What I learned was power. Don't get me wrong: The sensations of being kissed deeply, or having a mouth on my bare neck was wild and dangerous, and I felt as if I never wanted it to stop. I found myself pushing my hips against the hard bodies of those boys until it hurt, until I wanted to cry out with the ache of wanting—even though exactly what I wanted and how it would be achieved wasn't totally clear.

But I also found that these men—whether they were farm boys or the sons of businessmen and attorneys—were reduced to helplessness by what my body offered. Their hunger matched mine, but their response to our touching was almost gratefulness, a disbelief that these glorious feelings of flesh to flesh, mouth to mouth, lips on skin, were real. There were deep moans and sighs, often followed by begging and pleading for more; more of me and what my body could do. It was intoxicating, that power. Standing with my back against a tree, watching a boy's head lower to my breasts, I was struck by how vulnerable the neck of a football player could look.

"Rose, what has gotten into you?" George said at one point, pulling away from me. I had just kissed him, pushing his mouth open with my tongue—which, judging from his response, was a first.

"I want to be with you," I said, moving closer to kiss him again.

"You are with me," he said, reaching out a hand to my face as if to stop me.

"I mean, *really* be with you," I insisted. "All the way."

I kissed him again, and I could feel his body tense. I took one of his hands and placed it on the front of my thin cotton dress. I knew he could feel my body respond to his touch. I certainly felt his.

It took me the better part of an hour to end up straddling him in the back seat, my dress bunched around my waist and unbuttoned to my navel. George kept alternating between trying to stop me ("We really shouldn't, Rose.") and staring at the normally covered-up parts of me with wonder. I had been anxious about what it would be like to be touched by someone I didn't really know, let alone love. But I needn't have worried. To be handled so gently and with such reverence and awe was an aphrodisiac of a different type. And to my surprise, the kissing—which had begun so awkwardly—quickly got better, as he began to imitate the way I kissed him. The small rounded mound of my pregnant belly pressed against his reminded me of what I was doing, why I was here. I placed both of his hands on my tender, swollen breasts, covering the hard nipples which had lately grown so much darker against my white skin. Then I began to move my hips on top of him, not quite sure what I was doing, just trusting my body to take over.

I honestly think he came before he was inside me, but it didn't matter. I had only my one time with Dash to even surmise what was happening when George's body shuddered and I felt a warm wetness against one thigh.

Then with absolutely no warning, I began to cry; great, heaving sobs that felt like something inside me was trying to claw its way out.

George had collapsed back against the seat, but jerked up at my cries. He reached for my face in the semidarkness of the car.

"Rosie, have I hurt you?" His tone was genuine concern. "I never meant to!"

I cried harder. I wasn't sure why. It could have been simple physical relief from the touching and kissing and grinding that had my body so agitated. But I think it was more a deep sense of betrayal. I had calculatingly stolen my sister's life and her boyfriend. And his innocence—which I had taken without any regard for his feelings, just a selfish desire to keep the thin veneer of my new life intact. And worst of all, I had poisoned my sister's honor, doing things that she would never, ever do. I had gone further than even Violet, "the bad one," had ever thought possible. I hated myself.

I'm so sorry, Rose. I've mucked everything up. As usual.

"Rosie, please listen to me." George smoothed back my hair,

which had fallen across my face. "We'll get married. Everything will be okay. More than okay."

I shook my head. Here was George, offering me exactly what I thought I had wanted, exactly what I *needed*, and yet I couldn't allow myself to take it. I wasn't worthy of this boy, of his kindness or his love. This young man who, in my old life, I had disdained as boring. Ordinary. Plain. I was having a hard time remembering that life, when the things that turned my head were flash and fun. Things that didn't last. Like trying to grab hold of a sunbeam or catch a snowflake on my tongue.

Then all at once there *was* a sunbeam, only more concentrated and cruel, shining directly into my eyes. It came with a loud rap on the window across from us. Instinctively, I grabbed my open bodice, fumbling with the buttons to hide myself.

"George Steinkamp?" The voice was deep and muffled through the glass. George scrambled out from beneath me and scooted toward the far window, rolling it down a couple of inches. I kept my face turned away, but I could feel the cool air as it entered the steamy confines of the hearse.

"Hello there, Sheriff Sturtz." This night was full of surprises.

"I had a report of a hearse parked up here and I couldn't imagine why," the voice continued, genial yet businesslike. "Does your dad know where you are and what you're . . ." There was a distinct clearing of a throat. "Up to?"

"No, sir." I could practically feel the heat from George's face from across the back seat.

"I have to say, I'm a little surprised," Sheriff Sturtz continued. I felt the beam of the flashlight sweep across the near side of my face, and over my closed lids, making my view of everything briefly blood red. The color of shame. "That goes for whoever your girl is, too."

I said nothing.

"It's Rose. Rose Flowers. We're getting married," blurted George, and then it was my turn to blush. He wasn't the smoothest, but where had smoothness or fast talk gotten me? And although I was as dishonest as the devil, I admired George's earnestness, for being so genuine and loyal in that moment—qualities that I would count on during all of our years together, the good and the bad.

The sheriff swept his light back to George. "Is that right? I hadn't heard the happy news."

His voice conveyed his disbelief and, worse, his boredom. Despite my inner turmoil, my selfish preoccupation, I was in no way special. *We* were not special. Just two kids fogging up the back seat of a car—although the hearse was a dark twist—and getting caught in the act. The man had seen it all before.

Considering this made me feel even more upset. While George stammered about how we'd just decided tonight and begged the sheriff not to spoil the news for his mother and father, I sat in my seat and fumed. I was *not* ordinary. What had happened to me and to my sister, to the others at the dance hall, was anything but normal. Couldn't he see that? I tasted iron and realized I was biting my lip.

"I'm sure you'll be invited, Sheriff," I blurted out.

"I reckon I'll be honored to be there," he said, backing away from the car window and turning off his light. "Provided this glad occasion does actually take place. I suppose you'll be the one up front wearing white?"

He made an ugly sort of chuckle.

"You kids get on home. It's late. I was heading home myself before I got this call. Maybe you should think about saving something for your wedding night."

"Yes, sir."

"Too late," I said, my voice shrill. I had lost my ability to channel Rose and what she would say or do in this situation. Who was I kidding? She wouldn't *be* in this situation. But I needed to make sure this man knew he was not dealing with someone ordinary, boring him to tears with her petty trespasses while he was thinking about dinner, covered with a tea towel and kept warm in the oven.

"But I bet you'll be thinking about me on your way home."

"Rose!" George hissed at me. "Stop!"

But I was just getting wound up. "Or maybe you'll think about me later, lying in bed with your boring old wife with her fat ankles."

There was a crunch of gravel and suddenly the sheriff's face was back at the window, as was the brutal beam of his flashlight.

"You know there's nothing stopping me from writing you both up for lewd and lascivious behavior, Miss Flowers? Or indecent exposure. Or I could simply drag you home in my car and let your parents know about your shenanigans. Not to mention the neighbors who will watch us pull up in the driveway."

"Sir." The crisp fall air that came through the window held an electric charge, as if lightning were about to strike. George was trying to be the human voice of reason in a potentially ugly dogfight. "Rose just lost her sister, Violet, last month. At the dance hall? You can understand. She's just not herself lately."

I heard Sheriff Sturtz suck in the air between his teeth. "I see that." He paused. "I'm sorry for your loss, Miss Flowers."

"Thank you," I muttered, grateful that I was being given a graceful way out.

"But I need to warn you, Miss Flowers, and I don't mean any disrespect: You don't want to go down the path your sister was heading. I heard a little here and there, if you know what I mean."

I swallowed hard. Being Rose was like being at my own funeral—Violet's funeral—but not in a good way. I hadn't heard many praising my character or extolling my virtues. I had no idea I was so notorious. It took everything I had to answer with a respectful, sarcasm-free "Yes, sir."

After the sheriff's car door slammed, George and I sat primly in the back seat, watching the pair of headlight beams play across the dashboard and windshield before disappearing into the night. I stared straight ahead, afraid to look at him. Afraid of what the outline of his jaw or his posture might say.

Finally: "Rose, I don't know who you are or where you came from . . ."

"George, I'm so sorry . . ."

"No, don't be sorry. You made me feel . . . *alive* tonight. Like I could do anything if you were beside me, you know? Even a life in the funeral business."

He slapped the dashboard, which shocked me a little bit.

Then he laughed. I liked the sound of it, warm and honest, like butter on toast. I laughed, too.

"I better take you home, Rosie. You need your sleep. Tomorrow we're giving Mom and Dad the big news. Your mom, too."

I smoothed the skirt of my dress around and beneath me, checking my bodice to make sure I was properly buttoned. Then I felt around on the floorboard for my pumps.

"I'll be ready," I said. My mother would be thrilled, of course. She'd been dropping hopeful hints for weeks. But I knew to expect a chilly reception at the Steinkamps'. There was a reason they were in the dead people business.

As if reading my thoughts, George reached across the back seat and patted my leg. Then we got out of the car awkwardly on our respective sides, stretching and sighing, and slid back into the front seat.

At my house, I gave him a quick kiss on the cheek and didn't look back until I reached the steps. In the moonlight, the hearse hummed, dark and mysterious but no longer as frightening. I waved goodbye and watched the car slide away, through the circle of light from the single street lamp. I stood for the longest time, inhaling the smells of that night, a combination of sex and my own sweat, and the light sweet scent of the moonflowers. Their huge, trumpetlike white blooms glowed virginally against the dark, heart-shaped leaves; curling vines embraced the stair rail and spindles. When the sun came up, they would be closed and limp, like damp, collapsed umbrellas. But for now, they bloomed without a thought about daylight. It occurred to me how odd it was that my mother had planted the vines, since she was always so early to bed.

Perhaps, it was her little gift to me, to Violet. Or to anyone in

Possum Flats awake and wandering in the wee hours who needed a reminder of the fleeting nature of both beauty and night. The sun always comes up, making everything new and hopeful. Everyone knows that. The trick is to see the beauty in the dark while you are still in it.

I took in one last lungful of the rich night air, took off my shoes and quietly slipped inside.

I wish I could say that George's parents welcomed me into the family with open arms, that upon hearing the news, his father patted George on the back with pride and his mother collapsed onto the couch and wept grateful tears at the prospect of "finally having a daughter."

That sort of thing.

Instead, I was not even offered a seat in the small living room hidden in back on the main floor of the funeral home. No one sat, as a matter of fact. I remember my wounded feet aching in my black pumps as we stood uncomfortably in the wake of George's announcement. His parents looked as stiff and unemotional as the pair in the *American Gothic* painting that would cause such a stir in a few years—except that it was George's father who avoided eye contact, while Gladys stared with open hostility at my stomach, which I had tried to conceal with a drop-waist dress for the occasion. I am sure she would have gladly employed the painting's pitchfork, had one been within reach.

Of course, George hadn't told them I was pregnant. He didn't know! But—bless his heart—he was certainly taking responsibility for our actions in the back seat of the hearse last night (and mine with Dash in a different back seat on a different night). Whatever he had told them before he brought me over that afternoon, it was clear that he was not going to be talked out of his decision to marry me and to do it in a hurry. I could see that Gladys had her suspicions on both counts. I couldn't blame her.

"I hope you know what you are getting into," was all she said to George, moving her eyes from my midsection to his face, which was, of course, deep red. But he stood taller than his father—I hadn't remembered him being that tall—his chest puffed out. And I realized: He was proud to bring me here and introduce me as his bride-to-be. I was both grateful and deeply ashamed. His mother saw me as the fraud that I was. Maybe she didn't know the real truth, but she had surmised enough of the situation to know that I wasn't the type of girl she would have chosen for her son.

"Oh, I do, Mother," George said, looking at me with adoration. He reached over and took one of my hands, which I had clasped together in front of me, trying not to allow the loose fall of my dress any purchase on my small protruding belly. "*We* do," he said. "Don't we, Rose?"

"I highly doubt it," Gladys answered in my stead. "Neither of you have enough God-given sense to fill a thimble. Now, if you'll excuse me," she huffed, stomping her practical brown oxfords toward the basement, "some of us have work to do."

With Gladys gone, Hermann sighed deeply and hid his hands in his pockets, as if he could not extend one to me in good conscience.

He nodded instead, just a quick dip of his square head. "Welcome to the family, Rose," he said, looking toward the door to make sure Gladys hadn't heard his blasphemy. Then he, too, was gone, leaving me and George alone.

"Well, that went pretty well," he said, wiping his sweaty face with his sleeve. "Didn't you think?"

I couldn't help but burst out laughing.

"Yes. I thought it went swimmingly."

"Mother will come around," he said. "You'll see."

"I doubt it."

George laughed in a rueful sort of way and I realized that he had been trying to bolster himself up with his hopeful declaration— not just me. But deep inside, he knew I was right.

"Me, too," he said, finally. Then he pulled me close, and I put my arms around his back, pressing my face against the shirt that smelled of starch, nervous sweat and embalming fluid. "But remember, she's used to people who don't talk back. She's not as hard-hearted as she seems." He let me go, trying to read my emotions, my willingness to go through with our crazy scheme. *My* crazy scheme. "Almost, but not quite."

I did not think of her as hard-hearted. But I recognized in Gladys a determination, a stubbornness that I shared. Or, should I say, *Violet* shared with her. We were both survivors, strong women who wanted things done their way. I didn't have a problem with that. Goody Two-shoes Rose should be able to easily toe the line. If I let her.

Everything was perfect in the beginning of our marriage.

Well, as perfect as any marriage based on a heaping bushel-basket full of lies can be. George adored me, so grateful to me for making him a husband. A man. He followed me around like a puppy, affectionate and enthusiastic, blind to any faults or shortcomings. And the way he touched me! Of course, I hadn't a world of experience before George, but being with him was nothing like the panting, sweating backseat lust of Dash Emmonds— something I had wanted, but not particularly enjoyed. George would spend an hour just touching me, everywhere, his eyes asking permission to explore me with his hands and mouth and . . . well, I felt like a long-awaited, long-hoped-for Christmas package, opened with such love and absolute care. Never would I have thought that the awkward, sweaty-palmed boy who called on my sister would have been capable of making me feel so desirable.

And I wanted him, too. Not at first, when the guilt and weight of my lies felt like several layers of clothing between our bodies, an impenetrable second skin. But after a while, the way he looked at me began to make me forget a little bit. To think maybe there was something inside me that deserved to be loved, too. I started seeing him as my husband, not my sister's boyfriend. I felt lucky. I knew what I had done to give myself another chance at a life, and was resigned to simply endure the relationship I had wormed my way into. But I hadn't thought to hope that I could be cherished.

He cried when I told him—as soon as I thought believable—that he was going to be a father. As my body swelled, George was like a mother hen. He made sure I put my feet up (even if there was work to be done), rubbed my back, and brought me box after box of the chocolate turtles I craved from Morton's. He was bursting with pride and would spend our evenings with his parents speculating on our child's gender, listing the adventures he would have with each. Would his boy like baseball? Would a daughter want a swing in the backyard? His enthusiasm was a complete shock to me. I hadn't imagined anything would have shy, steady George so jovial.

Not everyone in the Steinkamp household was as enamored of me. While Hermann listened with quiet amazement to his son's nonstop chatter about the baby, Gladys kept casting a skeptical eye on the pair of us. Especially me.

One morning, I was alone upstairs in our little bedroom—which barely had room for the old iron double bed pushed up against one wall and a plain maple dresser. I was lining the top drawer of the dresser with a blanket to see if it might serve as a bassinet, when Gladys stuck her head in the doorway. Her sharp glance took in my efforts and she put her chin up as if something she had been thinking had been confirmed.

"I know what you're up to, Rose," she said. "While my son walks around with moon eyes—and his father not a fair sight better—thinking you're some fairy princess come to grace us with your presence, I've got a good idea what you're about."

Instinctively, I put a hand on my belly, nearly bursting from the uncomfortable casing of one of my old dresses. I couldn't stop the feeling of panic that crept upwards from my midsection and tightened in my throat.

"Don't act for a minute like you don't know what I'm talking about." Gladys looked behind her, as if to make certain that mine were the only ears that would hear what came next. "You tricked my son into getting married, like the low, grasping girl you are," she hissed, nodding at my belly. "My *only* son, who, as you well know, will take over the business one day. A girl with no father and a washerwoman for a mother could do much, much worse than George."

"I . . . I . . . don't know what you're talking about," I stammered. "I love George. And he loves me."

"About the last part, I am sure," she said coldly. "I'm not blind. But you better be certain about that first part. If you're just looking for a place to keep you and that child warm and fed, you've underestimated me."

Here, she moved into the room and held a finger in my face. "If you break my boy's heart, if you dare to do anything to make him unhappy, I will make you regret it every single day you're under this roof."

She gave a last reproving look at my belly. "I hope you haven't done it already."

After she left, my legs felt wobbly and I steadied myself with the bed. I didn't know exactly what Gladys suspected, but I had to hand it to her: she was shrewd. Maybe we were alike in that way, too. I would have to watch my step. I had been so wrapped up in my own pain, with Rose's death and my fear of being a single mother, I hadn't considered what our hasty marriage must look like to others. Gladys' appraisal hit close to home. I *had* tricked George. But the thing was . . . I truly had grown to love him. No one could have been more surprised about that than me.

Talk about surprises: I was in the bowels of Steinkamp & Son, watching my father-in-law carefully drain the blood from a large, bloated-looking farmer on the worktable when my water broke. Not just a warm trickle of liquid, but a large, splashing gush that caused Hermann to look up from his task in alarm: Had a tube gone awry?

The baby was three months early. At least in terms of our marriage, which was only six months young.

Everyone panicked—my father-in-law, George, me. Thankfully we had Gladys to hold everything together. I wouldn't have picked my mother-in-law as my midwife, but she took over just like she did for a funeral, delegating tasks. When Mother arrived after being informed breathlessly by George that it was "my time," Gladys eyed her warily. But in a nod to my mother's experience with laundry, she put her to work freshening sheets and towels. Meanwhile, Gladys made cool poultices for my forehead, ordered boiling water and kept the curious, fearful menfolk on the other side of the door. There was barely room for anyone to stand beside my bed, let alone maneuver, but the three of them—Gladys, my mother and, eventually, the doctor—made do for the next twelve hours.

"It's a girl," Doctor Tweedy said at last, holding up the shrieking red ball of baby for my inspection. A girl: of course! The long hours of jagged, sweaty labor fell away and I reached for her, wanting to calm her. I didn't know then that her angry, blood-curdling world debut would be a glimpse of our future. She started life pissed off and pretty well stayed that way. And she would let me know every day in a thousand different ways that it was all my fault.

I marveled at her then: that wide-open mouth, the slender fingers spread apart stiffly as if she were warding off the light and noise, her eyelids squeezed shut in annoyance. She was captivating and terrifying. I'd barely gotten to hold her when Gladys snatched her away, insisting the baby be cleaned and bundled for viewing.

"There's nothing premature about this baby," she said pointedly. But her eyes were soft, focused on the scarlet writhing baby girl with the shock of black hair. "What will you name her?"

The baby's eyes flew open. For the first time, I took in their deep baby blue. Without a second's thought, I said "Violet."

The baby stilled for an instant, as if considering what this name might hold for her. "Violet *Rose*," I amended. After both sisters who lost their lives at Lamb's that night.

My mother quietly cried her approval. And when Gladys finally opened the bedroom door to let the doctor out and my husband in, George was in agreement, too. He held her a moment—until the screaming started again. The baby's silence had apparently been to refill her lungs for another shrill blast. George quickly handed her back to me.

"She is perfect," he laughed, squeezing in at the head of the bed. "You're both amazing," he said, giving me a shy kiss on the cheek. Then he leaned down to give his howling daughter a kiss, too.

It is still one of my favorite memories, that time when Lettie was new and I had so much hope for us. For all three of us: George, me and the baby. That we could be a real family, even if we didn't come about it from the usual path.

I didn't know then, in my ignorance—it was my first baby, my only baby—that those dusky blue eyes would change to green. And that the dark mop would fall out, replaced by a fuzzy halo of white hair that eventually turned a rich, dark blond. She would look nothing like me, which was one thing. But she would also look absolutely nothing like George, which was devastating. No orange-red curls. No blue eyes. And not a single, solitary freckle to be found.

Fortunately, my girl was loved and adored by all. Lettie transformed the somber stillness of the funeral home with her energy until none of us could imagine the place without her. Even flint-hearted Gladys fell captive to her spell.

But that same magic and consideration did not extend to me. The more the baby evolved into her looks and personality—more of a Lettie, less of a Violet—there was a downward tick in my own status in the Steinkamp home. Gladys did not address me at all except through others ("Ask your wife if she needs help with the table, George"). It was as if her suspicions about Lettie's origins had not only been confirmed but further downgraded. It was one thing to trick a man into marriage by getting pregnant . . . but tricking him to save face for a pregnancy that wasn't even his doing? That was beyond the pale.

Of course, she didn't voice her doubts directly. She did it more

insidiously, causing our marriage to die a slow, poisonous death—
like the husbands or wives who add trace amounts of antifreeze
or arsenic to their partner's food until eventually he or she dies of
organ failure.

"Why, would you look at that blond hair? George, would you
ever have thought you'd have a towhead? And those green eyes . . .
Whose could they be? Not my George's. And Rose and her mother
both with those dark brown ones."

Or: "We need to put a bonnet on that child. George would have
been a freckled mess at this age if he were out in the sun like Lettie. But she doesn't have a one!"

Then one day, when Lettie was about a year old, Gladys went
too far.

We were all coming out of the Catholic church one Sunday
morning. I was the interloper, the Protestant who was always
suspect, even though I had chosen to convert. Lettie was in her
stroller, and George had taken charge of rolling it, even though
that wasn't what men did back then. He was just so proud of her!

We had just shaken hands with the priest, Father Donohue,
when he leaned down to take a closer look at Lettie.

"Why, where's the red hair and freckles, George?" the priest
said in jest, I'm sure.

"That's a question we've been asking since she arrived, Father," Gladys chimed in, and not in a joking manner. "We've been
wondering if we need to check out the milkman or the postman.
Because this little one doesn't look like her mama, either."

Here, she smiled, her teeth a set of yellowed daggers. My face
must have turned as white as the Father's alb. And unfortunately,
George chose to look at me instead of Lettie or the priest. I don't
know what he saw in my expression, but what I saw in his was
like an entire movie, played out on his open, honest face. From
surprise to worry, from doubt to sickening understanding. George,
who had such a good heart, who only saw the good in everyone. I
absolutely broke him.

Gladys had the satisfied look of a house cat who had finally gotten to the caged canary. Incredible that her tight, smug smile was not smeared with blood or feathers. But she killed me just as surely, without a drop of blood being shed.

The walk home was deathly quiet. Hermann feebly attempted small talk about the spring weather—how dry it had been, how the farmers were worrying about their crops taking hold in the cracked soil. The silence was as hard as the sidewalks, and broken up only by the intermittent squeak of a stroller wheel and Lettie's oblivious gurgles.

In our room, George closed the door and turned to face me, loosening his tie as though he were a desperate man about to get the noose.

"Rose, I'm only going to ask this once."

A shadow flew across my heart then, chilling me to the bone despite the warm April weather. George's eyes locked on mine and I couldn't look away, as terribly as I wanted to.

"Is Lettie mine?"

So many thoughts and feelings flashed through my mind: George carrying me out of the hospital, kissing newborn Lettie, caring for me so gently when I was lost and broken in the wake of my sister's death. Words were failing me exactly when I needed them to clarify, to solidify how I felt for George, feelings I neither expected nor deserved.

"I don't know what you mean by 'yours,' George," I stammered. "You've loved her since before she was born, before you knew she was Lettie . . ."

"That's not what I asked."

What was the right answer? I'm not sure if I could have given it that day. Or any day. I've worried the edges of this horrible memory ragged with endless replay.

Of course, I should have said yes. A no-doubt-about-it, take-no-prisoners yes. I should have gone to him and taken his face in my hands and kissed him like I had never kissed him before—hard and sure, with complete and utter confidence in my status as his beloved. Showing him that I was his and he was mine. And she was ours.

Instead, in my fear and shame, I stood at the foot of the bed by the wall while he waited catty-corner by the door. That expanse of off-white chenille might as well have been a nubby, unnavigable ocean. I didn't seize the moment; I didn't seize the man. I lowered my eyes and said, "She's yours in every way that matters."

I couldn't lie. I wish I could have. It would have changed everything that came after. Because what I said wasn't enough for George.

The silence in that tiny room with its faded floral wallpaper was awful.

When George finally spoke, his voice was not angry or broken, like I expected. It was worse: It was nothing. Just a voice one might use to ask for a pat of butter or recite a grocery list.

"My mother tried to warn me," he said, without bitterness. "I didn't believe her, that my sweet Rose could be so conniving. Even when Lettie was born just six months after that first time in my car . . ." He paused, as if embarrassed to recall the night that had sealed our fate.

"I love Lettie. She *is* my daughter in every way that matters . . . except one."

Here, I finally looked at him. I had crushed him. But still, he kept talking, the smooth, monotonous tone of his voice belying the devastation of the words that kept coming, like a river that had been too long dammed.

"I'll always love Lettie, Rose. I'll provide for her, of course. And for you. We—you and I—will put our very blood into this business my parents have built so that Lettie has a good life.

"And I'll be a husband to you, too, in all the ways that matter. Except for one."

Somewhere downstairs, we heard the muffled sounds of Lettie crying and Gladys trying unsuccessfully to console her. Normally I would have let my mother-in-law suffer a little longer, fail more completely with her granddaughter. But I was grateful for the excuse to leave the unhappiness that hung as thick as the velvet curtains in the rooms below. As I came around the bed, I held my body so as to avoid touching my husband in that narrow space. I reached for the brass doorknob, cool in my sweating hand.

"You've got nothing to say for yourself?" I felt his breath at my ear. He was so close I could feel the heat of his body and his anger. Then his hand covered mine on the knob. "I've been defending you since the moment I brought you home. So you really are a whore and a liar?"

He spun me around and before I could answer his mouth was on mine. It was as though he was trying to devour me, to tear at and grind against my lips, forcing my mouth open with his tongue, our teeth clicking together roughly as I tried to twist away. Frustrated, he grabbed behind my neck and pulled our mouths tightly together again, and when I tried to pull back he bit my lip so hard I tasted blood.

Then he was ripping at the front of my dress with his other hand, the small tan buttons of the shirtwaist falling to the floor with a pitiful popping sound. Something in me just died, stopped fighting. I don't know if it was shock at his behavior, so terribly out of character for the man I had come to love, or just the feeling that the ugliness of what was happening was exactly what I deserved. *A whore and a liar.*

George pushed me back on the bed and fell on top of me. He pulled away from my bleeding mouth and pulled my slip down in the front until one breast was exposed. He bit the tender skin so hard I cried out, feeling the broken rings of bruising forming. I felt him fumbling with his belt and fly, then reaching up under my skirt and yanking aside one leg of my underwear, all the while trying unsuccessfully to jam himself, hard, against my body. A body that felt like it wasn't really mine, as though I were watching things happen to it from some other place.

"Is this how you like it?" He was panting from the struggle. I lay stiff, eyes closed, trying to breathe, to survive the wave of his rage and hurt. I knew this wasn't him, that I had caused this desperate, awful act. How very, very stupid to have thought I could be someone else and ruin another innocent person's life in the process.

"Da-da! Da-da!"

Somehow Lettie was on the other side of our door, out of breath and gasping. She must have escaped Gladys at last. She was a holy terror as a crawler, fast as lightning and unafraid of stairs. I had found her once atop the dining room table, snapping a pair of sewing shears open and closed. I pictured her pulling up against the door, holding herself up with her palms.

"Da-da?"

Just like that, all the hate and frustration and violence of the moment was gone, evaporated. George collapsed on top of me, sobbing in a choking, pathetic way.

"I'm so sorry," he managed at last. Then he was off of me and pulling himself together, heading for the door to swoop up his girl, to rescue her like he always did, would always do, for the rest of his life.

"I've got you, love." I heard the door open and close again behind him and I rolled over on my side, facing the wall. I didn't know where this left us, me and Lettie. And George. All I knew was that something beautiful and miraculous had been destroyed.

How to pick up the pieces this time? I didn't know if I had the strength to keep going. I didn't know if I wanted to.

But children have a way of pulling you through, like a simple threading tool helps yank a thick strand through the impossibly small eye of a needle. Caring for Lettie's needs and doing the yeoman's share of the funeral-home work—both in penance and of necessity, as time went on—made the hours, days, months and years zip by.

My mother died when Lettie was nine—the toll of years of hard manual labor and grief—making me feel more alone. And when Lettie left, Steinkamp & Son became even darker and more somber than the day I had moved in eighteen years before. The four of us remaining were like ghosts, sliding quietly by each other without touching as we did our chores, sharing wordless meals in the cramped dining room. Sometimes an entire day would pass without anyone speaking.

Eventually, the ghosting began in earnest, as one by one, the Steinkamps took their leave of me and of this earth. Poor Hermann died of a heart attack in 1949, unloading a shipment of caskets, ironically—followed several years later by Gladys, eaten away from the inside by cancer. By the time she complained of the pain and saw the doctor, there was "nothing to be done." This pronouncement seemed to give her a measure of grim satisfaction as she returned home, took to her bed and waited impatiently to die.

George made it until 1953. That was the worst, watching him waste away from drinking and—I had to presume—heartbreak. His spirit, like his orange-red hair, thinned, faded and finally disappeared altogether. He was only forty-six years old when he left me to carry on the business.

But his death was just a formality. By that time, I had already been alone for years. I had gotten used to it. And I liked not answering to anyone and handling things in my own way, on my own time.

The colorful, extroverted Violet had become a thorny Rose.

"Until you came along," I say to Daisy now, this girl at my bedside. "I've gotten used to having you around."

"I love you, too, Grandma," she says. "Thorns and all."

Daisy

It is Sunday morning and I am dreaming of California. I'm on a soft sand beach, the sun so bright that my closed eyelids are a veiny vibrating red and I'm longing for a pair of sunglasses. I can't see her, but I know Mom is on a beach towel beside me. There is the rhythmic sound of water coming closer and then receding.

In a small corner of my mind, I know that what I am hearing is a good old-fashioned lawn sprinkler—not the Pacific Ocean—but I don't want to wake up. I want to stay with Mom a little longer in this perfect place. All the doubts and questions that have been gnawing at my insides are gone. It's just the two of us, washed up on the same shore, like a message inside its blown-glass bottle. Launched and landed, nothing more to be communicated. I feel peaceful for the first time in months.

The smell of bacon finally causes my eyes to open. Someone's making breakfast.

Roger.

He has taken to coming over in the mornings, cooking for Grandma and cajoling her into eating. For some reason, he is the only one who can convince her to take more than two bites of anything.

"I would have given my eyeteeth to have seen his face while he read that last article in *The Picayune*," she is saying. "Oh, whoops! I don't have any teeth to spare."

When I get to the kitchen, they are both guffawing. Grandma covers her tooth gap with her hand like a giggling schoolgirl. I feel like I have walked in on something.

"Good morning, Daisy," Grandma says. Roger busies himself at the stove, flipping over a bubbly pancake to brown the second side. "We thought you might stay up there all day."

"Not with bacon on the griddle. And pancakes, too? Roger, I don't know what's gotten into you lately, but my taste buds thank you."

He gives me a nod. I guess he's saving all his best one-liners for Grandma.

"Well, Roger says your last story has really got the town fired up," Grandma says. "I'm surprised there isn't a mob with pitchforks on the front lawn."

"I think it's *your* story that has everyone talking," I counter. "I'm just the writer. It's your scandal, remember?"

Grandma sighs. It is a weighty one.

"Well, I guess I am the blue-haired Hester Prynne of Possum Flats," she says.

"Better get that scarlet letter ready," I agree. "Or is it a *violet* letter?"

At that, all three of us crack up. Since Grandma "came clean" to me last week—and then to all of Possum Flats in the article that came out two days ago—it feels different around here. Lighter. Maybe she feels free after living a lie for so long. I'm not tiptoeing around the truth anymore, either. We're finally comfortable together.

And Roger is happy as a clam just to have her around. The very real fact of almost losing her has made him tender with her in a way he wasn't before. He's always been willing to do anything for Grandma, but now it seems like more than just business. It isn't enough to be her right-hand man anymore. I think he just wants to be her *man*.

But what do I know about friendship and falling in love?

I haven't seen Joe since the night we kissed. And then I had to spill my guts and ruin everything. I almost wish I could take it back and we could be buddies again, flipping crap on each other; Joe calling me "Flower Child" and me acting annoyed and keeping him humble.

Almost.

That kiss was amazing.

But I can't blame him for staying away. First I tell him that we are some weird kind of related. More than "kissing cousins"—which is way too cutesy to describe this mess. Now that the article is out, Joe knows the awful details: his grandfather got my grandma pregnant. That's no small news. It could blow Possum Flats apart, like the dance hall explosion all over again.

It's probably tougher to accept when your grandfather is Brother Emmonds, pastor and longtime conscience of Possum Flats. The bigger they are, the harder they fall, I guess. But Joe's known his grandfather for nearly sixteen years and me all of three months, so I'm pretty sure where his loyalties lie.

But still. Today is August 13th. The fiftieth anniversary of the explosion. And I wish I could be with him. To talk about it together. Mark the day somehow.

"Daisy, Fence called."

I snap back to the present. Fence? On a Sunday? He hasn't exactly been in the Daisy fan club lately, either. When I went back late last week to *The Picayune* with the final installment of my dance hall series, Patty had buzzed Fence's desk on speakerphone.

"Daisy Flowers is here to see you," she'd said, raising a finger for to me to hold up a minute.

"We don't have any business to discuss." Fence's tone was curt. "You can walk her to her desk to clean things out."

"But . . . I have the fourth article. The final story," I pleaded.

Patty didn't like being caught in the crossfire. She picked up the phone receiver.

"Tell him I won't leave until he looks at it."

"Um, Mr. Fence? She's not leaving until she can show you

something," she said, swiping at her eyes, fighting tears. "I didn't mean to sound like I was threatening you. It's just . . . well, you know Daisy." She shrugged at me apologetically.

I didn't care what she said as long as I got an audience.

She motioned with her head toward Fence's office. She didn't have to tell me twice.

He had been reluctant to take the pages from me, but the newspaperman inside him won over the irritated and exasperated boss. Fence knew a scoop when he saw one—and this story had it all: sex, betrayal, mistaken identity, death. When he'd finished the last paragraph, he looked at me with a bit of awe, in spite of himself.

"Well, I'll be good and goddamned," was all he'd said.

The story ran the next day.

In the forty-eight hours since, I haven't left the funeral home. Neither has Grandma. Mobs and pitchforks are more than a possibility. Her business might be done for.

"What did he want?" I felt a twinge of anxiety. Hopefully Possum Flats hadn't turned on him and *The Picayune*. He was just doing his job, publishing the story. Like I was doing mine.

"He wants you to meet him at the armory around five," Grandma says. "Maybe he's got another assignment?"

"The *armory*? That's a long walk. And on a Sunday? Why can't we just meet at the paper this week sometime?"

I don't like the sound of this.

"Maybe he's feeling you out after . . ." She pauses. "Well, after everything that happened. You know. It could be he's afraid of a scene."

"Me? Make a scene? That's stupid," I say, shaking my head. "But if anyone has a right to throw a fit, it's me. After what he said to and about me?" I sniff. "He outright said I killed Jimmy Jeffers! But I took the high road."

"That you did," agrees Grandma. "Maybe he just wants neutral territory to make an apology? Fence doesn't like to be wrong. Your articles are the best reporting we've had around this town in years.

He knows that. He knows that Possum Flats knows that. I expect it's difficult to own up to the fact that he was a complete ass."

"He published my last story," I say. "That's enough for me."

"Well, apparently it's not enough for him," she says. "Roger and I can drop you off. I could use a little Sunday drive, anyway. Right, Roger?"

"Roger that," says Roger.

"Oh, brother," I say. "You two are too much."

Fifty Years Ago in Possum Flats:
Remembering the Lamb's Dance Hall Explosion
Part IV: Rose & Violet Flowers

by Daisy Flowers

August 11, 1978

It was just another Friday night in Possum Flats and the Flowers girls were getting ready for the dance.

But it wasn't *exactly* a regular night. It was Friday the 13th. Rose and Violet's mother had mentioned the date, wondering if it might be bad luck to venture out. But the Flowers girls weren't superstitious—and, like most teenagers, felt invincible. They had no reason to expect anything bad would happen that night.

Although both girls were primping, their efforts were focused on the one twin who would be attending the dance. Her hair was freshly bobbed, the right dress picked out, makeup applied, accessories chosen.

Violet was supposed to go to the dance with her steady, Dash Emmonds. He and Charlie Walters would be arriving any minute in Charlie's father's car, with Hazel Sampson in the front seat beside him.

There was one small problem: Violet was sick as a dog. She had been vomiting all day. And the day before that, too.

So why would she go to the dance? Couldn't she beg off?

"A lot can happen in one night," explains Rose Flowers. "New romances. Slow dances. Big fights. Messy breakups. If you missed a dance at Lamb's, you might get left out in the cold."

Violet had the option that most of us don't: an identical twin sister—so similar to her in looks that even their own mother couldn't tell them apart without a) checking for the small purple birthmark hidden on the back of Violet's neck or b) asking about their social plans (Violet always had them; Rose rarely did).

But Rose didn't want to go. She had her own boyfriend—a budding romance with George Steinkamp—for one thing. And she wasn't sure she could fool Dash and his friends for an entire evening. A known wallflower, Rose's dancing was sub-par. Yet, the idea of stepping outside of herself, being adventurous and carefree for one night, enchanted her.

And Rose never could say no to Violet.

So she went to the dance. With a newly bobbed hairdo to match Violet's sassy cut and the necklace that Dash had given her sister when he asked her to go steady.

Rose went to Lamb's Dance Hall with Dash Emmonds the night our town's world blew up.

Not Violet.

It was a sisterly prank, pulled on an unsuspecting Possum Flats. Just for the evening. But when the building exploded in a rain of rubble and flame, the sisters' plan blew up, too.

Rose was dead.

And Violet was . . . pregnant.

Unmarried. And with no college education, practical job training or prospects.

She woke up in a hospital bed after passing out that night, hysterical over the loss of her sister and with her feet bandaged from running barefoot down the glass-strewn streets of Possum Flats. She was disoriented, confused. Why was George Steinkamp at her bedside? Why was her mother calling her "Rose"?

When she finally understood that they mistakenly believed Violet was dead, it was a split-second decision not to correct them. It was a way out of her troubles; a parting gift from Rose.

It couldn't hurt anyone . . . could it?

Daisy

The armory is a big, butt-ugly cement-block building with a curved metal roof, sort of like a Pringles potato chip. But even knowing it was built for military purposes, I think it could be a whole lot nicer. It's like a giant wart or hemorrhoid on the edge of Possum Park—a little town green with several rolling acres of manicured grass, and home to a playground, the Possum Flats swimming pool and a cracked red concrete tennis court. In the middle of the park, there's a community pavilion made of local stone, which sits above the ground by a good five feet, like a stage.

When Roger and Grandma drop me off at the armory, Fence is nowhere in sight. Looking out over the park from my seat on the steps, I can see something is happening at the pavilion. The one-way street that winds through the park is full of cars, and people are carrying covered dishes, lawn chairs and blankets. There are slower-moving old people, some gripping a cane or each other for balance as they make their way across the grass and up the steps. Other adults hold babies in their arms or small children on their backs, while older kids run up ahead of them, excited about whatever is about to take place—not the least of which is a table full of dessert options, I'm sure. Vinegar pie, sweet milk cake, coconut washboards, lemon bars, carrot cake. I've been in Possum Flats long enough by now to know the pride and pure deliciousness that goes into a community pot-luck, whether a church, club or a family or class reunion. Recipes are guarded more jealously than family silver or heirlooms. Grandma says some of the old ladies will just flat-out refuse to share their secrets. But even worse are the ones like Tillie Mason, who will copy out the recipe for her to-die-for crumb cake on a 3x5 index card in her best cursive handwriting with a flattered smile. Just try to duplicate her genius in your own kitchen, though. When you take that much-anticipated first bite, you are left feeling that she might not have transcribed *every* ingredient or the exact right amount of each.

"Daisy." Fence's bass voice booms behind me, always a surprise from his small frame, no matter how many times I've heard it. "Don't get up."

He pulls his pant legs by the front creases so that he can sit without wrinkling. Then he reaches inside his vest for his pipe, and gives a couple of quick raps on the bowl.

"Do you mind?"

I shake my head. I am not a fan of smoking, but the smell of pipe tobacco is heavenly to me, like sun-warmed earth. Maybe it reminds me of my mom and the faint scent of weed that used to linger in our apartment, even though she never lit up around me. Anyhow, it somehow makes me feel friendlier than I might have toward Fence.

"So, Daisy," he begins, pausing for a puff on that cherrywood pipe. "How's your grandma?"

"Better. She's got a ways to go. Still using a walker to get around and a wheelchair for longer distances. But she's Grandma." I shrug. "Tough as nails."

"Yes, she's that in spades," says Fence. "All of us in Possum Flats would agree on that, even as we recalibrate our idea of your grandma. Now that we know she is really Violet, I mean."

There is a silence as he seems to gather his thoughts. Across the way, children are playing tag around the pavilion, shrieking in delight at near misses and teasing each other by taking their hands off and on "base," which appears to be an old post oak.

"But I'm not here to talk about your grandma," Fence finally says. "Even though everyone else in Possum Flats has been and probably will be for the foreseeable future. At least until some other piece of gossip turns their heads."

Fence's gray eyes give nothing away.

"Well, what *do* you want to talk about?"

"Your future."

My *future?* From the man who as good as fired me a few short weeks ago?

"Um," I say. "I thought you wanted to string me up after . . ." I pause. "After Jimmy and everything."

"I did," Fence says, his eyes steady. "And even now, if I could figure out exactly what sent the chief into that dark place where he didn't feel he had a way out? I'd sure change it if I could.

"But we can't know, can we? And blaming it on you seems . . . well, like a lot to lay on the shoulders of a fifteen-year-old newspaper intern. What I mean to say is that I'm awfully sorry, Daisy."

"Apology accepted," I say, wanting to get past this awkward "buddy" moment I seem to be having with my former boss. "But it doesn't change the fact that my article must have dredged up something tough for the chief. I hate that. What if I'd never come to Possum Flats? Or taken a job with *The Picayune?* Or dug up the dance hall story?

"He would still be here, I just know it." I shrug my shoulders, as if trying to get free of the weight I've been carrying around these past weeks. It doesn't help.

"Well, we can't change anything, Daisy. And I would venture to say that I'm not the only one who is glad you came to Possum Flats. I'm hoping you'll want to keep on reporting for us into the school year."

The school year.

Here? In Possum Flats? It had not even crossed my mind. But Fence is right. School starts after Labor Day. I have been biding my time until Mom sends for me. I'm going to be a California girl. Aren't I?

"Daisy?"

I realize that I have just been staring at Fence, open-mouthed, for God knows how long. The reality is that Mom hasn't been in touch since she dropped me here three-and-a-half months ago. No letters. No calls. For all I know, she could be dead in a ditch.

"I haven't really thought about the future," I lie. My eyes are stinging as I struggle not to cry. "I wasn't planning on being here this long, I guess."

"Well, think about it," Fence says briskly, obviously worried that I'm about to go all weepy on him. "After school and maybe Saturday mornings? Do some of those glamorous obits you're so good at." He chuckles. "And maybe talk me into another feature that I won't want to say yes to . . . and then be glad I did. Is it a deal, Watergate?"

At that, I laugh, too. I extend my hand.

"Deal," I say.

Fence grabs my hand and gives it a firm pump. For a moment, I am taken back to the day he offered me the internship in that cramped office—on the heels of my very inappropriate pitch story. We've both seen and learned a lot since then. This is our fresh start. But maybe with a little more respect on both sides.

"And now, do you have time for dessert before you head home? There's an end-of-summer picnic over at the pavilion, and I've heard a rumor that Tillie is bringing her crumb cake."

"We better hurry," I say. "Because it won't last long."

Fence and I share a friendly silence as we head down the sloping lawn of the armory to the street in front of the pavilion. There is a slant to the sunlight through the high canopy of post oaks that signals afternoon easing into evening. While it is still full-on summertime hot, the nights have started to cool. And though leaves remain deep green, there is the musty scent of plants well past their prime.

Summer is in a death spiral, and I never thought I would be here to see it. But somehow, I am. And the prospect of staying here in Possum Flats beyond that—which only a month or two ago would have left me depressed or hysterical—doesn't seem terrible. I might even enjoy it.

I haven't given up on my mom. But if setting us up in California takes a little longer, I guess I won't be devastated. I'll have a couple of friends at school: Patty and, if I'm lucky, Joe. An after-school job. And I feel closer to Grandma since nursing her after her fall. And learning her secrets. I don't know how grandmas and grand-daughters are supposed to relate, but old Violet-Rose feels like a good friend who's been around longer and is a little wiser than me.

"Are you sure we should do this?" I realize as we reach the steps that I am arriving both empty-handed *and* uninvited, a double Possum Flats party foul.

Fence laughs. "I've got two words for you: crumb cake. And yes, you are definitely invited."

I don't feel reassured. I haven't been out of the house since Grandma's article. I'm not sure what people think of her. Of me.

At the bottom of the stairs, I feel frozen, afraid to join the hub-bub. What if I'm asked to leave? There's a not-so-gentle push on my back; Fence wants me to go on up.

The whole scene is surreal. The crowd of people casually hang-ing out on the steps pull apart, taking their places against the rail-ings as if clearing a path for me. I see Hazel's grandson, Will. One of Joe's paperboy buddies from *The Picayune*. But when I reach the top of the stairs, the crowd—laughing and visiting, chasing their kids, placing their dishes just so on the red-and-white-checked tablecloths—goes completely silent.

As if on cue, everyone pulls back to the edges of the pavilion, away from the picnic tables, leaving an empty space in the middle. There is so much to take in all at once: the podium with a micro-phone and boxy black speakers at one end of the open floor space, a large silver disco ball winking in the evening sun as it spins, like some strange bejeweled planet dangling above us. And behind the podium, a large hand-painted banner, red tempera paint on newspaper print:

LAMB'S DANCE HALL EXPLOSION: WE REMEMBER.
1928–1978
POSSUM FLATS, MISSOURI

The bottom of the banner is peopled with a crowd of whimsically drawn dancers that I immediately recognize as Joe's handiwork. Just as I am beginning to understand what is happening, the silence is broken by someone clapping. I turn to find Smiley, who has stepped forward from the edge of the crowd, sporting an ear-to-ear grin. The sound his hands make echoes off the cement pillars and ceiling of the pavilion.

It's as if he has loosened a brick in a dam and suddenly everyone has joined in, the applause like the roar of a spring creek. I am stunned, seeing so many faces that I've come to know and love. Right beside Smiley, there's Myra and Sedalia, with Patty peeking out shyly in-between. I see Betty from the diner, still wearing her apron; Ginger Morton with a fox stole around her shoulders, even in mid-August. Ruby Rae Watson, in her Sunday best circa 1940, is standing beside Mo Wheeler, dapper in his sunglasses and fedora. He has propped himself up with the help of his cherrywood cane and his daughter, Julie. And there, in the front corner: Grandma in her wheelchair with an expression that can only be described as smug, and Roger beaming behind her. I look over my shoulder and Fence is nodding and clapping, too.

I can't think, the noise is so loud. I don't know what to do. I almost start clapping—until it dawns on me that everyone is clapping for me. And just as the thunderous roar starts to die down, Patty steps forward into the empty space beneath the disco ball, her hair plaited in Dutch braids and denim skirt freshly ironed for the occasion.

As the crowd quiets, she shyly opens her mouth—but instead of words, the clearest note sounds. And then:

"For she's a jolly good fellow,
For she's a jolly good fellow,
For she's a jolly good fellow . . .
That nobody can deny!"

"Ladies and gentlemen, please join me in another round of applause for Daisy Flowers!" Another voice is speaking now, from the other side of the crowd.

Joe.

He heads toward me with a huge bouquet of daisies, swaddled in tissue paper and carried in his arm like a football. When he reaches my side, he places the flowers in my hands and then takes my arm, moving us toward the front of the pavilion. The crowd starts clapping again, and Joe turns to me with an extremely self-congratulatory smile.

"Did you do . . . all of this?" I feel like an awkward Miss America, walking down this makeshift catwalk with my bouquet, on the arm of a handsome escort. All I need is Bert Parks and a sash: Miss Possum Flats, USA? I look up into his eyes and see hilarity; he is enjoying my discomfort. Just like that, we are back to the way we were before. It feels amazing.

"Well, it *was* my idea," he says, in the not-too-humble way that only he could pull off. "But I had help. You've got a lot of fans around here, Flower Child."

Joe deposits me at a folding chair beside the podium, just as Fence slides in behind it with a microphone.

"Daisy, on behalf of Possum Flats, I just want to thank you," he says. "Taking on the story of the dance hall explosion was pretty brave. Especially for a fifteen-year-old green intern who many of us might have considered an 'outsider.'"

I look out at all the faces, some smiling, some somber, all nodding. There is a smattering of applause. "But you told us our stories. Hard stories. True stories. Stories that some of us needed to share and all of us needed to hear. Things we weren't sure we wanted to hear . . . until we did.

"Turns out, this story was really your story, too," he says. "You found out some things about your family . . . and about yourself. Like it or not"—he pauses to a few chuckles—"you're one of us."

Here he turns to look directly at me.

"I won't say it came without a dustup. And yes, I know I tried to talk you out of it multiple times along the way. But it was a reckoning of sorts," he says. "We needed to acknowledge that dark time so that the Possum Flats folk we lost that night aren't forgotten. So we could let a little light into some tucked-away corners of our souls. And heal.

"So thank you, Daisy, for helping us say today—to the survivors, the families who suffered loss, and to the dead, of course—we remember.

"Now Myra and Smiley will read the names of the victims of the Lamb's Dance Hall explosion."

I watch my two mentors make their way to the podium. They taught me in different ways that the key to good storytelling is understanding that it is more about people and their responses to life than any particular event. "Just the facts" isn't enough.

"Thank you, Fence," Myra says. She nods at Smiley and he takes a nervous gulp of air—poor introvert!—and begins.

"Beryl Adams," he says.

"Stanley Clapper," answers Myra.

"Dale Diggs."

"Rose Flowers."

It sounds so strange to have my grandma's name read in the roll of the dead that I have to look up. Grandma has her eyes closed; Roger is patting her reassuringly. The names continue, echoing off the cement ceiling before dissipating through the open sides of the pavilion, out into the sun-warmed air. In the strange quiet of this summer evening, the only sounds are the steady chirr of cicadas and the occasional car or truck passing by on Porter Wagoner Boulevard.

"Ralph Mitchell."

"Beebe Monroe."

"Nell Peters."

A hand on my shoulder gives a firm squeeze. Joe is behind me. Knowing that makes me feel less alone and strange during what has become an unexpectedly weird but cool night. I can't believe this is happening, that something I've done has brought us all together. But I know the real reason we are gathered is the people whose names we are sending up. Sneaking a peek around, I see most everyone has their eyes closed. Some are bowing their heads as if in prayer. There are some quiet sniffs and people dabbing their eyes. Ruby Rae hugs a black-and-white photo: a young woman with a mane of dark curls.

"Charlie Walters."

"Fern Watson."

"Timothy Woodbin." Smiley's voice sounds relieved. That's it. I've read enough of the old news clippings to recognize the end of the alphabetical list of the dead from the explosion. Heads lift, eyes blink and open. A baby babbles and is hushed.

And then the brief silence is broken.

"James Jeffers." A woman's voice is loud but a little wobbly. "Jimmy," she adds.

It is Mabel.

I see her in the far corner, short despite the dyed beehive hairdo that adds about six extra inches of height—along with the two from her practical black pumps. Her eyes are closed, but that does nothing to hide their redness.

Heads bob; someone from the back throws out an "amen." I find myself nodding, too. Because while he didn't share his own story with me—or with anyone else—it clearly killed him, what happened fifty years ago. It just took a while for those fatal injuries to take their toll. Like a slow-growing cancer or a thinning spot in an artery, waiting to burst. Jimmy Jeffers was as much a casualty of the Lamb's Dance Hall explosion as any of these other thirty-nine. Knowing that my story dislodged the small stone that gained speed and danger on the way down the dark hill of his mind still gives me a guilty pang.

I'm sorry, Jimmy.

Myra and Smiley return to their seats and Fence has the mic again.

"Thank you both. And now let's have a moment of silence for those thirty-nine lives we lost that night, August 13th, 1928." He pauses. "And for Jimmy, too."

DASH

Lord, not my will, but thine, be done.

These words from the Gospel of Luke are running through my mind as I make my way along the uneven sidewalks of downtown. It is not quite five o'clock, but Possum Flats' shops are shuttered, windows darkened, keys already turned in shiny dead-bolts.

With a jolt, I remember that it is a Sunday: Of course they are closed.

How can any preacher worth his salt forget the Lord's day? Suffice it to say that it has not been an ordinary Sunday. I was absent from my pulpit for the first time—outside a rare vacation—in nearly fifty years. Marilyn was adamant I stay home. I had given her a scare, she said.

For once, I was too worn out to argue. She called one of the church elders to fill in. Brother Barker enjoyed the spotlight, I'm sure. Perhaps too much. When I allow myself to think about the message he may have preached this morning, I am terrified.

I must not think of that.

For the moment, I am just grateful there isn't anyone out to see me struggling, dragging my bad ankle. Although the struggles inside me are the ones of which I am most ashamed. I am trying to keep my emotions in check as I push myself along.

I need to make it to the park.

Not my will, but thine.

314 Michelle Collins Anderson

So far, I am feeling no calming effect by relinquishing my life to the Higher Power. My will—if it could be exacted right now—would include a few choice lightning strikes from the heavens above. Like the prophet Amos, I want to "let judgment run down as waters, and righteousness as a mighty stream."

I want Daisy Flowers' head on a pike and Fence McMillan's right alongside.

There. I've said it. *Thought* it. Which is the same difference in the eyes of Almighty God. Just ask Jimmy Carter, damned by both God and the media for committing adultery in his heart.

I better watch the heavens myself.

Since Daisy's last article came out on Friday—two long, hellish days ago, to be sure—I have been in absolute purgatory, of both mind and body.

Joe stopped by my office late that afternoon with my rolled-and-rubber-banded copy of *The Picayune*.

"Fresh off the presses," he said, setting it in the middle of my desk. I had the strangest image then, of a faithful hunting dog presenting his master with the kill.

"You probably ought to stay sitting down when you read that, Bro," he said. The cheeky boy is regularly calling me his pet endearment to my face now.

"What do you mean?" I chose to ignore his impertinence.

"You're in Daisy's last article," he said. "You might need to gird your loins or put on the full armor of God or whatever." He paused as if he wanted to say something more, but didn't. Did Joe know how that exhortation ends? *Put on the whole armour of God, that ye may be able to stand against the wiles of the devil.*

For once, I did not think he was joking or poking fun at me. I sat still, digesting the fact that my grandson had made some scriptural references—as if he *knew* Scripture.

Miracles never cease.

"Good night, Bro," he said at last and was gone.

It did not take me long to figure out why I might need that full armor. Or which devil and exactly what wiles I would be called to stand against.

Daisy Flowers. And her final installment.

I found my hands trembling as I unfolded the newspaper and tried to smooth it, smudging the ink and leaving a dark stain like old blood on my palm.

Rose and Violet Flowers.

Ah, I see. It was not enough to showcase Hazel's recollections of my drunkenness or Jimmy's courage in the face of my helplessness that night at Lamb's.

Now I had to read about my days as a rake and Lothario through the eyes of my old steady's sister.

As I began reading, I was immediately transported back to those Friday nights at Lamb's. All those intermissions spent in Charlie's Plymouth and the uncomfortable jostling for position in the tight, hot confines of the back seat that smelled of gin, sweat, leather and, let's face it: human coupling. How much would Violet have shared of our romantic indiscretions? As I recalled, it was only that one time, although I saw and covered plenty of territory on other occasions.

We had been together longer than I usually lasted with any one girl, I remember that. But Violet was coy. I had to put in extra effort since she wasn't quite as susceptible to the Dash charm as most women were back then. I even gave her a gold locket—a small heart with even smaller diamond chip—to "prove" my love, and she agreed to go steady. It was the price I had to pay to get to what we crudely referred to then as "home plate." Was it worth it? Young Dash—that scoundrel—would have said yes.

But, no. The words I read made my old body shudder, as if the bones themselves had frozen, sending chills through my sagging flesh.

Violet was *not* Violet that night?

Rose was Violet.

So *Violet* was really . . . Rose. Rose Flowers. From the funeral home.

And she was pregnant.

Oh, dear God in heaven.

What had I done to deserve this?

I don't know how I made it home that evening after sitting para-lyzed at my desk, well past suppertime. I don't recall eating or watching television—not even my beloved Johnny Carson. I took to my bed and I stayed there that night and most of the next day.

Marilyn showed up last night with a Chinet plate covered in a hump of tinfoil and a concerned look on her face and I did not even get up to answer the door. She *tsk-tsked* at the sight of me, flat on my back in bed. She set the plate on my bedside table, while she felt my forehead and began haranguing me about not being in any shape to preach the next day. The smell wafting up from beneath the foil reminded me I hadn't eaten all day. And that my human flesh was, once again, weak. My mouth watered at what I knew lay beneath that shiny cover: roast beef with gravy, garden-fresh green beans and a golden-crusted biscuit. Yet how could I even think of eating? My life was absolutely, abysmally ruined.

Skipping a Sunday was one thing. But how could I ever go back now? Who would be my sheep? Who could I shepherd in my fallen state? I had done my level best to live by the law of the Lord for five decades, overcoming my first quarter-of-a-century of de-bauchery and foolishness. Or so I had thought.

I balanced the plate on my sunken chest and ate my daugh-ter's offering ravenously. I barely paused to chew or savor as I nor-mally would, eating being one of the few pleasures of my dull life. Meanwhile, I heard Marilyn on the phone, making arrangements for my Sunday substitute. She only left after extracting a promise that I would "take it easy."

I promised. But as soon as I heard her drive away, I was up and pacing my modest home like a caged animal, far past the time the late summer sun had disappeared in an electric-orange burst, leaving behind a bruised and darkening sky. My mind kept turning over what I had read, exhuming the horrific memories of that night at Lamb's. I swear it was as if my body was feeling the white-hot scorch of those long-ago flames; my ankle shrieking once more with pain as real as if I were still trapped beneath that fallen beam. I was drenched in sweat, yet shaking with chills.

I awoke this morning sprawled on the hard, humorless sofa in the sitting room, where we used to welcome parishioners and visitors when Susan was alive. She kept it covered in translucent plastic so that no stains or dust would mar it. My cheek stuck in a puddle of my own saliva on that cracking yellowed plastic. Who or what were we saving that couch for? It seems so ridiculous now.

In the light of day, I no longer felt the heavy, knee-buckling despair with which I had walked these floors.

Weeping may endure for a night, but joy cometh in the morning, the Psalmist wrote. But I would not categorize what I felt as "joy." Rather, I felt myself working up to a good, hot fit of rage.

Who was Daisy Flowers to write this story without corroboration of any kind? And why did Fence see fit to print it? The article all but names me as the perpetrator of Violet's out-of-wedlock pregnancy. But while she may have played hard-to-get with me, who is to say I was the only one? I'd seen her dance on tabletops with no regard for who might be receiving a show below, swill gin with the best of us, and reappear after a band break with her dark hair mussed and lipstick gone.

I felt violated myself, if I may say so.

And I needed some apologies. Not to mention a full correction and admission of shoddy reporting and publishing. I would not stand for having my reputation dragged through the sticky red-clay mud of this town.

So when Joe came by with Sunday dinner this afternoon and mentioned the memorial picnic for the dance hall explosion victims, I knew I would have my audience—and a chance to clear my name.

"You should think about showing up, Bro, if you're feeling better," he said. "It's shaping up to be a nice celebration."

"Wild horses couldn't keep me away," I said.

Joe had looked slightly puzzled but pleased. "See you there, then."

But I don't think he is going to be all that happy when I arrive. I'm not in a party mood. My watch shows I'm fifteen minutes late, thanks to this damned ankle and my old-man lungs. I can finally see the pavilion, which looks packed to the gills with Possum Flats' citizenry. Sweat drips down the back of my black long-sleeved clerical shirt.

Strangely, when I make it to the stairs, there is no sound coming from the people crowding there, leaning against the pillars of the old stone structure and spilling out from the edges. Even the small children are quiet, although one little towhead gives me what can only be described as the "stink eye."

Something must be wrong. I take the first stair and then a second, bumping into several men who nod—is it my imagination, or do they avoid my eyes?—and back away. An uneven path clears for me, an unlikely Elijah parting this Jordan River of humanity. But in my case, no one follows me. I feel as alone as I ever have in my years of ministry.

That is when I realize that I must have unwittingly barged in on a moment of prayer or silence. Up ahead, a homemade banner in memory of the Lamb's explosion undulates in the evening breeze. Fence McMillan stands behind a podium, hands clasped around a microphone, head bowed. To his right, sitting satisfied as you please with an armful of aptly chosen blossoms: Daisy Flowers.

My blood heats up ten degrees with a righteous surge as I take it all in. How perfect that the precise two people I came here to excoriate are front and center. Perfect. The crowd can watch them squirm as I enumerate their sins and shortcomings as they've seen fit to speculate on mine.

As if they've heard my thoughts, they raise their heads. Daisy's eyes widen. Surprise? Fear? *Just wait, my dear. I have a few choice words for you.*

"Thank you, everyone," Fence says into the mic. "And now it

would seem that Brother Emmonds might want to offer a prayer or thoughts on the occasion? Didn't know you were on the program, Pastor. But welcome, I'm sure."

I snatch the microphone from Fence's hand. I have everyone's attention. But all I can do is breathe as heavily as an overworked plow horse, a noise grossly amplified by the sound system. I sound almost as angry as I am.

When my breathing slows, I scan the expectant faces lining the edges of the pavilion. I see a few parishioners—like Patty Johns and Ruby Rae Watson. And so many of the people who make this town run in some capacity or other. Ginger Morton. Betty. Hazel. Rose Flowers—*Violet*—in a wheelchair. Dear God, she has aged since her fall!

While my ire had been mainly directed at the two people behind and beside me, seeing Violet makes me understand that she is truly the cause of all my woe. Daisy should not have done that shoddy piece of reporting—and Fence should not have published it.

But Violet! She *told* the story, for the love of God and all that is holy. Without pausing for a second to consider my good name would be besmirched along with her own. I have been maligned, tried and convicted in the court of public opinion without even a chance to defend myself.

"No prayers today, I am afraid, Fence." I notice with consternation that some people look positively relieved. That's a real shot in the arm.

"No. I speak today in response to the blasphemy that has been perpetrated upon me by this . . . this *woman*." I am looking straight at Violet now, who does not falter under my gaze. "Her outlandish portrayal of the people and events surrounding the Lamb's Dance Hall explosion are nothing short of heresy."

I watch one of Violet's eyebrows quirk up and that small insouciance infuriates me, drives me to say things upon which I should ponder long and hard before letting escape my mouth. But the torrent has been unleashed, and I cannot veer from this path.

"Why, in this so-called 'news article,'" I say, "we learn that she had danced and smoked and caroused and gotten herself in the family way—which is not a surprise. But must I be yoked to her sins, her lasciviousness, her shameless whoring because I was once her beau?

"How dare you, Rose Flowers—*Violet Flowers*—accuse me of creating a bastard child with the likes of you!"

There is a collective intake of air: I have shocked these people, these Possum Flats citizens who are used to my blustering against the devil and his wicked ways. But usually he is more of an abstraction, lurking in the shadows, some antiquated version of pointed ears and pitchfork. I do not typically give the devil a specific name and face.

In those next few seconds in between, after everyone inhales sharply in alarm but before they breathe out, there is an ear-shattering squeal of rubber tires braking on the road beside the pavilion. A door slams, a heavy, creaking exclamation point on the car's tumultuous arrival. There is jostling as those on the stairs move out of the way of whatever or whoever has arrived on the scene.

I've lost my audience.

And for good reason: a woman has broken into the circle of citizens ringing the pavilion's edge.

She stands there like a vision, in a long, loose shift of purple tie-dye, hands on her hips, an aura of dark gold hair streaked subtly with gray. Her chest is heaving with either exertion or impatience, pointing up the fact that she is not wearing a brassiere. I would not be surprised to see wings sprouting from her back, a terrifying angel of the times.

Her green eyes slit as she focuses her powers and indignation on me.

"Excuse me," she says in a husky voice. "But did you just call my mother a *whore?*"

I am struck dumb. Why hadn't I seen it before? In my blissful ignorance, I didn't realize what was right in front of me the entire eighteen years she lived among us.

Too late, I reach for the podium to steady myself. But I am already stumbling backwards. Hands are clamping both arms as I am guided into the webbed safety of a folding lawn chair. But still she remains, terrible to my eyes.

My own countenance in female form.

Lettie.

My daughter. My child.

VIOLET-ROSE

"Lettie."

She whirls to find where my voice is coming from. When she sees me at last, not standing, as she expected, but seated, her expression devastates me. I must look frightening, so much closer to death than when she last saw me three short months ago. Her mother, in a wheelchair with a beat-in face still ugly with bruises, stitches and a missing tooth. Mercy. I had not considered what I must look like to a stranger.

Because that is what she is to me. A stranger.

Before I can say anything else, Daisy has bolted from her chair beside the podium and thrown herself into her mother's arms.

"Mom!"

They are so beautiful then, these two strong women. I marvel at my good fortune to have brought one of them into being and to have delighted in the other, even for the few short months I've known her.

I watch—all of us do, this goodly portion of Possum Flats captivated by the drama unfolding in front of them—as Daisy pulls back from her mother at last.

"But . . . where is Ron? Why didn't you write?" Her voice breaks the slightest bit. "How did you know to come today?"

She is an excellent inquisitor, showing off the skills sharpened by her stint at *The Picayune*.

But the questions are too many and too fast—or likely Lettie opts to answer only the ones she prefers.

"I didn't have money to keep my post office box." Lettie shrugs. "But you can thank Hazel for using her U.S. Postal Service colleagues to track me down. She said my mother was in really bad shape. That she might not make it."

Bodies shift and necks crane to get a look at our postmistress, whose cheeks have brightened to the color of strawberry Jell-O. She bobs her head as if to own up to her indiscretions. Bless her heart.

Here, Lettie turns again to look at me, and I can see she is unsure of what to do. The few yards of concrete between us feel like a vast desert. All those years of taking a firm, hard line with my child. Meting out rules and punishments to make sure that . . . that *what*, exactly? That she stays as far away from me as possible? Out of my life?

In that split second, I decide to make it easy for her, for once.

I simply open my arms.

DAISY

Absolute pandemonium.

I don't know how else to describe it. The whole pavilion has broken out into crazy applause and cheering, whistles and shouts. My body is electrified, like when I would eat a sugary cupcake at a birthday party and my strictly monitored body couldn't handle the rush.

Mom is here with her arms around my grandma and everyone is going bonkers. The sun's rays cut in from the west, giving them a golden glow, like they are part of a play. I wish this moment could last forever: two of my favorite people that I wasn't sure liked each other, hugging. I can't see my mother's face, but I can see Grandma's over her shoulder and she is crying.

Rose Flowers going soft. That's not something you see every day. *Any* day.

Violet, I mean.

Mom left me in the middle of the pavilion, right under the disco ball, dazzling as it spins in the sunlight. I take a slow turn myself, beaming the same way. All these happy, satisfied faces, the cheering. Possum Flats is welcoming home one of their own, while letting the other know that she is loved, too—no matter what her story.

There are Myra and Smiley and Patty, clapping to beat the band. I see Joe with his humongous smile, applauding with his arms raised above his head; Dash, who is sitting with his legs out stiffly, a little peaked from shock or overexertion. Little kids are darting onto the dance floor, chasing each other, riding the mood of the crowd.

All at once there is a loud hum and eardrum-busting screech of microphone feedback. The insanity ends as abruptly as it began. Fence has reclaimed his mic.

"Thank you, ladies and gentlemen. And Lettie," he adds, making it seem as if she is—as usual—outside the bounds of propriety. Which, to be fair, she is.

But then he surprises me.

"Welcome back to Possum Flats. It's been a while. But now, if we could get back to our, *ahem* . . . regular programming? Our final tribute to the victims of the Lamb's Dance Hall explosion is a fitting one at the end of this gorgeous late summer day. Please join me in remembering the events of August 13, 1928, by listening to the last song the band played that evening at Lamb's: 'At Sundown.'"

There is a sharp, scratching noise over the speaker as Fence bends over a record player, trying to drop the needle into the right groove. I hear a crackling and a few pops before the music begins, and the sound of an almost jaunty piano fills the pavilion. But after a few upbeat measures, a woman's voice begins to sing, wistful and haunting:

"Every little breeze is sighing
Of love undying
At sundown.
Every little bird is resting
And feather nesting
At sundown.
Each little rosebud is sleeping
While shadows are creeping.
In a little cottage, cozy,
The world seems rosy
At sundown;
Where a loving smile will greet me

And always meet me
At sundown."

My heart is about to burst from the beauty of this voice, this song. Thinking about those dancers so long ago, "cozy" in each other's arms and unaware of what was just about to happen—I feel a sadness like a flinty, square box in my throat. I can barely breathe, it hurts so much. And yet, I don't cry. I'm drawn into the music, like the singer has put a scarf around me and brought me in.

"I seem to sigh, I'm in heaven,
When night is falling
And love is calling me home!"

But it's Joe who has pulled me in. He looks down at me and winks. Before I know what is happening, we are making a slow circle on the pavilion floor. And just when I think it can't get any more perfect, there is a sweet, low, mournful sound that takes over for the singer's voice. I look over Joe's shoulder and see the most amazing sight: Mo Wheeler is blowing his saxophone like he is breathing out his very soul. A man who cannot see, who can't talk and can barely hear—creating this crushingly beautiful sound, suffering and sweetness all at once.

The crowd responds to the sax solo with a spontaneous burst of applause. Then it's a free-for-all. Fence has gotten Mom onto the dance floor. Roger has wheeled my grandma out for a few circles. Smiley and Myra. Hazel and her little grandson, Will. Betty and her freshly shaven fry cook.

"In a little cottage, cozy,
The world seems rosy
At sundown;
Where a loving smile will greet me
And always meet me
At sundown."

As we make our own small circle around the dance floor, I am on sensory overload. There is the clean smell of sunshine and bleach from Joe's white T-shirt, the current of warmth where his chest touches mine. The old song fills my ears, but it feels like it is working its way inside me, touching my bones. All around, there are people who I love—I still can't believe my mom is here! Dancing with Fence!—and everyone looks genuinely *happy*. At peace.

Until we turn so that I am facing the podium. Instantly, I see that not everyone is at peace. Far from it.

Dash Emmonds has risen from his chair. His gray face is a study in emotion: confusion, disbelief, anger? He takes a step forward, heading to the dance floor. Then another. His progress is slow, but his target is clear.

He is making his way toward Grandma. His jaw is set, a lumpy blue vein above his left temple throbs. He looks neither to the left nor right. I wonder, briefly, if Joe or I should stop him. He looks like a man on a mission—and not the Christian kind—and I am a little afraid for her.

The couples on the dance floor give way to him as he passes. Roger is the only thing between him and his target now, but his back is turned.

Why can't I move? Joe and I seem to be paralyzed by what is happening. I'm scared that when Roger turns around, Dash will throw a punch. He looks that agitated.

Dash taps Roger on the shoulder. I want to look away. But I can't.

Roger is surprised to find Dash behind him, but he nods at whatever has been said to him and steps out of the way. Grandma looks up, startled to see her old beau there. Yet she doesn't look afraid—just curious—when he slowly leans down, placing a hand on her wheelchair while he says something in her ear.

He pulls away, and Grandma's smile is awesome, busting out on her face. Maybe it's worse for the wear, but I'm betting every bit as mischievous as it was fifty years ago.

DASH

"Forgive me, Violet."

I'm embarrassed at how hard I am breathing, how my voice cracks as I try to speak loud enough to be understood over the music. But dear God, I'm afraid to speak too loudly. My pride, already cut to ribbons, cannot bear for everyone to hear my confession. Shame on me.

But I've made it this far. If she rejects me now, it will be humiliating, of course. But it would pale in comparison to what I've been through in the shame department the past week. What Violet must have experienced herself these many years.

I wait for her response, which seems to me to take an hour. My chest heaves from the effort of walking out here.

Then she surprises and delights me by extending her hand. I must pull her up to standing—but can I on these tottering old legs?

Thank God Roger is there to steady us both.

"I'll forgive you, Dash. But only if you dance with me."

Damn you, Violet. She has always known how to get under my skin. Between me and the will of my Lord. Certainly, I should take my stand—those from my flock who are in attendance will expect nothing less. *We* do not dance. The peril of it leading to immoral behavior is too great. Why engage in activity with such potential for eternal damnation? That is much too high a price for social acceptance.

And yet.

I do not even pretend that I would feel the stirrings of lust that are so feared from this dread activity. That part of me died in the explosion. Or I tried to kill it off, allowing myself only the pleasures of marriage that could lead to procreation. And even those felt shameful.

But . . . here we are.

I cannot deny her. She has been denied too much for too long, her very personhood even. And I am partly responsible for that. Even if I didn't know it until now.

Let me be, Lord. I have not asked directly for my salvation for precisely fifty years. *I have kept my vow to be your faithful servant. I pray you will understand now. Or punish me accordingly.*

Eternal hellfire be damned.

Clumsily, I place my left hand on her lower back while we put our palms up together, yet not quite touching. It is as if we are in a prison visiting room, where the desperate can align their hands through a layer of heartless glass, but not feel each other. But who is visitor and who is the prisoner? I think I know the answer as our hands make contact at last, hers half the size of mine and sandpaper-rough from years of embalming.

The music performs its strange magic, taking me back to that night, to those moments on the dance floor so many years ago. Looking down at Violet now, I don't see the silvery white of her hair or the lines that cradle her features. The deep brown eyes are the same and in them, I can nearly make out the young Dash Emmonds—fool that he was. That I am.

> *"I seem to sigh, I'm in heaven,*
> *When night is falling*
> *And love is calling me home!"*

To my surprise, Violet has breached the space between our bodies, pressing close to me. I close my eyes. I feel myself swaying, ever so slightly, a giant oak about to be felled. To those watching—and I know there are many eyes on this not-so-upright man of the cloth—it must look strange, more trembling in place than dancing. Quaking.

Until Violet does what she always does. What she used to do back when we were young and wild and sort of in love.

She takes over.

She nudges me gently until I pick up my right foot and take that first step. And then another.

I am following her lead.

It is wonderful to behold. And to be held.

Daisy

Grandma and Dash brought the house down.

There might have been a few raised eyebrows as they danced—if you could call it that. Not to be too harsh, but they put the "slow" in "slow dance." But there wasn't a dry eye in the house, mine included. It felt like something had been put to rest. Not just buried or jammed aside, but held for a few heartbeats and gently let go.

Like everything in Possum Flats—from the crooked sidewalks and brick buildings of downtown to the deep green parks and playgrounds and cemetery—breathed a deep sigh. Not just relief. But peace.

And I was part of it. I *am* part of it.

The potluck after the memorial service and dance is a blur. I have never smiled this much in my entire life. My cheeks hurt and my teeth feel chalky and dry from keeping my mouth in a grin for so long. People want to shake my hand, introduce themselves. Some say they feel they already know me because of my writing. Others talk about how I am the "spitting image" of my grandma and my aunt Rose. Even Ginger Morton stops by to say, "I told you so."

"Yes, you did." I can see why Grandma finds her irritating. "Grandma wasn't who I thought she was. But she was right about you, too."

Ginger's eyebrows disappear into unnaturally orange bangs. Her face settles into calm, and I understand that she doesn't want to hear that particular truth. Then she nods before turning away, an action I can only interpret as "touché." More people press in on me. I try to come up with intelligent responses to all the questions and comments.

But it's so much. So crazy. And the whole time, Joe is beside me, smugly satisfied at pulling this whole thing off. Maybe proud of me, too.

"Flower Child, I want you to meet someone." Joe is tugging a short, squat woman toward us. Her dress is a simple chambray, and her brownish-gold hair, threaded with gray, is pulled back neatly. Behind her—an inch or two taller, but skinny as a rail—a brown-eyed, square-jawed man wearing a short-sleeved plaid shirt and a cowboy hat.

"Mom and Dad, meet Daisy Flowers."

"So nice to finally meet you, Daisy," the woman says, her dark eyes warm like hot chocolate. "Joe has told us lots about you. You're the one who encouraged him with these drawings of his? We had no idea." The man agrees with a quick dip of his head. I practically whiplash my neck as I turn from the couple to Joe and back again. I would never have guessed they belonged together.

"But . . ." I don't know how to formulate my question without being extremely rude.

Fortunately, Joe has read my mind. Or he's gotten this response before.

"Oh, yeah. I'm adopted. I thought everyone knew that." Joe picks up his mom in a bear hug and twirls her around. She pretends to be horrified but is obviously delighted by her son's antics. "These are my people."

The way his parents look at him gives me a sharp pang. Until I remember that I've got people, too.

And I don't want to let my mom out of my sight.

Mom also seems quite popular. She's perched at one end of a redwood picnic table, an exotic bird, with Grandma close by in her wheelchair. Grandma is a Cheshire cat, practically disappearing behind her grin. Pride, of course. But something else, too, that I haven't seen in her face before. I think it's pleasure, pure and simple.

Mom appears as charmed by all of the people and attention as they are by her and hers. She is surrounded by Possum Flats citizens vying for a word or even asking for a hug, which my mother gives without hesitation. Tillie Mason is pressing a piece of crumb cake on a fluted white paper plate into my mom's hand. Tillie usually stays out of the crumb cake fray, preferring to watch as the rest of Possum Flats jostle and elbow (and even cut in line) to claim a piece. Mom catches my eye. I think she must know how strange it is for me to see her here, so comfortable in this place she had insisted was only worthy of escape.

Maybe home is something you can't run from, a place you find yourself searching for even after you think you've gotten away. You look for it in every town or city, apartment or house—but it's slippery, shifty. Because home is a *feeling*, and the people and place that inspire that feeling. It's about their acceptance and your belonging, whether you feel conflicted about that or not; whether they always like you or not. You can't change where and who you've come from, only where you will go and who you will be. But that place and those people always call your name, longing for you—and you, in turn, long for them.

I didn't know Possum Flats was my home. Until it was.

Later that night, I am at Grandma's dining room table playing gin rummy with Mom, Grandma and Roger and eating popcorn. The way they are laughing and carrying on, you would think they had been holding Friday night card games forever. Roger lays down his sets as soon as he accumulates them; Mom and Grandma keep their hands to themselves, trying to go out all at once with a bang—despite the risk of being caught with all seven cards. In the meantime, they are trying to outsmart each other by the cards they keep and discard.

"Damn you, Lettie!" Grandma is exasperated as Mom tosses a seven of hearts on the discard pile. "I swear you knew I was collecting those!"

Mom laughs and shakes her head. "You're giving me too much credit," she says, but I can tell she is pleased with herself. It is weird how much alike Mom and Grandma are, now that they are together. I could only see their differences, their extremes, when they were apart. They are like two magnets, how their like poles keep pushing each other away, with that invisible but very real force between them—until one sudden flip and the opposites pull them together with a satisfying "click."

I feel like a little kid, desperately wanting them to stay together this time.

But right now, I could use that seven for a straight.

"Gin." I fan all seven of my cards down: a run of four and three aces.

Mom and Grandma are shocked. They were so hell-bent on beating each other that they forgot about me.

I can't help but feel that is the story of my life.

But it sure feels great to win.

"Daisy! You little sneak!" Grandma pelts me with a piece of popcorn. "Sitting over there on a gold mine while Lettie and I duke it out."

I bask in the glow of my big victory, while the two women count their points—they both gambled by collecting face cards, so they lost big. Roger rakes in the cards with a shake of his head, as if he doesn't understand them. Or maybe just in general. His careful style means he rarely wins—but he also doesn't lose.

"I hate to bail on you," I say, "but I think after everything that happened today, I'm going to bed. I'm exhausted."

Mom touches my arm. "I bet you are, baby. You go on ahead. I'll take the couch when I'm ready to crash. Grandma and I still have some catching up to do."

Normally, that would feel like code for arguing or hashing

things out. But the way Grandma is looking at my mom, I know everything is going to be okay. I kiss each woman on the crown of her head and go upstairs.

Of course, I'm not really going to bed.

Joe and I are meeting up at the cemetery tonight. He slipped me a note right before he took his grandfather home from the picnic, a little sketch of the two of us sitting on the memorial headstone with a full moon like a disco ball above our heads.

11? was all it said when I unfolded it. There was nowhere I'd rather be—and no one I'd rather be with.

The memorial and picnic were cool. Reading the names. Dancing. But Joe felt we needed to really *be* with those thirty-nine people tonight. So they didn't feel forgotten.

I agreed. But I wasn't sure how I was going to get out of the house undetected at eleven o'clock at night.

I hear chairs scooting across the floor, backing up from the table. Laughter and snippets of words float up through the heat register in my floor. Water runs in the sink. There is the clinking of bowls and the heavier thunk of the popcorn kettle being washed and rinsed.

I wait a few minutes to make my way down the back stairs. I know exactly how the screen door will creak, so I ease it open slowly against the rusty spring coil and it doesn't complain much at all.

Outside, the muggy August night is vibrating with its own noises: the chirrup of small tree frogs, the scratching throb of cicadas. A barred owl punctuates the rhythmic hum by asking "Who cooks for you?" again and again.

The grass is already damp with dew, and the toes of my new Tretorns are soaked by the time I reach the front corner of the house. I am skirting the edge of light from the streetlight when I breathe in the unmistakable mixture of skunk and burnt leaves that I haven't smelled since landing in Possum Flats.

"Hey there." My mom's voice from the dark front stoop is low and gravelly, the way it gets when she smokes. I see the small, dark orange flare in the blackness as she takes another drag. "Sneaking off to meet a boy?"

My face heats up in the pitch black. I'm glad she can't see it.

"Um . . . no."

"Daisy. I know every single solitary means and reason to steal out of this house. And at this hour . . . I think it's safe to say you're not heading to the library."

"Well, I *am* sneaking off to see a boy, I guess. But not like that," I add, flustered. "I'm meeting Joe at the cemetery."

My mother laughs. "Wow, okay."

I didn't mean that the way it sounded. Now I'm sweating all over. "It's part of the memorial," I manage at last. "We want to mark the exact time of the blast with the people who died. Joe doesn't believe in ghosts exactly, but he thinks they'll know we're there."

"Sounds kind of cool," she says. I watch as the little ring of fire brightens again, then disappears with her exhale. "Have fun."

I am dumbfounded. Really?

"Go on," she says. "Get out of here."

"Thanks," I say, turning to go. But I stop in my tracks. "Mom?"

"Yes, sweet baby?"

"You'll still be here when I get back, right?" My heart is pounding all the way up in my throat. It surprises me how anxious I am for her answer.

"I'll be here," she says. "I'm not going anywhere. At least, not right away."

"You're not?"

"No." She exhales slowly, as if buying herself time to think. "I shouldn't have let Ron turn my head and take me away. That was wrong.

"But I learned something," she says in the dark night. The insects and tree frogs fill in the blank spaces around her voice. "I belong with you."

"But what about Ron?" I ask, my voice shaking with relief. Not that I care about Ron. I just want to know she means it.

"You're my home," she says. Her tone is like a simple shrug of the shoulders. "He didn't get that."

I make my way in the dark toward her voice until I bump into her, as she is following mine. Our hug feels fierce and desperate and soothing all at once.

"I missed you, Mama."

"Me, too, sugar bear," she says. Her body tightens against mine, with its smells of sage, hemp and incense mingled with sweat. "And I'm sorry. But shouldn't you run along now? You don't want to miss the big moment with that boy."

Dash

Marilyn and Joe got me home from the picnic in their late-model Ford from the dealership; John stayed behind to clean up and said they could pick him up on their way home. Exhausted, my shirt plastered to my skin with sweat, I couldn't have walked another step. I was grateful for the plush seats and air conditioning.

Marilyn is banging around in the kitchen, likely horrified by my lack of provisions, while Joe gets me lowered into my La-Z-Boy. The black vinyl behemoth is the single indulgence I allowed myself after Susan died and it no longer mattered if an ugly chair would fit into the decor.

"Bro, you okay?" Joe's face is close to mine when I open my eyes. I'm surprised to see he has whiskers—blond and mostly soft, but still. Where has time gone?

"That's Grandfather to you," I say, trying for a bit of levity I don't feel. I don't like the worry in his eyes.

"Right," he says. "Want to change into a more comfortable shirt? Take off that collar?"

I shake my head.

"Always on duty, right, Bro? Wouldn't want the good Lord to think you were blowing off your responsibilities."

I want to smile but it is too much effort.

"Dad, don't you have a can of soup I can heat up?" Marilyn

sounds exasperated. But her habit of sending over plates of home cooking have only encouraged me not to stock many groceries.

Joe tucks me in with an old quilt made by the sewing circle at church; Marilyn puts a cup of warm chicken broth and a few saltines within my reach. Then, dissatisfied but resigned to their limitations with this stubborn old curmudgeon, they leave me in peace.

It is a relief not to feel the constant buzz of electricity that comes with their frenetic busyness and need for conversation. I'm simply not used to it.

Involuntarily, I sigh deeply, shiver. Now I can't seem to get warm after the AC in the Ford. Perhaps I should have let Joe help me into a dry shirt.

I am tired like I have not experienced before, a shimmering weakness that I feel to the very marrow of my bones. And yet, my mind is racing, unable to join my body in its lethargy. It wants to puzzle things out, to categorize and bring order to that which will not be ordered. That which does not fully make sense.

I learned today that I have a third daughter. And another granddaughter. And that my old girlfriend whom I thought I watched die one night fifty years ago is alive and—while not altogether *well*—persevering. I am frankly overwhelmed.

I close my eyes.

There is only the sound of my own ragged breathing against the house noises I've grown used to, as it complains before settling in at last. The old rectory is feeling its age deep in its bones, much like I am.

I don't know how long I have lain here or if I've slept off and on or maybe even been awake the whole time. But all at once, I feel that I must get up now, at this exact moment. I don't need anything; I am not thirsty. My bowl of broth and crackers lie untouched beside me. It's more as if someone has called for me— *Pastor? Brother. Dash! Paul?*—and I must answer.

I am amazed at how easily I pull myself up from my recliner.

My body feels refreshed in a way it hasn't for years. Decades. There is a lightness to my whole being, something I can liken only to absolution. Nothing weighs on my heart. At some central point of me, not quite my brain but not in my body alone, I honestly believe that I could fly.

And to my amazement, I do.

At first, I am not high off the floor at all. It's more like hovering— not with the frantic intensity of a hummingbird, but more like a hawk sustained above the earth by an air current. Then, as I rise, I find myself looking down from the vantage point of the ceiling and drift back until I am settled into the upper corner of the room.

From here, I am disconcerted to see that I am still in my re-cliner, sleeping peacefully beneath the heavy flowered quilt, mouth slightly open. There is no sound, no rough gasping like when I first got home, my chest tight and lungs exhausted from the physical efforts of my day. No snoring, either. My face, as deeply lined as the farmland my father once plowed, is relaxed. I find it hard to look away from my corporeal body, so familiar but so strange. I am not sure we ever stop seeing ourselves as eighteen or twenty, no matter how many years or mirrors we pass, and this picture is not compatible with the aged relic I see beneath me. I'm not tethered to that old man at all anymore, and yet I feel a great tenderness for him.

As I do for this room, this house. The wooden floors where my daughters crawled, then walked and eventually left me be-hind. The kitchen, where Susan could still be standing, crimping the crust of a peach pie or cutting our potato soup with water to stretch it further.

I am receding now, pulling further back and *up, up, up* until I am outside in the starry night, near the top of the shingle oak that has shaded this place beneath its broad arms since before I was born. I do not wonder at my ability to do this, to see my humble home and neglected yard from up here, where the slightest of warm breezes rustles these shadowy boughs around me.

"Brother."

Is it just the wind? Or a whisper? As I turn toward the sound, I am spirited away from my little patch of earth in a rush of black night and trails of glittering stars. I stop suspended over the downtown square, floating near the steeple of my beloved church with its fragile brick-and-mortar walls which protect the even more delicate souls fed and nourished within them. My heart could burst for love of every single one of them: the broken, the lonely, the lost . . . the bitter and crotchety. I wish I could tell them it will be all right. More than all right.

Like Patty. I can see her profile near the window of her attic room in the rundown bungalow a few blocks away. The rest of the house is dark at this hour, but Patty is at her desk with a single bare bulb overhead. She has her right hand on her Bible—yet she is not contemplating Scripture or saying her prayers. Instead, the fingers are carefully splayed on that black leather book and in her left hand, she holds a tiny plastic brush that she traces painstakingly across a pink oval nail, then dips in polish before moving on to the next. She pauses to hold that hand up to inspect it, turning it one way and then another, catching the light in the shine of her wet nails.

It's good, I want to say. It is good to test and try on different ideas of what it means to be godly, a good person. To push back against what you are taught and preached until you find what is true. And follow it—relentlessly, exhaustively—holding it up constantly against the changing light and asking hard questions. Doubt is just the dark, necessary side of understanding. Of reconciliation. Of peace. I can't tell her this. But she is figuring it out on her own.

Down Main Street, I see Morton's, with the lights still on behind the locked door. Stooped at the cash register is Ginger, counting the till and stacking her receipts. There is something endearing about the way her too-red lipstick is smeared slightly atop her cracked lips, as though she can no longer color within the lines. So many lines. But I do not feel a pang for her in her aloneness. She is content, surrounded by the friends in her own manicured hands—Ben Franklin, Abe Lincoln, George Washington—and the tidiness of her aisles full of little packages of hope: body lotions, anti-wrinkle creams, wart removers, aspirin, nail polish, emery boards, hair dye, deodorant, mouthwash, toenail clippers, Kleenex. Comforts and cures for the physical body designed to reverse or stave off decay. It all seems so unnecessary to me now, and yet, I would not discourage her or any of her customers from these small comforts and vanities that make life bearable. I see that Ginger will die there in Morton's, a fall off of a stockroom ladder—as tenuous as she is shaky—on a late night like this one. No one will find her until morning, when she will be long gone.

There, too, is *The Picayune*, dark inside. I no longer feel a burning hatred toward Fence or that girl. Any of them. Smiley. Myra. Instead, there is a flush of something else that courses through me. A warmth. An understanding. People need to tell and be told their stories to know who they are and where they came from; where they are headed. Truly it is not all that different from my sermonizing and attempts to spread the Gospel. We were just coming at it from two different places, above and below. Earth and heaven. All part of the same. All one.

I see the lights on at the back of the funeral home. Instantly, I'm outside the brightly lit scene framed by the window—it's like I'm watching a movie, except I know what is going to happen. Violet is at the dining room table, stretching a dirty, flesh-colored rubber band around a deck of cards; Roger rests his chin on one hand, smiling at whatever she's just said.

But he isn't really listening. He's thinking how he is going to ask her—maybe tomorrow, if he can muster up the courage—to marry him. He's a little afraid of her, like everyone else. She will be completely shocked, and for once she will struggle to find words. When she does, she will say they are too old. That she is too set in her ways. That she is a pain in the ass.

Then she will say yes.

This pleases me.

I feel a presence beside me and see that Lettie has crept back here to spy on her mother, too. She hangs back out of the circle of light, but she is as transfixed by the scene as I have been. The ember of one of those "wacky weed" cigarettes glows between her fingers, and her face is a study of emotions: curiosity, joy, wistfulness, relief. Sadness for her own loneliness and failures. She resolves in this moment to stay here, to be truly present for her mom and for Daisy.

She will be gone by New Year's. Another false hope for true love. This is not her fault. It is in her DNA and I certainly bear some responsibility for that. But this time, she will offer to take Daisy along with her.

Daisy will say no.

Daisy.

My *granddaughter*.

The thought of her tears me away with such force that I must close my eyes, or whatever is allowing me to view this world. My world. I am an energy thrust into blackness, tearing breathlessly through a tunnel, until suddenly I am floating once more, suspended high above Possum Flats.

There she is, running as fast as she can, a blur in her new white sneakers, one of her small concessions to trying to *be* a part instead of standing apart. She is heading toward the cemetery. She flashes in and out of the streetlights, fully illuminated, then immersed in shadow. Yet I see all of her.

Her beauty, yes. But also her beating heart, so strong, so determined to be true to itself and yet yearning for love. For acceptance. A home. She will keep putting herself out there, even having suffered abandonment and uncertainty. She is a seeker, and that open, bleeding heart will always find its way. It will draw people in, enchant them, make them want to protect her, to be good for her.

Like that boy sitting there, impatiently tapping his foot on the lowest granite step of the monument marking the dead from the explosion.

Joe.

I can't help it, I am pulled toward him. Just another one of his paparazzi, I suppose. My golden boy. Then, it is as if I am inhabiting him, feeling the nervous sweat beneath his arms, his pulse beating fast in his wrists. He is anxious to see Daisy—is she coming?—but worried, too. Not just about the time—though he desperately wants her to make it by eleven—but how she feels about him. His thoughts are a jumbled mix of adoration, lust, insecurity, bravado. He thinks he loves her, but he doesn't understand all the strange feelings he has. He wants to touch her, hold her, stay up all night talking to her, laugh with her, get out of this town with her, stay here together forever. He hasn't met anyone like her, and he wants to hang on to her like a drowning man to a life raft. Even just as friends, if she decides that's what they should be.

Just when I think I cannot bear to be inside the male teenage mind anymore, heartbreaking and harrowing as it is, Daisy is here. She is racing toward us, toward Joe. There is the skittering crunch of tennis shoes on the gravel path and thumping as her feet find the grass shortcut. Her face is a knot of worry and questions.

"Flower Child!"

Joe is opening his arms and just like that, he is holding her so tightly to him, to us. I am sandwiched between the two of them now, a warm, red, pulsing force. I am the beating heart outside both of their bodies, perfectly syncopated.

Joy.

That is what this is, this living, throbbing thing that I am inside of. It is so pure, so splendidly sublime, that I long to stay in it. I recognize the lack I had been experiencing prior, in my life before tonight, but it doesn't make me bitter or bereft. Instead, I feel complete, as if someone has seen the hole and filled it, every last nook and cranny.

These two blessed creatures don't need me. Daisy and Joe will not always be as blissfully happy as they are together right now, but I see many flashes where they will come close in the long, unfurling ribbons of time that extend in front of them both, parallel at times, veering off here and there, crossing and concurrent at others: high school. College for her, art school for him. There was a time I might have envied them that unspooled time and unspoiled experience. Like when I was a child atop a wooden sled on a glorious hill, a virgin snow before me, no tracks, nothing ahead but possibility. Yet now I feel only contentment. As if everything in my life to this point has been for this moment and it is extraordinarily rich and gorgeous and more than enough.

Now: a rumbling, a vibrating at my core. A low, deep moan seems to come from both inside and outside my being, a blend of ecstasy and pain, exultation and keening, all bound up in a voice of magnificent timbre.

The eleven o'clock train.

"Do you feel it? Do you feel *them?*" Daisy is asking, while Joe nods, closes his eyes and tightens his arms around her.

Dash? Dash!

Something, someone is pulling me away from this safe, sweet spot. I am loosed, pried reluctantly from this couple, their embrace. I see the headlight of the approaching train, barreling down the tracks, a fist of brilliant light punching through the inky darkness and growing larger with every passing second.

The sound increases, too, from a resolute mechanical chugging to a full-throated thunderous cry. I am transfixed, enchanted by the increasing intensity of that circle of light and the noise, the shaking of the very air surrounding me and what I see in the brilliant beam that reaches out and pulls me in, like a lover reaching for a partner on the dance floor.

Because that is exactly what I see in what is now a giant, enveloping light: a dance floor. It is as if someone has opened up a door into Lamb's, back on that night in 1928; as if I am being welcomed into the raucous party that has been going on without me ever since.

"Dash!"

There is Charlie Walters, leaning up against the bar, chatting with Fern and looking just as I remembered him in his well-made shirt and tie and expensive leather shoes. He recognizes me, and waves me over impatiently, as if he has been waiting too long already. But before I can move, I see Nell Peters in all of her peaches-and-cream perfection, her face peering happily over the broad shoulder of her dance partner.

That young man whips his head around and I am nearly overcome with feelings of relief but not surprise: Jimmy Jeffers. His hair is the slicked-back black of his youth and there is no pot belly or evidence of worry in his face from fifty years of caring—too much—for the people of Possum Flats. He is all grin and vinegar, proud to bursting of his partner and delighted to see me.

But before I can reach him I am yanked toward the dance floor by a girl with luminous dark eyes and hair that shines like patent leather. She wears a familiar locket at her throat. She lowers her eyes and the skin of her white neck blushes beneath my stare.

Violet.

No.

Rose.

She smiles up at me and nods, as if I finally understand. I am holding her somehow, she is as light as air. I feel her lips against me as she whispers so softly, shyly: "We've been waiting for you."

Standing off to one side, close to the coat room, I see Susan, my dear wife. She was never a dancer—that would have been a sin—but she smiles at me as if to say that she doesn't mind that I have just this one dance. That she knows in her deepest, unswervingly faithful heart that she is my girl and that she will be here afterwards. And the band—*the band!*—has started up "At Sundown," the gentle chords from Beebe's piano tugging at me. She is arching an eyebrow over the top of her upright while Dale Diggs bobs his head, keeping time on his trap drum.

> *"The world seems rosy*
> *At sundown;*
> *Where a loving smile will greet me*
> *And always meet me*
> *At sundown."*

The dance floor is full now, all of us circling, planets and their moons, turning and revolving in our miniature orbits. We are next to Daisy and Joe, who are slow dancing awkwardly, barely moving from side to side. I am mesmerized by the entire scene: so much light and shadow, movement and noise, with good-natured talk and laughter creating another layer in the music. All of these people, these friends I had thought were gone, exulting in their youthful perfection, their innocence, their potential. I want to weep, yet it is not sadness that fills me. As I look down into the face of this gorgeous young woman and feel her body supremely relaxed against me, I am happy, whole. I feel an unwavering confidence in all of us, that we have lived the best we could within our countless limitations. That I am forgiven, understood, accepted. Even celebrated. We all are.

"Paul."

I do not want to look away from Rose, but I must. That voice. It cannot be. My mother.

She is seated at a table at the far edge of the dance floor, wearing a flowered dress and holding my infant sister in her arms. Oh! She is so young and her expression is that of someone who has not known hardship, only love. Not just for the baby she holds, but for that man who stands proudly behind her, one protective hand on her shoulder.

My father. The grin that is spreading across his fresh face is goofy and shy, but shines with pride. In this wife he chose. This child she holds. In *me*. I feel it as purely and fully as if he had spoken it aloud. He nods—just once—but slowly, surely. It sends a vibration through me and I find myself buzzing, humming.

That humming vibration becomes louder and louder, until it is no longer just inside me but everywhere; I am shaking along with every other being here. The tumult ratchets up until it is nearly unbearable, as though we are caught up in an earthquake or tornado, some force of nature or the supernatural, swallowed up in a crazy convergence of light and deafening noise.

And just like that, we are all of us swept up into sky, streaming upwards in a glorious blaze of light.

Then: sudden silence.

The last train car has passed, its single red taillight blinking steadily, like a watchful eye, and receding into the black night. I am floating once more, we all are, circling dreamily above that one young couple that remains in the cemetery, reluctant to pull away from each other, to end their dance. And why should they?

Faintly at first, there is a tinkling, almost like chimes, and then I recognize notes from the very upper keys of a piano. Soon they give way to the full-throated chords of the bass clef, the melody clear and bright as these souls surrounding me, these brash, brilliant stars in the night sky:

"I seem to sigh, I'm in heaven,
When night is falling
And love is calling me home!"

A slight summer breeze is causing the ancient oaks to sway, and they stretch their crooked boughs out and upwards, as if to reach me, to pull me back in a leafy embrace. There is the lingering smell of smoke and slightly overcooked hamburgers from an evening barbecue. Somewhere close by, the vigilant bark of a lonely yet hopeful spotted dog, chained to a stake in his backyard: *Is there anyone out there?*

How can I let go, abandon them? All of this?

But then the girl reaches up and puts a sweat-slick, tentative hand on the boy's soft cheek; he covers it with one of his own. Life can and will go on without me. Painful and gorgeous. Breathtaking and gut-wrenching. Messy and mundane.

"Brother. Dash! Paul?"

You must excuse me now. Love is calling me home.

Author's Note

I grew up in West Plains, Missouri—a small Ozarks town about ten miles north of the Arkansas line. But in my seventeen years there, I never heard a word about the Bond Dance Hall explosion of 1928, even though it killed thirty-nine people. My grandfather was born in 1919 and lived in the area all his life, and his parents before him, yet he never mentioned it—nor did anyone else I knew! There is even a huge memorial tombstone in the local cemetery marking the mass grave where the unidentified remains of many of the dead are buried, but I never knew to look for it.

It wasn't until I read local writer Lin Waterhouse's nonfiction book, *The West Plains Dance Hall Explosion* (2010) that I learned about the tragedy. I was fascinated to think how something of this magnitude could shake up a little town like mine. There were only three thousand people in West Plains in 1928, which meant that everyone knew someone who died or was injured. Many of the dead were young people, the up-and-coming leaders of the town. And the fact that this happened during Prohibition in the heart of the Bible Belt meant that a lot of people felt that the young revelers had brought the wrath of God down upon themselves. The actual mystery of why the explosion happened was never solved, either.

All of these elements made my "writer radar" go off! I just *had* to tell this story. I renamed West Plains as "Possum Flats," and populated my beloved Ozarks hometown with people who were struggling mightily—even fifty years later—to live in the aftermath of this terrible disaster. But even though the characters are fictional, there are lots of real West Plains places, from the Dog 'N' Suds to Porter Wagoner Boulevard. In the novel, I took the liberty of changing the date of the explosion from April to August so that Daisy could have a summer internship to uncover the story.

Speaking of: I, too, enjoyed a wonderful summer internship at *The West Plains Daily Quill*, where I learned to write obits, take "grip-and-grins" and photograph all manner of strange flowers, vegetables and prize livestock! And besides my research into the music, dances, clothing, hairstyles, slang and more from the 1920s through the 1970s, I learned a lot about the evolution of the funeral business over the past hundred years. My visit to the Heaton-Bowman-Smith Funeral Museum in St. Joseph, Missouri, was a highlight.

ACKNOWLEDGMENTS

As I write this, we are settling into our new home in St. Louis—and I am so grateful to be closer to family at last. I've loved everywhere that I've lived, from Palo Alto, CA and Denver, CO to Houston, TX and various towns and cities across Missouri. But, as Daisy puts it in this novel, "home is a *feeling*, and the people and place that inspire that feeling. It's about their acceptance and your belonging."

I'm back where I belong. Thanks, fam. To my husband, Clay, for his love and belief; and to my kids—Benjamin, Levi and Vivian—for inspiring me every day, cheering me on and celebrating the victories, large and small. You truly are the best (and the cutest!). That goes for Finn and the kitties, too.

Thank you to all the Benson, Collins and Anderson family members—I love you so dearly! How lucky I am to be a part of this wonderful oddball assemblage of comedians, artists, teachers, philosophers, engineers, farmers, adventurers, seekers and humanitarians.

Special thanks to my mom, Maureen, for helping me go to grad school and follow my dream; I miss you every day. To my dad, Marvin, for sending me the book *The West Plains Dance Hall Explosion* by Lin Waterhouse and sparking my imagination. To my Aunt Carlene and Uncle Ed, for always buying me books. Thank you to my brother, Kevin, my first creative collaborator and fierce Scrabble opponent (could I just win a game now and then?). And my sister, Dacia, who shares my taste in all things beautiful—art, decorating, nature, plants—a true "flower sister"!

I have so many people to thank for their inspiration and assistance in making *The Flower Sisters* a real, live book. First and foremost, my agent, Marlene Stringer, for plucking *The Flower Sisters* from a crowded field (!) and believing in these characters and this story. And John Scognamiglio, my editor, for his enthusiasm and careful reading and suggestions—I'm so proud to publish under your imprint! Likewise a huge thanks to the entire team at Kensington—especially Jackie Dinas, Vida Engstrand, Carly Sommerstein, Tory Groshong—and the entire creative team that so perfectly captured the essence of the novel with a jaw-droppingly gorgeous design! And Kim Wade, for sharing your time and considerable talent for the author photo.

Thank you to my beloved Warren Wilson College community. The mountain experience lingers and colors all my creative efforts for the better. Particular thanks to my generous and genius advisors: Liam Callanan, Debra Spark, Sarah Stone, C.J. Hribal and, most especially, David Haynes. You were the first to read the opening chapters of *The Flower Sisters* and tell me that I had "an engine"—and you've picked me up in some tough moments over the years. Let's have lunch in the Central West End soon, my treat.

I'm beholden to many Warren Wilson colleagues and friends, especially my first reader, butt-kicker, cheerleader and super-unselfish writer friend Katie Runde: you *insisted* that I finish this book and I wouldn't have without you. To Elisabeth Hamilton and Virginia Borges, for support, sharing and generally cracking me up over the miles and text chains. To early readers Lynette D'Amico and Leslie Koffler: your encouragement meant the world. And Somayeh Shams, for your friendship and shared sisterhood of writing while mothering.

I'd like to thank Iowa Summer Writers Festival faculty Amber Dermont for making me apply to MFA programs, and John Dalton, who also saw glimmers of this novel in his workshop at Washington University's Summer Writers Institute. Thanks, too, to Elizabeth Marro, my "Binders" mentor. Heartfelt gratitude to Phillip Howerton, editor of *Elder Mountain: A Journal of Ozark Studies,* for publishing one of my short stories and then kindly asking if I had anything more! You read *The Flower Sisters* cover to cover and told me to dream big. Thanks also to Craig Albin and Faith Collins, for recognizing a kindred Ozarks spirit and putting her into print. And to *The Missouri Review*'s Speer Morgan, Kristine Somerville and Evelyn Somers for championing new writers and great writing. Finally, to fellow writer Carlynn Trout: what a gift to have had those hours at your dining room table, reading our work out loud and making each other better.

To Rick Cotner, for pointing me toward invaluable resources about the Azusa Street Revival and the rise of the Pentecostal movement.

And my friends: so many! Thank you to all the tennis ladies who hit the ball with me before I hit the library—especially Carrie Bastin, Lisa Fujima, Raquel Madison, Cheryl Morton and Dana Haines, who unfailingly asked how the book was going, even when it wasn't! Special shoutout to Cathi Reinmiller and Jayme Paul, for insisting on a "sneak peek" of *The Flower Sisters* and giving such kind feedback. And Samara Pernice, for hair and chair therapy.

To Elaine Johnson, Catey Terry and Judith DelPorto: truest friends who have shared my life in the trenches of childrearing over coffee, tea, wine and good books as we attempted to maintain our senses of humor (and our personhoods!). My Theta sisters Janis Jones, Shari Johnson, Leslie Hutter, Tina Schnelle, Ann Walters and Mary Rudder. And my West Plains High School friends Carla Smith, Michelle Moody, Sonya McDonald, Myrna Asberry (miss you) and Ann Kinsella, who lost her great-grandmother in the 1928 dance hall explosion.

Finally, thanks to all the book groups I've been a part of, especially The Red Tent Women of Calvary Episcopal Church in Columbia, MO and the Liberal Ladies of Liberty, MO. And to the public libraries that have provided my office-away-from-home for years: the Withers and Woodneath branches of Mid-Continent Public Library in Kansas City, MO and the St. Louis Public Library's Carpenter branch. Let's keep the doors open and the shelves full in these essential, magical places for *all* people.

THE FLOWER SISTERS

ABOUT THIS GUIDE

The suggested questions are included to enhance your group's reading of Michelle Collins Anderson's *The Flower Sisters*!

DISCUSSION QUESTIONS

1. *The Flower Sisters* opens with a prologue set in a 1928 Ozarks dance hall that introduces us to most of the main characters in the novel. What are your first impressions of Dash, Violet, Jimmy, Ginger, Hazel and the gang? How did your assessment of any or all of them change throughout the course of the book? Why?

2. As Rose is preparing "the Mayor" for his funeral, she muses, "Maybe we can't always be the person we want to be. Maybe not even most of the time." The Mayor's not-so-secret extramarital affairs didn't align with his upstanding public persona. But who else in the novel is not exactly as they appear to be on the outside? Does this cognitive dissonance cause any problems?

3. Rose's position as a small-town female funeral home owner and operator from the 1950s on makes her unique for the times. Even in 1970s Possum Flats, we meet Mabel as a secretary, Betty as a waitress and even Myra—employed as a newspaper editor—is assigned to the more female-focused "society page." Discuss the choices that women had career-wise during this era. Can you relate to the limitations that these women experienced? How do you think this will change for Daisy? What are your hopes for your own daughters and granddaughters?

4. When Daisy bargains her way into a summer internship at *The Possum Flats Picayune*, Rose admonishes her to "Write the truth, but make sure the truths you write are yours to tell." What does she mean by that? Do you think Daisy ends up telling any truths or secrets that she shouldn't? What happens when her stories about the dance hall explosion are printed?

5. Identical twins look alike—but often have extremely different personalities. Are you more of a Rose or a Violet? Did your perception of each sister change or solidify when you discovered the secrets that were revealed in Daisy's final installment?

6. A major theme of *The Flower Sisters* is identity. Can we truly choose to be someone other than who we are? By intentionally changing ourselves and our actions, how does that create a ripple effect on those we love and our greater community? For instance, do you feel sympathy for George, who made major life decisions based on misleading information? What about the twins' mother and the loss she grieved?

7. Dash says, "Sometimes the punishment doesn't fit the crime, the price too high for that one unthinking moment, one ill-advised decision." This is true for Rose, Violet, Dash, Hazel and Jimmy. Have you ever made a split-second decision that you regretted for years? Or one that changed your life for the better? Can or should people be held accountable for the actions and decisions made by their high school-aged selves? Would you want to be?

8. When Myra teaches Daisy how to write an obituary, she introduces her to a lot of euphemisms for death—like "passed away" or "received his heavenly reward"—which Daisy doesn't understand: "Why not just say he *died*?" But Myra says the town likes its obits "with a little optimism." Do you think this language is simply old-fashioned? Or is it a way of avoiding the truth or reality of death? How does the town's attitude play out in the larger story of the dance hall explosion and its aftermath?

9. Rose says: "I'm a real stickler for getting everything just right with the dead. Sort of helps to make up for what I haven't been able to put right with the living." Rose's personal failures include everything from marriage to parenting to family rela-